THE WINTER OVER

ALSO BY MATTHEW IDEN

{The Marty Singer Mysteries}

A Reason to Live

Blueblood

One Right Thing

The Spike

The Wicked Flee

Once Was Lost

{Stand-Alone}

John Rain: The B-Team (Kindle Worlds)

Stealing Sweetwater

{Short story collection}

one bad twelve

THE WINTER OVER

MATTHEW IDEN

THOMAS & MERCER

This is a work of fiction. Names, characters, organizations, places, events, and incidents are either products of the author's imagination or are used fictitiously. Any resemblance to actual persons, living or dead, or actual events is purely coincidental.

Published by Thomas & Mercer, Seattle

www.apub.com

ISBN-13: 9781503942851
ISBN-10: 1503942856

Cover design by Edward Bettison Ltd.

Printed in the United States of America

For Renee, who continues to make the whole thing possible.

For my family.

For my friends.

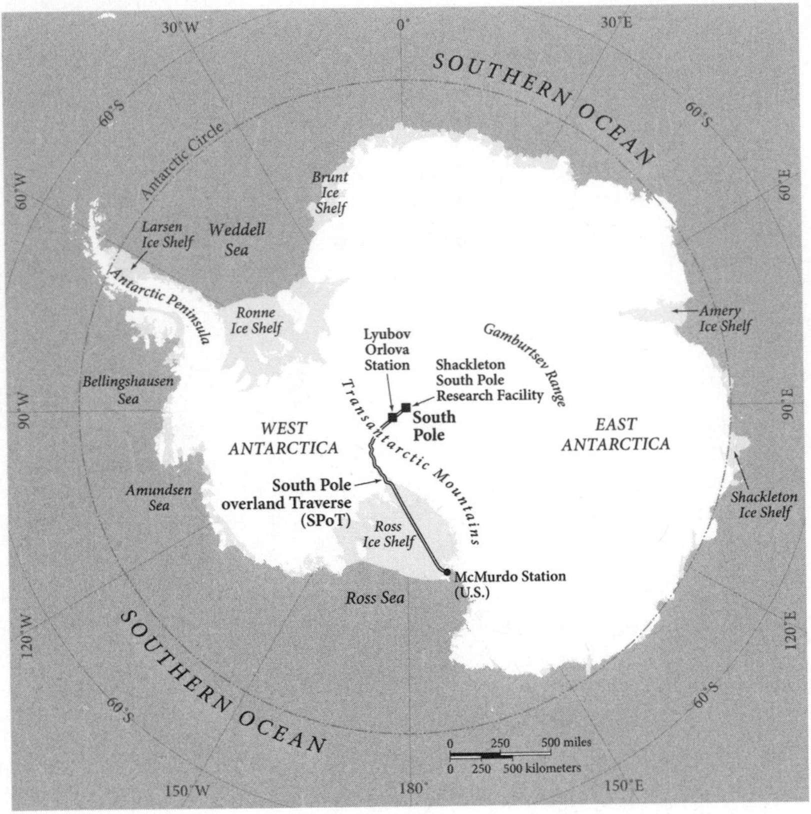

30°W
0°
30°E
SOUTHERN OCEAN
60°S
60°S
Antarctic Circle
60°W
60°E
Brunt Ice Shelf
Larsen Ice Shelf
Weddell Sea
Antarctic Peninsula
Ronne Ice Shelf
Amery Ice Shelf
Gamburtsev Range
Lyubov Orlova Station
Shackleton South Pole Research Facility
Bellingshausen Sea
90°W
90°E
South Pole
Transantarctic Mountains
WEST ANTARCTICA
EAST ANTARCTICA
South Pole overland Traverse (SPoT)
Amundsen Sea
Shackleton Ice Shelf
Ross Ice Shelf
McMurdo Station (U.S.)
Ross Sea
120°W
120°E
SOUTHERN OCEAN
60°S
60°S
0 250 500 miles
0 250 500 kilometers
150°W
180°
150°E

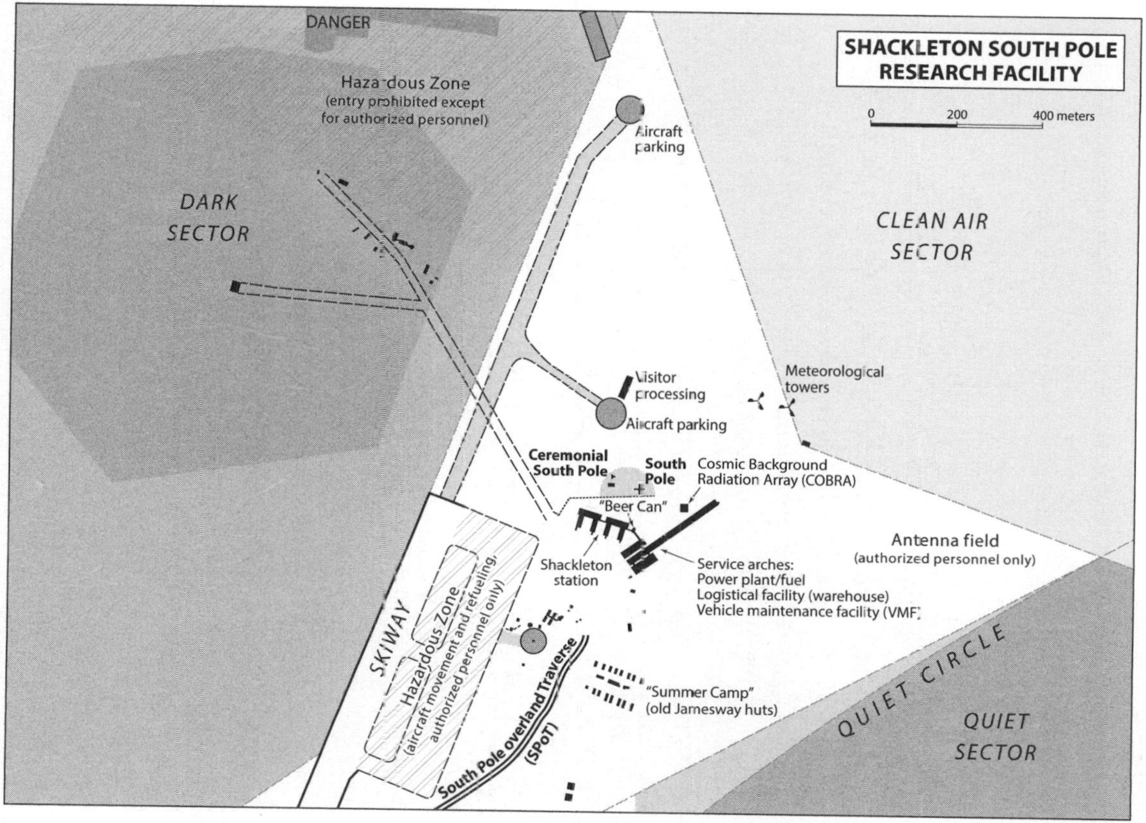
SHACKLETON SOUTH POLE
RESEARCH FACILITY
0
200
400 meters
DANGER
Hazardous Zone
(entry prohibited except for authorized personnel)
DARK
SECTOR
Aircraft parking
CLEAN AIR
SECTOR
Visitor processing
Aircraft parking
Meteorological towers
Ceremonial South Pole
South Pole
Cosmic Background Radiation Array (COBRA)
"Beer Can"
Antenna field
(authorized personnel only)
Shackleton station
Service arches:
Power plant/fuel
Logistical facility (warehouse)
Vehicle maintenance facility (VMF)
SKIWAY
Hazardous Zone
(aircraft movement and refueling, authorized personnel only)
South Pole overland Traverse
(SPoT)
"Summer Camp"
(old Jamesway huts)
QUIET CIRCLE
QUIET
SECTOR

"Men wanted for hazardous journey. Small wages, bitter cold, long months of complete darkness, constant danger, safe return doubtful. Honor and recognition in case of success."

—1912 expedition recruitment ad attributed to Ernest Shackleton

PART I

February 12

Two days until Austral Winter

Shackleton South Pole Research Facility

South Pole, Antarctica

CHAPTER ONE

The woman's arms were spread wide, open to the world, as though she were asking for a hug or just starting a snow angel.

One boot—ridiculously oversized—was turned at an obscene angle. The other, held rigidly in place by its thick plastic and neoprene, pointed toward a dishwater-gray sky. Reflective goggles and a thick balaclava hid her face, but a delicate lattice of ice crystals framed her mouth and nostrils, a ghostly "o" and two dashes where her once hot breath had frozen instantly in air that was forty degrees south of zero. Ramps of snow leaned against the body's windward side, brought to rest against her by the constant Antarctic gales. Had they not found her, she would've been buried in eight hours, maybe less, and she could've been someone else's discovery a hundred days or a hundred years from now.

Through the rising wind and flurries, Cass stared at the body. It was tempting to imagine that there wasn't a person inside the cocoon of Gore-Tex and fleece, that it was just a pile of clothes stuffed into boots and gloves, a scarecrow dropped half a klick from the west door of the Shackleton South Pole Research Facility to frighten the crew. Not a woman named Sheryl Larkin who had been vibrant and warm and alive twelve hours before.

Each time Cass tried to wrap her head around the fact that she was looking at what was left of Sheryl, the thought wriggled away like an eel, refusing to be caught. Behind her own mask and scarf, her breath came in short, ragged plugs. Echoes of parting advice from her instructor back in Colorado Springs resurfaced now, counsel she'd laughingly taken for granted at the time. *Never forget. Antarctica wants to kill you.*

"Jennings." She jumped and turned to face Jack Hanratty. The station manager's voice, already gruff, came through his balaclava sounding like a wood rasp. "Help Taylor get that body on the sled or there're going to be three more out here."

Frozen, but not from the cold, Cass turned back to the figure sprawled on the ice. She did not want to touch it. The marionette-like lifelessness invoked another memory, and with it, a rising tide of fear and anger. *I'm a mechanic, not a medic. I fix snowmobiles and broken engines, not people. What in hell am I doing out here?*

"Jennings!" Hanratty's voice crackled again. "I said, give Taylor a hand before we all freeze to death. I'm going to take a look around."

Reluctantly, she helped Taylor maneuver the body onto a banana sled hitched to a 120-horsepower Skandic snowmobile. The cadaver felt like a piece of lumber—frozen solid or in the process of succumbing to rigor mortis or both. She'd hoped the mechanical stiffness of the corpse would make it easier to forget what she was doing, but the arms remained open and wide, still asking for that hug. Behind her mask, Cass bit down hard on her lip. Together, she and Taylor muscled Sheryl's body onto the sled. Once it was balanced inside, he pulled a nest of nylon straps from the Skandic's trunk and began the process of tying Sheryl down like she was a set of tent poles.

Dizzy and numb, Cass watched him work, unable to look away. Like Sheryl, all of them wore the polarized, reflective ski masks that were standard issue at the South Pole, a layer of protection that was necessary to stay alive, but which swallowed up most of one's face and nearly all of the humanity. Cass knew she was just as devoid of expression as the others, but for some reason, Sheryl's facelessness bothered her—the cold landscape, the cold death, the cold reality, combined with Taylor's and Hanratty's stilted, businesslike attitude. It seemed as if a great and ancient law was being broken or ignored. Not thinking, she reached to move Sheryl's mask away.

Taylor's hand shot out, grabbing her wrist. "You don't want to do that."

Cass flinched, then retreated a step. Taylor had a dark reputation—Shackleton's chief of security was rumored to have history with everyone from Blackwater to Israel's Mossad—but he was probably right. If the sight and feel of Sheryl's dead body, hidden by layer upon layer of clothing, was almost too much for her to take, the image of her face would definitely send her to a place she didn't want to go. She moved farther away and watched Taylor finish tightening the crisscrossed straps. The body rocked with each tug.

Hanratty approached, stomping through the snow. "Taylor, you drive the body back. Doc Ayres should be waiting for you in the garage. No one except you two are to look at it . . . at her . . . before I return. And not a word to anyone."

"You aren't coming back now?" Taylor's twang—Southern Comfort with a hint of backwoods bayou—came through in the five simple words.

"I want to keep looking around. We'll join you in a few."

"The met report said the next storm is due at fourteen-thirty." Taylor would never come out and chide his boss, but the warning was clear. "Con two."

"I know it," Hanratty replied, turning his face southwest into the thickening flurry. "The blow that caught Sheryl probably covered anything worth seeing, but if we don't look now, for sure it'll be gone in another hour."

"What was she doing in the Dark Sector, anyway? I thought she was with the weather gang."

"No clue. She liked to jog. Maybe she thought she'd go for a long loop. Jennings, you're a runner. You ever come out this far?"

She shook her head. Was she a runner? Yes. Ten miles a day, every day, for years. Running away from something, running toward something. But never on the ice, where she didn't trust she would ever come back if she dared venture out.

"On the far side of the skiway?" Taylor pressed, gesturing. "In bunny boots?"

"Hell if I know, Taylor," Hanratty said, annoyed. "Maybe she spaced out and started chasing sun dogs. Get the body back to the station and we can spend the rest of the winter guessing."

Back stiff, Taylor nodded once, then hopped onto the Skandic. The snowmobile's engine caught on the first try and he motored back toward base, nothing more than a blue-gray Lego block at this distance.

Cass turned to Hanratty. "You want me along?"

"You're not going to walk back, I assume," he said, swinging a leg over the saddle of the other snowmobile. "And I want to be there. I can trust Taylor not to talk."

Cass mounted behind Hanratty, but underneath her mask and gaiter, her face burned. Rather than put her arms around his waist for support, she gripped the bottom of the seat instead. More precarious, maybe, but she'd rather fall off the back than give him the satisfaction of holding on to him.

As though reading her mind, he took off with a jolt that snapped her head back. For a long second, she teetered on the edge of pitching backwards off the seat. Hanratty, known for his object lessons, probably *would* make her walk back to base then. But she regained her balance as he slowed the snowmobile in order to follow Sheryl's tracks.

Or, rather, where the tracks should've been. In the arid, desert-like climate of Antarctica, little snow fell day to day, but tens of thousands of accumulated years of the stuff blew around the continent in curtains. The rest was sculpted into frozen waves of glass-like hardness, what the old ice-heads called *sastrugi*. A single footprint appeared occasionally, but there was no reliable trail thanks to the crystalline surface. And since bunny boots had been standard Antarctic issue for decades, any footprint they spotted could've been Sheryl's . . . or it could've been laid down by any other Polie in the last twenty years. At certain points, there seemed to be a cluster of footprints, but again the temporal element was missing: they could be prints from a group of two or three or those of singular individuals inscribed over years.

Snowmobiling over sastrugi was no picnic, and Cass's teeth clacked together painfully as the Skandic bucked up and down on the icy fins. Thankfully, Hanratty kept their speed to a crawl so they could look for clues as to why Sheryl had been outside the base, alone and without a radio. None of it made sense. Leaving base without a radio was a violation of policy; doing so during the previous day's storm was a violation of logic.

As was keeping up a fruitless search while visibility began to fail. Cass tapped Hanratty on the shoulder and leaned forward to be heard over the snowmobile's whine. "We're running out of time."

"I'm aware." The reply was terse, metallic.

Veering south, they drove farther onto the plain. Shackleton, glimpsed over her shoulder, was nothing more than a dot on the horizon, and when she turned to look front again, wind drove the snow directly into her face. They continued for several minutes, bucking over the troughs of the sastrugi, eyes glued to the ground, trying to spot one man-made anomaly in an ocean of natural deviations.

But there was nothing. Cass rose in her seat to look over Hanratty's shoulder. The white, featureless expanse expanded in endless iteration and continued—as she knew rationally but had difficulty believing—for eight hundred miles over the Transantarctic Mountains and the Ross

Ice Shelf before meeting the sea. Between here and there was literally nothing. Sheryl's death had not come from that direction.

A gust slapped them with such force that Cass had to snatch at the seat to hold on. The leading edge of the storm was coming at them fast. Despite multiple layers of expedition-rated clothing and the massive gloves they called bear claws, the cold was stupefying, spawning a knot of fundamental, animal fear in her gut. *We shouldn't be out here. I shouldn't be out here. I came to Antarctica to lose myself, to find myself, not to die.*

Hanratty, feeling her anxiety, relented. "All right, Jennings. Take it easy. We're heading back."

He hit the gas and they took off from their previous crawl with a jerk. *To hell with pride*, Cass thought, letting go of the seat and wrapping her arms around the waist of the thin, hard body in front of her. In tactile terms, Hanratty seemed not so different from Sheryl's corpse.

Within a few seconds they were doing fifty miles an hour, flying across the snow and ice so fast it seemed they were hovering rather than plowing through it, though they still caught several of the sastrugi hard enough to jar the bones in her knees and hips. Hanratty was careful to follow their double-wide tracks back, both as a backup to GPS and to avoid the ever-present danger of falling into a crevasse. At their speed, they wouldn't have a chance of spotting the slightly darker aqua-blue shade of ice that was the only warning—the two of them would hit bottom before they even knew they'd found a chasm.

For most of the trip, the wind pressed on Cass's back like an invisible hand, then a gust of swirling, katabatic wind hit them unexpectedly from the side, lifting the right side of the snowmobile off the ground and threatening to dump them onto the ice. Cass instinctively leaned into the tilt, bringing her body weight to the fight to force the snowmobile back down. They landed with a jolt, the whining track bit back into the snow, and Hanratty piloted straight for the hump that was Shackleton base.

As they neared the compound, the dozens of outbuildings that surrounded the base became dimly visible: the skiway where the planes came in, the Summer Camp of old red Jamesway huts, mounded berms of supply pallets, and a scattering of other buildings, sheds, and shanties. Thanks to the oncoming storm, all were obscured as though seen through a translucent white curtain, present but indistinct, and she only knew they had crossed the skiway when the punishing ride stopped thanks to the runway's compact surface. Somewhere off to their left was the candy-striped ceremonial South Pole, surrounded by the flags of the Antarctic Treaty signatory states and topped by the reflective metallic bulb that everyone took their picture with. Then, as if erupting from the ground, the main building of Shackleton—the beating heart of all research efforts at the South Pole—loomed in front of them, looking like a colossal double-tall shipping container hovering on a cluster of pillars.

Hanratty continued past the facility, then slowed and banked left, following a gentle slope around and down that ended at a man-made snow cliff some forty feet lower than the plateau on which the main base rested. Taking gradual shape out of the flurries were the half-moon entrance arches of Shackleton's garage and warehouse, embedded side by side at the base of the cliff. Taylor must've been watching for them: the mouth of the garage gaped wide. Hanratty drove straight toward the white LEDs and crossed the open doorway with a clatter and a roar, then cut the engine. Cass took a deep breath, trying to lose the feeling of dread that had built up as the storm chased them across the Antarctic plain.

"Jennings. Let go."

Cass jerked back, releasing her hold on Hanratty. She swung off the saddle of the Skandic, stumbling a little as she did; her legs were numb from the thighs down. Stamping her feet to get some of the feeling back, she began peeling off layers, looking around while she did her little warming dance. Sheryl's body was gone, presumably already in the medical lab undergoing an autopsy or an exam or whatever was supposed to be done in a situation like this. Cass fought down a wave of nausea. The garage workspace, normally comforting and familiar, now felt abandoned and dismal.

Taylor punched the green button to close the bay door and it slowly obeyed, rattling and grinding on the way down. Wind keened as the descending door increased the pressure, then was cut off altogether as the rubberized bottom section slid into the protective socket in the floor. The two formed an almost airtight seal, although if a Condition Two storm was on the way, snow would find its way through regardless, piling in drifts on the inside of the door.

"Jennings." She turned to face Hanratty, who had doffed his goggles and balaclava. His gaunt, stern face—a Puritan minister's face, an inquisitor's face—was twisted into a scowl. "Not a word of this to anyone until I can make an official announcement, understand? Only you, Taylor, and I know about Larkin's accident and I need to keep it that way until I can get some idea of just what the hell happened out there."

"I got it," she said. "Who found her?"

Hanratty frowned, but said, "The Herc pilot for today's run back to McMurdo thought he saw something odd as he took off from the skiway. He called it in about an hour ago."

"Why didn't you scramble one of the trauma teams? Why did we go out?"

"We checked Larkin's tag-out. She was gone twelve hours by the time the pilot saw her," Taylor said, joining them. Stripped of his gear, he was a man of average height but had a gymnast's poise and strength. His large nose and receding gray hairline were reminiscent of a bald eagle, though no one at the base dared say that to him. "This was a recovery, not a rescue."

"God," Cass said, sick. "Why tap me to go with you?"

Hanratty shrugged. "We needed two vehicles and some help. You were here in the garage and seemed available. Do you have a problem with that?"

Cass raised her hands and dropped them in exasperation. "I have a problem with the cavalier attitude. One of our own people just *died.* This is a big deal. She was a . . . a good person. She deserves better than to be strapped to a gurney and carted off."

A flicker of emotion—sympathy or impatience, it was hard to tell—passed over Hanratty's face. "Antarctica is antithetical to life, Jennings. Every minute we're here is stolen from the ice and sometimes the ice takes it back. Sheryl, for whatever reason, forgot that fact and paid for it. We don't have to like it, but it's happened before and it'll happen again. So, in regards to my attitude, as much as I regret this . . . accident, I will not let it compromise our work here."

Cass was silent.

"Look, I don't need panic taking hold while we're getting ready for nine months of isolation. When we know what happened, I'll be fully transparent to the rest of the base personnel. You know Sheryl wouldn't want us to handle it any other way."

The silence stretched longer, then Cass nodded once, curtly.

Hanratty blew out a breath. "Okay, then. Taylor, let's go see Ayres and hear what he's figured out, if anything." He glanced back at Cass. "Living and working down here has always had the potential to be lethal. I'm sorry Sheryl had to be the one to remind us of that."

The two men left through the base-side exit door, heads close together as they conferred.

Cass stared at the sleds and the snowmobiles while the wind battered and screamed at the garage door. Idly, she picked up a wrench, then dropped it with a clatter. Tears formed at the corners of her eyes, resting there but not spilling until she leaned over a workbench, holding on to the edge for support.

Images she'd hoped to forget splashed across her memory. Crumbling walls. Stricken faces. One long arm draped over the side of a stretcher, bouncing gently as it was pulled hand over hand out of the debris. Incomprehension growing into horror.

It didn't matter that *this* wasn't *that.* Sheryl's death summoned forth the same bottomless, sinking, sucking hole of blame and self-loathing she'd felt then; it opened up at her feet once more, tugging her downward. She rubbed her face against the rough material of her jumpsuit, trying to pull herself out of the spiral, whispering over and over again, "It's not your fault. It's not your fault. It's not your fault."

CHAPTER TWO

"So why did he pick *you* to go?"

Cass tugged the card table away from the wall so she could run the vacuum behind it, wrinkling her nose at the rising cloud of body odor and stale carpet. That question, among others, had cost her a full night's sleep and had gnawed at her mind. But when Biddi said it with her lilting Scottish accent—normally employed to tell a dirty joke or dish out gossip about one of the other Shackleton staffers—it possessed all the drama of asking her if she'd seen the mess someone had left in the men's room.

"Earth to Cass," Biddi said. "Anyone home?"

"I don't know." Cass bumped her hip into the table to jog it left another half foot, then plugged in the vacuum. "He claimed I was just . . . here. Available."

"And?" Biddi ran a dust cloth over the tops of the bookcases, the door frame, and the pictures of past Antarctic explorers. Her arms jiggled as she wiped. She was the heaviest member of Shackleton's winter-over staff and a source of wonder to everyone at the base, where—despite doubling caloric intake—most of the staff lost fifteen pounds over a season just trying to stay warm.

Cass folded the chairs from around the poker table and leaned them up against the wall. "He got the call that Sheryl was missing, ran down to the VMF to grab some wheels, and found me there working on one of the snowcats. He realized a little too late that he might need help getting . . . getting the body onto a sled. I was the only one around, so there you go."

"I thought Mr. 'Have You Reported Your Hours Yet?' Taylor was with him."

"Later. He followed us out."

Cass stopped speaking as the door to the lounge opened with a loud *clack*. A pale man with a sandy blond mustache took a step inside. Without raising her head, she snapped the vacuum cleaner on, filling the small space with a roar like a transport jet taking off. The man made a face and retreated from the room. She waited for the door to close, counted to five, then turned the vacuum off.

"Which one was that?" Biddi asked.

"Schaffer. One of the beakers from the geophysics lab. Taking a last look around, probably."

Biddi made a rude noise. "That one. Eats like a two-year-old. He's always spilling milk on the table after breakfast, like he can't find his mouth yet. Bless him for shipping out with the other summer people."

Cass smiled, despite her anxiety. Since the very first base had been founded in Antarctica there had been friction between staffers and scientists—"beakers" to the rough-and-tumble support crew—and it would continue until the last base shut its doors. The former knew they wouldn't be there without the scientific need in the first place, but it was aggravating to be treated like an afterthought. Conversely, the latter's work couldn't exist without around-the-clock support, but most scientists were oblivious to the effort that entailed, or worse, simply accepted the service of others as their due. Biddi had put more than one astrophysicist in his place when she'd been treated like the hired help.

"I think there's another reason he picked you," Biddi continued.

"Oh?"

"We're the low persons on the totem pole, my dear." Biddi helped her pull a couch away from the wall. "It doesn't matter that you have a mechanical engineering degree and keep every damnable snowmobile and -cat in the 'vehicle maintenance facility'"—she put air quotes around the VMF's formal name—"running. And it doesn't matter that I'm a registered nurse and went to culinary school, we're both—"

"Bloody fucking janitors," Cass finished for her. It was Biddi's favorite phrase when she went on an anti-oppression rant. At least she wasn't singing from *Les Mis* this time. "What does that have to do with anything?"

"Because Hanratty thinks he can control you," Biddi said, snapping the dust rag. "Do you think the head of the neutrino collection program is going to keep his mouth shut just because Hanratty says so?"

"And I will?"

"Yes. Not because of who you are, but what you are. Face it—it doesn't matter what else we know or what else we've done, we really *are* bloody fucking janitors and not much else for the next nine months."

Cass stared at her. "Where is the real Biddi Newell and what have you done with her?"

"I don't like class distinctions any more than you do, my sweet, but the way to survive an Antarctic winter is by keeping your head down. You don't want to stick out as a troublemaker before they've even shut the doors, do you?"

Cass thought about it. She didn't feel good about the stigma of being a staffer, but it especially stung to think that Hanratty might be banking on the double standard of some kind of class hierarchy to keep her quiet about Sheryl's death.

Artificial class divisions had never made sense to her. Even when there was a full crew of two hundred over the summer season from November to February, staffers were expected to wear several hats, which meant most of the crew were competent, educated, and resourceful—and no one came to Antarctica if they didn't already have guts and drive on top of that. The breakfast cook could also be a core member of the fire response team; the carpenter might be a backup IT specialist. But over the nine months of the austral winter, when Shackleton's crew was cut down to forty-four, each person on staff really *was* a walking jack-of-all-trades, capable of backstopping four or five jobs.

Cass herself was Shackleton's winter-over mechanic, plumber, and carpenter and was expected to be able to stand in for the physical-plant engineer and run the fuel, HVAC, and waste systems without batting an eye if she had to. Biddi was on the base's emergency medical team, lent the cooks a hand with dinners, and had recently learned enough electrical engineering to help out in the e-systems lab. With those kinds of skills, not to mention the ambition it took just to *land* a job in Antarctica, you'd think you'd garner some respect. But, at times, what most people recognized Biddi and Cass for was being, well, bloody fucking janitors and not much else.

"What do you think happened to the girl, anyway?" Biddi said, switching gears. "You never said."

"I shouldn't have even told you that much."

"Oh, look who's caving to authority now. You'll walk in here and announce that you just strapped the body of a friend of mine to the back of a snowmobile, but you won't tell me what you think happened?"

"You were not friends with Sheryl."

"Not in the traditional sense, no," Biddi said. "She always was a bitch to me. I'm not so sorry to see her go, to tell the truth."

"Biddi!"

She waved the dust cloth dismissively. "I'm just pulling the piss. It's sad, no doubt about it. Even if she did tell me she found dust in her room after each time I cleaned it."

"She did that once."

"Once was enough. Anyway, what happened to her?"

"She'd twisted her ankle. Definitely broken, not just sprained."

"Poor thing went hypothermic and tried crawling the whole way, did she?"

"Well, she was heading back toward Shackleton when we found her," Cass said, then frowned at the memory. Victims of hypothermia were almost always discovered in the fetal position, or at least that's what all the training manuals had said. Why had they found Sheryl flat on her back?

"A terrible way to go." Biddi shuddered. "Was it like going to sleep, do you think?"

"I suppose . . ." Cass's voice trailed off, the image of Sheryl's arms and legs rocking stiffly back and forth as she was loaded onto the sled so much like the time before. Other arms, other legs, other people.

"Cass, hon, are you all right?" Biddi was suddenly next to her, a hand under her elbow for support. "Don't go passing out on me."

"I'm fine. I'm okay."

"Bollocks," she said, pushing her down onto the couch. "I'm sorry I made a joke out of the poor dear's death. It's the only way I know how to handle tragedy. But it's not everyone's approach, I know."

"It's just not what I signed on for, that's all." Cass smoothed her hair back with both hands. "I knew that coming here could be dangerous, but for Christ's sake, when's the last time anyone *died* at the South Pole?"

Biddi clucked sympathetically. "It's a shock, no doubt. We're supposed to have every technological advantage, every modern device, yet people can still freeze to death. The unfairness is enough to drive you mad. But I suppose what's important is how we handle it, don't you think?"

"I guess so." Cass pushed herself off the couch and took up her station at the vacuum. "Could we talk about something else?"

"Of course," Biddi said, her voice suddenly brisk. "Let's rank, by attractiveness, the men who are staying behind for the winter."

"Biddi."

"'The goods are odd, but the odds are good.'"

"I've heard that in every oil rig and lumber camp I ever worked in."

"Maybe so, but the phrase was invented down here. Besides, was it ever not true?"

"No," Cass admitted. "But you'd have to be pretty desperate to play the odds down here."

"You say that now, but nine months is a long time to go without a bit of bandicooting. And that's assuming you managed to snag yourself a piece over the summer." Biddi looked sideways at her. "Which I don't think you did, did you? Although, I swear, how you held them off with that red hair and those lips, I'll never know."

Cass felt herself blush up to the roots. "So what if I didn't?"

"It's not healthy."

"Says who?"

"My grandma. In her immortal words, ''Tis better to get a frig than give one . . . to yourself.'"

Their laughter was cut short when the door opened and someone poked their head into the room. Cass moved to turn the vacuum on again, but stopped when she saw it was Deb Connors, the deputy base manager. Deb scanned the room, then waved at the two of them.

"Cass, we've got an early morning tour group that's missing its early morning tour guide. You're up."

Cass gestured to the vacuum cleaner. "I'm kind of busy, Deb."

"Vacuuming? Drop it. This is a VIP group and the last one of the season. Senator Graham Sikes with an entourage. We need him to go out with a bang before he heads home to tell America that it's okay for TransAnt to be in charge down here."

"Can't Elise do it?"

"Elise is working comms, you know that. And most of the other guides either left for the summer or they're just about to. You're it."

"Damn it, Deb," Cass said, her voice cracking. "I just . . . I had a rough day yesterday, you know?"

Deb looked at her with perpetually sad eyes. "I'm sorry, Cass. We all liked Sheryl. Nobody is feeling good today, you especially, but life goes on. If I didn't have to show them the external sites after they land then hustle back to the office and whip up some press info, I'd do the tour myself. Now that everyone's flown the coop, you're the only inside guide left."

Cass nodded wearily. "When do you need me?"

"I'm heading out to greet them on the skiway in five." Deb glanced at her watch. "The external show-and-tell should take about ten more, so you should still have plenty of time to meet us at Destination Alpha for a handoff if you get moving."

"Jesus. Why don't you cut things close?"

"Remember. Senator Sikes, Destination Alpha." Deb pulled her head out of the room and the door slammed shut, then opened again. "And Cass?"

"Yes?"

"I know you're not in the mood, but don't be afraid to put on a show. Sikes is on the Senate subcommittee that handed Shackleton to TransAnt. And word is that he's something of a letch. We could use some good press. Make sure we get it."

Cass flipped a middle finger in the direction of the closing door. "Good press, my ass."

"I believe that was her very point," Biddi said, grunting as she shoved the couch back against the wall with a hip. "Better get going. Mind what I said. The key to surviving a winter-over is getting along."

"You said the key was to keep your head down. Or was it the part about getting a frig?"

"It all amounts to the same."

CHAPTER THREE

Taylor stood on Shackleton's external observation deck, watching the off-loading and on-loading of the season's last flights. The workhorse of the continent, the Hercules LC-130, was used to fly new crew members, fuel, and supplies in from McMurdo Station, and to take old crew members, waste, and scientific data out. On the surface it wasn't all that different from any other day of the past two weeks—summer crew had been cycling out constantly as the season had wound down.

Officially, however, today was the final day to travel, the last chance to leave the base, and there was a frantic pace to the scene as hundreds of crew members prepared to either flee an Antarctic winter or endure one. The only group above the fray was Senator Sikes and his boys, who'd come in on their own private flight from McMurdo, an unheard-of extravagance that had pissed off more than a few old-timers. But one of Taylor's jobs over the summer had been to remind the base's personnel that TransAnt was running the show now. When they said *jump*, you said *how high?* and not *why does the senator get his own plane?*

Halfway between the ob deck where he stood and the skiway, a knot of fuelies hovered around one of their trucks. The vehicle was apparently on a return trip from the giant bladders that acted as temporary storage for the AN8 jet fuel until it could be siphoned into the ten-thousand-gallon tanks in the fuel arch under the station. Taylor had blanched the first time he'd heard that the entire station was powered by avgas. The source for much of it was the very planes used to bring people to Shackleton, which meant that the nearly thousand-mile flight back to McMurdo was routinely done on fumes. When he'd asked the pilots on his arrival flight about it, they'd joked that there was always enough left in the tank to walk back. Taylor hadn't laughed.

He stamped his feet to warm them, watching the activity below and wincing at the tang of AN8. The cold always seemed to make sharp smells sharper, and the fumes from the Hercules seemed to be riding the low temperatures straight into his skull, giving him a headache to write home about.

The cold itself was no picnic, either, especially for a kid born and raised south of Shreveport. Only in Antarctica, he thought, would thirty degrees below zero be flirting with a record high for this time of year. And that on one of the prettiest days he'd seen yet. Yesterday's storm had cleared out a week's worth of scud, leaving a sunny, cornflower-blue sky straight off a postcard. *Hello from the South Pole! Colder than a witch's tit and dropping just as fast. Wish you were here.*

The beautiful day, unfortunately, barely registered; the pervasive chill and piercing headache put him in a foul mood. Easy enough to solve, of course; he could've just walked inside and warmed up away from the fuel dump. But it wasn't just a migraine and the god-awful temperature driving his bad attitude.

The business of getting Larkin's body back to base, of recruiting Jennings to help, had been foolish. And waiting to tell the rest of the staff about Larkin and the circumstances in which they found her—that was just stupid. Maybe Hanratty had some kind of larger plan, but sitting on information that radioactive was precisely how rumors got started.

Not that Taylor had anything against rumors, per se. Scuttlebutt was fine, as long as you were the one controlling it, or at least out in front of it. Ignore it and gossip took on a life of its own, no longer yours to use. He'd learned that from a lifetime of pushing and pulling people in directions they didn't want to go. His knack for manipulation had been honed doing six years of dirty work around the world for TransAnt and, after four months at Shackleton, he didn't see any reason the same approach shouldn't work at the South Pole.

He hawked and leaned forward to launch one over the rail—and caught himself just before he spat in his mask. *Damn it.* His bad humor wasn't going to go away with a cup of coffee and a sit-down by a heater; he needed to be in motion, he needed *action.* He stomped down the steps to the ice field, setting his sights on the little group, and double-timed it over. The fuelies were crowding around the truck's engine, not the tank in the back or the lines on the side, so there was something wrong with the truck and not the equipment on it. He might as well find out what they were doing.

As he got closer, a tingle of satisfaction trickled down to his nuts. One of the fuelies was Dave Boychuck, an ice-head left over from the National Science Foundation days. The two of them had nearly come to blows on a host of issues already, with the foreman obstinately sticking to the way things had always been done and Taylor insisting he follow TransAnt's protocols, from wearing the company-issued shirt to tagging in and out. It was all petty shit, really. The brass at TransAnt had mandated minimum change during the takeover of Shackleton. But some, like Boychuck, resisted change the whole way, which made Taylor's job a frequent pain in the ass.

It would be his absolute pleasure to return the favor.

❄

"Aw, hell," Jeremy swore, his voice muffled by a scarf.

Dave looked up from the engine. "What?"

"Taylor. Heading our way."

Dave straightened and squinted into the glare bouncing off the ice, shading his eyes with one hand and rubbing his thick beard with the other. There was no way to do good work on an engine wearing a ski mask—you couldn't see anything in the shadow of the hood—so his goggles were high on his head or dangling under his chin by the strap half the time. All he saw now was an indistinct shape striding toward them from base, but the shape's cocksure walk told him Jeremy was right.

Dave growled something unintelligible. Normally, he wouldn't mind locking horns with Shackleton's new chief of security—*Chief of security? Security for what? There was nothing to steal and nowhere to take it*—but squeezing three flights out on the last day of summer had pushed his crew and his equipment to the edge. His boys could handle it, but Antarctica wasn't kind to mechanical devices and half their time had been spent doing field repairs instead of moving fuel. After a hard summer's work, everything was ready to fall apart, although just as often the culprit was the most obvious: it was too damn cold. Engines of all kinds simply up and quit when it was forty below and colder. Whatever the reason, you couldn't tell that to a Herc pilot with an ETD of twenty minutes. You just had to get it working.

"Looks like he's got a burr under his blanket."

"Like I give a damn." Dave went back to tinkering under the hood of the truck.

Taylor strode up to them, eyeing each of them until they looked away. "What's the problem here? That Herc's got to take off within the hour."

"Engine's frozen," one of the other fuelies said.

"I can see that." Taylor's voice was scornful. "What's the plan?"

"It's the South freaking Pole, man," Jeremy said. "We have to wait for the NGH to come from the garage so we can heat 'er up."

"And when is it going to show?"

"It'll happen when it happens, Taylor," Dave said, not bothering to raise his head. "Things freeze. We thaw 'em out. Nothing gets done in between."

Taylor ducked his head under the hood across from Dave. "I don't need back talk, Boychuck, I need answers. What am I supposed to tell Hanratty when the fuel isn't off that plane and the next one is coming in for a landing?"

Dave shrugged. "You want the gas out so bad, put your lips on the hose and suck it out yourself."

Jeremy guffawed and the other two fuelies turned away to look into the distance, shoulders shaking.

Taylor yelled an obscenity, Dave tossed his wrench down and straightened to his full six foot four, and the pissing contest escalated until the other fuelies moved forward to separate the two before Dave took a swing at the chief of security. Taylor stormed off toward a group of flight techs and pilots in a hail of curses.

"That guy's a bag of dicks without a handle," Jeremy said.

"No argument there." Dave shook himself. "Forget him. The real question is when is that NGH going to get here? Sam left for the garage twenty minutes ago."

"Busy day today," one of the others said. "NGH might've gotten swiped by someone else."

"Hail him and find out, will you?" Jeremy pulled out a field radio from an inside breast pocket. They all turned at the squawk coming from the front of the fuel truck.

Dave threw his hands in the air. "For Christ's sake, Sam didn't take his radio?"

"We could call in, have him paged."

"He'd never hear it." Dave straightened again, fumbling with the ski mask. "Damn it. If you want something done right . . ."

"Cass ain't in the VMF," Jeremy said as Dave started heading toward the arches. "Last I saw, she was with Biddi on second deck, cleaning."

"Got it," Dave said, changing course. "You all head back to the Herc and see if you can lend a hand. I'll get the NGH and bring it back. If you run into Taylor again, tell him to jump in a hole."

Dave marched to the base, aiming for one of the station's ground-level doors instead of Destination Alpha, Shackleton's main door—with the Hercules's arrival, the regular entrances were jammed with knuckleheads and he didn't have the patience to deal with them. Summer crew leaving, winter crew arriving, guests and visitors and onetime drop-ins from McMurdo . . . they were all knuckleheads. Even now, he could see Deb leading a gaggle of muckety-mucks around, pointing out the architectural wonders of the main building, which, as much as he loved the place, had all the panache of a boxcar. At least it wasn't his responsibility to fake excitement over airshafts and antennas. He shuddered at the thought of having to lead a tour or deal with the day-to-day administration of the base. When he worked, he needed a job, not a job description.

Dave banged through the door and climbed the stairs, the metal steps ringing like chimes. He nodded to the few workers he recognized and skated past newbies still trying to figure out A wing from B wing and first deck from second. One tall, lanky guy with a sketchy blond goatee stared out a window with watery blue eyes, watching the world go by. His mouth hung open and his wet lips moved silently.

"Careful, friend," Dave said without breaking stride. "You'll catch a fly."

He climbed the stairs to the second floor, feeling bad about not stopping, at least for a second—the kid looked really out to sea, worse than most first-timers—but there just wasn't time to meet-and-greet every fingie coming through the door. He'd buy him a beer later.

Dave started poking his head into rooms, looking for Cass. Dwight, her old boss, had been okay; he and Dave had seen eye to eye on most things. Cass, on the other hand, was a question mark. He didn't know much about her, despite the fact she'd spent the summer season at the

Pole. Quiet, smart. Seemed competent enough. But if he couldn't get the NGH out of her garage, that estimation would be readjusted, and quick.

As he passed the greenhouse, he had just enough time to spring out of the way as the door to e-systems banged open. A woman, her face stormy, burst out of the lab and marched down the hall toward the Beer Can. Almost on her heels was a worried-looking man in a white polo shirt and jeans. Oblivious to Dave, the two continued an argument that had apparently started in the lab.

"Diane, just think about it," Dave heard the man plead as he struggled to keep up with the woman. "Please. They've got you under contract."

"She fucking froze to death out there, Rick. If you think I'm going to stick around . . ." Their conversation faded away as they moved down the corridor.

Dave watched them disappear, a sour feeling in his stomach. Being at the other end of Shackleton's work spectrum from Sheryl, he hadn't known the woman well, but you didn't have to be chummy with someone at the Pole to feel their death keenly.

In all the years he'd been coming to the Pole for work there'd been only two other deaths, both heart attacks. Even those casualties—unavoidable—had hit that year's crew hard and cast a pall over the rest of the season. To lose someone to the cold, to allow the continent itself to claim one of their own, especially in this day and age, was a bitter pill to swallow.

He shook his head and continued down the hall. He'd nearly reached the end when he heard a vacuum cleaner kick on in the reading lounge. When he peeked in, though, it was only Biddi running the machine in broad-armed sweeps across the floor. The opening door caught her eye and she turned the machine off, a smile on her face.

"Mr. Boychuck! Whatever can I do for you?"

Dave's beard bristled outward as he shyly returned her smile. "It's just Dave, Biddi. Did you happen to see Cass?"

Biddi made a sad face. "And here I thought you'd come to see me."

"I . . . I'm not really here to *see* Cass," Dave said. "I just need her NGH."

"Goodness. I never heard it called that before."

"What? No, the NGH is a heater. On wheels. We've got a fuel truck stuck out on the field and need to get it warmed up to start it."

"You need something to get your motor running, you say?" Biddi batted her eyelashes, then laughed at his discomfort. "Oh, relax. I'm just giving you a hard time, love. Cass was yanked away to play tour guide for some high-and-mighties in for the day."

"She's a tour guide?"

"You wouldn't think so with that demure little countenance, would you? She's trying to break out of her shell, I think. You'd be surprised at what she's capable of."

"Well, shoot," Dave said, nonplussed. "I guess I have to page Sammy, after all."

Biddi glanced out the window. "What's the NGH look like, by the way?"

He spread his hands wide. "Little yellow box on two wheels with a smokestack and a big hose on the side. You have to tow it with a Skandie or a tractor."

She pointed. "Is that what you're looking for, hon?"

He walked over and squinted. Sure enough, Sammy was chugging across the ice field on a snowcat, the NGH trailing faithfully behind. He sighed. "It's a wonder I get any work done around here."

Biddi swatted him on the arm. "You let me know if I can help out any more. And if I can start any more engines."

CHAPTER FOUR

Anne Klimt put her hands on her hips and assessed the contents of the lab. By Caltech or MIT standards, it was barely adequate. Grad students had assembled better systems in their dorm rooms. And, of course, this facility was dwarfed by Shackleton's COBRA lab, which was in its own freestanding building. But the difference was that this tiny, second-rate lab, stuffed inside the base with ten others just like it, was her domain and she was its queen.

Well, not entirely. She'd have to share it with Jun Takahashi and two other beakers who'd come in with the latest winter-over drop-off—newbies, so new she hadn't even learned their names yet. But still, it beat bumping up against fifteen other astrophysicists. Winter, with its perpetual darkness, was the better season for astronomy by far, but it was not always the most sought-after assignment. A bevy of her fellow astro-nerds, hoping to pad their résumés, had flocked to join the summer crew, but virtually none of them had opted to stay for the next nine months. They were already heading stateside to apply for post-docs and lab positions with their shiny new South Pole credentials.

Anne didn't begrudge them their priorities; she knew how the game was played. But she'd wanted to prove something beyond her capacity for science, and there was no better stage for that than a winter season at Shackleton. Well, being assigned to the next spacewalk, perhaps. But who said that wasn't in the cards, too? At thirty-eight, she was young, in shape, and attractive enough to become the next face of space exploration. Her academic credentials were pristine, and if they wanted to know how she performed in a stressful environment, a winter-over at Shackleton should lay just about anyone's fears to rest. Even the most skeptical, chauvinistic review board in existence would be impressed that she'd survived months at the world's coldest research facility and not ended up as a popsicle—

She put a hand to her mouth. *What is wrong with you?* Barely a day had passed since the news that Sheryl had died out on the ice and here she was making jokes, even if it was unintentional. Colin had told her that Sheryl had frozen to death, unable to make it back to the station after going for a long run past the skiway. Anne imagined what it must've been like as the cold crept into your bones, to feel your life ebb away . . .

She gave a little shriek. Standing in the doorway was a tall man wearing black denim overalls over a waffled long-sleeved undershirt. He had corn silk–blond hair and blue eyes that reminded her of fishbowls. A patchy goatee and mustache decorated his face. Judging by the expression on his face, he was as startled as she was.

"Jesus Christ." Her voice crackled, the fear turning her angry. She put a hand to her throat, feeling as though her heart had stuck there. "Who the hell are you?"

"Sorry, ma'am. I didn't mean to scare you." He gestured at the wall behind the door. "Can I take a look at the panel over here?"

"What?"

"I'm the electrician," he said, enunciating the words in a flat Midwestern accent. "I got to do a first inspection for the winter season."

"God, you startled me," she said. Now that her heart rate was returning to normal, she saw he was holding a workbag and had trailed a cart full of tools behind him. It was a wonder she hadn't heard him coming down the hall. "Go ahead."

He placed his bag on the floor with a light metallic clatter, then pulled the cart into the room and shoved it against a wall. She watched him for a minute, uncertain if she should leave and let him do his thing, or if she should continue working, or if she should hover and act like she was interested in his work. Then it occurred to her that maybe she should hang around and make sure he didn't do anything to the actual equipment, the stuff a wire jockey shouldn't touch.

If he's doing the first inspection of the season, then he's a winter-over, just like you, Anne reminded herself. *And you don't want to get off on the wrong foot with one of the people you're going to be stuck with for most of a year.*

Putting on her best smile, she walked toward him, sticking her hand out as she went. "I'm sorry. Let's start over. I'm Anne. I'm one of the astrophysicists wintering over. And please don't call me ma'am. It makes me feel so old."

The man glanced up from sifting through the items on the cart, then back down. He slowly extended his hand. "Leroy Buskins."

I wonder if he's ever shaken hands with a woman outside of a church before. "You're staying on for the winter, Leroy?"

He nodded. "Just got in."

"They don't give you much time to rest, do they?" she asked, putting some sympathy in her voice. "A day to get your wits about you and then you're on your first shift."

"Yeah." His eyes flicked to her hair and she pushed a stray lock behind one ear self-consciously. "You were already here? From the summer, I mean?"

"That's right. I was one of the lucky few who got to stay on through two seasons. A full year. You can get a lot more work done that way."

He nodded, then turned back to his tray with a trace of a smile. "You don't have to worry about your instruments, ma'am. I know better than to touch anything except the wires behind the panel over there."

"Thank you, Leroy," she said, ashamed. She'd taken him for a country bumpkin, something she'd vowed never to do at the Pole. Nobody down here was an idiot, even if they looked like a hayseed and wore overalls. "How about I leave you to your work, then? I'd probably just be in your way."

"Yes, ma'am." Leroy pulled out a screwdriver and went to work removing the panel. "I'll be about half an hour."

"Then that's when I'll come back." Anne went over to her desk to grab some papers and her coffee mug, then headed for the door, her long hair swinging with each step. It was going to be a busy couple of days and she needed to meet with the other astrophysicists—or at least learn their names—and now was a good time to do it.

Just before she reached the door, she thought she heard Leroy say something and she glanced over with an expectant smile, but his attention was focused on the mess of wires that sprouted from the wall, frowning in concentration and whispering to himself as he worked.

CHAPTER FIVE

Cass hurried down the hall to the A4 wing and along the narrow corridor to her berth, a five-by-ten-foot box that resembled a small dorm room at a state school where the funding had dried up.

A single bed was built into the left-hand wall. Next to it was the only horizontal surface in the room aside from the bed: a tiny nightstand that acted as both desk and bookshelf. Resting on it was a well-thumbed copy of *The Worst Journey in the World*, a mug with three-day-old coffee in it, a portable alarm clock, a reading light, and a handset phone. A large, single piece of cardboard had been cut to fit into the room's only window so as to block out the light that spilled through it twenty-four hours a day during the summer. It had been there when she'd arrived back in November and she'd never removed it. Judging by the packing label that said "FEB 2008," she was just the latest in a long line of people who hadn't bothered to take it down.

Overhead, chipped ceiling panels fit poorly in their flimsy metal frames, loosened and damaged by Polies pulling them down to check for leftover booze and other treasures hidden from season to season. All Cass had found was a deflated soccer ball and three bottles of mint Irish cream liqueur. The gray-green liquid sloshing around in the bottles had apparently looked so gross that even booze-hungry Polies hadn't broken them open.

A closet near the entrance was just big enough to hold three pairs of jeans, three shirts, several sets of cargo pants, sweaters, and two fleeces that could function as work outfits or casual wear as needed. The rest of the space was taken up with the two backpacks and five pairs of running shoes she'd brought on the long commercial flights from Logan to LAX, and from LAX to Christchurch, then—courtesy of the USAF—from Christchurch to McMurdo on the battleship-sized C-17, and on the final flight to Shackleton.

The small space wasn't meant for comfort, but at least she could reach everything from the door. In four quick moves, she grabbed a makeup kit, a "nice" sweater that showed off her modest chest, and a relatively clean set of jeans. She changed in the shared bathroom, chucked her work clothes into her berth as she ran by, then left the dormitory and entered Shackleton's main artery, where she slowed her pace. No one liked to see running down the halls—it put people on edge, made them glance around for the emergency. But a brisk walk put her inside the foyer of Destination Alpha, where she glanced at her watch. Thirty seconds before her guests were scheduled to appear. Alpha, the main entrance to the base, was on the second floor. The stairs slowed all but the fittest visitors.

She took that half minute to settle her ever-present butterflies. Leading visitors through the station was one of her least favorite things to do, and that included cleaning restrooms. The forced social interaction went against every instinct she had—she was shy, retiring, geeky. But that's precisely why she'd volunteered as a tour guide. The engineer in her knew that a system's potential was discovered only when pushed to its limit. If she wasn't in Antarctica to find out more about herself, then why was she here?

A gust of cold air blasted through the meat locker doors and hit her full in the face, whisking those thoughts away. Deb stomped through the door, trailed by eight people stuffed into the ubiquitous scarlet Antarctic parkas with the faux-fur trim around the hood. They shuffled forward like penguins, forced by the awkwardness of many layers to turn their entire bodies if they wanted to look around. Deb gestured toward Cass.

"All right, everyone. I'm going to leave you in the capable hands of one of the station's best guides. Besides keeping the place spick-and-span, Cass can drive, maintain, or fix just about anything ever built."

"And she's not hard to look at either," said one of the men in front. He was of late middle age, with a doughy face and capped teeth. The men around him, younger versions of him, laughed.

There's our VIP. Putting the face to the name finally clicked for Cass. Senator Graham Sikes, most likely visiting Shackleton in order to reassure a vaguely troubled public that the one-hundred-and-fifty-million-dollar base—the crown jewel of NSF research stations little more than a year ago—would be just fine under the control of the giant multinational corporation TransAnt.

Cass smiled, ignoring the senator's remark but inwardly imagining her fist connecting with his face. "You can take off your shells now that we're inside, everyone, but hold on to them. It's a toasty seventy degrees in the upper station, but I'll be giving you a full tour today, which means we'll be going down into the service arches below the station, where it's a constant sixty below."

She waited patiently through the rustling of Gore-Tex, the mechanical rasp of zippers unzipping, the jokes and groans about having just put all this junk on. "Welcome to Ninety South and the Shackleton South Pole Research Facility, formerly the Amundsen-Scott South Pole Station. You're visiting us at an interesting moment—we're just a few days from starting our winter-over season, the first under the auspices of TransAnt. Wintering over means when the final flight leaves today, it'll be the last plane the crew will see until mid-November, two hundred and seventy days from now. For most of that time, the South Pole is in complete darkness, outside temperatures can drop to as low as one hundred degrees below zero, and the base is, in effect, completely cut off from the rest of the planet."

She'd memorized the lists of salient facts that she threw at them now, from the two miles of ice under their feet to the average wind speed at the station to reiterating the most significant fact of all: once winter arrived, there was no physical way to reach the outside world.

An aide raised his hand. "Isn't there a snow road from here to McMurdo Station?"

Cass nodded. "The South Pole overland Traverse, or the SPoT. When your plane takes off from here, look out the window to your right and you'll see it, a trail of thin blue sticks leading away from the base. It ends almost a thousand miles away at McMurdo Station. But it's operational only during the summer, when the sun shines twenty-four hours a day. Even then, it takes more than a month for a fully loaded convoy to reach Shackleton. If it made the run without freight, it might make the trip in half that time. And, of course, there are frequent flights, like the one you'll take back to McMurdo. But during winter, neither is possible due to the constant darkness and the potential for extreme winds."

"So what would you do in case of a real emergency?"

"We'd have to take care of it ourselves," Cass said. "We're equipped to handle almost any contingency. We have a full trauma center—you'll see that later—and possess the power, food, and emergency equipment to last the nine months until the summer crew arrives."

"No one can fly in, even in an emergency?"

"There *have* been three recorded winter flights, all of them small craft performing life-saving medevacs," Cass conceded. "But winter winds have been clocked at hurricane force and the skiway has no lights, which, as you can imagine, is particularly inconvenient when there's complete darkness for half the year. No plane can take off or land in those conditions. Those three flights were major exceptions."

"So it can be done, but only *in extremis* and, I imagine, only for one or two lucky—or unlucky—souls," Sikes said.

"Exactly. The reality is, we're stuck here." She smiled, getting ready to deliver the punch line in three . . . two . . . "During winter-over, what happens at Shackleton stays at Shackleton."

That got the expected chuckle and, rapport established, she coaxed them into moving with her down the corridor, showing them the science lab, the gym, the galley and mess hall where everyone took their meals. If one ignored the setting, it was the stuff of tours at college campuses and army bases everywhere and not the most scintillating stuff. To snap the group out of its complacency, she paused to point out the flags and medals from various visiting dignitaries from around the world, as well as memorabilia—South Pole markers from years past, a harpoon from a nineteenth-century whaling ship, and the station's prized possession, a page from Ernest Shackleton's journal during his time as a young mariner on the *Tintagel Castle*. Sikes and his clan murmured and hummed their appreciation, then they climbed a short set of stairs to continue to the library, the lounge, and the movie room.

"They didn't spare any expense, did they?" This from one of the young staffers who had laughed the loudest at the VIP's joke. "I guess TransAnt wants its people to be treated to the best."

"The shortest staff assignment at Shackleton is the summer rotation, at just four months," Cass explained patiently, "but the winter crew is required to stay for nine, and some elect to stay for the entire calendar year. You can see how morale can be a problem if there aren't at least a few comforts. Over that long winter, we also have to combat T3 syndrome, a mental fugue state brought on by the lack of sunshine and the repetitive environment. Four decades of human behavior studies concluded that it would be foolish to spend millions on a scientific research facility only to fail because the crew had cabin fever."

"Speaking of research, the experiments are still conducted to the standards set by the NSF?" He furrowed his brow.

"Yes," Cass said, then plunged into the corporate message she'd been told to memorize. "TransAnt maintains a one hundred percent commitment to preserving the original mission of the base, which is to advance science in any and every capacity."

"Except that TransAnt is assured of research and patent exclusivity, correct?"

Cass hid a grimace. The benefits their employer would receive for taking the reins of Shackleton away from the NSF were well known and difficult to defend. With the possible exception of TransAnt employees like Hanratty, Taylor, and the base psychologist, Dr. Keene—those who were not either new hires or remnants of past South Pole crews like the rest of them—no one on base was excited about increasing TransAnt's bottom line instead of working purely for science. But that was beyond their pay grade. For most, the South Pole was a once-in-a-lifetime opportunity, and if they needed to be employees of TransAnt to come here, so be it.

"I'm personal friends with most of TransAnt's board of directors, Jimmy," Sikes broke in testily. "I'm sure there's nothing untoward about the situation."

"I understand, sir, but you're going to be fielding some tough questions when we return—"

"It's nothing I can't handle. In any case, all the public wants to know is that less of their tax money is going to pie-in-the-sky science projects and whether or not we've found the cure for cancer under a block of ice. No one cares if TransAnt makes a small profit at the same time, especially considering the risk they ran taking charge down here. We'll work on messaging on that long flight back."

"It's bad optics," Jimmy groused, unsatisfied. "This place is outfitted like a resort."

"Don't begrudge them a few creature comforts, son. You've never lived in subzero temperatures for nine months."

"I don't know about that, sir," a third man interjected, a handsome, Harvard-looking type. "Have you met Jimmy's mother?"

After the laughter had died down, Cass pulled the group along to the berths and the greenhouse, the e-systems control room and the IT pit, but the big belly laugh at Jimmy's expense had popped the cork on the formality of the group. Snickers and side conversations picked up as they waddled down the corridor, a sign that attention spans were shrinking. Time to wow them a little. She stopped in front of a door set into a black-and-orange-checkered wall.

"If you take a peek in here, you'll see a room with a kitchenette, some comfortable couches, and shelves full of books. It looks just like one of our extravagant lounges." She glanced at Jimmy. "We call it the

Lifeboat. The thick wall you noticed is a three-hour-rated firewall, the kitchen is stocked to keep a skeleton staff alive for weeks, and the whole mini-wing has its own dedicated power supply."

One of the men cleared his throat. "Why three hours on the firewall?"

"Our engineers have calculated that's the maximum amount of time it would take for the rest of the station to burn to the ground." Cass let that sink in. "There's some extra margin built in, but not much."

"I thought you said you were stranded here, that no one could reach you from McMurdo, even if the station were in trouble," Sikes said, curious. "The existence of the Lifeboat implies a rescue would be forthcoming."

"I exaggerated a bit. The three medical flights we discussed were successful, of course, but there's no way to safely or efficiently remove more than one or two crew members at a time, so we currently have no protocol for transporting ten or twenty people during the winter-over. However, if the base itself were in jeopardy, with all hands at risk, there's a plan in place to initiate a rescue."

"At which point, it's not about the ability to do it, but the time to make it happen."

She nodded. "The expectation is that an overland rescue operation could make it here from McMurdo in about two months. Hence, two months of survival supplies."

"Isn't there a Russian station fairly close, though?"

"Yes," she said. "Lyubov Orlova. It's only about fifty kilometers to the southwest—quite close to the SPoT highway, in fact—but its full-time crew is tiny, smaller even than the winter-over numbers here at Shackleton. In an emergency, we'd overwhelm them, putting both populations at risk."

There were nods and murmurs of assent. After passing the fire lockers and more display cases, they reached the end of the hall, where a set of steel doors blocked their path. Cass stopped and turned to face the group.

"This is the point where I give you the choice of how we proceed. We can return to the first floor and look at more labs, berths, and maintenance facilities. But"—she gestured behind her—"this is the top of the tall, vertical tower I'm sure you saw on your way in. We call it the Beer Can. It's a massive corrugated metal cylinder protecting a stairwell that not only provides access outside at ground level, it keeps going fifty feet down into the substation ice. That's where our service arches are—the place where we fix things, build things, and store things."

"So, what's our choice?" Harvard Man looked at her quizzically.

"We only have time to do one. The first floor is warm, safe, and dull. The service arches are cold, crude, and interesting."

"You're not really selling the physics lab," Sikes joked.

She smiled. "I'm the station's mechanic. I don't need no stinking room-temperature work environment." Light laughter and gestures toward the Beer Can. "All right, then. Put on your parkas and gloves. Except for the lack of wind, this is just like heading outside."

After running her eyes over them to make sure they were geared up—it would be her fault if frostbite took the tip of someone's nose and ended a promising political career—she motioned them through the two thick metal doors that led to the most intriguing section of the base.

Sikes and his group gave a soft, collective grunt as they stepped into the frozen air, inert and so cold as to be almost hanging in front of them. It caught in the chest with hooks and instantly froze the soft, moist membranes inside the nose.

The Beer Can was just as Cass had described it—a towering, unheated silo with the sole function of protecting the station's outer staircase from getting buried in drifts of snow and ice. Amenities included a frozen handrail and one stark white lamp at each curl of the stair. Narrow, quadruple-paned thermal windows provided some illumination now, but as the austral winter progressed and the sun fled the continent, there would be nothing beyond the glass but a bruise-colored twilight followed soon after by a velvet darkness.

Cass guided the group to the edge of the landing and gestured for them to peer downwards. The flooring was an industrial gridwork of steel that was both functional and allowed them to see through each step to the one below it.

"As you no doubt saw when you came in, the entire station is elevated about fifteen feet in the air on thirty-six concrete pilings. This allows snow to pass underneath the station rather than build up against the sides, as happened to the original domed station from the seventies, eventually burying it. The angled construction of the station's underbelly actually increases wind speed, causing it to scour the built-up snow away.

"The Beer Can allows access to the first and second living floors, as well as outside access to the ground level. But, as I mentioned before, the stairwell continues down fifty more feet below the base. It's not technically under*ground*, as all the space has been carved from solid ice. What we call service arches are large hangars that have been constructed inside these spaces to house most of the maintenance and storage facilities for Shackleton. We'll take a short peek into each area, then hurry back before we freeze solid. Everyone ready? Hold on to the handrail as we go."

She led the way down the steps, the silo filling with the sound of eighteen rubber boots thumping on steel. Despite being a descent, she stopped at the bottom floor to give everyone a rest. Shackleton was almost ten thousand feet above sea level, which meant things like altitude sickness and high-altitude edemas were real possibilities, especially for amateurs who'd flown in from sea-level McMurdo just for the day. The only thing more embarrassing than the VIP losing the tip of his nose would be him keeling over from a high-altitude-induced heart attack. Once Sikes had stopped sucking in air and blowing it out in billows, she turned and took them into the bowels of the station.

What she showed them wasn't much different than a tour of the vocational departments of a large high school—carpentry, plumbing, and auto shops. In her own domain, the VMF, she gave a quick summary of the work she did on a normal day, pointing out the cherry picker that let her work on the tallest vehicles as well as the snowcats and massive Mantis construction crane, laid up for winter storage.

Despite the clutter, the arched ceiling and massive scale gave the entire area the feel of a chapel devoted to vehicle maintenance.

Back in the hall, Cass gestured to the ice that bloomed on the ceiling, on the walls, on all the metallic surfaces of the lights and structure around them. "The hallways connecting the shops and arches are as cold as the Beer Can, so the moisture from our breath causes small icicles to form on the ceiling. It's a far cry from the labs above, where most folks wear shorts and Hawaiian shirts to work. Any questions?"

She waited, but the sheer presence of the ice around them was palpable in a way it hadn't been in the station; its density smothered all sounds. Footsteps died almost instantly, leaving only muffled breathing and the occasional sniff. The silence was contagious; aside from a few whispered comments, the banter and mumbled conversation was gone.

Leading them single file down the hall, she let them experience the heft of the place until they reached a bump-out in the corridor. The set of pipes that had followed them overhead now joined a host of others in an alcove before shooting off in three directions. She stopped and turned to the group.

"This intersection is one of the most interesting parts of the sub-ice section of the base, though not because of the pipes." She pulled out a flashlight and pointed it at the alcove. Hidden deep in the tangle of pipes was a short corridor. At the end was a plain, plywood door. "That's the entrance to the ice tunnels. Not ones framed by corrugated ceilings and walls, but passages literally carved out of the ice."

"Are they part of the regular station?" Sikes asked. His voice started at just above a whisper.

"Yes and no. Most are remnants from past stations and utility corridors for fresh water, sewage, electricity, and fuel. We've repurposed some and left others."

Harvard cleared his throat. "I heard a rumor that past crews have used the ice tunnels to make—what do you call them?—shrines to commemorate their time here."

"It's not officially permitted, of course, but personnel at Shackleton are allowed to go almost anywhere on base, so it would be almost impossible to keep them from making the shrines."

"I'd think you'd want to stop that kind of thing," Jimmy said.

"A little bit of illicit behavior goes a long way toward improving morale. Better to let a few of the crew blow off steam putting some memorabilia in a niche than going postal halfway through a winter-over."

The group nodded. Probably thinking about being trapped with Jimmy for nine months.

"Can we see the shrines?" Sikes asked.

"I'm sorry, we can't for safety purposes."

"Can you tell us what's in them? I've seen pictures of some."

"Well," Cass said, hesitating as she thought of one cubbyhole that had a set of four upright, brightly colored dildos named Fred, Ted, Ned, and Red. Polies had a strange sense of humor. "They're really just small spaces with personal effects. A compass, an empty beer can, that kind of thing, although one year someone smuggled an entire sturgeon to the base and made a shrine to it. Since it's almost zero percent humidity and below freezing in the tunnels, nothing ever rots. So there's a gigantic, mummified fish back there that means a lot to somebody, somewhere."

She moved on before they could try to pressure her into taking them into the tunnels. The hall's narrow mouth disgorged them into another hangar-like arch. Everyone's eyes turned upwards at the metal ribs seventy feet above them; they were all Jonahs in the belly of an Antarctic whale.

"This is our next stop, the logistical facility, which is a fancy name for warehouse. All of our food, emergency extreme cold weather gear—ECW, for short—and base supplies are kept here. It's the coldest deep freeze on the planet, so dry goods are perfectly preserved. When the end of the world eventually comes, there will still be powdered milk and freeze-dried coffee here."

Sikes glanced at his watch, no mean feat through three layers. Cass took the hint. "If we had more time, I'd take you outside through one of the exits through the VMF or the fuel station, but that's definitely the long way around. So, let's retrace our steps, get something hot to drink in the galley, then I'll hand you back over to Deb. I'm sure she's got plenty more to show you before you get on the plane to McMurdo later today."

There was an overall sound of murmured relief. With the tour essentially over, the aides fell into chatter and jokes again as they followed Cass back through the arches. Freed of the obligation to guide the group, she set a brisker pace than she had coming down, but the senator caught up with her and matched her stride.

"You talked a lot about the facilities, Ms. Jennings," he said, "but you didn't say much about the people."

She shot him a sidelong glance, wondering what kind of answer he was after. "The station was designed with the people in mind, Senator. As you say, we've got the lounges, movies, music . . . even the menu in the galley was put together to keep morale up. There's also enough space to be alone, which is just as important as being part of the community."

"That's a fine answer," he replied drily, "no doubt provided by the TransAnt handbook. But what about the human side of things here? What do people do to relax that *wasn't* designed for them by a team of shrinks back in DC? Do you have drunken orgies? Are you sober as monks? And what happens when none of that works? You can't tell me someone hasn't gone batty down here before."

"Sorry to disappoint you, but things don't get that crazy. Everyone's too cold and tired." When she saw he was unconvinced, she tried humor. "You had to notice that everyone down here is a geek of one kind or another. We have trouble talking to other people, never mind organizing drunken orgies."

They passed the bump-out and he shot a glance into the darkness toward the door to the ice tunnels. "Humph. What about when someone loses their marbles down here? What happens then?"

"I haven't seen it happen," she said. "All I can say is, the selection testing for station personnel is some of the most rigorous in the world. People are stable, happy, and well balanced."

"You'd put yourself in that category, then?"

Not really. "Yes. Although I'll admit you have to be a different kind of crazy to come down here in the first place. They say everyone who comes to Antarctica is either running from something or to something."

"And which are you?"

"I'm somewhere in between, Senator." She put a note of finality on the end of the sentence. *Subject closed.*

"How do you feel about the death of that woman . . . Sheryl, was it?"

She stumbled, feeling like she'd been kicked in the stomach. "You know about that?"

He smirked. "Mr. Hanratty told me. He figured, rightly, that word would get out sooner or later and that it was better to be transparent about the tragedy now than have it appear later when it would suggest a cover-up. Since Shackleton isn't under NSF purview anymore, the day-to-day situation isn't a governmental concern, of course, but there's still intense public interest in what happens down here."

"We'll all miss Sheryl," she said, choosing her words carefully. "But if officials determine her death was an accident, then it's important to keep the base moving forward."

"Do you think her death was an accident?" He peered at her as though examining a specimen.

She started. "Of course."

"Ah. Your answer seemed to suggest . . . well, never mind."

To forestall another battery of questions, she picked up the pace and within a minute they found themselves at the base of the Beer Can. She would normally point out the cheerful, handwritten message "EARN THAT COOKIE!" some wag had scrawled on the bottom step in permanent marker, but she didn't spare anyone a break, marching directly up the stairs until Jimmy called for her to stop. Months of high-altitude work at the Pole had paid off; her pulse had barely bumped past normal. Based on the number of aides holding on to railings or bent over, sucking wind, however, they hadn't enjoyed a similar training. Sikes looked ready to stroke out.

She gave them a minute, then flogged them upstairs to the top level and down the hall to the galley. Most were too tired to take their parkas off before they sank into the plastic chairs in the mess hall. Sikes, ashen-faced, sat at one end of the table, eyes closed and pinching the bridge of his nose.

Cass spoke to the cook to line up coffee and hot chocolate for the group, then stood at the head of their table, her hands folded in front of her, smiling sweetly. "I hope you enjoyed the tour. Do you have any questions for me before I call Deb?"

"Yeah." Jimmy groaned, rubbing his temples. "What the hell are you people made of?"

"It takes a special breed to want to come here." *And you're not it.* "It's been a pleasure showing you Shackleton station. Have a safe flight back to McMurdo."

She turned and left. As she opened the door into the hall, she heard Sikes say, "Gentlemen, there goes the only thing more frigid than the ice this station is built upon."

The door swung closed on not only the last group of visitors she'd have to guide this season, but maybe her career as a tour guide, as well. After that performance, it seemed doubtful that she'd be asked to reprise the role. In fact, if Sikes had any pull at all, it might be doubtful she'd be allowed to come back to the station. And maybe that was okay.

CHAPTER SIX

The stack of files behind Hanratty's chair towered like some kind of totem pole, each pale manila folder telling a story, though most were as enigmatic or inscrutable as the carved wooden face of a god or a demon. Each contained enough paper to make the whole stack over a foot and a half high.

He poked his head out of his office door. Deb was at her desk shuffling through activity reports. He cleared his throat. "Would you mind running interference for me if anyone comes in, Deb? If I don't clear my in-box, my ass is grass."

She shot him a thumbs-up without raising her head. Hanratty backed into his office and sat down at his desk, spinning in place to address the tower of files. He thumbed the stack, glancing at the names typed in small caps on the tabs at the top. Klimt, Takahashi, Simon, nearly a dozen others. He'd sifted through them so many times that they were no longer in alphabetical order, so he'd fallen into his own classification scheme.

First came the most obvious way to tell them apart: the thickness of the folder. A wad of paper didn't necessarily mean there was a problem; it just meant a lot had been written on the subject. His next criterion was more illuminating: the swatch of color created by the papers inside. White was innocuous. Splashes of green and pink were concerning.

Dark pink bordering on red was what his old buddies at DoD would've labeled *roundhouse:* . Hanratty had managed to visually distinguish the roundhouse folders—four in all—from the others at a glance.

A very few folders could be separated by his last criterion, his personal touch: the number of inky thumb stains on the outer folder and name tab. He'd read and reread the contents of those files so often that the tabs had been worn down to rounded bumps peeking out of the pile.

He'd fought to have physical folders at all. TransAnt's administrative branch had battled him tooth and nail to digitize the records, reminding him that every scrap of written word on base could be contained on a single hard drive or sent over the network in a burst less than a minute long. Physical objects had volume, space that equaled expense when it came to shipping things to the bottom of the earth.

He'd stood his ground. Being old-fashioned had been part of it, of course, but the real reason was that digital files could be stolen and replicated a million times without anyone knowing. If only a finite number of physical copies—in this case, one—existed, then their theft would be obvious. Sometimes the simplest measures were the best.

The base psychologist possessed his own dossiers on the staff, of course, though in reality, Keene had been given no more than half the contents that existed in Hanratty's files. Sometimes Keene gave him a look when they spoke about Shackleton's crew and Hanratty wondered if the man knew he'd been given the *Reader's Digest* version.

Hanratty found the folder he'd been looking for and set it aside from the others, though he didn't open it, not yet. He knew its contents intimately, and he wanted to have it at hand, but he also didn't want to taint his recent observations with a fresh read. Better to jot down his impressions, add them to the growing pile, and synthesize later.

A single white sheet of paper with no lines or holes was his preferred scribbling pad. He pulled out a red, felt-tipped pen and wrote at the top:

E1. SUB1. DISCOVERY OF LARKIN BODY

Next to that, he placed the date. It seemed faintly ridiculous to do so—he'd have as much chance forgetting the day Sheryl Larkin had died as his own birthday—but he'd learned over time that any and every bit of information was valuable.

He took out a ruler and marked off an inch of white space with a tiny dot of his pen, then proceeded to write using bullet points and acerbic sentence fragments. He kept at it for the next thirty minutes, sometimes with speed and confidence, but more often with his eyebrows knotted in concentration and tapping the pen's cap against his teeth, a habit his wife had found infuriating. *Ex-wife*, he corrected himself, then sealed off that line of thought like he'd closed a tank hatch and spun the wheel.

He frowned when he'd nearly filled the page. The unrelieved red scratches gave a sense of alarm to the whole thing, which hadn't been his intention. Most of his notes were only observations, with just a few items that deserved special attention. Sighing, he reached into his drawer and pulled out a blue pen, this time to underline only the critical parts, the most significant of which was the last line on the page.

Yesterday, after returning to Shackleton with Larkin's body and leaving the VMF, he'd acted on a hunch and told Taylor to head back without him. Creeping like a thief, he'd rested his ear against the garage door, then peeked inside to confirm with his eyes what he'd heard with his ears. The intel had been valuable, but he'd slunk away, ashamed of himself. Even now the memory caused him to curl his lip.

He exhaled through his nose, long and slow, consciously purging the thought and the emotions that rode shotgun alongside it. Too much depended on this project, professionally and personally, for him to get squeamish or sentimental about his conduct. If a brief moment of shame was the worst casualty of the winter, it would be a ridiculously small price to pay. He circled the last bullet point and read it once more.

Subject distraught upon return (expressed privately). Seemed to feel personal culpability. Highest—lowest?—emotional point observed to date.

He capped the blue pen and tossed it into the drawer, then blew on the ink to make sure it had dried—an old habit—before the page went into the file to join the others. He let the folder's leaf fall shut, then tossed the well-thumbed file beside the stack and picked up the next one. Sparing a glance at the name, he slipped another single sheet of unblemished paper from the ream, picked up his red pen, and got back to work.

CHAPTER SEVEN

The two men stared at each other for a pregnant moment until the one behind the desk said, "You just came in on yesterday's flight with the other fingies, didn't you?"

"The what?"

A smile. "Sorry. It's local slang. Fingie stands for 'fucking new guy.' It's just a term we use. No insult intended. Anyway, you just came in?"

"Yes, sir."

"First time in Antarctica?"

"First time." He nodded.

"Why don't you tell me something about yourself?"

"What do you want to know?"

"Like where you grew up."

He smiled nervously. "Isn't that all in my file?"

"It tells me where you were born, where you went to high school, where you've lived. But those are just facts." The man gestured extravagantly. "My file says I was born in San Francisco and earned a degree at Stanford. Those are facts, and true, but they mean very little. Millions of people live in that area and tens of thousands have gone to that school. If I said instead that, as a child, I lived in a small town on the coast and woke up smelling pine trees every morning, that tells you something no written record can. Do you see what I mean?"

"I guess so." He considered. "Though there's nothing much to tell. I was born on a farm in Iowa, learned how to fix tractors and turn the lights on when they quit, then got the heck out of there as soon as I could."

"What did your family farm?"

"Boredom."

Smile. "What did you sell?"

"Soy and corn, like everyone else."

"Did you have any brothers or sisters?"

His jaw muscles bunched once, then released. "A sister."

"Was she older or younger than you?"

"Older."

"Much older or just a few years?"

"She was seven years older than me."

"Most older sisters boss their younger brothers around. Did yours?"

He paused. "Yes."

"Did you push back?"

"When I could. There were chores. And work to be done. She whipped me when I didn't carry my share."

"Did you run away or did you have to take it whenever she dished it out?"

"I ran when I saw it coming." He laughed. "She was pretty good about hiding it until it was too late."

"And where did you run?"

"It's Iowa. There wasn't no place to run *to*. I just picked a direction and went."

"Out into the fields."

"Yes, sir."

"What did you do out there? How long did you wait before you went back?"

He tilted his head and smiled again. "You ever sat in a cornfield?"

The other man pushed his glasses up to the bridge of his nose. "No, I haven't."

"If you had, you'd know there's nothing to do. I sat and thought and I listened. When I figured I could sneak back into the house without getting a whipping, I went."

"To what did you listen?"

He hesitated. "The wind."

"Why the wind?"

"It was the only thing out there."

"What did it sound like?"

He paused. "Like wind."

"Was it the same every time?"

His eyes flicked around the room, following the shelves, counting the books. He was unaware his mouth moved as he did so. After a moment, he answered. "Not always. When it went through full cornstalks, it was different than later in the season."

"After the corn had been harvested."

"Yeah."

"And what was different about it?"

"It hummed, a little."

The man nodded. "Did you ever fight with your sister?"

"I told you, she whipped me."

"How about when you got older? Bigger? Seven years isn't much of a physical difference when you're sixteen or seventeen."

He shrugged. "I guess. Yeah."

"Did you hit her when she wasn't expecting it? The way she hit you?"

"Once or twice."

"When you were bigger and started to hit back, did you hurt her when you hit her?"

"No."

The man said nothing.

"I told you, I didn't."

"A lot of people would want to get back at someone who had punished them so much. Are you saying you never felt the urge to dish out some retribution?"

He gave another shrug, provided from an endless supply. "I made myself head out to the fields when I felt that come on real strong. When it got to be too much. When I got the jumps."

"And you listened to the wind?"

"Sure, if it was blowing."

"Do you still feel them?"

"Feel what?"

"The jumps."

"Sometimes."

"What do you do when you feel them?"

"I take a walk outside."

"Does the wind sound different here?"

"Yes."

"How is it different?"

He grinned. "Hell of a lot colder's all I know."

The man smiled back at him. "Winter is coming and it'll be dark all day, every day. That makes taking a stroll pretty hard. What are you going to do then?"

"I guess I'll have to walk it off in the halls. Work out in the gym, maybe."

Another nod. The man reached a long arm back to his desk and flipped through a stack of papers at the edge of his reach. He found what he was looking for, then studied the paper for a few moments, flipping it back and forth to check something. "Are you on any medications?"

"A few."

"And you brought those with you? Enough for nine months?"

"Sure. I don't need them all the time."

The man nodded, thoughtful, then smiled again and stood. "I think that's all I need for now. But I'd like to talk to you next week, if you don't mind."

"Why? Do you think I'm crazy, Doc?"

"Of course not. No more than any of us. But I get the jumps myself, sometimes. I find it helps to talk things out. What do you say?"

He thought about it. "Sure. But I can handle it. I'll be fine."

The other man smiled like his teeth had been painted onto his face. "I'm sure you will, Leroy."

CHAPTER EIGHT

Cass sat backwards in a plastic chair, resting her chin on her forearms, savoring the peaceful moment now that she'd put the tour with Sikes and his crew behind her. She squinted into the morning sun, her face almost pressed against the glass of the library window like a three-year-old ogling a fish tank. The view swallowed her entire field of vision. For a thousand miles in that direction, there was not a single human habitation.

She felt a rush of gratitude for the architect or site planner who had decided that the east-facing view from Shackleton would be of a vast, pristine expanse of ice. The western and southern sides—marred by outbuildings, the airstrip, and the deep-ridged tracks of hundreds of industrial vehicles—seemed to her to be the worst kind of accumulation of people and their things. It couldn't be an accident that there was nothing man-made visible on this side of the station. Someone had planned this view.

Interestingly, while the vista might be unblemished, it wasn't uninterrupted or uninteresting. The base had been built on a plateau and the escarpment it capped ran for hundreds of meters in a half-moon shape to the right. If she leaned away from the window and used a little imagination, she could curve her arm so that it matched the proportions of the ridge exactly. Angular shadows cast by frozen cliffs broke up the landscape while subtle blue variations in the sastrugi made the whole look more like a choppy sea than an unending field of very solid ice.

In time, probably, the technology would improve and the number of residents at Shackleton would increase until today's bustling research station would be merely the central building of a larger complex. Traffic and everyday commerce would compromise the land, and it would take a monumental effort to find a place where the past and present hadn't infiltrated the panorama.

Cass lowered her forehead and rested it on the thin muscle of her forearm, closing her eyes to preserve the searing afterimage. She liked that every detail appeared in perfect, monochromatic detail to her inner eye, fading like an old photo or a memory, so that she had to invent the missing pieces as they disappeared. When nothing of the memory-image remained, she raised her head and opened her eyes.

Without items, *things*, in it, the scene was empty, devoid of the meaning that objects and people would give it. And while it was comforting to stare into space for a time, to imagine unlimited potential, an empty canvas *was* a void if nothing was ever painted on it. At some point, potential had to be realized, or you simply ended where you began: a blank, empty, meaningless frame of white, waiting for effort to give it meaning.

She dropped her head to her forearm again. Each time she thought she'd found a place—a job, a relationship, a home—to begin the process of forgiving herself, some part of the memory would catch up with her and shove the past in her face. She'd move on to the next stop in the journey to rebuild herself, pushing out to more dangerous work in more remote locations, only to find her past had closed the gap after a few weeks, a month, a year.

Antarctica was different. She'd felt it the moment she'd touched down on that great snowy expanse. A place with no context, no limits, and with room to grow, to start over. She needed just a little more time. Time and a blank canvas, empty of the past, open to the future. A chance to start over. Again.

Cass savored the feeling a moment longer before quietly packing it away. One thing working at Shackleton was good for was keeping you too busy to make navel-gazing a habit. There was equipment to tend to in the VMF, tests to run, reports to file. She was pushing the chair away from the window when the door opened behind her. She turned to see Deb poking her head in and Cass's heart sank. Maybe Sikes had been less impressed with his tour than she'd thought.

"Don't tell me there's another tour."

"Not this season," Deb said as she walked over. "Hanratty wants you to report to Keene's office."

Her stomach twisted. "Keene? Why?"

Deb hesitated. "Sorry, Cass. I didn't ask."

"Right now?"

"Afraid so. And I wouldn't keep him waiting. I heard he puts that kind of thing in your profile." She turned to go, then stopped. "Nice job this morning, by the way. Sikes couldn't stop talking about you."

Message delivered, Deb returned to the main hall and disappeared around a corner, off to ruin more of someone else's day. Cass sat back down and put her forehead against the cool metal of the windowsill, the little bit of inner peace she'd achieved gone.

❄

Cass stopped at the nameplate. GERALD KEENE. Just the name, no title, which was appropriate. Few people at Shackleton really had titles, at least none that could be tacked to a door frame. On the other hand, the station "morale officer" seemed to merit one if any of them did. Had he asked to have it removed, afraid a small thing like a title below his name would cause people to shy away? It wouldn't have mattered. Everyone on base knew who the resident shrink was.

You're stalling.

She reached out to open the door when the latch moved under her hand, startling her. Keene stood in the doorway, looking at her impassively.

He was a walking contradiction, she thought, both robust and professorial, like a fourth-generation lumberjack who'd stumbled into higher learning and kept going until he'd crashed through the other side with a PhD. A full, reddish-blond beard, a broad set of shoulders, and a pair of fleshy hands inherited from his grandfather meshed poorly with a wave of academic indifference.

"Cass? Come in." Pale gray-green eyes behind gold-rimmed glasses sized her up from knees to chin before he turned back into his office, leaving it to her to catch the closing door and follow.

The room was something of a nonfunctional anomaly at the station. Bookshelves packed with manuals and academic journals lined the room wherever a soothing periwinkle-blue paint job didn't peek through. Three of the only comfortable chairs on base were grouped in a chummy circle around a coffee table while prints of Antarctica's landscape—Wilson's watercolor of Cape Crozier, Hurley's stark portraits of the *Endurance* trapped in pack ice—hung from the walls. And somehow, incredibly, Keene had smuggled in a small column aquarium that he'd placed on a narrow étagère. Cass watched as a flame-red Betta swam up and down its tiny cylindrical world.

Keene followed her gaze. "Not a bad metaphor for life here at Shackleton, is it? One-gallon personalities caught in a pint-sized environment."

She smiled woodenly. Keene waved her to a seat, then rounded his desk to sink into an office chair. It squeaked like an old mattress as he leaned back. "Normally I'd say, I'm sure you're wondering why I asked you here."

Cass nodded.

"But I think, under the circumstances, to do so would be insulting to both of us."

Cass waited, but Keene didn't say anything. He simply looked at her with an expectant expression.

She ducked her head. "Do you mean what happened to Sheryl?"

"Yes." Keene nodded in encouragement. "And your role in it."

"My role?" Cass blinked. "You mean helping Hanratty bring back her . . . body?"

"If that's what you want to talk about."

"I didn't ask to talk," she said, confused. "You did."

"Certainly, but I'd think you'd want to talk out the circumstances."

"I would?"

He shrugged. "It's not a small thing, a dramatic death at the base, right before a winter-over. Reduced staff, increased tensions. We haven't even shut the doors, officially, and we're already off to a rocky start."

"Rocky?" She stared at him. "Is that what you call Sheryl freezing to death?"

He waved a hand, like he was clearing smoke. "I apologize. A poor choice of words. Her accident has shaken the base to its core, is all I meant. Carrying on as if things were normal has been difficult for some people."

"I thought Hanratty said it was to be kept under wraps?"

"Cass." He gave her a look of profound disappointment. "Everyone on base knew about Sheryl before you were done taking your gloves off."

"Oh."

"Hanratty knew such a thing would be impossible to contain, so he told you to keep quiet in order to check a box, so to speak. Had he not done so, he could be accused of not maintaining decorum or enforcing protocol. But by making a show of telling you not to talk, he puts the onus on you and whoever knew about Sheryl when she was brought back."

"I see."

Keene nodded, apropos of nothing. "So, was it what you were expecting?"

"Was *what* what I was expecting?"

"How you felt? How the people you've spoken to about the accident felt?"

"I didn't speak to anyone."

The look of disappointment was back. "It's statistically and intuitively impossible that you didn't tell someone about Sheryl's accident. Biddi, perhaps?"

Cass's face flushed. She knew from experience that her color was especially noticeable around her hairline. Milk-white skin was nice except when it highlighted the slightest blush. "Well, if statistics say so, I guess I did."

The wave again. "Ninety-nine out of a hundred people will unburden themselves to a friend or colleague after a traumatic event, especially in a confined stressor environment. It's normal and, frankly, expected. You're in the clear."

Had she been in that much trouble? "Great."

Keene tipped forward in his chair, putting his elbows on the desk. "Let's forget that for a moment. Tell me what's in your head."

Cass hesitated, confused. "I'm not happy, naturally. Sheryl and I didn't work together, but I liked her. And you don't have to like someone to be horrified. To die out on the ice . . . alone, in a storm? It's terrifying. It's exactly what everyone fears the most down here."

"Yes, of course," Keene said. There was an impatient note in his voice. "But what were you *thinking*?"

"I . . ." Cass struggled to understand what he wanted from her. His words technically made sense, but they didn't fit the conversation. It was as if he were speaking to a third person in the room. "I was thinking how terrible it was to die like that, how much I didn't want it to be me, how glad I was that it *wasn't* me. If someone with her experience could die out there, then I could, too. Then I felt ashamed, I guess, because my second thought was that I wondered if we'd all be sent home even before we started and what a waste that would be . . ."

Cass trailed off. A change had come over Keene's face as she spoke. It was subtle, a soft unwrinkling around his eyes and relaxation of his mouth. Now that he'd leaned closer, she could see a fine spray of perspiration along his forehead, glistening over his eyebrows. She had the strange sensation that the third person in the room had suddenly disappeared.

Keene cleared his throat, then reached for a stack of folders resting on a corner of his desk. "Of course. Those are all perfectly natural emotional reactions. Anger, fear. Frustration at the waste of life, of time and effort. Yours and everyone else's. If you haven't already, you may find yourself blaming her, as well. You'll wonder why Sheryl wasn't more careful. What was she *doing* out there, risking herself and others? And, lastly, there will be some survivor's guilt, as well. You've had some experience with that, I believe?"

There it was, the cannonball to the gut, the simple reminder that nothing would ever be normal for her. Cass fought to keep her voice steady. "Why am I here, Dr. Keene?"

But he'd already opened a manila folder stuffed with printouts and forms. It wasn't difficult to read JENNINGS, CASSANDRA typed across the tab. Keene leafed through the dossier like a deck of cards. In the hands of the station's psychologist, she could only assume he was looking at her psych evaluations, all of the comments and judgments and pronouncements that experts had made about her mental state. Maybe even from before she'd submitted her application for Antarctica.

He raised his head and held the folder up, giving her a smile that she supposed was meant to put her at ease. "Strange, isn't it, seeing your mental and emotional makeup boiled down to a few sheets of paper? I've always despised my colleagues' crude renderings of something so complicated as the human psyche, but what can you do?"

She stared at him.

Unperturbed, he carried on in a light, conversational tone. "Your SOAP scores are remarkable. Not to mention the other battery of tests you took. Your MMPI and 16PF are fine, although I have to admit, those two are of limited use. Would you believe that real estate agents and violent sociopaths score almost identically on the MMPI? Now, the FFI—sorry. I'm using a lot of lingo. The FFI is a personality survey—"

"I know what it is."

The Five Factor Inventory was the psychologist's scalpel, the tool with which they flensed a patient's emotional core. It was the most popular of the tests that revealed where a subject landed in terms of the psychological Big Five: openness, conscientiousness, extraversion, agreeableness, neuroticism. OCEAN, for those fond of acronyms.

Following the accident, when she couldn't sleep, couldn't hold on to a relationship, grew simultaneously bored and frantic at every job, she'd been subjected to a dozen different tests and batteries, many of which TransAnt had repeated. She'd managed to sneak a look at one of the summaries. Even now, she found herself remembering the words from the report. *Closed to experience . . . chronically introverted . . . unwilling to extend herself emotionally or intellectually . . . has turned to intense physical exercise as an emotional crutch . . . a classic neurotic.*

She flushed again. Her lips had been moving, mouthing the words of that report, and Keene had been watching her. She needed to pull herself together or he'd stamp "NUTS" on her personnel file and she'd be thrown onto the last plane along with Sikes and his circus.

"I've read the literature, Dr. Keene," she said, trying to reassert some control over the conversation. In her lap and out of Keene's sight, Cass squeezed her hands together, feeling the fingers bend under the pressure. "The crew of some of the most successful Antarctic missions exhibited exactly my kind of characteristics . . . they often excelled because of traits usually thought of as antisocial, in fact. You can't boil a person down to a five-point test or know how they're going to behave under stress from a set of questions."

"That's technically correct," Keene said slowly. "But those batteries are the best tools we have to predict emotional and mental behavior."

"People find a way to cross hurdles, regardless of their personal handicaps."

He shook his head. "Each year's crew faces isolation, confinement, and an extreme physical environment. We'd all like to think that they made it through those nine months of winter regardless of the mental or emotional makeup of their staff, but that is a deeply dangerous presumption. We can't let familiarity breed contempt. A winter-over at Shackleton is an almost unique human living situation and the margins for error are razor thin. What were manageable events for other crews might become a life-and-death crisis for this year's staff. If I see behavior or even an attitude that threatens that, it's my responsibility to call it out."

"What are you suggesting, Dr. Keene? That I'm too mentally unstable to work on snowmobile engines? That I'm unfit to do my job as a *janitor*?"

A smile tugged at the corners of his mouth and she realized she'd been baited. Would that go on her record? *Quick to take offense, dissatisfied with her role on base*. "Of course not, Cass. Nor do I think that your function as a . . . sanitation engineer should be looked down upon. I know all about the staffers versus the eggheads. If you think about it, I'm a staffer. I might have a PhD, but my work isn't tied to deep space astrophysics or neutrino analysis. And I've got the stigma of being on staff *and* the base shrink. Nobody wants to sit at my lunch table, I can tell you."

"Forgive me if I don't feel sorry for you."

"I'm not asking you to. I'm saying that I understand my role here and I'm comfortable with it."

She shook her head to clear it. "Dr. Keene, why am I here? I get it. I have a spotty psych profile. But I cleared every hurdle the recruitment team at TransAnt could throw at me and passed. I was asked by the station manager to help bring in a poor woman who'd died in the cold, yet I haven't broken down into a puddle or locked myself in my berth. What's the problem?"

Keene held up a placating hand. "It's precautionary, Cass. Nothing more. Your behavior at the station has been completely normal and, you're right, you've handled the situation with Sheryl in stride. As well, or better, in fact, as almost anyone on base. My only goal in talking to you today is to see if your . . . history and Sheryl's death, taken together, formed a third, synergistic, problem."

"Would her death be a trigger for me, you mean?"

"In short, yes."

"And?"

He closed her folder and tossed it back on the stack in the corner. "I don't see that it has been or will be. I'll be frank; your personal history and FFI profile concerned me before you even landed at Shackleton. But I simply see a skilled and dedicated woman doing her job in an exceptional environment under stressful conditions. Even your occasional verbal barbs are what would be considered a normal level of aggravation and aggression at being subjected to a psychological interrogation. As far as I'm concerned, you're fine."

Her hands relaxed, gently unfolding on her lap. She managed to keep from sighing with relief.

"However," he continued and the knot in her chest clenched again, "these are early days. We aren't even technically in the winter-over period. As you say"—he smiled—"you've read the literature. You know that the stressors that form the staple of the winter-over experience don't even begin to occur until later in the season, perhaps not even until midwinter."

"There's still plenty of time to go crazy, in other words."

"Something like that. So, I want you to come to me if you exhibit any kind of somatic issues. Things like sleep disturbance, poor appetite, constipation, fatigue, that kind of thing. They may seem like minor medical issues—and more in Dr. Ayres's bailiwick—but they can also be the precursors of profound psychological disturbance. Unfortunately, they're so incremental that they often go unaddressed until it's too late."

She nodded, but Keene waited her out until she said, "I'll do that."

"Good." He clapped his hands together and rubbed them like he was attempting to warm them. "Well, I hope this hasn't been too much of a burden."

"No, it's fine," Cass lied. The meeting was over and she was obviously free to go, but she hesitated, left with the feeling that she hadn't defended herself very well. Keene raised his eyebrows, but she had nothing, really, to say. She got to her feet and turned to leave.

"Cass?"

She turned back.

"Historically, the people who weather crises the best are those who adjust their expectations to fit the reality of the situation." He paused and his eyes flicked over her face. "And life at the South Pole is nothing more than a potential disaster held temporarily at bay. Isn't it?"

CHAPTER NINE

Keene sat at his desk long after Jennings had left, listening to the bubbles rising in the aquarium and doodling ever-widening circles on a notepad.

He'd like to believe that the girl wasn't who he'd thought she was. He'd run her through a series of confrontational and ambiguous questions prepared in advance and she'd responded to all of them as obtusely as one could expect from someone completely out of the loop. She'd looked like a duck and quacked like a duck, so he very much wanted to believe she was a duck. But—and he couldn't shake the *but*—a well-prepared graduate psychology student who'd taken a turn in a summer theater could've done as well.

Keene knew he was a first-rate psychologist, but he was also a realist; psychology wasn't mind reading and for every victory his field had made in behavioral prediction, it had accumulated a thousand failures, especially in the perilous field of individual predictive analysis. *Groups* were relatively easy to manipulate. Assess the synergies, conduct a few probing questions to test the water, and it was likely you could prod a mob into doing just about anything you wanted it to do. But put your figurative thumb on a single individual and it was like pressing down on a watermelon seed. They could go shooting off anywhere.

He grunted and put the pen down next to the pad with intentional precision, resisting the urge to throw it across the room. One individual's behavior he could definitely predict was his own, and what he saw in his immediate future wasn't good. He would stew and steam over all of the possible contingencies and tangents until he'd worked himself into knots. None of it was constructive; on the contrary, it was psychologically destructive. If he wasn't careful, Shackleton's station psychologist would be halfway to barking mad by midwinter. Not good.

He sighed and stood. *Tanto monta, monta tanto*. He could sit in his office for the next week and try to unravel the tangle of his suspicions, or he could just go and get the answer from Hanratty. And since he didn't have any more information after the interview with Jennings, he might as well go beard the lion in his den. If the station manager didn't like what he had to say, he could send him home. A disappointing end to his Antarctica career, perhaps, but he wasn't going to be played for a fool.

He pushed through the door of his office and went out to the hall, turning right to head for the administrative offices. On the way, he passed four or five of the scientists and staffers. A few gave him the standard Polie nod in greeting—eyes sliding off to one side, a flat-lipped bob of the head, a lengthening of the stride to discourage conversation—but most of the expressions he received were universally flat and blank. No one cozied up to the guy who held everyone's mental and emotional secrets.

Ironically, aside from a few exceptional cases, he rarely had cause to read any histories or, frankly, give two whits about them. On the other hand, he couldn't forget what he already knew, and he couldn't help but do a quick analysis of a few of those he passed in the halls.

"Dr. Keene," Biddi said as they passed each other at the entrance to the B2 wing.

"Biddi," he said, nodding, then did a double take, but she was already past him and heading down the hall. For a split second, he was sure she'd stuck her tongue out at him.

Frowning, he continued down the corridor. Hanratty's office was past the labs on the second floor of the B3 wing, the administrative heart of the station. Communications, base management offices, and the station's only conference room took up most of the wing.

He opened the door to the admin suite, nodding to Elise Simon, the station's only comms specialist, who had looked up from her console as he walked in. She turned away, ignoring him, and he smiled thinly at the back of her head. Elise had not reacted well at their first encounter when he'd suggested—after she'd admitted to insomnia and latent hallucinations about her work—that she apply for a less stressful position at McMurdo.

"Is Hanratty in, Elise?" he asked unnecessarily.

"His office is in front of you," Elise said without bothering to turn around.

His smile widened and he pushed through the steel door to the admin office. He nodded to Deb as she glanced up from her screen and got a cautious nod in return. He'd been careful to avoid pushing Deb's buttons, either in their initial meeting or since. The deputy director was one of the few people at the station with enough clout to make the next nine months hell for him, not to mention taint future assignments if she wished. Granted, he could do the same to her.

"Do you know if Hanratty is free, Deb?"

She tapped a pen against her teeth. "I think so. He's probably just making sure the Herc is on time for takeoff tomorrow. All routine stuff, though, so he's probably got time."

Keene thanked her, then reached out and rapped on Hanratty's door, two short, sharp knocks.

The answer was muffled by the door. "Come."

The manager's office, tiny by stateside standards, was vast compared to any other private space at Shackleton. Behind the desk, however, was what distinguished this room from almost any other on base—a wide picture window that was a thermal engineer's nightmare. The heat loss probably ran in the thousands of dollars per season, but the extravagance had been deemed necessary to both draw and reward the kind of administrative talent that would run a base at the bottom of the world.

The window had a broad view of the skiway, revealing the snowplows and blowers that were busy clearing the runway. Keene watched for a moment as the machines groomed the snow in precise lines.

Oblivious to the view, Hanratty was seated at his desk with his back to the window, frowning at something he saw on one of his three monitors. One hand was on a mouse, the other holding the receiver of an antiquated phone handset. He was dressed in a blue short-sleeved button-down with the TransAnt five-pointed logo emblazoned on the breast. The man was never cold; Keene had seen him stand outside for twenty minutes in the same outfit.

Hanratty's eyes flicked toward him, then back to the screen. "What can I do for you, Gerald?"

"I need a minute, Jack." Keene moved one of the guest chairs closer to the desk.

"Not a good time."

"It rarely is." He sank into the chair, crossed his legs, folded his hands, and waited.

Hanratty spared him an irritated glance. "I'm trying to make sure the last flight of the season gets off the ground in one piece. It's bad form to slam a US senator into the firn on his way out."

"The pilots have a lot more to do with that than you. It's what they're paid for, after all. Why don't you let them do their job and relax for once?"

Hanratty's already austere face tightened even further, but he took another minute to finish what he was doing, then turned his full attention on Keene. "All right, Dr. Keene. What can I do for you?"

"I just had an interesting conversation with our sanitation engineer extraordinaire."

"Jennings? Or Newell?"

"Jennings."

Hanratty showed mild surprise. "Did she ask to see you?"

"No, you did."

Hanratty frowned. "What are you talking about?"

"I sent word to Jennings that you required her to see me."

Hanratty folded his hands together, rested them on his desktop. Keene could see he had the man's full attention now. "And why would you do that?"

"I don't have the authority to require a staff member to undergo a psych eval unless they pose an immediate threat to the base or other crew. So, at best, all I could do was send her a politely worded request to chat, something she might've agreed to, or might not have. I wanted to guarantee that she would show up. And in the right frame of mind."

"Which was?"

"Cooperative."

"And you used my authority to do so."

"Correct."

Keene watched Hanratty's mental struggle play out on his face. The muscles of his jaw rippled up the side of his head. The man had a famous temper, but he was also sharp enough to know that his base psychologist wasn't here simply to push his buttons or indulge in an ego trip.

Hanratty got himself under control. "You'll explain."

Keene steepled the tips of his fingers together. "You subjected Jennings to quite a trauma yesterday with no warning and no subsequent emotional support. It was all the more extraordinary considering her past."

Hanratty shrugged. "She wasn't closer to Sheryl than anyone else on base, so I don't see how she was put in any more of an untenable emotional position than, say, Taylor or myself. I supposed I could've checked up on her today, but the reality down here is that that's not always going to happen. I assumed she'd been cleared by the stateside psych team. Was I wrong?"

"No," Keene said slowly, "but the question is, cleared for what?"

"To handle the emotional and mental adversity of a winter-over, obviously."

"And the death of a colleague?"

The station manager shrugged. "If necessary. It wasn't exactly listed in the season's work agenda."

"Is that all?"

"Christ, Gerald. Spit it out. What are you asking?"

Keene paused. "Jack, I've looked at Jennings's records. I've interviewed her. I called the head of the psych eval team back in Colorado Springs. I reached out to her therapist at home and stopped just short of ringing up her family doctor."

"Yes?"

"They all agree, she's a hot mess."

"None of us are perfect—"

Keene interrupted. "Psychologically speaking, there's no way in hell Cassandra Jennings is fit for work in Antarctica, never mind Shackleton, never mind a nine-month night at the South Pole."

Hanratty said nothing.

Keene leaned forward. "She's not the only one, Jack. The winter-over crew always has a few oddballs in it, which is perfectly fine and understandable. Personality diversity is one of the basic tenets of group success in a confined environment. But there are a dozen people on staff right now who I wouldn't trust to make it through a rainy weekend at the shore without cracking up, never mind a winter-over at the South Pole."

Hanratty cleared his throat. "What's your point?"

"My point is—considering the rigorous standards that every South Pole crew has been subjected to in the past—this can't be a mistake. Someone at some point knew exactly what Jennings and the other crew members were like and instead of selecting them *out*, they put them *in*." Keene stood and put his hands on the edge of Hanratty's desk. "Jack, what the fuck is going on?"

CHAPTER TEN

Cass shot a look over her shoulder as she walked, her boots squeaking on the compacted snow of the tunnel floor. Still stinging from her meeting with Keene, replaying the odd and humiliating exchanges in her head, she hadn't paid attention as she'd clomped down the steps of the Beer Can and into the arches. But the chance that anyone was following her was unlikely in the extreme; deep in the service tunnels, in the middle of the workday, no one was simply wandering around in the sixty-below, wondering if the station's mechanic was goofing off. And since the VMF was accessed via the tunnels, she was one of only a handful of people who had business under the base, anyway. If she ran into anyone, she was simply on her way to work.

Had there been anyone there, however, they might've gotten suspicious when, instead of continuing straight to the base's garage, she took a sharp turn at the conduit intersection, pulled out a flashlight, and headed straight for the ice tunnels that she'd discouraged a certain senator and his tour group from exploring.

She yanked at the plywood door, stuck after being squeezed and compressed over the years by the sinking ice, stepped through, and closed it behind her gently, then fumbled in the darkness for the switch embedded in the wall. The tunnel flooded with a sterile light. White bouquets of icy peonies and crystalline scales clung to every non-natural surface: off the bulb cages of the lights, along the metal framework, even to the insulated pipes. She stood perfectly still and listened. It was so cold that she had to breathe, painfully, through her mouth or the sound of air passing through her nose would cover the noise of anyone moving in the tunnel. Although the majority of sounds were swallowed by the crushing ice, most people made small sounds along the way simply to keep themselves company.

But those were no guarantees—she'd also come across people in the tunnels before who hadn't wanted anyone to know they were there. At least she could invent an excuse about conduit inspections. It was a little harder for two amorous meteorologists to come up with a good reason for rolling around in an ice tunnel in the dark. She continued moving. The sleeves of her parka, when they rubbed against the walls, made a noise like a dishrag being torn in two.

Maybe it was her introverted nature, but the ice tunnels were one of the first things she'd set out to explore when she'd finally made it to Shackleton. The thought that there was an entire subterranean complex below the world's most exclusive research facility gave her a thrill. The small secrets that had been hidden in the tunnels—the shrines, the doors to nowhere, the buried equipment—only added to the mystique.

One of those secrets was coming up at the tunnel's first turn, and she forced herself to stare straight at the wall as she rounded the bend. It was the first shrine and the one everyone who ever made it into the tunnels knew about.

Jerry.

Sitting in a square niche was the crude bust of a man, his mouth open in a frozen scream. It was made both more horrible and more comical by the fact that—while the eyes were clearly flange gaskets, and the mouth was the end of a vacuum hose—the entire sculpture was made of something . . . brown. Cass had heard theories that it was old cheese, or snow mixed with axle grease, or even leftovers from the latrine, but since almost nothing smelled down here and no one had

had the brass to . . . well, *taste* Jerry, the composition of one of the station's most famous shrines remained a mystery. He was worth a laugh in the light once you knew about him, but of course no one warned the fingies, and the screams of first-time fuel techs rounding the corner were sometimes heard as far away as Shackleton's galley.

The tunnels went on for hundreds of yards, peeling off from the main artery at various points toward old storage rooms, sewer bulbs, and dead ends. The tunnel was perfectly, almost eerily, rectangular, with only slight deviations and scallop-shaped patterns on the surface of the ice to show where the hydraulic tunneler—built specifically for the purpose—had shaved and carved out the shaft more than twenty years before. A very few tunnels, rough-hewn and rounded at the top like the entrance to a medieval chapel, were handmade, and sure as shit not on any station schematic.

She'd heard various reasons for the tunnels during her time at Shackleton. Some people had heard they were originally meant to be year-round pedestrian walkways between labs, living quarters, and maintenance hangars, but that funding dried up before they could be built. Others were sure that the tunnels had been—and still were—meant to connect to military facilities that none of them knew about. It was typical tinfoil-hat bunk, but she'd been in the tunnels when odd noises came to her from hundreds of feet ahead, or boot tracks that she'd never seen before disappeared after heading down one of the branches.

Cass knew that the primary reason for the tunnels, the one that disappointed everyone when they heard it, was simple: they harbored the sewage, fuel, and electrical lines for the station. All of it needed to be protected from the punishing environment and as a result, the main tunnel went on for nearly a half mile under the ice, with a dozen or more tangents branching off to carry the necessary resources to, or away from, every corner of Shackleton. Access hatches with ladders leading to the stub-ups on the surface had been built every five hundred yards as a safety measure, but the reality was that the doors and latches in most of them had frozen years ago and even those that might work were probably buried in drifts on the surface. That left the tunnels as the best way to access the more mundane needs of the station.

Of course, it was foolish to think you could keep smart, adventurous—and most of all, bored—people from doing crazy things in a place as strange as an ice tunnel. She'd heard of one attempt to start an ice bar and at least three attempts to sleep overnight in ice niches until the campers found they couldn't feel their toes after the first hour. There were the truly creepy and hidden utilidor tunnels, left over from the original 1950s station that had been abandoned and snowed in decades before. "Spelunking" had, in fact, been a popular Shackleton pastime until someone had slipped and broken an arm in a freak accident, and now the old tunnels were off-limits. Naturally, that just meant people were more careful to not get caught.

About halfway down the long, long tunnel was the one bit of civilized relief: the warming hut, a small cube cut out of the ice and lined with insulation. There was room enough for about three people to stand over an electric heater that was kept bolted to the center of the floor.

But her destination was far short of the halfway point. Not far past Jerry was a metal ladder leading to an emergency hatch. Iced over, uninviting, and seemingly impassable. While the bottom ten rungs were, in fact, solid ice, she happened to know it was *not* iced over on the remaining five rungs, nor was the hatch itself sealed by ice. She knew that because one night, several months ago, she'd dragged an acetylene torch and a portable tank to this very spot and spent two hours carving out the topmost handrails and melting the access hatch open.

She'd been inspired to do it because a little time studying the base's engineering schematic had showed her that this hatch had to pop out either very close to, or actually in, one of the old wooden Jamesway huts that dotted the outer perimeter of the base. The collection of red shanties, nicknamed the Summer Camp by adventurous Polies who would take over residence in them when the temperature stayed above freezing, had been part of the original base. More than half of the two dozen huts were buried in the snow. The rest, while still standing, had been officially condemned.

Never a group to waste a resource, Shackleton base staff had, over the years, appropriated the ones that remained and made them into impromptu gyms, bars, and lounges. There was even a climbing wall in one of them. Every few years, some desk jockey in Washington heard about the huts and filed orders for them to be torn down to maintain order. Each time, of course, the directive was somehow lost, ignored, or destroyed. Cass was thankful that the order had never been carried out.

She paused in the small closet-like space that housed the ladder and listened one more time, waiting for a scrape of a boot on the ice or laughing banter of two friends daring each other to go deeper into the ice tunnels than they'd ever gone before.

Nothing.

Reaching into a parka pocket, she swapped the handheld flashlight she'd been carrying for a headlamp. With a hood, balaclava, and scarf all competing for space on her head, she had to wrestle the thing to get it in place. Once it was secured, she turned on the light, letting her eyes adjust to the strange red light. All of the headlamps and many of the flashlights had their lenses covered in a red gel to keep from interfering with the sensitive astrophysics sensory equipment in case a worker forgot and stepped outside. While the precaution made sense if you were, indeed, going outside, it was strange to experience the gaudy red illumination in the tunnels underneath the station.

Once her eyes were ready, Cass mounted the first rung, moving carefully both to protect herself and to keep from knocking ice off the rungs and leaving evidence of her passing. The climb was easy enough at first, but at twenty feet, she was sniffling and gasping from the effort; this wasn't like humping up the steps in the Beer Can.

Between the thickness of her gloves and the ice that rimed the ladder, her hand felt like it barely wrapped around anything solid, which was unnerving enough. But at the halfway point, she spared a peek between her boots at the ice tunnel below. A mistake. The light below seemed no bigger than the size of a plate. Cass closed her eyes, took a deep breath, and continued moving slowly and deliberately up the twenty-three rungs until the lamp revealed a closed hatch above her.

Resetting her grip on the top rung, she grunted as she one-handed the latch open. Taking another step up, she crouched at the top of the ladder and pressed her back against the stubborn door until it gave an inch, then a foot, then banged all the way open like the attic door of an old house.

She turned her head in semicircles to pan her headlamp over the inside of the Jamesway she'd discovered over the summer and had been covertly visiting ever since. A quick glance showed no one in the hut and nothing out of place, if you could call a jumble of chairs, tables, and random junk nothing.

Cass climbed the rest of the way out of the tube, then wrestled the hatch back down, dropping it into the floor with a dull thump, a sound barely audible over the wind that rattled and hummed like a train was passing outside. It was an unsettling difference from the absolute stillness of the tunnels.

She straightened up and made a more careful inspection of the tiny space, exactly sixteen square feet, reduced to about the distance of her outstretched arms by the junk that had been chucked into the hut over the years.

The hut had probably started out as a temporary shelter for a mining or construction crew, but the NSF had officially stopped using Jamesways in the seventies, which meant generations of Polies had probably commandeered the hut for a thousand different things since. Nosing around like a rat, she'd found broken drill bits, survival blankets, a part of a parachute from the original navy base from the 1950s, and the remains of a dozen eggs that had long since given up the ghost—cracked and frozen but not rotten.

The geek in her had been thrilled to find the curiosities, but she'd been even happier to see the sheer amount of crap in the hut, since she'd had an ulterior motive for poking around.

Moving carefully, she lifted a thick piece of shag carpet from a section of flooring that looked a lot like a wooden packing crate, which was exactly what it was. Kneeling, she pulled out her multi-tool and flicked open the knife blade. Slipping it into a gap between the boards, she pried up the floor, revealing a small, shoebox-sized depression in the ice. In the niche was a spaghetti-like mess of wires, circuits, and diodes, all mounted on a scrap of plywood.

Cass folded and punched the shag carpet into something like a pillow, gingerly lowered herself onto it, then reached into the depression and lifted out the hodgepodge of electronics with a surgeon's care. She rested the whole thing on the floor beside her. Slipping a hand deep into her parka, she extracted a small black box about the size of two stacked paperback books. It was a twelve-volt SigmasTek rechargeable battery that would've lost its charge in an hour if it had been sitting in the ice below the hut, but lived most of its life safely on a shelf in her berth. Kept warm by her body on the trek to the Jamesway, it was juiced and ready to go.

All of this was done by the light of her headlamp. She pulled off the elastic band and, stretching her arm to the limit, hung it from a nail in a sidewall to act as an impromptu overhead light. Pawing at her cuff, she pulled back the sleeve of her parka and checked the time. Two minutes to go. She pulled one glove off and went about connecting the electrodes to the battery, sparking to life the crudest shortwave crystal radio in the history of amateur electronics.

Electrical work had never been a specialty of hers, but you couldn't graduate from an engineering school without taking a few courses here and there, and every student had a friend in EE who had kluged together a homemade soldering iron, hacked an ATM machine, or built their own robot. Eventually, some of it rubbed off. In her case, she'd learned to build her own ham radio.

Another glance at her watch. Twenty seconds. She blew on her fingers, put the earpiece in—wincing at the sudden cold in an unexpected place—and began fiddling with the tuner.

"Vox," she said, but the cold clutched at her throat and her voice came out in a rasp. She cleared her throat and tried again. "Vox. Come in, Vox. This is Blaze."

Only the empty void of static answered her. She repeated the call every ten seconds, giving a self-conscious grimace each time she had to say her call sign out loud. The handle hadn't been her idea.

After three minutes of constant calling, the answer came back, like a missive from deep space. "Blaze, this is Vox. Are you there, over?"

The voice was heavily accented and the radio waves gave it a hollow, tubular sound, but she grinned. "I'm here, Vox. What took you so long?"

Pause. "I keep telling you, my dear, you don't know the Russian mind. Stalin might be a wax statue in the Kremlin's front lobby, but Soviet-style paranoia is alive and well. It takes me an hour to put all the excuses in place to get to the radio. And I can't talk for more than fifteen minutes, or someone is bound to come looking for me to make sure I'm not plotting against them."

"It's not that bad, is it? You're ten thousand miles away from the nearest KGB agent. Or whatever you guys call it these days."

"*Federal'naya sluzhba bezopasnosti Rossiyskoy Federatsii*," Vox said. "Not KGB, FSB. And, yes, they are on the other side of the planet, but it's still a part of the planet I'd like to return to someday. So I do my work, watch over my shoulder, and report on my fellow scientists whenever I can."

"You're plotting against your other team members?"

"Of course." It was difficult to tell with the static, but she thought he sounded surprised. "How else am I supposed to keep *them* paranoid enough to leave me alone?"

She laughed. "That's crazy."

"Russians invented crazy," he said. "But you can't tell me you Americans don't do something similar."

"Of course we don't."

"Please. Give me one break. No competition? No gossip? No secrets?"

The smile melted away as she thought about Sheryl. *Not a word of this to anyone until I can make an official announcement, understand?* Hanratty's face floated into view from a murky corner of the hut, followed by Keene's bland, bearded face. *Everyone on base knew about Sheryl before you were done taking your gloves off.*

She hesitated. She'd met Vox—real name unknown—during an unexpected hiatus at the Christchurch base on the last leg before the flight to McMurdo. The layover was usually a no-nonsense twenty-four-hour pause before the crew shoved off, but a surprise storm along the coast had grounded aircraft for a week. With hundreds of scientists, workers, and other Polies trapped in a mid-sized New Zealand city with nothing to do except indulge in bouts of epic drinking, every bar in the city had turned into an intoxicated, impromptu United Nations. Cass had met Vox, a shaggy-haired, gap-toothed, thirty-something radio astronomer in the company of six Swedish physicists en route to borrowing time at the Lyubov Orlova station.

The lot of them had been amazed to meet a female engineer who didn't have "a face like a wrench," as Vox put it, and had challenged her to prove her bona fides. Grinning, she dove into a description of Lami's theorem and the basic principles of kinematics until their eyes glazed over and they begged her to stop. She did shots of vodka and aquavit the rest of the night, then gave herself permission to follow Vox back to his hotel and screw him until they both passed out. The next day, mortified, she'd tried to slip out, but he'd stopped her, laughed at her discomfort, and told her he wanted to stay in touch.

"How the hell are we supposed to do that?" she'd asked. "We're going to be at the South Pole for the next nine months. What do you want to do, meet for coffee?"

Which was when he told her, if she were half the engineer she claimed she was, it should be a snap to build, borrow, or steal a shortwave that could reach across the fifty klicks separating Shackleton from Orlova. She laughed, told him he was crazy, but they agreed—if they each managed to get their hands on the parts—on a time, date, and frequency. They'd had their first broadcast less than a month after she'd gotten to Shackleton and had managed a radio "date" every week or two since, whenever their schedules would allow.

So, aside from radio contact, she'd known this guy a total of twelve hours. Severe and threatening, Hanratty's face appeared before her again, warning her not to shoot her mouth off. Then she remembered Biddi's theory that Hanratty was counting on her to keep her mouth shut, just because of her so-called rank.

Her lip curled. *Screw it and screw him*. She launched into a description of the situation around Sheryl, starting with Hanratty's orders to help retrieve the body and ending with the strange interview with Keene.

"Jesus P. Christ!"

"H," she corrected.

"H? H what?"

"It's Jesus H. Christ," she said. "Not P."

"Why is it H?"

She paused. "I have no idea. Use P if you want."

Static ate up part of his reply. ". . . are you feeling?"

"Better than I thought I'd be." *Better than I have a right to be*. "It's a terrible thing, but I wouldn't be dwelling on it so much if Keene hadn't acted so strangely."

"Keene is your psychiatric officer?"

"Yes."

"Tell him nothing. He will only use it against you. The thought police are always the same. Believe me, this is something we Russians know about."

"I thought the Soviet era was over," Cass said with a small smile. "The wall came down decades ago, didn't it?"

"Same play, different cast," Vox replied. "But about this man Keene, Blaze: remember. No one wants in your head if they don't plan to use it for themselves."

She snorted. "He can dig around all he wants. He's not going to find anything of value."

"A painful memory to you is an item of value to him. We all have skeletals in our closet."

"Skeletons," she corrected absently, her mind dwelling on remembered forms and shapes different—yet not so different—than Sheryl's. *There will be some survivor's guilt, as well. You've had some experience with that, I believe?*

"Blaze?"

"I'm here," she said. "Vox—why do I have to call you that, anyway? You know my name."

"Maybe I like mysteries. I am dating you, no?" He paused. "That is joke. My name is Alexander Mikhailovich Krestovozdvizhensky."

"What the hell? I can't pronounce that."

"That is why I pick Vox, no? Simple. Elegant. Latin. You can call me Sasha if you want, is short for Alexander. Though, I prefer if you call me Vox."

"Sasha," she said. "I like it. It's dashing."

"No one has ever called a Russian radio astronomer dashing before, but I accept your compliment." He laughed. There was a short pause, then, "Blaze, I'm sorry, I have to go. Comrade—excuse me, *First Researcher*—Konstantinov is thundering up and down the hall, looking for me."

"Same bat channel, same bat time?"

"Yes, whatever that is. *Poka*."

And, suddenly, he was gone.

Lying still, her body heat slowly leaching away, Cass felt herself on the verge of shivering, and the smell of the shag carpet filled her nose with must and a disagreeable synthetic odor, but she continued to recline on the Jamesway floor for long minutes after the connection was lost, pondering the randomness of things. Besides Biddi, she'd made few friends at Shackleton and, after yesterday's events, there really wasn't anyone at the station she'd feel comfortable telling about the horror of seeing Sheryl's body lying on the ice.

Instead, she'd turned to a Russian national with a lopsided smile and a sense of humor for support. His motives, outlook, and background? Unknown. She sighed and rolled to her feet. A one-night stand and a few months of radio dating weren't much to build a relationship on. But a disembodied voice coming out of the darkness seemed the best she was going to do.

CHAPTER ELEVEN

My name is Cass Jennings. I was born west of Boston, Massachusetts, about a five-minute walk from the Waltham Watch Company. I visited almost every weekend as a kid, which might explain why I've always wanted to take things apart and put them together again—

Cass jumped as someone hammered on the door to her berth. *Bang, bang, bang.* Biddi's voice came through, muffled but distinct. "I'll huff and I'll puff and . . . you bloody well better let me in, is all."

Self-consciously, she closed the little, nearly blank diary and shoved it under her pillow, then swung her feet over the side of the bed to answer the door. Had the closet not been in the way, she could've reached the knob from the bed.

Biddi was standing in the hall on the other side, wearing an admonishing expression. "What are you doing?"

"I was trying to relax and get some reading done. What are you doing?"

"Bothering you."

"I can see that," Cass said.

"Actually, I've come to see why you aren't out on deck to see the plane off."

"I thought it wasn't due to leave for a couple of hours yet."

"It's not, but that shouldn't keep you from ogling it from the observation deck with the rest of the winter-overs."

"Why would I do that?"

"Because it's a singular bloody occurrence, something we won't get much of in the next few months. The station's next big news item will be if Dr. Ayres farts in the galley during lunch. We have to enjoy these events when they present themselves. So, put down your bloody book"—she pronounced it *booook*—"come outside, and celebrate with everyone. You know I won't take no for an answer."

Cass made a face. "Biddi, that just isn't my thing. I don't go in for big parties or manufactured events—"

"Manufactured?" Biddi snorted. "Our whole fricking existence down here is manufactured, if you hadn't noticed. We'd all be nothing more than a collection of sorry-looking ice crystals if not for some *manufactured events*." Her face softened. "Cass, I'm a wee bit older than you and I've got my regrets. One of them is not making the most of every moment. Don't let even the little things slip by."

Cass looked at her friend's face, trying to formulate an argument, some reason to say no. She didn't need one, of course. She could simply utter the word "no," shut the door, and forget about the whole thing. The morning with the irksome Senator Sikes and his groupies was already forgotten. She wouldn't be missing a thing if she stayed in her room.

But Biddi was right. If she was going to reconstruct herself and her life, she needed to populate it with new experiences, not old habits. Ten years from now, if someone asked what she'd been doing when the last plane of the year left the South Pole that one time she'd worked there, her answer couldn't be, *I was in my room writing in my diary*. It just couldn't. Not if she had any hope of forgetting her past and making something of her future.

She sighed, then laughed at the victorious expression on her friend's face. "Give me a second."

Cass shut the door on Biddi doing a victory dance, switched out sweatpants for jeans, then grabbed her parka, mittens, and hat. Thirty seconds later, she was in the hall and following Biddi toward the observation deck that overlooked the skiway. A dull hum—no louder than a refrigerator or the buzz of a heat pump—reached her ears as she approached the airlock doors, but as they opened the second set, a colossal roar made it almost impossible to hear, let alone think. Why hadn't she remembered the sound from her flight to Shackleton a few months before? Too excited to notice, maybe, or unimpressed after the flight from Christchurch—eleven bone-bruising, eardrum-shattering hours in a C-17, a plane so big it could hold the Hercules in its belly. Since then, she realized with surprise, she'd never had or made time to watch another flight.

Squinting against the glare, she looked at the Hercules, parked on the skiway like some temporarily grounded sway-bellied dragon. Its four turboprop engines were idling and ready to go despite the fact that takeoff was an hour or two away—engines were not shut off at the South Pole unless you were done for the day or had an affinity for futility; it could take forever to resuscitate a cold engine. Squatting on the skiway with engines going might blow a swimming pool of wasted fuel out the tail, but everyone involved considered the idling worth it.

After a moment, Cass's attention slid away from the plane. The skiway was full of people: fuelies checking lines, staffers driving Skandics and snowcats full of gear and supplies out to the plane's loading platform, a dozen people simply standing around with their hands in their pockets, talking.

Biddi tugged on her arm to get her to join a small knot of winter-over crew standing to one side of the ob deck. Thanks to the noise, conversation was limited to hand signals, so they all stood in a strange gaggle, side by side, but almost entirely unable to communicate. *So much for getting out and interacting with friends*, Cass thought. But she knew there were other events planned, old Polie traditions to mark the severing of the last thread connecting Shackleton to the outside world. There'd be plenty of time to catch up.

So, she gave herself permission to watch the prep for the last flight, looking on as scores of tiny workers bustled around the Herc like ants crawling over the carcass of a giant beetle. As much as the Antarctic ice and snow would allow, it was a smart, efficient operation, with snowcats and snowmobiles running supplies back and forth to the service arches, downslope, around the corner, and out of sight. She grinned as she saw that even the old LMC 1800, "Little Tug" painted on the side in white, had been pressed into service. With a top speed of eight miles an hour, no one took the little crate on tracks to make time, but it had enough torque to pull the station across the ice if you could find cables strong enough. And, sure enough, daisy-chained behind the Tug were six sleds stacked man-high, chugging along slower than a person could walk . . . but moving nevertheless.

There were hiccups in the process, naturally, and she watched as one of the snowmobiles bucked and stalled out on the ice en route to the Hercules. Even from this distance, she could tell the driver was frustrated as he or she slammed the controls in an effort to coax it back to life, then yanked the brake lever and climbed off. Whoever it was stood and faced the snowmobile with hands on hips for a minute before looking around helplessly.

Cass nudged Biddi, pointed out to the stranded vehicle, then leaned in close. "I'm going to give them a hand. It's my kind of work."

Biddi gave her a gloved thumbs-up. Cass climbed down the outer stairway to ground level, then set off across the ice, purposefully steering wide of the Herc itself to keep the gung-ho air force guys from running over to save her from getting chopped into bits in case she didn't know what a propeller was.

By the time she reached the stranded snowmobile, the rider had the side hood open and was tinkering with something inside. To her amazement, the snowmobile wasn't one of the newer standards, like a

Skandic or a Tundra; it was an Alpine. A great machine, but it was a little like finding a Model T at a truck rally. She knew the inventory of the VMF pretty well and wondered where they'd found it.

"Hey," she called from about twenty feet away, barely audible over the roar of the Herc's engines. "Don't do that."

"What?" A hooded, masked face popped up from behind the hood. "Why not?"

"It's too cold and that Alpine is an antique. If half the engine isn't frozen already, it will be by the time you actually figure out what's wrong. It'll be easier to just tow it back to the VMF since we're so close."

Despite the layers of cold weather clothing, she could tell the person was irritated. "Who are you?"

"Cass Jennings."

"Who?"

"*Station mechanic*," she yelled. "Stop screwing with that and let me get you a tow so we can get it to a museum in one piece. Why don't you go warm up while I take care of this?"

"Oh." The driver's shoulders didn't exactly slump, but she could tell he was at least partially contrite. "Okay."

Cass veered off, stomping across the ice and down the long, gradual decline to the outer doors of the VMF and warehouse. Deep ruts left by the thick tread of utility vehicles had frozen in place, making the walk precarious—it was like trying to hike over a landscape of upraised and uneven glass teeth on a slope of maybe twenty degrees, and she had to windmill her arms more than once to keep from pitching forward. It was a short walk, however, and while the mouth of the large VMF garage door—the one she'd come through with Hanratty the day before—was shut, next to it was a more reasonably sized door for people. She steered for the latter, banged it open, then stopped short.

Standing in the middle of the VMF, as though caught playing with themselves, were Hanratty, Taylor, and Keene. Cass couldn't have been more taken aback if she'd found the Three Stooges in the middle of her garage. Judging from the look of surprise on their faces, the feeling was mutual. She peeled off her goggles and pushed back her hood.

Hanratty was the first to recover. "Jennings, what are you doing here?"

"I work here," she said evenly. "What are *you* doing here?"

"We came to oversee the loading situation," Taylor said. Hanratty winced.

"From the VMF?" she asked. "Wouldn't you see more in the warehouse?"

"Of course," Hanratty said. "We were just on our way there."

Cass turned. "What about you, Dr. Keene?"

He shrugged, his hands in his pockets and his shoulders hunched. Of the three, he was the only one not in a parka. His breath steamed as he spoke. "Just bored, Cass. I don't get down to the service bays very often. Actually, since you're here, this is a great chance to ask you about some of the things you do. For example, what in the world is this thing—"

Keene was interrupted by a crash from the back of the shop, where the spare parts for every vehicle on base were stored in a labyrinthine collection of racks and shelves. Frowning, Cass turned and walked toward the noise.

"Jennings!" Hanratty called, but Cass ignored him. The racks were in a darkened alcove of the VMF and she fumbled for a light switch. As she did so, a splash of light lit the muddy gloom as the adjoining door to the carpentry shop was thrown open and a slim form dashed through the opening.

What the . . . "Hey," Cass yelled and hurried after the form. Behind her, Hanratty and Taylor called to her again, but she ignored them, more than a little pissed. It was one thing to find three of the base's highest-ranking managers in her garage; it was another if someone was screwing around with her inventory. She stretched her hands out in the darkness to keep from impaling herself on a protruding crankshaft or jack, piloting to the carpentry door by memory, then threw open the door.

The white overhead lights were on full blast in the carpentry shop and she squinted at the sudden glare. The door on the far side was just closing shut, and she raced across the little workshop, zigging and zagging between benches and counters. Moving awkwardly in her outdoor gear, she cut a corner too close and caught the toe of her boot on a definitely immovable object. Her ankle was wrenched the wrong way. The thick walls of her boot kept it from turning further, but she still hissed as pain lanced up her leg.

Pushing through it, she hobbled to the door and flung it open. A blast of freezing cold air hit her in the face—this was the long tunnel connecting the service arches that she'd brought Sikes and her other charges down earlier that day. Shielding her face with her hands, she peered through the gap of her fingers. The figure she'd been chasing was pelting down the tunnel and moving fast. Cass limped after, but in just a few seconds, the form had disappeared into the gloom and shrinking horizon of the tunnel walls.

Cursing, she shambled back through the carpentry shop and into the VMF, full of questions. But when she got back to the garage, Hanratty, Taylor, and Keene were gone, leaving nothing behind but the buzz of the overhead lights and the muffled roar of the Hercules in the distance.

CHAPTER TWELVE

"I didn't even want to come to the Pole," Colin Sutter was saying. "What I really wanted to do was study the Gamburtsevs."

"Ah, yes. The Gamburtsevs." Tim Kowalski shot a glance at Carla Bjorkholm. "The Russian circus family? From Moscow? I caught their show in New York once."

"No," Colin said, confused. He pushed his glasses up a long nose. "It's a subglacial mountain range east of here. It's quite famous."

"So is the circus," Carla said, straight-faced.

Anne took up the thread. "Amazing contortionists. Their show is something to see. You should get out more, Colin."

"The Gamburtsevs? Really?" Colin frowned. "I suppose it might be a common name in Russia . . ."

The three glanced at one another. Tim popped an eyebrow, Carla shrugged, Anne smothered a grin. Colin's cluelessness bordered on the obtuse, but after having spent the summer season together, they were used to his quirks. Tim, a materials engineer, had suggested that, as a geologist, his friend had taken on the properties of the object he studied and, in fact, they probably all had. When Carla asked how that applied to her as a biologist who studied molds, he backpedaled, although he returned to his theory in a clumsy attempt to compare Anne to the stars.

He gave up when Anne told him she dealt mostly in radio astronomy and hadn't looked through an optical telescope since she was in college.

The four were sitting in the first-floor TV lounge. The galley, their preferred haunt, had been taken over as a staging area for the final flights of the season, making the simple acts of getting a coffee or finding a seat nearly impossible. They'd already said their tearful farewells to friends and colleagues, with promises of getting together in the future. Better to stay out of the way for a few hours until the last flight had taken off.

In groups of four, six, or eight, travelers were summoned via the PA system to report to Destination Alpha so they could begin the shuttle process to the Hercules. Each time the speaker crackled to life, the group of friends would pause, listen to the call, then pick up their conversation.

"None of you have wintered over, right?" Anne looked at the other three, who all shook their heads. Although they'd been at Shackleton for the summer season, it was surprising how little they knew about each other.

"I've heard things can get pretty squirrelly," Tim said. "A crew of two hundred shrinks to forty. Nine months together. Dark for two-thirds of it. We'll have our work to save us, of course, but that only goes so far."

"I'm sure we'll think of something," Carla said, glancing at Colin.

The geologist nodded. "I already mentioned to Deb that I'd like to start a chess tournament. Someone told me Pete has a rating over two thousand! I'd love to go head-to-head with him."

Carla mocked smacking her forehead, but as Tim started to laugh, Colin caught his eye, and the geologist winked at him, which just made him laugh harder. Anne, puzzled, asked, "What's so funny?"

Before Tim could say anything, the PA speaker screeched to life. "*Senator Sikes. Senator Sikes. Please report to Destination Alpha and ask your group to do the same. This is the last load of the season. If you're not on that plane in the next five minutes, then you'll be our guest for the next nine months. Senator Sikes. Please report to Destination Alpha.*"

The voice disappeared with an electrical snap and the lounge went quiet.

Carla cleared her throat. "Anyone else thinking about running out and stowing away on the senator's plane?"

"Of course not," Tim said. "I had a very good reason for almost jumping up and sprinting out the door in the general direction of the skiway just now."

Anne smiled. "It *is* going to be weird, isn't it? Do you remember how strange the winter-overs acted when we landed last summer?"

"They huddled together in one corner of the galley and wouldn't look at us as we came in," Carla said, her eyes unfocused as she remembered. "I mean, I wasn't expecting a brass band, but some of them looked like they wanted to claw my eyes out just for being there."

"One lady actually snatched a chair away from me when I tried to sit at her table," Colin said, his tone still injured. "I swear she almost growled at me."

"I heard one of them call us the 'orange people' because we actually had some color to our skin," Tim said.

"Pasty, mean, and anthropophobic. Great," Anne said. "I hope we'll be a little different."

"Don't count on it," Carla warned. "Your biology is a slave to your environment. In nine months, another crew is going to land and wonder what happened to all those bitchy lunatics in the corner."

They debated the point until the PA suddenly crackled again.

"*Ladies and gentlemen, this is station manager Jack Hanratty.*" The voice came across the system as gruff and flat as it did in person. "*As you no doubt heard, in just a few minutes the final flight of the season is about to leave for McMurdo. I urge you to head outside to watch it take off. It will be the last plane you will see until November.*"

"Guy really knows how to improve morale," Tim said. Carla shushed him.

"*Now that our guests have left, I wanted to ask you to take a moment to remember our friend and colleague, Sheryl Larkin. As many of you already know, she was found yesterday unresponsive, alone, and without a radio several hundred meters from the station. We don't know why Sheryl wandered so far from base, but she appeared to have sustained an injury in her attempt to return and, unable to walk, had unfortunately succumbed to exposure.*"

The quasi-permanent grin that Tim normally wore melted away. Anne leaned forward, bowing her head so that her long hair hung down, covering her face. Carla stared at the coffee table in front of them and Colin absently rubbed the tips of his fingers together, as if to make sure they were all there.

"*I know Sheryl's death has been a terrible shock to you all, as it has to me. She will be remembered as one of our team and, more importantly, one of the Shackleton family. I can't claim to know why she died, but I do know she wouldn't—not for a second—want us to compromise the work we do here. Please think of Sheryl as we enter this winter season and know she stands behind us every step of the way.*"

Hanratty cleared his throat, a strange sound that came across as a flat bark over the PA system.

"*If any of you would like to talk over this situation, counseling is available. Please see myself, deputy station manager Deb Connors, or station morale officer Gerald Keene. Thank you for your attention.*"

The speaker snapped off once more, leaving the lounge in silence again. Anne looked around. This time, however, none of them had anything to say, and eventually they left the room, one by one.

CHAPTER THIRTEEN

Cass composed herself, trying to keep her face blank, but the man's fingers and thumbs were pressing deep into the flesh of her ankle and the back of her calf like he was trying to separate the layers of muscle and tissue into their individual strands. The skin from her lower leg to the top of her foot was already a multi-shaded purple-green around the joint and, while there wasn't any single spot that hurt more than another, the whole thing was throbbing to a beat that made her suspended foot swing rhythmically in place.

"I'm glad I caught you when I did," Dr. Ayres said mildly, kneeling at her feet like a suitor. Only a small hint of reproach colored his voice as he continued to roll and probe her bare ankle like it was a piece of meat. "If I hadn't seen you limping down the stairs over by the greenhouse, you might've gone on to do some real damage here."

Cass grimaced. After losing the mystery figure in the tunnel and finding the VMF empty, she'd gone back to work rescuing the stranded Alpine. The pain in her twisted ankle had grown, however, until she'd been forced to hobble up the Beer Can steps in search of the stash of Advil she kept in her berth. But one unlucky encounter in the hall later and she was in triage, getting her ankle wrapped and praying Ayres wouldn't think her injury bad enough to find her a seat on the last flight of the season.

More lightly than she felt, Cass joked, "I figured I'd wait so you'd have more of a challenge."

He gave her a small smile. "You're the one with the challenge. I see some impressive runner's calluses here. I bet you haven't skipped a day in years. Except for that plantar fasciitis, I think I see here. What did you do then?"

"I switched to century rides. You can bike when you can't run," she said, then hissed as the doctor's thumbs hit a spot that she didn't think she'd had. Pain lanced from the sole of her foot to her heel. He held on gently as she pulled away.

"Take it easy. I'm all done. With the inspection, at least."

He stood and rummaged around in a side cabinet. Ayres was a slender man in his fifties, sandy hair cropped close, but prematurely bald. Some people called him the Bartender because his mild manner and sympathetic ear had Shackleton staff coming to him as much for advice as twisted ankles. But Cass had also heard that Ayres had gotten his medical training in the Marines, and earned his stethoscope on the battlefields of Iraq, Afghanistan, and a half-dozen other hot spots around the world.

"What got you into running in the first place?" With his head buried in the cabinet, Ayres's voice was muffled.

Escape? Distraction? Survival? "Just a fitness nut, I guess. I ran in high school and college."

"Competitively?"

"In high school, yes. In college, no. Club. I wasn't even close to making the team."

"Sounds like my love life."

Cass smiled. "Am I going to live, Doc?"

"I think so. You have a mid-level sprain. A Grade One that was probably eight degrees' torque away from a Grade Two. Nice work, actually. It should take you, oh, a month to get your normal mobility back. A bit more than that before you can train for the Ironman, so take it easy in the gym."

Cass swallowed. "So, I get to . . . stay?"

"Stay?" He smiled quizzically. "For Pete's sake. Was that why you tried to slink away when I found you? Cass, you'd have to cut your foot clean off to get eighty-sixed this late in the season. You're staying."

"Oh, God." A wave of relief washed over her. "Thank you."

Ayres grunted and stepped back from the cabinet with two boxes of bright purple medical wrap. He pulled a stool over to the table where she sat, took his place back at her feet, and began gently winding the spongy fabric around her ankle, starting at the joint and working his way up to her calf, then back down to encompass half of her foot.

Biting her lip, Cass watched, expecting the pain to blossom and swell, but the rigidity and extra support actually reduced the consistent hammering down to a dull throb. Ayres's hands were sure and gentle and he had her entire foot wrapped in a few minutes.

He handed her the other box of medical wrap. "Swap the wrap every few days. Try not to get it wet or they'll smell you coming from down the hall. Not too tight or you'll be back in here for gangrene. Stay off your feet—"

She snorted.

He gave her a look. "—as much as possible. Which I know is unlikely. But do what you can to give that ankle a chance to heal or you'll limp for the rest of the winter. Everyone down here winds up with a nickname eventually. You don't want yours to be Gimpy."

"Okay." Cass leaned over and put her socks back on with difficulty. Ayres watched her struggle for a minute, then took pity on her and helped her get the sock over the wrapped foot.

"Do you have any painkillers?" he asked, then caught himself. "I mean, like aspirin. I don't want to know if you've got anything stronger than that."

"I brought a few bottles of over-the-counter stuff for bumps and bruises." She smiled. "Nothing stronger, unless you count mint Irish cream liqueur."

"I said painkillers, not rat poison."

He fished a ring of keys out of his pocket, unlocked a steel cabinet in the corner of the room, and rummaged around for a moment before pulling out four or five square envelopes. "I'm going to give you some Percocet if you need it to help you sleep at night. And only at night, okay? Normally I'd say don't operate any heavy machinery, but that's what you do. So, take your OTCs to get through your shift and before you go to bed. Rip an envelope open if the pain gets too much to rest. Got it?"

She nodded, then hesitated. "Can I ask you something?"

His eyebrows shot up. "Please don't tell me you're pregnant."

Cass flushed. "Of course not."

"In that case, shoot."

She paused, trying to put the words together. "When we brought Sheryl in. Did you . . . did you perform. I mean, did you—"

"Are you asking if I did an autopsy on Sheryl?"

She swallowed. "Yes."

Ayres walked to a sink on the far side of the examination room, pulling off the latex gloves as he did so and chucking them into a biomed bin. Then, taking his time, he turned the water on, adjusting the hot and the cold just so, and began gently but thoroughly washing his hands.

Cass cleared her throat. "I'm not sure why I want to know, but I suppose it's because no one's really talked about it. Hanratty made that announcement, but other than that, everyone's acting as if it didn't happen. I don't know if they're in shock, but part of me doesn't think it's right to brush it under the rug. On the other hand, it wouldn't do anyone any good if the entire base was freaking out about it, either . . ."

Ayres shut the water off and turned around as he patted his hands dry on a towel. "First of all, time was tight. I've done them and I'm fast, but you need at least twenty-four hours, sometimes more, to prep the body, perform the autopsy, make sure you have tissue samples for toxicology, then put everything back in place for safe transport back to

McMurdo and eventually the States. Sorry if that's a little graphic, but that's the way it is. There's no halfway with it. I had just enough time, but very little wiggle room."

Cass was silent.

Ayres leaned back against the sink and tucked his hands into his pockets. "On the other hand, you get the best information on cause of death and the like right after the event that caused the death. So, even if an autopsy can't be performed for some reason, it's still a good idea to do an exam."

He stopped talking and simply watched Cass's face. When he didn't go on, she raised her eyebrows. "And . . . what did you find when you examined her?"

Ayres continued to look back at her impassively.

"*Did* you examine Sheryl?"

He pursed his lips.

"Stomp your foot once for yes, twice for no."

That got a slight grin that quickly melted away. Ayres pushed off from the sink and stuck his head out of the room to check the hall, then took his place against the sink again. "Did you ever play Twenty Questions as a kid?"

"We were more into I Never, but I know the concept."

"Why don't we try my game. Even if you never played, the concept is pretty simple. Ask me yes or no questions. If you don't get your answer in twenty, you lose."

Voices rose in the hall outside the office and they both froze, but the voices passed on and faded quickly. Cass licked her lips. "Did you examine Sheryl after Taylor brought her back to base?"

Ayres crossed his arms over his chest. "No."

"Did you get a chance to examine her later, before she . . . before her body was loaded onto the plane?"

"No."

"Did you *try* to examine her?"

He shifted his weight. "Yes."

"And you couldn't," Cass said. When Ayres didn't answer: "You weren't allowed?"

"No."

"No, you weren't allowed or no, I'm asking the wrong question?"

"No, I wasn't permitted to look at her."

Cass paused. *Hanratty had made a point of saying he'd be talking to Ayres about examining Sheryl.* "Can you elaborate?"

Ayres leaned his head back and looked at the ceiling. "I was told that what was done was done. Shackleton personnel were upset already, and since McMurdo had better facilities, the autopsy would be done there, so there was no need for me to do an examination. Taylor made some kind of joke that it's not hard to keep a body cold, so what was the harm in waiting?"

"Do you find that strange?"

Ayres hesitated for the first time. "Yes. And no. From one perspective, it makes sense. A quick examination wouldn't tell us much, certainly not as much as a full autopsy. And there's no doubt that morale would have taken a beating if I'd done the autopsy or an exam, even if nothing extraordinary was found. People don't actually want to know causes of death when it hits so close to home. Hell, *I* didn't want to do it, not really. I . . . I had lunch with the woman, I played poker with her in B1, for Christ's sake. I didn't want to take a knife to her."

"But?"

"But what if she'd wandered out on the ice because she was hypoxic from a bad air circulator? Or had gotten a bad dose of meds or recreational drugs and was hallucinating? Or was simply weak and dizzy from food poisoning? Any one of those scenarios could decimate the population of Shackleton. Half of them could be revealed with a visual exam. The rest would come out with a simple blood panel or toxicology test."

"So, the negative consequences of doing an exam don't even compare with the upside."

"It's not even close."

"Who told you not to do the exam?"

Ayres huffed a laugh and pushed himself away from the sink. "You don't make it twenty years as a corpsman by shitting where you eat, Cass. I'm sure you can figure out how many people at Shackleton can tell me not to do something and I've got to pay attention."

"But—"

He held up a hand. "Sorry. I've already said too much. It's water under the bridge. Whatever happened to Sheryl was terrible, but we're not going to let it happen again. Right? So, wrap that ankle, take your pills, and you'll be better in no time."

Cass could see the subject was closed. "Take two Percocet and call you in the morning?"

"Yes, except don't bother calling. There's nothing more I can do for you."

"With advice like that, I'm glad I didn't gash my leg open." She slipped off the table, hissing a little as her bad foot took some of the weight.

"Well, as they said in med school, the bleeding stops eventually." Ayres stepped forward and helped her to the door. As she reached out to open the latch, he put a hand firmly on the door, holding it shut. She looked up at him.

"Cass," he said. The smile was gone. Pleasant wrinkles around the eyes and laugh lines around the mouth were now trenches of experience. The kind mask of the healer—the sympathetic ear of the Bartender—was gone, revealing the warrior beneath. "What we talked about here. Let's keep it our little secret, okay?" When she didn't reply, he continued, "I don't like it any more than you, but I've learned over the years that crusades don't help anyone. We'll find out soon enough what happened to Sheryl."

"Thanks," she said, which wasn't agreeing. His smile returned and he held the door for her as she left the room and hobbled into the hall.

CHAPTER FOURTEEN

For Cass, rebuilding a motor or flushing brake lines had always been the best form of therapy. Methodical, mechanical, hands-on tasks had a way of pushing her anxieties aside, giving her time and space to grapple with the thornier problems in her life. Over the course of her lifetime she'd left a trail of repaired engines, gearboxes, and motors in her wake, a testament to how well the tactic worked . . . and how many troubles she'd faced.

And the trick had worked this time, too. After leaving Ayres and once more navigating the Beer Can steps, she settled into the garage and dove into an inspection of the derelict Alpine, checking off items on a mental list before getting her hands greasy in an attempt to settle her mind. *Plumb the engine with a bore scope. Doodle with the combustion chamber and piston skirts. Lube up the grease zerks.* Familiar work turned the growl into a happy hum as she started wrenching away on the busted snowmobile.

As machines went, however, the Alpine wasn't all that complicated and soon her hands were on autopilot, running over the engine with a will of their own, the tasks so routine that her mind returned to the strange still life of Hanratty, Taylor, and Keene staring back at her in surprise and dismay.

The fourth person had been with them, they must've, but how was she supposed to pin down the station boss, his security chief, and the base psychologist about just what the hell had been going on? All three had the authority to be in the VMF any time they wanted, so she'd have to accuse them of something really out of bounds if she wanted more than excuses or blank stares . . . and, even then, they were under no compunction to answer her. Demand answers from Keene about the mad dasher she'd chased and he'd simply shrug and say, *who?*

Which was a very good question. Cass's movements slowed, then stopped. She leaned against the Alpine's frame and closed her eyes, calling forth the image of a silhouette framed against the white ice, fading into darkness. The form had been slender, insofar as anyone in cold weather gear could be called "slender." Which meant Cass had thought of the form as slenderer—*was that a word?*—than other parka-clad people around the station. Had it been a woman? She compared her mental picture to the height of the tunnel, relative to the pipes and cabling that ran along near the top of the wall. The runner's head hadn't come close to the lowest pipe. Short, then, or at least shorter than she was. Only a few men on base met that mark, but more than half the women did.

Something else nagged at her, plucking at the edges. Something about the way the woman moved or how she'd run . . . her mind snatched at the image, tried to pin it down, but it curled away and evaporated. Cass shook her head, frustrated. She'd watched the figure for, what, three seconds? Not many clues you can pick up in the space of a few heartbeats.

The garage phone rang, its electronic chime jarring her out of her thoughts and surprising her, as well. No one ever bothered to call down from the station since the little beeping noise always lost to the VMF's routine combination of heavy machinery, protective headphones, and loud music. Cass limped over to the phone.

A familiar lilting voice responded on the other end. "Love, did you really think you could hide down in that cave and I wouldn't find you? You only go there and your room, you know."

"Oh, shit, Biddi. I'm sorry. I wasn't trying to blow you off. That snowmobile was in lousy shape and I started in on it and totally forgot about you guys topside. And you wouldn't believe what was going on down here when I opened the door—"

"You can tell me later," Biddi interrupted. "Drop what you're doing and get up here. You're in luck. Sikes's flight was delayed for a good hour or more, but it's almost ready to leave now. That cute man Dave promised to lead the group in singing a special good-bye song to the senator and his bloody brownnosers."

"Biddi . . ."

"And Peter hinted the kitchen made a cake for everyone to share later while we watch the trifecta." Biddi paused. "I don't even know what trifecta he's talking about, but I know I like cake."

"It's a tradition," Cass said. "The winter-over crew is supposed to watch a bunch of bad horror movies to celebrate the start of the winter season."

"As long as there's cake. Now, no excuses. Get up here. Or I won't speak to you all winter. And that's a very long time, chickie." *Click.*

Cass hung the receiver on its cradle and limped back to the tray, where she wiped her hands, shrugged on her parka, and headed for the door to the tunnel. Twenty painful minutes later, with a fat ankle that pushed against the sides of her boot in a way that couldn't be normal, she walked down the corridor to the ob deck and threw open the door.

She was just in time. Fifteen or twenty parka-clad bodies—half the winter crew—were crowded onto the small platform, all of them facing the Hercules as it barreled down the skiway. Biddi's short form turned as Cass came onto the deck, shaking her fist at her, but at least she couldn't hear her friend bitch at her: Dave Boychuck was belting out the verses to "So Long, Farewell." The entire group pitched in at the end, their voices rising in muffled falsetto and their arms waving in exaggerated sweeps as the Hercules lifted off and lumbered into the sky.

A tattered cheer went up as the plane, rather than just taking off into the distance, banked and came back for a farewell waggle of the wings before swinging over the station again and setting a course for McMurdo. Voices around her died off as they strained to catch the fading roar of the plane's engine over the swishing of their parkas and the sigh of a light wind. After there was nothing left to hear, the little group still watched as the Hercules became a block, then a line, then a tiny dot in the sky. When it finally disappeared, Cass sighed. The last flight of the year had departed.

Summer was gone.

"I wish Sheryl could've seen this," Biddi said clearly into the silence. A flush ran through Cass, followed by a wash of nausea. Someone gasped; someone else made a noise between a sigh and a cough. They stood in an uncomfortable semicircle.

"I do, too, Biddi. Why don't we take a moment of silence for her right now," Dave said in his big, booming voice and the group, as one, bowed their heads. The only sound was the soughing of the soft breeze on the plain.

After a moment, Dave raised his head and turned to the crowd. "Thanks, everyone. I think she would've liked that." He shook himself like a bear. "All right, no moping. Off to the galley for cake and then we'll do something fun, like watch someone get eaten by a monster from outer space."

Shaky laughter rippled through the group, but it was enough to pull everyone out of their downward slide. Crew members peeled off in twos and threes to head inside, led by Dave's shambling form.

Biddi laced her arm in Cass's and tugged her along to follow the others. "So you got to see it take off, at least. Glad you could make it, love."

"I am, too," Cass said, surprising herself. A small lump of anxiety made her stomach sour at the idea of hanging out with forty people, and she thought longingly of the Alpine and all the great work she could do on it, but . . . the snowmobile wasn't moving anytime soon. It would be there tomorrow and the next day. The last day of summer, by definition, wouldn't.

Their cohort made its way down to the galley, which was already buzzing. Buckets filled with Antarctic ice and bottles of cheap champagne decorated each table. People grabbed plastic cups and chatted noisily. Tinny seventies disco spilled out of a small speaker in the corner. Ceiling- and wall-mounted monitors, normally filled with endlessly scrolling weather and work reports, now looped graphical displays of exploding fireworks.

"Is it cake time, Petey?" Biddi called to Pete Ozment as they stood in the doorway watching the party.

"You betcha," he said, slipping behind the counter and toward the kitchen door. "Grab a seat. I'll be back out in a second. You're not going to believe what's coming your way!"

Cass scanned the crowd, looking for a friendly knot of people they could break into. For an event like the last day, the normal staffer versus scientist barriers melted away, but people still tended to flock to the group they knew the best, so the nerds in the astro crowd clung to each other while the fuelies—still reeking from off-loading fuel into Shackleton's storage tanks—were bunched up in a corner, sipping from dirty coffee mugs and watching the others.

"Oh, no you don't," Biddi said, reaching out and snagging Jun Takahashi by a bird-thin arm as he shuffled toward the corner to join the astro group, no doubt the only people he knew on base. "You've got two beautiful women right here, ready to drink bubbly and indulge in an epic sugar rush, and you're going to run off to a gaggle of beakers? I don't think so."

Cass grinned as someone else had become the target of Biddi's social bullying. Jun, looking like he'd just swallowed an iceberg, allowed himself to be led by the hand to a table in the middle of the room where the action, such as it was, was thickest. Waving to get everyone's attention—among others, Dave was already there, deep in conversation with Dr. Ayres, while Colin was nodding as he listened to something Carla was saying to him—Biddi led them all into shouting a greeting to Jun. Cass laughed as everyone at the table roared, "*Hi, Jun!*" The little astrophysicist looked ready to crawl inside himself and disappear. Then it was her turn and she could feel herself flush beet red as the table turned in her direction and bellowed, "*Hi, Cass!*"

Before she could die of embarrassment, Pete rolled a cart from the kitchen that held a sheet cake the size of a door. The partiers gathered around, oohing and aahing at the monstrous dessert, a masterpiece of creativity and limited resources. The icing was white, of course, with blue and gray highlights and shadows. Penguins and chirpy killer whales patrolled the outer rim, while in the center was a passable likeness of the old South Pole base, the geodesic dome that had been torn down to make way for the current station. Across the top, written in rainbow sprinkles, was the line "DOMED TO FAILURE . . ." A wave of laughter rolled through the crowd, replaced by a shriek as the first bottle of champagne was opened with a startling *pop!* and then everyone rushed for the remaining bottles as Pete started cutting the cake. Someone turned up the disco until it was louder than the Hercules had been.

Biddi pushed a plastic cup into Cass's hand. "You're on your own, love. I'm off to talk to Mr. Boychuck about his hose."

"Biddi, my God."

Her friend put a hand to her chest in feigned shock. "He's a fuelie, Cass. I'm just interested in his job, is all. Though if he wants to show me any of his *equipment*, I can't say I'll stop him." She winked and sashayed toward the seat next to Dave.

Cass found herself suddenly alone with Jun, who cradled his cup of champagne in the palm of his hand like it was a Fabergé egg. She turned to look at him, thinking that the little astrophysicist couldn't be more of a stereotype. With the top of his head barely coming up as high as her chin, she had to look down to speak to him, which meant she got a bird's-eye view. He was thin to the point of transparency, with a white polo shirt tucked into creased, unbelted department store jeans that, as small as they were, were still too big to keep his waist from swimming in them. The ensemble ended in a pair of tatty Keds sneakers, worn by elementary school kids everywhere.

"This is fun," she said, thinking to start out simple.

Jun smiled and nodded, said nothing, and the conversation landed with a thump. When nothing else was forthcoming, she pivoted back to look out at the galley.

The sounds of the party swelled around them, but never strongly enough to pull them in, and they stood shoulder to shoulder in silence for more than a minute. Cass groped furiously for a topic, but the harder she tried, the blanker her mind became.

She finally cleared her throat and tried again. "I know you're with the astrophysics department, but I'm not familiar with what you actually do here, Jun."

"Observational cosmology," he said, pushing his glasses up his nose with the knuckle of his thumb. His voice was soft and difficult to hear over the party noise.

"That's great." Cass smiled. "What is that?"

"I measure the cosmic background radiation," he said. When he saw that didn't help, he said, "The Big Bang."

"Oh." She took a slug from her cup and grimaced. The champagne was dry to the point of sour. "Which lab do you work in?"

"COBRA," he said.

"The microwave telescope?"

"Yes."

Cass finally nodded in understanding—not about his work, but at least she knew where he was going to spend his days. COBRA, the Cosmic Background Radiation Array, was one of the few outlying buildings that would be staffed throughout the winter. The astronomers who worked at COBRA slept and ate at the Shackleton station, but would spend most of their time alone in the blocky, two-story lab. COBRA was just a hundred meters away from the main base, but in a dark Antarctic winter, it would seem like another planet.

She gave a little shudder. Personal time was important, but there was no way she could spend the lion's share of the winter stuck in an otherwise empty building, staring at a computer monitor.

"There is only darkness in the winter," Jun said. "No light means less solar radiation to interfere with the readings."

"I guess that's why the lab is in the Dark Sector," she said, more as a joke than anything.

Jun smiled. "Yes! That is exactly why."

Mistaking her quip as a wish to know more, Jun embarked on a complicated explanation of the age of the universe in terms so ridiculously large and abstract that the whole thing had the whiff of a joke, then went on to describe those terms with words that sounded as if they'd been plucked from a Dr. Seuss story. Cass didn't consider herself an intellectual lightweight, but her brain tended toward the concrete and real, not the theoretical, and, despite Jun's enthusiasm, she found her attention floating away. Her eyes roamed over the crowd.

Pete, tired of cutting the cake into dozens of pieces, had given up and now people were simply grabbing plastic forks and shoveling chunks of cake into their mouths straight from the pan. Biddi already had her arm woven through Dave's and he looked down at her with a quirked eyebrow and a knowing expression. Cheeks were rosy and easily half the noise in the room came from laughter, although it had a shrill note, as if, upon finding something to laugh about, people wanted to make sure their response was noted and they were *having fun*. It flavored the celebration with a taste of desperation.

Cass felt a light touch on her arm and turned to Jun. His face was serious. "I'm very sorry."

"About what, Jun?"

"About Dr. Larkin. You were in the party that found her?"

She felt as though she'd been kneed in the stomach. "I . . . I was, yes. It was sad."

"Does anyone know what happened?"

"I don't know . . ." Her voice trailed off as she caught sight of Hanratty at the far end of the galley. "Actually, there's someone who might. Will you excuse me for a second?"

"Sorry?" Jun asked uncertainly, but Cass had already stepped away, setting a course for the far side of the long room. With his austere expression and skeletal features, Hanratty always stood out, but he was even easier to spot now, as his was the only unsmiling face in the crowd. Maybe a staff party wasn't the best time to corner the base manager about some unfortunate and uncomfortable events, but he could hardly claim he was too busy to talk. No one was doing any work now, nor would they for the next twenty-four hours.

Cass waded through two dozen people, many of whom smiled and said hello for the first time, showing that the champagne or euphoria of the last day of summer—or both—had gone to work. When she was halfway across the galley, Hanratty seemed to sense her approach and his head rotated in her direction like a gun turret. Without acknowledging her gaze, he turned in place and headed for the exit.

Asshole. Cass got ready to chase the man down, when a hand reached out and gently grabbed her arm. She spun around.

It was Gerald Keene, standing close. He held a cup topped off with champagne. "Leaving so soon, Cass? The party just started."

"Sorry, Dr. Keene, I really have to go—"

"Nonsense, Cass. They haven't even fired up the movies yet." Keene clucked his disapproval. "It's important to take part in the on-base events, you know. Social interaction is key to long-term psychological health. There won't be another party like this one until midwinter."

"Yes, I know," Cass said, trying to pull her arm away, but his grip tightened.

He leaned in, his breath yeasty and his eyes shining. Cake crumbs decorated his beard. "Be my Valentine?"

She stared at him. "What?"

"A joke, Cass, merely a joke. Tomorrow isn't just the start of a new season, it's Valentine's Day, remember?" He tsked. "You have to learn to loosen up a little. It's been a trying last couple of days, I know, but winter at the South Pole is a long time to be friendless and alone."

A knot of disgust formed in her gut, a mélange of anger at Hanratty, her distaste for the circus atmosphere, and Keene's repulsive demand for levity. Cass backpedaled away from the psychologist and the rest of the party, shoving and pushing her way out of the galley. Plans for confronting Hanratty were forgotten. All she wanted was to get to her room or the garage, lock the door, and forget about Keene, Hanratty, and everything else.

As she reached the door, she heard Biddi shout her name and she turned. Her friend waved at her to wait or not to go, she wasn't sure which. Behind her, watching, smiling, then lifting his cup in a mock toast, was Keene.

PART II

March

CHAPTER FIFTEEN

"I haven't seen you lately. Have you been spending more time down here in the tunnels?"

He nodded.

"It's quiet down here."

Another nod.

"Tell me more about your sister."

"Why?"

"She sounds like an important part of your life."

He scowled. "Everyone asks about her."

"You don't have to tell me if you don't want to."

He was silent. "What do you want to know?"

"What did she look like?"

Leroy's breath puffed into tiny clouds. "She was pretty, I suppose. Long hair. Brown eyes. Tall."

"Brown eyes? Not blue, like yours?"

"Brown," he said firmly.

"Was she older or younger?"

"Older."

"And your mother was . . . not present?"

Leroy shook his head and tugged the flaps on his trooper's hat down. His balaclava covered most of his face. "She left my dad when I was a kid."

"Was your mother also your sister's mother?"

A long pause. "No."

"Your father had a girlfriend."

"Yes."

"Is that why your mother left?"

He shrugged. "I guess."

"And your father didn't remarry?"

"No."

"So, neither you nor your sister grew up with a mother?"

He shook his head. A shudder rippled through his shoulders.

"I'm sorry, Leroy. That must have been very hard to understand as a young boy."

Leroy nodded.

"You only found peace when you ran into the fields. And listened to the wind."

He started to speak, coughed, tried again. "Yes."

"When you listened to the wind, did it say things to you?"

Leroy made a sound, then said, "Yes."

"Did you understand what it said?"

"Yes."

"The wind blamed you, didn't it? It told you that *you* were the reason your mother left. That you were the reason your father was all alone."

He said nothing.

"What else did it tell you, Leroy? That maybe your sister was as much to blame as you were? That she reminded your mother of your father's infidelity? That maybe she deserved punishing for hurting your mother, your father, you?"

Leroy leaned against the icy wall.

"Do you sometimes see other women, other girls, who remind you of your sister?"

Leroy shook his head again, but made no answer. His upper body quivered as though pulled by a million tiny strings.

"Ah, well, we'll leave that for now." A pause. "It must be difficult. Lying in your bunk at night, the wind constantly talking to you. Is it hard, Leroy?"

"Yes." He twitched.

"Is that why you come down here, Leroy? To get away from the wind? To stop it from talking to you?"

"Yes," he whispered.

"Did you know these tunnels are just the beginning? They keep going far, far under the station. Almost no one ever goes there. You should explore them sometime. Perhaps you could find your own little getaway. Away from the wind."

Leroy's shoulders stopped quaking. "Below the base?"

"Yes. You'll have to be careful. If anyone hears you've started spending time down there, they'll stop you. But if you don't tell anyone and only go down there when you need to, you can do it. You can start to create your own space, away from the others. Away from the wind."

Leroy stared for a moment longer, then nodded and shuffled away.

CHAPTER SIXTEEN

Cass ran her mittened hand along the ice wall as she moved down the tunnel, wrinkling her nose as she went.

In the supernaturally cold air below Shackleton, smells didn't actually travel far, but master pressure gauges and the computer monitoring system had suggested something was wrong with the station's sewer pipes, and it was pretty easy to fool herself into thinking she smelled the accumulated sewage of hundreds of people over decades of use. Or maybe she was being hypersensitive; a busted shitter was a five-alarm mechanical emergency for a small group stuck together for nine months and it was her job to fix it. Or else.

Finding the problem was the challenge. In the early days of Shackleton, leaving sewage at the site where it had been deposited was a distasteful, if necessary, reality. When simple survival was in doubt, no one bothered to haul out months of accumulated excrement. Even as technology improved and year-round residence at the South Pole was established, it was still considered impractical to remove waste, despite the environmental impact.

Hence, the invention of the sewer bulb, which was a fancy word for shit hole. Two dozen of them had been plumbed when the new station had been built but, like anything else involving fluid mechanics and pipes at the bottom of the world, the delivery system sometimes failed.

Unfortunately, the only way to discover whether the problem was a split line or a busted conduit or a malfunctioning pump was to descend the Beer Can, take a right past the intersection at the service arches, walk the length of the main utilities tunnel past the shrines and stub-up ladders, and maybe even haul your butt down to the old ice tunnels, the ones that went to the original parts of the base, using nothing but your eyes and nose to find the problem.

Dwight, the departing engineer who had trained her, had warned Cass that, with jobs like this, you had to make a choice right off the bat: drag a banana sled full of tools with you, prepared for anything, or walk to the problem empty-handed to perform a diagnosis, then return with only the tools you needed. If the leak was right around the corner, the first choice paid off. If not, you were in for a serious workout.

Cass, prudent and hardworking, would've normally gone for the first option and humped half the tools in the VMF with her, but Doc Ayres had been right: although it had been a month since her sprain, her ankle was still tender. The last thing she wanted to do was reinjure it or prolong the healing process, so dragging a sled for a mile-long round-trip wasn't a possibility. Making two round-trips? Not a savory option, either, but she didn't have a choice. Unless she wanted to supplant Keene as the most unpopular person at Shackleton, she had to find the problem before the toilets stopped working.

As she passed it, she glanced down the alcove at the access ladder that led to her hidden radio spot and felt a twinge of guilt. Busy with countless tasks around Shackleton, she hadn't gotten in touch with Vox lately. She imagined him waiting by his own shortwave—hidden who knows where—listening to the hiss of empty airwaves. She promised herself she'd make it up to him.

She continued down the tunnel, each segment looking exactly like the last. Bright overhead lights lit the way, although as an energy-saving measure they were spaced farther apart than in the main tunnels. The radius of each light died out just as the next one picked up the slack, forming modest pools of illumination interspersed with wedges of darkness. Since she'd want her hands free in order to inspect the pipes thoroughly, Cass pulled out her trusty headlamp and secured it in place as needles of cold sprang along her forehead and scalp. She switched the red light on and pulled the hood back over her head, giving the lamp just enough room to shine through.

The work was slow going. To do the job right, she had to look over each section of pipe, running her light along and behind the sections where the overhead illumination didn't reach. After the first hundred meters, however, there was no sign of a leak and she felt a small surge of vindication—if she'd taken a chance and pulled a sled full of tools with a bum ankle, she'd already be regretting it.

But the air seemed colder here, if that were possible, and she shivered as she thought about losing her way at the far end of the frozen tunnel. Wandering and alone, unable to find the path back to the surface as the heat slowly left her body . . .

"Jesus. Get a grip," she said out loud, regretting it instantly as the sound died in the still air. She calmed herself and kept moving, continuing on to the Section D branch, different from the others in that—eventually, after many twists and turns—it connected with the ancient tunnels from the original base. At least, that's what her schematic said. Before he'd left her in charge, Dwight had told her it was worth a look at the old rat warren and abandoned vaults just to see the wood beam and rivet construction the first Polies had used to shore up their tunnels.

She stopped in front of the plywood door to Section D, then shook off a mitten so she could pull out her copy of the tunnel map. At a guess, it was a half mile back to the Beer Can. Tucking the map into her parka, she tugged open the door and tried the sniff test, regretting it immediately as the inside of her nose turned into an ice cube.

Not surprisingly, there was no smell, but she hesitated and looked back the way she'd come. For one of the planet's foremost research facilities, there was a sometimes surprising lack of rhyme or reason to where utilities had been placed, with sewer bulbs plumbed and dropped in different areas over the decades. Abandoned bulbs sat next to some currently in use, while still others had been drilled a decade ago but were waiting to be filled.

Coming to a decision, she passed through to Section D, closing the plywood door behind her. The lights here were even fewer and farther between than in the main ice tunnel, spaced maybe twenty meters apart. The puddles of darkness were now three or four times larger than the spread of light, making the lamps less a source of illumination and more like beacons guiding her onward.

She kept her eyes fixed on the pipes running near the top right corner. After another hundred meters, she paused to work the kinks out of her neck, then pulled the schematic out once again. According to the plan, she wasn't far from the switchback to the 1950s base. She grimaced under her mask. If she didn't find the leak in the next thirty meters of ice tunnel, there was a good chance it was in the original construction. It would be a major undertaking just to reach it, never mind fix it.

The thirty meters came and went. No leak. At least none that she could see. The downslope switchback to the original base peeled away to her left and she dutifully followed the pipes down the narrow tunnel. The lights were even more infrequent here, the exception instead of the rule—each lamp was barely within sight of the next.

The light from her headlamp swung back and forth as she walked. Smooth, sculpted walls gave way to hand-chiseled passages so tight that she could almost reach up and touch the ceiling. After a minute, those began to seem spacious as the walls and ceiling closed in until Cass's shoulders brushed the ice and she had to duck her head to keep from banging it on the suddenly low-hanging pipes. The walls were now supported with the wooden shoring and steel rivets Dwight had described to her.

Eventually, the tunnel squeezed down into a passage no larger than a crawl space.

"You've got to be kidding," she said, looking at the four-by-four opening. With the pipes in the way, she'd have to get down on her hands and knees to squeeze through.

It was time to call it quits and go back to the base. Fixing the plumbing and emptying trash cans was one thing, but doing major repairs in a seventy-year-old ruin was another. She turned to leave, then stopped.

A vision of the contempt and disappointment on Hanratty's face materialized in her head. *Who, exactly, is supposed to do the work, Jennings?* she could hear him ask. *Biddi? One of the astrophysicists? Want someone to fly in from McMurdo with some duct tape? This is what wintering over means. Like it or not, you're it.*

Encumbered by her layers of clothes, she sank to her knees awkwardly, like a bear kneeling to pray. She inched forward, wincing as she brushed her head against the crawl space ceiling. The timbers and fasteners around her were not only decades old, they'd no doubt been compressing under the millions of tons of settling ice above. Dwight had warned her that the risk of collapse was small, but there was a chance that the wood—desiccated, aging, and under tremendous pressure—could essentially explode from even a modest amount of friction. Say, like the top of your parka brushing against it.

She sank until her belly made whisking sounds along the icy ground. Crawling was more work than she'd thought. The balaclava was moist from her breath and the outer layer began to freeze. The crawl space in front of her, revealed in patches from the light of her headlamp, looked like a miner's shaft instead of the access tunnel to a relatively modern scientific installation.

Cass swallowed. She wasn't claustrophobic, but she didn't have to be to feel the weight of the continent above her head. The threat of Hanratty's sarcasm was melting away in the face of the shrinking tunnel in front of her.

Just as she was contemplating turning around, the tunnel broadened, expanding until it transformed into a room. She shuffled forward on her hands and knees, then gingerly stood up into what looked like a grubby old lounge or galley. Steel desks and plastic chairs were gathered in random groups around a musty central table, while a counter in the rear seemed to be the focal point of either meals or drinks or both. Sniffing cautiously, she picked up the clear stink of sewer gas, making her wish for the frozen air of the tunnel behind her.

She swung her lamp to the ceiling. The sewer conduit had obviously been installed long after the space had been abandoned; the silver pipes shot rudely across the room in complete disregard for its original purpose. They passed through the lounge and out the other side, exiting through another crawl space. As she played the light along the pipes, her heart leapt in her chest when she saw something she'd never thought she'd be excited to see: a sluggish stream of sewage dripping from a gash in the side of the pipe. Much of it had frozen to the outside of the pipe, forming a stalactite of shit that reached to the floor.

Placing both of her mittens over her face to guard against the smell, Cass picked her way around the furniture and debris, dodging frozen pools of sewage.

She frowned as she got closer. *What the hell?*

The leak's source was a ten-inch vertical slash, but structural failures usually occurred horizontally, following the length of something like a pipe or cable. This breach looked like someone had whacked the pipe with an axe, which was stupid. If you were going to sabotage the pipe, you'd do your damage a quarter mile back up the tunnel and save yourself the hike. But, of course, that missed the point. Who would want to vandalize the sewage system?

She stared at the damage a moment longer, then shook her head. Forensic work on the failure would have to wait until she returned to make the repair, but at least she had her answer to the *what* and *where*. The *how* and *why* would have to wait.

Sighing, she turned and knelt to reenter the crawl space. It would be a hell of a lot of work to get her tools down the tunnel, into the crawl space, and set up in the old base lounge.

Cass's mind was busy making calculations and decisions on what tools to bring, crawling forward on autopilot and simply letting her body work its way to the string of lights ahead of her. She looked up only once to reassure herself that the crawl space was coming to an end.

Which was when the lights went out.

Frozen in place on her hands and knees, she stared straight ahead, trying to make sense of what had just happened. *Okay okay okay.* Even with the lights on, she told herself, visibility had been poor at this end of the tunnel. Maybe she just wasn't seeing the halo of the nearest light. She wagged her head to move her lamp's beam back and forth, comparing the illumination she was seeing to what had been there.

Wherever the beam went, there was red light out to fifteen feet in a soft, diffuse spread. Anywhere else, it was pitch black. Dead black.

An instinctive panic grabbed her, and her chest tightened as though a belt had been cinched around it. The layers of clothing that had kept her warm and alive felt instead like they were suffocating her. She clawed at her scarf and mask, her nails scratching her face. She took a deep, piercing breath that sent her into a coughing fit.

But the frozen air sliced through her panic like a razor, halting the fear and giving her enough presence of mind to stop what she was doing and take stock. Moving deliberately, she replaced the scarf and mask, imagining how her instructors back in the States would've told her to tackle the situation.

Stop and think. Assess the situation. Where are you and what's going on?

"I'm in the tunnels underneath Shackleton," she whispered. "I'm probably a half mile from the basement level."

What else?

"The lights are out."

Are you in any danger?

"No. Maybe. With visibility down, I'm more likely to brush the tunnel shoring, causing a burst or even a collapse."

Which means?

"I better be careful and take my time going back."

Is there something wrong with being cautious, Jennings?

"If I don't freeze to death, probably not."

The voice had no answer to that.

Cass swallowed, wincing at the stiffness in her elbows and knees. In the few minutes it had taken to get herself under control, the cold had seeped through the layers of clothing and into her body. An inactive body provided no heat; she'd begun to freeze without even knowing it.

Newton's first law is truer in Antarctica than any other place on earth. The voice in her head was back. *What is Newton's first law?*

"A body at rest will remain at rest."

And what happens to a body at rest on the ice, Jennings?

"It dies."

Do you want to live?

"Yes."

Then . . .

"Get moving." She whispered the words, or thought them. Alone, in a dark tunnel half a mile from base, it amounted to the same thing.

She moved.

In a few minutes, she'd progressed through the crawl space and out into the upright tunnel. It was still cramped by any normal standard, but it seemed infinitely larger than the crawl space. With visibility reduced to the length of a pool table, the urge to put out a hand for support was hard to suppress, but the shoring was still the timber and rivet construction here, so she kept her hands tucked close to her sides and shuffled along the icy floor in hesitant steps, fighting the sensation that the walls were creeping inward.

To keep her rising fear in check, she turned her situation into a mechanical problem, examining her predicament like she would a clogged line or a bum engine.

Why had the lights gone out? The bulbs in all of the lamps were the best the industry could offer, guaranteed for a minimum of ten years.

Although, in the staggering cold of Antarctica, all bets were off. She and Dwight had routinely laughed at performance guarantees.

But that only meant *single* bulbs should fail sporadically. The tunnel she was in, roughly straight for a hundred meters or more, was impenetrably dark. Surely it was impossible that every bulb had conked out simultaneously. Which meant that the electrical system had failed.

Yet that was as unlikely as every bulb blowing at the same time. She knew firsthand that the base had been wired for triple redundancy. Three generators were in place in the unlikely event of a cascading electrical failure. If the system was down, then the entire base was in jeopardy, and the chances of that happening precisely while she was in the most remote location on base seemed infinitesimal. Which left only one possibility.

Someone had turned the lights off.

Stating it didn't surprise her as much as she thought it might. An image of the gash in the sewage pipe, obviously man-made, had been sitting in her head, waiting to be acknowledged. Matched with the almost complete darkness around her, the two realizations completed the problem set with the precision of a geometry solution. Unfortunately, that conclusion wouldn't just sit there, either. Another possibility tickled her mind, demanding to be examined.

Whoever had smashed the pipe must have done it days, even weeks, ago, for the pressure to have dropped over time. They'd planned that part in advance. But the lights were a different story. Short of planting an explosive or rewiring the system, it was unlikely anyone could shut them off remotely. They would have to have done it manually.

So that person was somewhere in the tunnels with her, right now.

This conclusion *did* startle her and she stumbled. Her bad ankle took the weight of her misstep and she careened to one side, crying out at the pain that lanced up her foot and into her shin. She threw out a hand to brace herself. Her hand found the icy wall, slipped along the slick surface, and plowed directly into a wooden beam with most of her weight behind it.

With a crack like a gunshot, the timber burst next to her ear, followed instantly by a blizzard of flakes and splinters of wood that showered her like a thousand drops of rain hitting the pavement. Without the protection of the hood, she would've been deafened from the noise and probably blinded from the shrapnel. Even with it, slivers of seventy-year-old lumber stippled her parka, her pants, and her boots. The thinnest cover was at her forehead and dozens of tiny painful pinpricks erupted where the splinters pierced the fabric.

Lying supine on the icepack, stunned, motionless, Cass waited for the creaks and groans that would mean the roof was about to collapse. She dropped her head to the ground, relishing the restful moment even while she waited for the final crash that meant she'd become Shackleton's first known "crushed ice" casualty.

She thought of the memorial they'd erect for her. Given Polies' macabre sense of humor, it would probably be an empty parka and mitten sandwiched between two blocks of ice. Biddi would write the epitaph and get Dave to chisel it with a pneumatic hammer. *Between these blocks lies my girl Cass. She slipped on some ice, said, "Isn't this nice!" and now she rests flat on her ass.* The image hit a nerve and Cass started to laugh so hard tears began to run down her cheeks and pool around the seal of her goggles.

But a long minute passed without a sound except her dying laughter. The collapse wasn't coming. Cass opened her eyes.

Or thought she did. Her eyes were wide open but the darkness in front of her was as total as if she'd kept her lids squeezed shut.

She wriggled her hand free of her mitten and reached to her forehead where her lamp was. *Correction*, she thought as she felt jagged shards of plastic where the bulb's housing should be. *Had been*.

The hard knot of anxiety in her gut yawned wider. Like an idiot, she hadn't brought a backup flashlight, instead relying only on her headlamp. No flare, no acetylene torch—she would've had those if she'd dragged the tool sled along. She had a miniature magnesium flint and striker fire-starter attached to a keychain almost as a joke, but was she willing to risk a fire, even a small one, in a tunnel filled with desiccated wooden timbers that had been sitting in an ultra-arid environment for more than half a century?

Hell, no. The only thing worse than being squashed by a collapsing roof would be finding herself trapped in a raging tunnel fire she herself had started, drowning in the resulting ice melt, *then* having the ceiling collapse in on her.

A shudder went through her. The safest thing—the *only* thing—she could do was to walk the tunnel in the dark.

While her hand was still out of her mitten, Cass passed her hand around her mask and hood to check the damage. She'd been lucky. None of the tiny fléchettes had done much except prick the skin. She pulled the largest splinters out, then put her mitten back on and got to her feet painfully, ready to set off into the complete darkness.

It was disorienting. Thinking carefully, she replayed her fall, the bursting timber, hitting the ground. Obviously, she'd been walking toward the base. If she'd hit the ground in one motion, her head should still be pointing the right way. It seemed unlikely she'd spun in a circle before falling. Unless she'd sprawled sideways *across* the tunnel?

Then she cursed, wondering if she'd hit her head on top of it all. *Come on, Cass*. What was the one ever-present structure in the tunnel, the reason she was down here in the first place? The sewage pipe. And it consistently ran along just one side of the tunnel. Which meant all she had to do to get back was reach out, find the pipe, and keep it on her left. Assuming she didn't smash her arm into another timber support and kill herself this time.

Cautious in the extreme, she sent her left hand out on a scouting expedition at about thirty degrees up and out from her shoulder, sliding her mitten up the ice at a slow, measured pace until her hand bumped into the cushy insulation that wrapped every inch of the sewage pipe. She cupped her hand around the underside of the conduit;

then, moving forward with short, wary strides, she let the pipe guide her forward.

As step followed step, however, she struggled to keep herself grounded and calm. In the complete absence of light, she had nothing to indicate her progress, which fostered the disturbing sensation that she was endlessly repeating herself. Cass found herself taking longer and longer steps, wanting nothing more than to get back to the cheap plywood door that meant she'd made it at least halfway home. But she forced herself to slow down and stick to the shallow stride that would keep her safe.

Counting helped. Picturing the schematic in her head and factoring in what she knew about her own stride, she did some rough calculations. Safety was still many paces away, but any problem could be quantified and, if it could be measured, overcome.

A memory hit her then, hard and visceral, so real that she gasped, fighting to keep her balance. This wasn't the first time she'd counted off steps or followed a schematic. Measuring, assessing, noting. It had been a tunnel then, too. It was amazing she hadn't seen the similarity sooner.

Maybe it was understandable. She'd had a hard hat on then, and jeans, not a parka and mittens. And she hadn't been in a squat, claustrophobic wormhole, but in an arched, rounded cavern so colossal that it resembled a cathedral more than the transit tunnel it actually was. She hadn't been frightened and alone; she'd been surrounded by welders and drillers and engineers working round-the-clock shifts. The city had been pushing for completion—constant pressure rained down from the mayor's office, it was an election year, transportation was that season's cause célèbre. Sparks flew at one end of a run while her team took measurements at the other.

Tight lips and flattened mouths spoke of mute disapproval, but no one had the brass to stop the process. They were a tight, professional group—a rarity in city government—and they prided themselves on never being the bottleneck in a project, doing their work on time and under budget. The unrelenting pressure had given all of them a fever, though, and they'd scrambled over pipes and scribbled in their notebooks at a pace they'd never allowed before. They made the numbers work, and when they didn't work, they made them right. Boxes were checked, lines were signed, and assurances given. There'd been much patting on backs and handshakes all around, until five months later when those same hands were being wrung in agony or covering their faces in horror.

A noise somewhere ahead brought both her feet and her memory to a halt. A clacking noise, followed by a thump, but having heard it through three layers of clothing, she couldn't be sure. The only sound she'd been hearing for long minutes had been her own breathing and the silvery whisper of her mitten's synthetic fabric against the slick insulation.

She hesitated, then pulled her hood back and loosened the scarf over her face. She wouldn't last long in the cold without both, but it was the only way she'd be able to hear anything louder than her own heartbeat.

There it was again. *Click-click-click, thump*. The bottom of her stomach dropped to the floor. Willing herself to move, she shook off a mitten and slid a hand down to her belt where she kept a multi-tool in a nylon sheath. Working fast, she ran a thumb along each tool, fumbling in the dark to find the one with the blade, cursing softly when the edge sliced into her thumb as she unlocked it.

With her left hand on the pipe and her right holding the knife, Cass resumed her tentative steps. If she was right about the distance, she should be near the door to the main artery. But was the person who killed the lights on her side or the other?

Her face and hand prickled with the bite of subzero temperatures. With her hood and scarf pulled down to hear and her right hand exposed while it held the knife, her skin was directly exposed, but she needed to hear.

And there it was again. A clacking, followed by a thump. Then she heard a soft, whisking sound, like a cornstalk broom being brushed across a hardwood floor. Cass strained to hear. Slowly, the whisking noises became a whisper, and the whisper became a word.

"*Cass*."

Sweat stung the punctures caused by the bursting of the wooden beam. She squeezed the knife, unsure what to do. After a long wait, crouching slightly and leading with the knife, she pressed forward. Five steps. Then ten.

"*Cass*."

The sound was barely there and seemed swallowed by the ice around her. Was it farther away? Or so close she could feel someone's breath? She recoiled.

After a moment, the whisking sound began again . . . and this time she realized what it was.

Laughter.

White rage flooded her from somewhere deep inside. Screaming something incoherent, she dashed forward, swinging the knife back and forth like a flyswatter . . . but the blade made no contact, encountered nothing. The cold whisking sound faded. Cass stumbled forward, stabbing and punching and slashing at whoever had tried to turn her fears and memories against her. Even in the complete darkness, she felt like she could sense the other person so well that she could actually see them. Hysterical, she swung for the imagined face.

But there was nothing there. Staggering forward from the swing, her foot kicked something hard and unyielding—the door frame?—and she pitched forward with a yell. The knife flew from her hand; her breath was nearly knocked out of her body. Pain tore through her ankle.

She pulled herself off the ground and crouched in the dark, whimpering, terrified, ready for someone to attack. When nothing happened, she listened intently, hoping to catch a telltale sound. But all she could hear was her own tattered breathing.

After an infinite minute, she put a hand to the wall for support once again and pulled herself to her feet. Limping, cursing, and crying, she made her way blindly through the darkness.

CHAPTER SEVENTEEN

"And then you walked back to base." Hanratty's face was as blank and unreadable as a stone. "But didn't tell anyone."

Cass matched his stare. "I'm telling you."

It had been a day since her harrowing journey through the tunnels. The tiny wounds she'd received from the exploding timber shoring weren't serious, but the resin or the preservative in the wood had caused a reaction and her normally clear skin blazed like she had the measles. After staggering back to her quarters, she'd spent an hour picking out splinters, debating what she should do about her experience in the tunnels. Report it or keep the whole thing to herself? Expose herself to questions and potential ridicule, or act like it hadn't occurred? She went back and forth with herself until, exhausted, she'd simply crawled into her bunk, giving herself permission to sleep on the issue.

The next morning, she'd decided there was no way she could simply ignore what had happened; her only choice was to tell either Hanratty or Taylor. Of the two of them, and despite her innate dislike of the man, her instinct told her Hanratty would handle the situation more professionally. But now looking at him across his desk, faced with his icy indifference, she had her doubts.

His gaze slid off her and over her shoulder. "Jennings, some of the infrastructure down there is nearly seventy years old. It's not beyond comprehension that the lights might stop working."

"What about the sewer pipe? The vertical split? That's not natural."

He shrugged. "Says who? I respect the fact that, of the two of us, you're the one with the degree in mechanical engineering. But strange things happen at the Pole, and just because a pipe broke in a different direction than you expected doesn't mean there's a grand conspiracy."

She gritted her teeth. "And the person in the tunnel? The one who turned the lights out? The one who I almost *knifed*?"

"But didn't." Hanratty ran his hands wide along the lip of his desk, like he was smoothing a wrinkle in a tablecloth. "You said you returned later."

"Yes." *With three flashlights and a crowbar.*

"You found evidence of this other person? Blood, maybe, or a footprint?"

Cass paused. "No."

"Was the . . . assailant a man or a woman?"

She swallowed. "I don't know."

He nodded, as if expecting the answer. "And the voice . . . no help there?"

"No."

"What did they say, again?"

"They whispered my name."

"Demonstrate."

She looked at him. "What?"

"Say it to me like you heard it."

"Why?"

"I want to hear what you heard."

"You're serious?"

"Yes."

Cass cleared her throat and lowered her voice to a whisper. "Cass."

It sounded profoundly ridiculous. What had been sinister and life threatening in the darkness of the ice tunnel sounded like the soundtrack to a bad movie in the warmth of Hanratty's office.

He looked down at the surface of his desk for a beat, then back up at her. "Jennings, how are you sleeping?"

"Oh for Christ—"

"How well?"

"Shitty," she said, exasperated. "Just like everyone else on base. And that has nothing to do with what happened yesterday. I didn't hallucinate this. Just like I didn't hallucinate that person in the back of the VMF the day you, Taylor, and Keene were in my garage. Which I'd like to know more about, by the way."

"What would you like to know?"

"Why were the three of you there? And who did I chase down the tunnel?"

Hanratty tilted his head as though unable to understand her. "I told you at the time that Taylor and I were overseeing the loading for the last flight. We'd just come from the warehouse and Keene had joined us because he was tired of sitting in his office. There isn't much for a morale officer to do when eighty percent of the staff has left."

Cass gritted her teeth at Hanratty's infuriating equanimity. So helpful, so curious, so full of shit. "Was the person who ran down the tunnel also there to inspect the loading of the last flight?"

"I didn't even know there was anyone in the back of the VMF. In fact, the three of us were surprised when you took off like a shot toward the carpentry shop."

"You didn't hear anything? See anything? Nothing out of the ordinary."

The manager shook his head. "No. The only strange event was you sprinting out the back of the VMF like you were on fire."

"You were gone when I got back."

He shrugged. "Were we supposed to wait for you?"

Cass looked at him, sure he was lying, but unable to comprehend why. "You saw no one? Really?"

"I know you want me to say yes, but I didn't. That doesn't mean there wasn't anyone there. It means I didn't see them."

"Why would they run away?"

"It was the last flight of the year. Everyone at Shackleton was trying to get that bird off the ground while conditions were good. Whoever you think you saw could've simply been one of a hundred different people trying to meet a deadline. You yourself were pulled in about a dozen different directions that day, correct?"

Cass put a hand to her head, then winced at the contact with the miniature puncture wounds. *They weren't running to do something. They were running away from something, from me.* Was the runner the same person who had been in the tunnel yesterday, whispering her name? She opened her eyes to suggest that, then stopped.

Leaning backwards, Hanratty had reached a long arm out to a counter behind his chair. Stacks of folders lined the surface. He fished through the tallest pile, found what he was looking for, then straightened up, his chair making a creaking noise. Taking his time, he leafed through the dossier. Sheets of colored paper—white, pink, and green—lay in the folder like stripes of candy. Cass gripped the arms of her chair, all thoughts of continuing the discussion about the mysterious runner gone. She knew what was coming.

"You had an unfortunate accident several years ago, I understand."

"Yes." Her voice jumped and she had to take a second to get it back under control. But as she spoke, it climbed the scale again. "I put that behind me, I passed the tests, I've paid. Goddammit, I've paid every day and every night since that happened."

"Jennings—"

"Don't." She skewered him with a finger. "Don't you fucking dare. If you had a problem with my fitness to be here, you had plenty of time to review my file. I didn't imagine what happened to me yesterday in that tunnel. My history doesn't change that. I'm fit for the position and I'm more than mentally stable enough to remember when I've almost been *attacked*."

His eyes so blank they might've been glass, Hanratty stared at her. "Jennings, I'm responsible for the lives of forty-four people on this base. Every one of them is important, their well-being paramount."

"Then do your job and support me."

Hanratty gently closed the folder. "I'm *doing* my job by questioning the veracity of what appears on the surface to be an outlandish claim. Can you see where I'm coming from?"

She said nothing.

"I'm glad we have an accord," he said drily. "Now. I've officially heard your complaint. I'll ask Deb to look into this. She may ask you to take her down to the tunnels and walk her through the . . . incident. Is that satisfactory?"

"Yes." It was the best she could expect.

"I'm obligated to ask if you'd like to see Dr. Keene about this incident. Would you?"

"No."

"You understand, also, that I have to tell him about this event. He may take the initiative to speak to you. Keene is allowed to conduct psych investigations that are beyond my purview to control. You can refuse to speak to him, but I don't think that would be . . . wise."

She closed her eyes, opened them, nodded.

He stopped speaking, as if considering something, then, "I would also ask you to keep this to yourself. Not to cover anything up. But let's consider this from an extreme range of possibilities. On one hand, it could be a prank by somebody with a sick sense of humor, in which case making it public will just encourage them to do it again. Somebody *will* get stabbed eventually if he or she doesn't stop."

"And at the other end?"

He shrugged. "If someone was preparing to attack you, making it public knowledge would not only encourage them, it would tip them off that we're watching."

Cass felt something unclench inside her chest. Was this lip service? Or a modest effort to help her? Examining Hanratty's face, it was impossible to tell. Residual aggravation from his early questions and the nagging sense he was just patronizing her still hung in the air, but at least he wasn't throwing her out of his office.

"Is there anything else?" His tone indicated he didn't think so.

"No." She stood and had walked to the door when he stopped her.

"Jennings."

She turned, but couldn't bring herself to look at him. He waited until she'd raised her eyes to his. His face, normally severe, showed sympathy.

"You won't believe it, but I'm on your side. More than you know."

Cass had nothing to say. He nodded once, though, as if she had, and bent his head to look over a report open on his desk, dismissing her. As she left, she saw him reach for a single, white piece of paper from a stack on the corner of his desk.

CHAPTER EIGHTEEN

Cass looked out the narrow window, trying to imagine a world without light.

"It will be dramatic," Anne explained, holding her hands wide, "but not like a light switch being thrown. Refractive light from the sun will continue to bounce off of the atmosphere for several hours after it goes over the horizon. That's what makes sunsets so pretty, right? Same thing here. The big difference is that *our* sunset starts six months of night."

A week earlier, the astrophysicists had reminded the crew that the last day the sun would be above the horizon, March 23, would be coming soon. Anne had offered to bring a telescope to the galley and lead a vigil of sorts to watch it go down. A small group had taken her up on her offer and were now gathered in the galley to grab coffee and peek through a filtered telescope. Cass had debated whether she wanted to take part or not, but finally joined the group to clear her head and take her mind off of recent events.

"So, it won't get dark instantly?" Pete asked.

"No. In fact, it will be dusk for quite a while. Technically, there are three stages—civil, nautical, and astronomical twilight—to describe how far below the horizon the sun is. Back home, we're used to seeing each stage occur with every sunset and sunrise. But here, since our day is actually measured in months, each twilight will be weeks long."

"So, when will it be totally dark?" Cass asked.

"To our eyes, it will seem dark in just a week or two," Anne said. "But officially? Astronomical twilight ends in early May. After that, there will be zero celestial illumination except that coming from stars, the moon, and the auroras. That's when it will be *dark* dark."

"And, if I remember right, you guys will still have to hump out to COBRA for work," Tim said with a matter-of-fact tone. "When it's pitch black out, the wind is howling, the temp is eighty below, et cetera and so on?"

"That's right, Tim," Anne said sweetly, scratching her nose with an extended middle finger. There were a few chuckles, then she looked down at her watch. "Oh, get your cameras ready, everyone. There may be a green flash as it sets, just like at the beach. You'll only get one chance to snap a picture before it's gone."

The small crowd was quiet as they all turned to stare out the windows. Cass, the only one without a camera, sat at one of the windows, her chin resting on her forearms. She preferred to commit the vision to memory instead of being ruled by what she could see through a viewfinder. Watching it, thinking about it, focused her mind more than worrying if she had the correct exposure setting or filter enabled.

And it was a sight worth her attention. The sky was clear and blue, with only a few scudding clouds high in the sky that were no threat to their view. Something about the quality of light had turned the ice fields a deep indigo that set off the weak yellow rays to perfection. The sun itself hung in the air like a flare on the horizon, although it was smaller than she would've described it had she been asked, and it seemed faintly ridiculous to think the small golden disc could heat their planet.

"Get ready." Anne's head was bent to the eyepiece of her scope.

Almost as one, cameras were raised to faces. Cass blinked her eyes several times and stared at the sun. The orb didn't appear to move at all, and then the rounded bottom was sheared off by the flat horizon as the sun ebbed downward. In a matter of a minute, the sun went from three-quarters, to half, to one-quarter full. Cass watched as its tip seemed to cling to the lip of the horizon, and then it slipped away. A small green sprite flashed just at the point of the sun's departure, and then there was nothing.

The group let out a collective sigh, murmuring appreciatively and peppering Anne with questions. Cass continued to watch long after the flash, admiring the clouds turning scarlet from the reflective light, until they were bruise-colored and indistinct. The light was not gone by any means, but it was clear that a profound change had taken place. She straightened in her chair and looked around. Only she and Anne were left in the galley.

"Last light," Cass said. Then, realizing that it had sounded overly dramatic, quipped, "The end of an era."

"Yes," Anne said. "Winter is here."

PART III

May

CHAPTER NINETEEN

Leroy stumbled through the door to his berth, locked the door, and fell facedown into his bunk. The little bed was barely big enough for him—his feet hung over the edge if he stretched out all the way—but right now he would've curled up on a pile of rags, he was so tired.

It wasn't the work, which kept him busy enough, he supposed, but he'd been on tougher jobs and even the farm where he grew up had a more demanding schedule. Which is to say, when something broke, you fixed it whether it was night or day, rain or shine, whether you were exhausted or not.

No, it wasn't the job. It was the constant push and pull of dealing with so many people, so many personalities, while all the while the wind was blowing and bullying, speaking to him as it thrashed the sides of the base. For weeks, his only solace had been the tunnel system below Shackleton, a place so quiet that his breathing was often the loudest thing he could hear. He'd explored farther and farther, inventing jobs so that he could pass entire shifts simply walking the warrens, old and new. He felt a small flush of pride—there probably wasn't anyone alive who knew more about the lost tracks and empty rooms below the South Pole than he did.

But his work had to get done sometime or they'd start asking questions, maybe even following. So, up he would come, like a prairie dog popping its head aboveground, taking the Beer Can steps to the surface where the wind would scream at him, berating him for hiding, setting his nerves on their bleeding edge.

When he wasn't in the tunnels, the crew was so small that he was constantly bumping into exactly the people he didn't want to see. Taylor, who looked at him with a sideways squint. Keene, acting like a long-lost uncle while wearing that phony, three-dollar smile.

And *her*. He didn't want to say her name, not even in his head. Meeting her in the hall, seeing her from across the galley. The pretty smile and long, swinging hair. He was always polite, his upbringing wouldn't let him act any other way, but every time he saw her coming down the hall, the wind seemed to pick up, screaming and rattling against the outside walls so loud that half the time he couldn't even hear her say hello or ask him how he was doing.

He groaned and rolled onto his side, his eyes squeezed shut, willing himself to sleep. Lord knows he was weary enough. But all he seemed to hear was the wind. Whistling in his head, whispering in his ear, telling, demanding, wanting.

Sleep wasn't happening, not right now. Maybe if he went to the lounge and put on a movie he'd pass out and finally get some rest. He sighed and opened his eyes, preparing to roll back out of bed, when he frowned. On his nightstand were two small, orange pill bottles, standing side by side. He hadn't seen them when he'd come in.

He reached out and grabbed one, bringing it closer. The pills inside rattled like teeth in a jar. The label read:

LEROY BUSKINS – TAKE 1 PILL PER DAY AS PRESCRIBED

He opened the bottle. Inside were perhaps forty pink, hexagonal pills. They barely filled the bottle to the halfway point.

A gust suddenly slammed the outside wall of his berth and he froze. A prickling sensation ran from the crown of his head down to his toes and he held his breath as he waited for it to speak. But the gale died away and he slowly relaxed.

Leroy put the lid back on the first bottle, then sat up and reached for the second. The label was identical, but inside were much larger blue capsules. They filled the bottle to the brim. He glanced at the labels again. They looked official enough, but neither had the name of the drug printed on it. That was okay; he'd been on so many meds over the years, with so many different names, it made no difference to him. The important thing was that he'd been taking two kinds of pills before he got to Shackleton. Here were two kinds of pills, right on his nightstand. The math added up.

Normally, he was supposed to pick up his meds from Doc Ayres at the clinic, but maybe they were trying to simplify the process. It had always seemed a little silly for him to have to go down there, show his ID, then sign for the drugs they both knew damn well were his. It only made sense to streamline things. And he couldn't complain about the service . . . delivered right to his room. No more BS trips to the clinic.

Leroy shook out a pill from each bottle, knocked them both back with a swig from an old can of soda he found sitting next to the bed, then rolled out of bed and started donning his cold weather gear again. He grunted a laugh as he pulled on his boots. A *movie*? He thought a movie would help him? With the wind thrashing outside and moaning through every crack and crevice? There was only one place he could find peace in this little patch of hell. He shrugged on his parka and grabbed his hat, then headed out the door for the tunnels fifty feet below the station.

CHAPTER TWENTY

It was late and the galley was nearly empty, populated by support staff and the few scientists who had to work as part of a twenty-four-hour shift. Most sat alone, staring at the TV with its endlessly scrolling weather report, out a window, or down at their tray. From time to time, one would give a little start as if remembering why they were there, and mechanically lift a fork or a water glass to their mouth. The wind pushed against the outer walls, but was ignored as nothing more than background noise.

Cass had made a point to sit down with Jeremy and Sam, two of the fuelies, in an effort to combat the lethargy that seemed to be grabbing hold of everyone at the station. The conversation was painfully stilted, but with the three of them working at it, they made it through a handful of topics before running out of steam. Still, it was a victory of sorts, and they beamed at each other for having beat T3, if only for one meal. Cass looked around at others not so lucky: those who seemingly sat for hours looking out a window; Elise, who still had her hand wrapped around a glass, though she'd emptied it thirty minutes earlier; even Taylor, his face set in a scowl, gazed unblinkingly into some middle distance.

The fuelies pushed back from the table, excusing themselves just as a neat, trim figure approached, a tray in his hands. Jun nodded at them as they passed, smiled at Cass, and sat down.

"It is nice to see you," Jun said as he methodically lifted each plastic bowl from his tray and placed them on the table in an array around his plate. He wore the same white short-sleeved shirt she'd originally seen him in and the same—or identical—too-blue department store jeans. She couldn't see them now, but she was sure he had on the battered Keds as well; they'd become a running, mean-spirited joke around the station.

"It's nice to see you, too, Jun," Cass said mechanically, though beyond the greeting she found herself tongue-tied, having talked herself out of trying to keep up the conversation with Jeremy and Sam.

"Are you having a good day?"

"I am," she said. "How about you?"

"I'm okay," he said, then looked down at a bowl of salad. He pushed the contents around with his fork as though the actual food was somewhere underneath.

Cass cast around for something to say, latched onto an easy topic. "How's your work out at COBRA?"

"It's good, thank you for asking," Jun said, brightening. "It's lonely sometimes, but I've gotten used to it."

Cass swirled the last inch of coffee in her cup. "I don't know how you guys do it, spending all that time alone monitoring the equipment."

"It's not as bad as it sounds," he said. "I take my books, some music. There's lots of time to think. I pretend I can hear the stars talk."

"Oh?"

As though a dam had burst, he began talking fast, building up speed as the words tumbled out. "Whales communicate through their songs and dolphins through ultrasonic clicks, but not many people think they are actually talking to us. It's a form of information delivery, but not necessarily speech. What if we thought of distant suns as communicating in a similar way? Radio astronomy is an accepted subfield of the science, but it's passive observation. What if we could interpret the language of a star like we do a whale's song or a gorilla's sign language or a human's speech?"

After months at the South Pole, the theory didn't sound nearly as batty as it might've in a previous life. "Have you mentioned this to the other people on your team?"

"Oh, no." Jun's face registered shock at the suggestion. "They'd think I was crazy."

Cass smiled. *You're kidding.* "Maybe when this is all over, you could test the idea back at home."

"I don't think so. They are not much more open-minded than my colleagues here."

"Where is home, again?"

"Pasadena." The answer came easily enough, but Jun's face fell as he said it. "Caltech."

"Not a good place?"

"Oh, no. It is a very good school. Many opportunities for research, grants, post-docs."

Cass nodded hesitantly. There was something there, but most Polies weren't fond of prying. Either someone offered personal information or they didn't. Jun tore open a sugar packet and stirred it into a glass of iced tea, focusing on it like it would talk to him like his stars. Cass watched him.

"My wife is in Pasadena," he said finally. "It is very hard to have her so far away."

Cass nodded again. The rattle of metal pans and utensils being washed filtered to them distantly from the kitchen.

"What does she do?"

"She is a physician's assistant at a local practice." He said it as if reading from a script.

"The two of you sound very successful," Cass said awkwardly.

He looked up and smiled briefly. "Thank you."

"No kids?"

Jun's face fell again. "No."

Idiot, Cass chided herself. "Well, I'm sure it's hard on her to be away from you, too, Jun."

He nodded, but not like he was agreeing. He pushed his salad around more, then said to it, "She was not happy that I came to Shackleton. But it is very rare to be invited. This will be very good for my career."

Outside, a capricious gust flung a spray of ice against one of the windows. Even through the thick glass, it made a sound like gravel being thrown at a wall. Jun didn't flinch. Moments passed.

"I came here to punish my wife," he finally continued. "I wanted to make her miss me."

Cass said nothing.

"At home," he said, "we had very different schedules. She always left work before me. Long hours, early in the morning. I study space, so my work is late at night, like here. But, no matter how late I came home, I would still get up every morning before she went to work."

A knot of pain formed at the base of Cass's throat. She found herself unable to speak.

"Every day, I would stand on our little porch and wave as she drove away. I waved. I waved as long as I could see her car," he said, almost in a wondering tone. "But, after all the times I waved, she never looked back."

Jun's face pulled inward then, and tears welled in his eyes. It was made worse by the fact that he made no sound. He simply cried.

Cass's mouth opened to say something, but nothing came out. She shared some amount of his loss and pain, but it was as if she had no ability to empathize, as if her emotions had been walled away and made unavailable for her to use on behalf of others or for herself. She could only watch as the man wept silently, his tears spilling down his cheeks and falling into his salad.

CHAPTER TWENTY-ONE

Aside from the smell of sweat and institutional cleaner, the gym was empty. Cass flicked the lights on and wandered the small but well-equipped room, spinning the wheels on the bikes and stabbing the buttons on the machines.

In addition to the treadmills and rowing deck, there were two stationary bikes, a punching bag, four weight machines, and some kind of stretching device with pegs and straps that looked like it had been invented during the Inquisition. Poking her nose into a utility closet revealed mats, some weird-looking rubber bands, and other odds and ends left over from various workout crazes. She sighed and shut the closet.

Since spraining her ankle, Cass had reluctantly turned to her non-running options for exercise, trying to rest an injury that, thanks to the fiasco in the tunnels underneath Shackleton, was still tender and occasionally buckled when she walked down a set of stairs. Ayres's suggestion when she'd asked what she should do—not exercise—wasn't an option. In recent years, she'd grown accustomed to throwing herself into each run, exhausting her mind as well as her body, punishing and pushing herself to accomplish a kind of therapy through fatigue.

Rowing, biking, and lifting weights all helped satisfy in part the physical and emotional craving running had created, but it was no substitute for actually picking 'em up and putting 'em down. Unlike Sheryl and some of the more adventurous in Shackleton's crew, she couldn't bring herself to run outside, but the miles stacked up the same on a treadmill.

But she hadn't been able to put those miles in since the end of the summer season. Desperate, she'd tried a light jog a few weeks ago, hoping enough time had passed that the ankle had healed. She'd put in three miles, encouraged by the lack of pain during the run . . . only to find the next morning that her ankle had blown up to three times its normal size.

Enough time had passed since for the ankle to heal, but she was skittish, remembering the tweak she'd felt deep in the tendons and muscles when she'd initially sprained it. She could probably run again . . . but what if she couldn't? *Give it one more week*, she thought. *You have the entire second half of the winter to get back in shape.*

Whatever she did, whenever she did it, Cass knew she had to do something to stretch her body and mind. Between the darkness outside the station and the lassitude she felt inside herself, exercise seemed the only weapon against the creeping sense of depression gripping everyone on base. She'd been ashamed that she hadn't been able to summon any empathy for Jun when he'd broken down in the galley; maybe with enough time in the gym she could beat some humanity back into her soul.

Grumbling, she mounted one of the stationary bikes and started pedaling. Thirty minutes later, having built up a decent sweat at the expense of a throbbing in her ankle, she strapped on a pair of boxing gloves and began slugging the punching bag, careful to put most of her weight on her good ankle. Imagining Keene's or Hanratty's face in place of the bag helped the throbbing go away.

She kept it up until her arms and shoulders burned and she felt a twinge in one wrist from hitting the bag at an awkward angle, but her pent-up anxiety slowly leaked away. The familiar and welcome feeling of serenity that came with an intense workout took its place.

Cass was about to wrap it up when the door opened and Anne Klimt came in. She flashed a smile at Cass, then walked by and headed for one of the treadmills. Anne, tall and lithe, was a runner, too, and Cass looked on enviously as the other woman started jogging effortlessly, her long hair pulled back in a ponytail that swung back and forth with her stride. Feeling peevish, Cass forgot about quitting and went back to slugging the bag despite the pain in her wrist.

She has good form, Cass thought grudgingly as she watched Anne segue into a full-stride, six-minute-mile pace after just a few minutes of warm-up. Elbows tucked to the sides. No wasted, bouncy, up-and-down motion. Heel-to-toe rocking motion, minimizing impact and compression.

Cass's hands slowly dropped to her sides as she watched. The other woman's running brought another's stride to mind: a floppy, arm-swinging figure dashing down a tunnel of white ice. She visualized the form over Anne's, comparing the sleek movement in front of her to the mystery runner's awkward sprint.

Anne, maybe feeling the weight of Cass's gaze, turned her head. Caught staring, Cass blushed.

The other woman smiled a little uncertainly. "Are you okay?"

Cass limped over to the treadmill. "Sorry, I was just watching you run. You make it look so easy."

Anne wiped a hand across her forehead and smiled self-consciously. "Thanks. That's a real compliment, coming from you. I know you're a runner yourself."

"I was."

"What do you mean?"

Cass gestured at her foot. "I twisted my ankle down in the garage back in February. I'm still worried about putting all my weight on it."

"*That's* why you were beating the hell out of the punching bag. I wondered why I haven't seen you on a treadmill."

Cass hesitated. "It's funny how you can spot another runner, isn't it? I saw you take three strides and knew you'd run all your life."

"It's true." Anne nodded. Her pace hadn't slowed one bit and her words came easily.

"There are people who run, but they're not *runners*. Do you know what I mean?"

"The ones who do this?" Anne lifted her knees almost to her chest and flapped her arms like a bird. They both broke out laughing at the pantomime of the world's worst form.

"There's someone who does this," Cass said, throwing her elbows out and swinging her hips wide to imitate the run of the mysterious figure she'd seen the day she'd towed the Alpine back to the garage. "But I can't remember who."

"Like a model on a runway, but with the arms going, too."

"Exactly!"

"It looks familiar." The smile died on Anne's face. "Oh. Sheryl Larkin used to . . . used to run like that. She was never very good, but she tried awfully hard. Is that who you mean?"

Anne's words came together like the missing parts of a clock, confirming what Cass had known but hadn't been able to articulate. A roaring sound flooded her ears. She could see the image of the fleeing figure and over it she superimposed the few times she'd seen Sheryl in the gym.

"Cass? Are you okay?" Anne stopped her treadmill and stared at her, alarmed.

"I'm okay," Cass heard herself say. "I'm fine."

"You don't look fine."

Cass realized she'd put out a hand and grabbed a nearby machine to steady herself. Anne looked like she was a second away from calling for a medic.

"No, I'm really okay. I just . . . you know, I was one of the ones who brought her in that night and I . . ." she babbled, trying to cover the confusion and anger her real thoughts had created. "I can't believe I didn't make the connection."

Anne nodded. "It was a shock for everyone, but it must've been really bad for you."

"It was. I . . . I think I'm going to go back to my berth and lie down for a while."

"That's probably a good idea," Anne said, her face sympathetic. "Try to put it out of your mind. Sheryl's death was just a terrible, tragic accident and it won't happen again."

She said a few more things in an attempt to comfort, but Cass didn't hear any of them as she stumbled out of the gym and down the hall. Images of Sheryl alive—laughing and eating in the galley, nodding to her at a meeting—mingled with those of the body on the sled, frozen and unresponsive, then morphed, in turn, into the shadowy figure sprinting down the ice tunnel. Cass felt sick.

It won't happen again . . . because it never happened at all.

CHAPTER TWENTY-TWO

"So what does it all mean? What should I do?"

There was a pause before the answer came across, crackling and hissing. "Are you really asking that of a child of Soviet-era dissenters who were sent to Siberia for asking too many questions?"

Lying on her side, cradling her parka'd head in the crook of her elbow, Cass smiled. It wasn't all that funny, but any joke was welcome these days. "I'm asking you as a scientist and a friend."

"A friend?"

"Well, yes," Cass stammered.

"Oh. In that case, how could I resist?" Vox replied in a mocking tone. Cass couldn't tell if the comment was sarcastic or self-deprecating. "But you should treat your friends better. You have missed our last two dates."

"I'm sorry, Sasha," she said, exasperated. He'd already chided her twice. "I don't know about life at Orlova, but things are pretty crazy here. Even when you don't think there's a major conspiracy going on."

"Call me Vox. I forgive you. But you owe me," Vox said. "In any case, you have asked for my help with a problem. I will solve this for you, but let us treat this as an academic issue. First, what is your evidence?"

"I never saw her face or checked her body."

"Next."

"Our station doctor told me he had not been permitted to inspect the body."

"Noted."

"I saw a person fleeing the vehicle facility who had a very distinct running style. I couldn't identify it at the time, but when I described it to someone else, they knew who it was immediately."

"The day you saw the figure," Vox said. "This was on the same day as the last flight back to McMurdo, yes?"

"Yes."

"And your vehicle maintaining faculty has an external door, does it not?"

"Vehicle maintenance facility. Yes, it has two entrances. One is human-sized, one is big enough for the snowcats to pass through."

"You said several of your station's administrators were also there," Vox continued. "This was your base manager, the security person, and your psychologist?"

"Yes."

"If you lived in Moscow, I would say they were there to interrogate you," he joked. "But you say they were gone by the time you came back to the garage?"

"Nowhere to be found. I've tried to ask them since that time what they were doing there, but they avoid answering me."

"No news is good news, I think you say. But, I agree, it is weird. Is there anything else? You told me that your psychiatric officer had asked to see you, no?"

"That's right. He wanted to do a psych evaluation."

"Why would he do that?"

"To see if I'd gone crazy."

"Did you pass?"

"*Pashol na khui.*"

Vox burst out laughing. "So someone knows how to use the Internet! Very good. Remind me what this psychologist said about you."

Cass rolled onto her back; her arm was falling asleep. "I thought that he'd brought me in to make sure I wasn't traumatized by the accident, but his questions were strange."

"How so?"

"He seemed to want to steer the conversation toward things I didn't even understand." Cass groped for words. Even months later, Keene's interview made no sense. "He seemed to think I had something to do with Sheryl's death. He asked about my 'role,' then seemed disappointed, maybe even worried, when I didn't have the answer he was expecting."

"I am going to assume that a psychologist acting unstable is an unusual situation in America," Vox said. "In Russia, they are the very first to go around the corner."

"Bend. Go around the bend."

"Whatever. Do you have anything else for me to consider, Miss Jennings?"

"Only that the base manager and head of security seemed to take Sheryl's death pretty lightly. They made a few announcements and asked a few questions, but it's been a closed subject since it happened."

"But you have a theory?"

"Yes."

"Tell me what it is. I will test it using the undisputed rigors of the scientific method."

"I don't think Sheryl died," Cass said. "I think her death was faked."

Silence greeted her statement. It stretched on for so long that Cass asked, "Vox? You still there?"

"Blaze, I must apologize. This whole time, I didn't think you were paranoid enough to survive in Russia. I was wrong."

"Don't joke, Vox. I'm serious."

She imagined him taking stock on the other end. "All right. Tell me your thesis."

"I think the body they sent out there was just a frozen . . . mannequin or something. Wrap a side of beef or a crash test dummy in enough layers of Gore-Tex and let it freeze for a few hours, and it would seem like a dead body. Especially if they didn't get a chance to see the face or check for an injury."

"Where is this woman now?"

Cass swallowed. "I think they were trying to sneak her on board the last flight when I found them in my garage. Sikes and his people had no idea what she looked like; she would've been just another face to them. But that's why Hanratty and the others were so shocked when I showed up and why she ran—she was probably minutes away from getting on board that plane. They must've found another way to sneak her on board later."

There was no sound on the other end. Cass continued.

"Then, Keene interviews me, but shows no sympathy or compassion. Instead, it's as if he thought I knew something, was part of something. Like I was part of a conspiracy or a plan. Say, like faking a crew member's death."

"But if he knows what is going on, why would he ask those questions?"

"Vox, hold on." Cass, lying on her back with an earpiece in one ear and three layers of clothing around her head, could barely hear the wind rushing outside. But she felt, rather than heard, something—a thud, a bang, something—come through the floor, nearly stopping her heart. Moving slowly, she rolled onto her belly, pushed herself to her hands and knees awkwardly, and crawled to the hatch that led down to the ice tunnels.

There it was again. Softer now, barely felt through the floor, but noticeable. Pulse pounding, she got a flashlight ready in her right hand, then yanked the hatch open with her left. Cold air wafted upward, hitting her in the face. The beam shone down the tube, illuminating the white ice riming the metal walls and rungs.

Nothing.

Ignoring the shock of cold, Cass ripped away her parka and hood so she could listen to the empty space, hoping the tube would act like an amplifier.

Was there a scratching, scuffing sound? Or was it the fabric of her parka? Her mouth was dry and her pulse pounded in her temples as she strained to hear.

Nothing.

After a moment, she heard Vox's tinny voice calling over the earpiece. Reluctantly, she lowered the hatch over the tube and crawled back to her shortwave, but kept her flashlight on. She screwed the earpiece back in.

"I'm here."

"Good. I thought they'd kidnapped you and were performing mind-control experiments."

"The first one, no," she said. "The second one, we're still trying to decide. Anyway, what were you asking?"

"Why would your psychologist ask you those questions if he already knew what was going on?"

Cass pulled the drawstring of her hood tighter. It was *cold*. "I don't know. Maybe he wasn't in on the entire plan to begin with and was hoping to learn more? Like I said, when I didn't give him the answers he wanted, he seemed worried. Or scared."

"Which leads us back to the big question. Why would your superiors fake a crew member's death?"

"Right."

"In my country, when such deceit is used, it is to observe how you *would have* acted had such an event happened."

"A test," Cass said, slowly, thinking aloud.

"Yes. Now, what would they be trying to test? Your loyalty?"

"No. You're still thinking like the KGB is after you. There's no cult of personality at a research base. Not one that matters, at least."

"What, then?"

"Maybe they wanted to rattle everyone, see how they reacted to a terrible event. Like one of their own dying right before the doors close for the winter."

"Surviving a winter here isn't enough?"

"Hundreds, maybe thousands of people have wintered over and survived more or less intact," she said. "A series of short, sharp shocks might send different people around the . . . corner in different ways. Ways you could study or report on."

"How did the woman Sheryl's death—or fake death—affect you?"

How did it affect me? Good question. Should I say picking her legs up reminded me of watching the first responders carrying bodies out of a tunnel? Or that I couldn't see past the ruse of Taylor not allowing me to lift her ski mask because I knew it would bring back all the faces of the people who'd been suffocated after the mooring collapsed?

A particular, caustic burn caught at her throat, a clutching of the muscles there. The imagined feel of Sheryl's wooden body—to hell if it hadn't been real, the emotions it dredged up *were*—mixed with the memories of a subway tunnel, an engineering failure, a knot of people trapped in the urban equivalent of a miners' cave-in.

"Blaze? Are you there? Cass?"

She cleared her throat. "I'm here."

"How did Sheryl's death affect you?"

"Why do you want to know?" It came out as a harsh accusation. She hoped the radio's white noise took some of the edge off. But she had the wild, unreasoning thought that maybe Vox was involved somehow and was baiting her, asking her to confide in him.

Vox continued, oblivious. "Because *their* reaction to *your* reaction might tell us something. Nobody does nothing in a case like this. Is not possible."

"What do you mean?"

"Most base administrators, even Russian ones, would offer you some kind of support after the death of a colleague, yes? The compassionate ones would offer sympathy, while even the most heartless would want to know when you could get back to work. But saying nothing, doing nothing? Then you are being studied."

The simple sentence made her mouth go dry. "So what should I do? What's coming next?"

"You're an engineer," he said, the distance and static making his voice robotic and impersonal. "Suppose you have a mysterious substance whose tensile strength is unknown. How do you find out how strong it is?"

"A stress test," Cass said automatically.

"And what happens if the test doesn't break the subject?"

A hollow feeling opened up in her chest, like a rock falling down an unplumbed well. "You keep trying until it does."

CHAPTER TWENTY-THREE

Alone, Leroy sat at one of the galley tables facing the outer wall and talked to the wind.

People passed him, trays or cups in hand, sitting or conversing within arm's reach. No one spoke to him. Had they, he would not have heard them.

But no one did. Behavior thought of as strange back in February was taken for granted in May. Most of Shackleton's crew had started to fade in and out, victims of the lack of light and mental stimulation. T3. The Antarctic stare. Long-eye. Whatever you called it, people recognized it and appreciated the right of others to indulge.

Hours slipped by. Someone asked Leroy to move slightly so he could wipe the table down. He lifted his arms, then put them back down on the tabletop without blinking or recognizing who had made the request. Gale-force winds on the other side of the wall surged and faded, ripping across the face of the station. They'd long since passed into winter's full darkness and almost nothing could be seen out of any of the galley's windows; only rarely did a gust throw snow so violently against the glass that it could be seen.

Leroy's lips moved as he answered the wind. He did so without a sound except for an occasional whimper. From time to time, a shudder would ripple through him from the skin on the back of his head down to the muscles in the small of his back, but he was otherwise motionless.

Throughout his vigil, the wind was constant, thrashing against the walls of the station then subsiding to a low hiss. Only once did it build into such a towering wave that it seemed to actually shake the building. The few people left in the galley glanced up, then went back to their conversations, relegating the wind to nothing more than background noise.

But Leroy, rigid in his seat, listened to the keening wind with wide eyes. When it finally tapered off, he let out a long, low groan, then rose unsteadily to his feet. He stumbled over to the buffet and grabbed handfuls of crackers and dry goods before tottering out of the galley. He proceeded directly to his berth, where he threw the food in a sack, gathered a few essential things, then headed to the Beer Can and followed the stairs down, deep into the dark.

PART IV

June

CHAPTER TWENTY-FOUR

Ron Ayres frowned at his laptop. According to his records, Leroy Buskins hadn't refilled his bimonthly prescriptions in more than three weeks.

What was he on, again? Ron clicked through several screens, having trouble even remembering much about the man. Leroy was one of those quiet, self-effacing types who, despite his size, had seemed to be perpetually in a corner, even if he was sitting in the middle of a room.

Oh, hell. That's right. Amoxapine and iloperidone. How'd he forgotten *that*? His frown deepened and he flicked through several more screens. The automatic e-mail alert he should've received when Leroy was three days delinquent had been turned off.

Without taking his eyes from his laptop, he called to the front room. "Beth?"

Beth Muñez, the station's nurse, poked her head around the corner, eyebrows raised.

Ron tapped his screen with a fingernail. "You haven't been making any changes in the pharma software, have you?"

"No, of course not. Why?"

"Leroy Buskins is way overdue for a pickup, but his alert's been toggled off."

She came fully into the room to look over his shoulder. "Wasn't me. Now that I think of it, though, it has been a while since he's come in. What's he taking again?"

Ron pointed at the screen. "Something he shouldn't be missing."

She grunted. "Not good."

"Definitely suboptimal." He pushed his chair back. "Hold down the fort for me, will you? I'm going to check up on him."

Ron left the tiny medical complex, rubbing his face to try to smooth out the grimace that was gathering there; no one liked to see a worried doctor walking the halls. But he *was* worried. When one of your charges was missing his dose of psychotropic drugs to stay on balance, you ought to be.

When he'd first seen Leroy's prescription, in the early days of the winter-over, he'd approached Keene to make sure the psychologist was aware of just what kind of challenge they might have on their hands. Keene had assured him he had the situation under control and gone back to reading his copy of *Applied Psychology*, leaving Ron frustrated but powerless. TransAnt had cleared the man to work, he was taking his medication, and Shackleton's shrink said everything was okay. It had bothered him at the time, but after that early push, work and life on base had swept the issue away. Until now.

A knock at Leroy's berth went unanswered and no one he asked seemed to have seen the electrician, not his neighbors in the dorm or Pete scrubbing down the breakfast grill or a weary Dave Boychuck climbing the Beer Can steps. Growing progressively more concerned, Ron struck gold when he spotted Biddi coming out of the e-systems lab carrying a bucket and a mop.

"Biddi!"

Biddi smiled. "Dr. Ayres?"

"Have you seen Leroy Buskins around?"

"No need to use his last name, Doctor, he's the only Leroy on base," she teased. "As a matter of fact, I haven't. Not for some time, in fact. Why? Is there something wrong?"

Ron ran a hand across his forehead. "I need to find him and I've looked everywhere."

"Is it possible you've simply missed him? Shackleton isn't that big, but there are a bunch of nooks and crannies to this place."

He mentally ticked off the places he'd looked and crew he'd asked so far. Discounting the locations Leroy simply wouldn't bother to go, like the skiway or COBRA, then he'd damned near covered the entire station. It was always possible that they'd both been moving and missing each other, of course—he was on the second floor when Leroy was walking the first; he'd checked the galley when Leroy was in the library—but he'd been thorough and asked nearly a dozen people if they'd seen the man . . . and almost to a person, they hadn't seen him in recent memory. Out of a crew of forty, that was the equivalent of sending out an APB. Unless he'd missed the obvious.

"Biddi," he began slowly, "you've got keys to the berths, don't you?"

"I do. Though Leroy specifically asked me not to clean his room. I shudder to think what state it's in." She cocked an eyebrow. "He's not in any trouble, is he?"

"No, not like that. He's simply due for a checkup and it's strange he hasn't shown up for it. And no one's seen him around. You don't think . . ." His voice trailed off as he thought about what he was considering.

"Yes?"

Ron blushed. "Do you think you could perhaps give me a peek into his room? If he's sleeping soundly, I'd hate to pound on his door. But if he is in there, it would put my mind at ease. What do you say?"

She made a motion like she was clutching an imaginary necklace of pearls. "Why, Dr. Ayres, are you asking me to break into a fellow crew member's private sleeping quarters?"

He gave her a weak grin. "Something like that, yes. It's for his own good."

"Then we'd better hurry before anyone catches us."

Biddi pushed the mop and bucket into a niche and they hustled to the E1 berth. When they got to Leroy's room, Ron rapped lightly on the door as a final courtesy to roust the man if he were in there, then motioned for Biddi to unlock the door. Flipping through her keys, she located the master and had the door open in a few seconds. She stepped back and presented the door with a flourish.

He paused for a moment, staring at the knob. For the people who worked in Antarctica, privacy was cherished above almost everything else. Living cheek-by-jowl with the same people for nine months meant that absolutely nothing replaced a sense of ownership over the space that was your berth. Breaking into someone's room was a violation on a level that was hard to match short of physically attacking someone.

Weighted against that was everything he believed in as a physician, both in what he considered his medical obligations, but also the social ones. He was responsible for the crew's well-being, dammit, whether that was a broken leg or a serious mental issue. There'd only been one time he hadn't listened to his inner voice and followed up on a patient. The blank, sad stares of the other VA doctors. The glancing, sliding gaze of the nurses. No one had wanted to tell him. *Where is Gary? Where is my son? He should be getting treatment, he should be getting help, goddammit. He doesn't need an IV drip full of poison, he needs his father. Yes, I took him off of that shit. You'd turn him into a vegetable instead of talking to a man. Where is Gary?*

Jaw muscles worked at the memory. You could only be told so many times that something wasn't your fault before you became convinced that it was.

He grasped the knob.

The lights were off inside. He slipped out a small pen flashlight he normally used to look at tonsils and panned it across the bed. No Leroy. He moved the beam over the rest of the room. Jeans, overalls, and dirty shirts hung from every peg and littered the floor. Candy wrappers had been crumpled and tossed into a corner as if the corner itself were the wastebasket, and the tiny quarters smelled faintly of bleach and foot odor and the general stale, stagnant odor of a human confined to a small space.

Ron hesitated, then turned to Biddi and said in a conspiratorial tone, "Would you be able to act like you're cleaning the hall, Biddi? And, perhaps, rap on the door if you see Leroy coming?"

The woman waggled her eyebrows and snatched a dust rag from a back pocket. "Of course, Doctor."

"Good girl." He shut the door gently, turned the lights on, and proceeded to search the room quickly but thoroughly. As a physician, he had no training in how to toss a room, but as a former marine, he knew every nook and cranny people used to hide things in a bunk. Five minutes later, however, having lifted the mattress, run his hand along ledges and under frames, and peeked behind drawers, he had to admit defeat. If there was anything to be found, he wasn't going to be the one to discover it. The man could use a lesson in personal hygiene, but there was nothing out of the ordinary. Except that its occupant was nowhere to be found.

He took a look around the room, decided it wasn't any messier or neater than how he'd found it, then cracked the door to the hallway. "All clear?"

"As a pane of glass." Biddi was dusting the door frame and walls. He slipped out of the room and watched as his accomplice locked it.

She looked at him. "Should we sound the alarm?"

"No, not yet. Though, if you see him, would you call me?" Biddi nodded. He paused. "And let's keep this to ourselves, please?"

She mimed locking her mouth and tossing the key. "Not a word, Doctor."

He smiled. "Thank you, Biddi."

She winked and went back to dusting the frame. Ron strode down the hall, a small knot of worry growing in his stomach.

CHAPTER TWENTY-FIVE

Carla had been running a difficult set of tests on crystalline structures, a task that required her to be glued either to the small electron microscope in the biology lab or to the two computer screens that were capturing and recording the results in real time. Even as a grad student, her reputation for total concentration on a test had been legendary, to the extent that she'd often gone sixteen, twenty, and once twenty-four hours without leaving her chair.

But today, the first phase of the test wrapped up early and she sighed in relief as she backed away from the microscope, stretched with both hands on her lower back, and rolled her neck in circles. Grinning, she grabbed a cup of cold coffee and put her feet up on her desk with relish, something that would've surprised her colleagues, who assumed she thrived on the unblinking concentration her tests usually required.

In fact, Carla would've liked nothing better than to fire off a few lines on a command prompt and go to lunch, like the stargazers over at COBRA. But, in biology, if you missed a few significant tics, the results were inconclusive or mixed or open to interpretation. So, if you were going to bother running an experiment at all, why wouldn't you put everything you had into the process? If you couldn't take ten hours of frowning into the eyepiece of a microscope, maybe you should try a different field of science. Like geology, where the time scale ran into the millions of years and the tons of rock. Make a mistake? Wait awhile or bust open another geode.

She smiled a little, thinking of how peeved her favorite geologist would've been if he were there to read her thoughts. Cute, serious Colin. Brilliant in his field, but as obtuse as the samples he tapped apart with his rock pick, capable of flaking apart millimeter-thick layers of shale but clueless at doing the same for the simplest social cues. She wondered if he were as baffled in bed. *Talk dirty to me, Colin.* Pause. *What do you want me to say, Carla?* Scenarios along those lines coaxed her into a daydream for long minutes and, had anyone come into the office, they would've found her staring raptly into the depths of a skuzzy tank of Antarctic pearlwort like she was in love.

Thinking about sex always made her hungry and, after a quick check of her watch, she jumped off her lab stool. It wasn't every day that she could still make regular lunch hours in the galley instead of begging for scraps across the counter in the odd hours after her experiments wrapped up. She made sure everything was powered down or in a holding pattern as needed, then strode out the door and down the hall to the galley.

Halfway down the corridor, she frowned and wrapped her arms around her body. Living and working at the South Pole, *it's cold* seemed a perverse statement. But the main part of Shackleton station was normally kept at a steady seventy degrees year-round. It was a rare day that she felt a chill, and even then it was from wandering too close to one of the outer doors when someone was coming in from the outside.

She shrugged to herself. Sometimes she caught a chill when all of her attention was focused on something in the lab, so much so that she wondered if her body, trying to help, shunted all of the blood and energy to her brain when she was working on a particularly thorny problem. She just needed to grab a bite and move her sedentary scientist's butt.

When she reached the galley, however, she was still cold. She waved to Anne, who was already sitting with Tim and Colin. Anne wore fleece that was zipped all the way, with the collar covering the lower half of her face. Tim was rubbing his hands together, while steam rose from Colin's cup of coffee like it had just been poured from the pot. At other tables, crew were hunched or hugging themselves.

"What the hell is going on?" she asked by way of greeting as she sat down.

"What do you mean?" Anne's voice was muffled. "It's like this all the time."

"Deb did a drive-by earlier," Tim said. "She and Hanratty and Taylor are going around, trying to reassure people."

"About what?"

"The heating system went down about an hour ago. Some kind of problem with the furnaces." He delivered the news contritely, as if apologizing on the administration's behalf.

"Is it the power plant? Are the fuel tanks okay?" Carla had only a rudimentary idea of how Shackleton was powered, but she did know that the base's furnaces were electrical and therefore relied on the energy produced by the diesel generators in Shackleton's power plant buried deep under the ice.

But the generators ran off just one source of energy: the jet fuel that had been convoyed to the base over the SPoT road or flown in on the Hercs. If there had been a simple mechanical failure in the generators, that was bad enough—heat and electricity would be compromised and, okay, that wasn't good—but it had always haunted her that they were sitting on top of several ten-thousand-gallon tanks of highly combustible petroleum product. If the fuel tanks or lines had a problem, an explosion would have the potential kinetic energy of a bomb. She didn't want to freeze to death, but neither did she want to get blown into the sky.

"I think so," Tim said. "Or we would've been evacuated. Which would be a little inconvenient right now, considering it's a bit chilly outside."

Carla shivered. "What happened to the backup systems? If it's just an electrical problem and not something wrong with the power plant, they should at least be able to get the fallback furnaces going."

"They're having trouble with those, too."

"Jesus." Carla glanced around the table. "Isn't that, you know, cause for concern?"

Colin shrugged. "I'm sure they have it under control."

She shot the geologist an irritated glance at the empty statement. Her daydream about him, still fresh in her mind, frayed around the edges. "How long ago did Deb come by?"

The three looked at each other. "Fifteen, twenty minutes ago?" Tim ventured.

Carla, appetite blunted, glanced around the galley. No one was on the verge of panic, but neither did anyone seem motivated to get answers. She bit her lower lip and considered her tablemates. An astrophysicist, a materials science engineer, and a geologist. Brilliant people, all, but perhaps not as in tune with biological functions and what subzero temperatures might do to those functions as, say, herself.

"Anne, what's the temperature in here, do you think?"

Her friend tilted her head. "In Fahrenheit? Sixty degrees, maybe high fifties?"

Carla grimaced. Sixty and dropping. Hypothermia had occurred at temperatures as high as fifty degrees, although that normally took place in extreme conditions where the victims didn't have access to such things as fleece sweaters and hot coffee. But her breath steamed when she exhaled.

She glanced out one of the many galley windows. Gusts whipped the snow savagely, making it appear as though the wind itself were white. Sweaters and hot drinks were nice, but with an outside ambient temperature of eighty below and the wind constantly peeling away radiant heat, real trouble could be just an hour away if they didn't get those heating elements back online. How did that constitute the situation being "under control"? Someone needed to light a fire—figuratively and maybe literally—under the administration's rear end.

Electing to do it herself, Carla had just started to stand when the intercom crackled. She eased back into her seat.

"*Hello, everyone. Deb Connors here. As you are no doubt already aware, we've been having some issues with the station's main and backup heating systems. We're currently working on the problem with the engineering team. Please stay calm. If you find the low temperature distressing, all non-GA and DA staff should feel free to take temporary leave to go back to your berths or the galley.*"

Carla looked around the room, watching faces. Stating the problem had made it worse rather than better and what had previously been a shadow of apprehension was now transformed into definite concern for some, fear for others.

"*Jack Hanratty or I will update you every half hour until we resolve the problem. In the meantime, please carry on with your regular duties. We hope to have the problem diagnosed soon and—*"

Like a candle being snuffed, Deb's voice stopped at the same time the lights went out, plunging them into darkness. Someone in the galley gasped, followed by a dozen low, moaned exclamations. Carla reached across the table and found Anne's hand, cold and bony, likewise fumbling for hers. Dim footlights—battery-powered emergency illumination meant to come online only when the main circuit was broken—flickered to life, giving off a weak, muddy light that barely lit an area a foot off the floor.

"Easy, everyone. Take it easy," a voice boomed nearby, making her jump. A cone of light appeared out of the dark, highlighting the face of Pete Ozment, the cook. He held a fat-headed, industrial-sized flashlight.

"It's just the lights. We'll be okay. Everybody just stay seated. I'm sure they'll get the generators going in a minute."

Just like they got the heat turned back on? Carla thought, but she wanted Pete to be right. Still holding tight to Anne's hand, she snaked her other out toward Colin's.

"Colin," she hissed. "Give me your hand."

"Why?"

"Give me your hand, you stupid man."

She could almost see his shrug in the dark and then she felt his rough, dry fingers wrap around hers. He had calluses on the palm of his hand.

Pete panned his flashlight around the room, then trained the beam on the galley door. "Everyone stay put. I'm going to see if I can round up any stragglers and lead them back here."

"So we can all freak out in one spot instead of separately?" Anne asked *sotto voce*. They watched the comforting glow from his light bounce and fade as he turned down the corridor.

Each small group began murmuring amongst themselves in the dark; the collective conversations became, in some ways, a comforting chatter. No one made it to Antarctica, and certainly not to Shackleton, without being resourceful, smart, and well balanced. Most of the people Carla had met, from the kitchen workers to the head of the neutrino program, had diverse skills and broad experiences. This wasn't a group to panic or to wait on a problem that could be fixed with ingenuity.

But as each minute built on the last, the room seemed to get colder and darker. Ozment didn't return and there were occasional flickers of fluorescent green dials as people checked their watches. The chatter died as there was less and less to talk about that didn't directly address being stranded in the dark.

"Twenty minutes since the juice went out," someone called.

Thanks for nothing, Carla thought. But it was better to know than to guess. She leaned forward. "Anne? Guys? How long are we going to sit here and freeze?"

"As long as it takes to get the electricity on." Colin, obdurate and blunt as a river rock.

"I don't remember anyone making Pete Ozment station manager," Anne said. "It's nice he tried to keep everyone calm, but he's not doing anyone any favors by being gone for so long."

"That's what I'm thinking," Carla said. "If the station is in real trouble, I'd rather get ahead of it than be a team player and freeze to death. We've all got cold weather gear in our rooms. I'd feel better about sitting tight in the pitch black if I'm ready for what's coming."

"Don't you think it would be better to stick together?" Tim asked.

"For Christ's sake, the station is two long halls connected by stairwells," Anne snapped. "My house has a more complicated floor plan. We could make it to our berths, get suited up, grab some flashlights, and be back here before Pete is."

"Go then," Tim said, his voice wounded.

"Colin?" Carla asked.

"I'll stay."

"Suit yourself."

The sound of rustling preceded Anne's hand pulling Carla to her feet. They continued to hold hands as they navigated their way around the tables. Carla stubbed her toe on a table leg and cursed.

"Is somebody leaving?" A woman's voice from the other side of the galley.

"This is Carla Bjorkholm. Anne Klimt and I are going to our berths to get our cold weather gear now," Carla called out. "I'm sure Deb is working hard to get the heat and electricity back on, but I don't see any reason not to hope for the best and prepare for the worst. If no one panics and we keep things orderly, we can all feel our way to our rooms and be ready for anything."

The suggestion prompted a swell of talk as the idea was debated at twenty tables. Anne tugged Carla close and said into her ear, "Come on. Let's keep moving or there'll be a big crush to get out."

So much for keeping things orderly. But Anne was probably right. She could already hear the scrape of chairs being pushed away from tables. They scampered for the door, their free hands reaching out to find a wall or the counter near the entrance that would guide them to the door and then to the hall.

She hissed as she bruised her hand against something cold and metallic on the wall—the fire extinguisher case. Just as she brought her scraped knuckles to her mouth, however, a thick body blundered into her, cross-checking her to the ground. He grunted at the impact, but she hit the ground hard, barely managing to break her fall with her injured hand. Anne's hand was yanked away.

"Carla?" she heard her friend call, but then the bumbling man who'd run into her also kicked her in the shin. Crying out with pain, she reached down to grab her throbbing leg.

No doubt the accident had been just that, accidental, but the sudden, unexpected pain—perhaps because it was heaped onto her worry about the loss of heat—enraged her, causing her to lash out angrily with her other foot. The man bellowed and fell beside her with a crash that shook the floor. Shouts filled the air. Someone brought out a small flashlight, but the tiny beam only added to the chaos as more people, confused and acting as a single organism, began piling toward the exit.

Ignoring the pain in her hand, Carla pushed against the floor, trying to gain her feet. But the position left her head down and vulnerable. A rising knee caught her in the side of the face and her world exploded with a parade of brilliant colors before turning as dark as the South Pole winter.

CHAPTER TWENTY-SIX

"Dismal. Disastrous. A complete failure." Keene turned away from the panoramic view. "Does that summarize it succinctly?"

"I think we get the picture." Hanratty had his hands folded across his stomach, rocking his office chair from side to side in small swings. "Have a seat and we'll take this one step at a time."

"I'll stand, thanks."

Hanratty masked his irritation and turned to the rest of the room. Gathered with him in his inner chamber were Deb, Taylor, Keene, and Ayres. It was the day after the heat and electricity failures that had paralyzed Shackleton's crew and Hanratty had summoned his top team members to do a postmortem. Normally, the station's doctor wouldn't have been part of that group, but Ayres had pushed his way in when he saw the others gathering.

Of everyone in the room, Hanratty was the only one who seemed comfortable sitting. Taylor stood broom-straight in the corner, his wiry forearms crossed and a blank expression on his face. Keene slouched by the window with his hands in his pockets, remaining irritatingly in Hanratty's peripheral vision. *Which is no accident*, Hanratty thought. Deb leaned against a bookcase, looking unsure whether she should adopt her boss's easy confidence, Taylor's readiness, or Keene's world-weary posture. Her eyes flicked over the others, assessing. Ayres had his hands on the back of one of the chairs for support, watching Hanratty.

"So the psychological makeup of the crew is hovering somewhere between severely damaged and irretrievably spooked. We'll work on solutions to that in a second." Hanratty swung his chair. "Ron, would you give us a rundown on the medical situation?"

Ayres's expression was sour. "It could've been worse, which isn't saying much. One sprained wrist, a black eye, and about three dozen contusions, goose eggs, and cuts. One anxiety-induced asthma attack and several people reporting GI problems probably brought on by stress and latent T3. Carla Bjorkholm was our worst injury."

"What happened to her?"

"She sustained a concussion that put her out for about fifteen minutes, based on what Anne and Colin said when they found her. She was just coming to when the lights *finally* came back on."

"We did the best we could, Ron."

"What good are backup systems if they don't work, Jack?"

"We're looking into it. The reason for the failures isn't clear yet," Hanratty said. He scratched something on a sheet of paper.

"Well, I'd love to know how you're going to find out without our electrician."

Hanratty frowned. "What's that supposed to mean?"

"No one's seen Leroy Buskins for nearly a month." Ayres looked over at Deb. "I sent a report that he hadn't picked up his medication."

"Deb?" Hanratty asked.

She held her hands up. "I forwarded Ron's e-mail to Taylor."

All eyes turned to the security chief, who shook his head. "Too much on my plate."

"Just what *is* on your plate, Taylor?" Ayres asked. "I've never quite understood what a security professional is supposed to do at a South Pole research facility. Especially one with such a distinguished career."

"Fuck is that supposed to mean, Ayres?"

"Nothing. It's just I knew a lot of folks in Baghdad, Kabul. Your name never came up."

"Those are big places," Taylor said, his eyes glittering. "No one knows everyone."

"They're not that big," Ayres said, grinning back at him. "And somebody with your . . . reputation would've been known, believe me."

"Enough," Hanratty said. "Ron, if you can't help contribute to a solution, leave. And Taylor, if you're that easily baited, maybe you should, too."

The room was silent as the two men stared at each other. Neither seemed prepared to give an inch until Hanratty stood, walked in front of Taylor, and said quietly, "Stand down."

Taylor gave Hanratty a venomous look that abruptly turned into a smile. "Sure thing, boss."

Hanratty watched him for a moment more, then turned to Ayres. "We were talking about the situation at hand. Do you have anything to add?"

"No, not add, but I'll repeat my original question," Ayres said. "How were you trying to get the power back online without the base electrician?"

Hanratty paused. "We thought it was a problem with the fuel supply at first, so we were working with Boychuck and his boys. By the time we thought of it as an electrical problem, it was too dark to go try finding Leroy. And from what you're saying, it looks like we wouldn't have had any luck anyway. Anyone have any ideas where he went?"

"I asked around when Ron first mentioned it," Deb said, "and Dave told me he's down in the tunnels all the time."

"I would hope so. That's where half the electrical is."

"Not near the arches. In the old, old tunnels. Like past the shrines. He was going down there and nosing around after his shift, apparently."

Taylor frowned. "I don't like that."

"No rule against it," Deb pointed out. "People like to explore down there just for something to do. If you seal it up, you're going to have some pissed-off crew."

"Christ. Like we need one more thing," Hanratty said, displaying dissatisfaction for the first time. "He's got to be on the job and we have to be able to find him. If we have another outage, we're screwed. I don't even know if we have another licensed electrician on base."

"I'd be more worried he hasn't taken his medicine. He's on some strong psychotropic drugs," Ayres said. "Maybe our psychologist could speak to that?"

Keene shrugged. "I've had a session or two with Leroy. The man had a rough childhood and mentioned a physically abusive older sister. If Taylor can find him and we can get him back on track with his medication, he'll be fine. I'd say we have bigger fish to fry, however."

Hanratty scrubbed his face with his hands. "Agreed. Let's get back to Leroy in a minute. I assume Carla will be laid up for a while?"

Ayres nodded. "The best thing for a concussion is bed rest, which she can do in her berth. I'll call on her as much as I can, but it wouldn't hurt if we made sure someone checked up on her once or twice a day."

"What about her work?" Deb asked, then flushed as she saw frowns around the room. "I'm not criticizing her. Carla's famous for working until she drops. She's going to want to get back to the lab as soon as she can stand."

"She can try, but she'll have headaches, nausea, and dizziness if she pushes herself beyond a light walk." Ayres shrugged. "I'd recommend she do very little except sleep for the next few weeks. But if she doesn't listen to me, her own body will take her out of the equation."

Hanratty wrote a few more lines on his paper, then raised his head. "Ron, thanks for your help. We all appreciate how quickly you got on this."

The doctor ignored the pat on the back. "Bumps and bruises. Nothing compared to the mental damage the event seemed to cause. I have to say I was totally thrown by the reaction in the galley. I mean, the lights went off and it got cold. I thought our people were made of sterner stuff than that."

Ayres's remark was aimed at the back of Keene's head, but the psychologist continued to keep his eyes on his footwear. An awkward silence filled the room.

Hanratty cleared his throat. "Thanks again, Ron. We'll get you somebody to check on Carla. Give me a shout if you need anything else, okay?"

Ayres had spent enough time in the Marines to know when he was being dismissed, but that didn't mean he liked it. He walked out of the room stiff-backed and shut the door behind him with a bang.

The room was silent for a moment, then Hanratty spun in his chair to face Keene. "Gerald, give us a read on the situation."

Keene shifted his weight. "Twenty-six people were involved with the episode in the galley. The rest of the crew was aware of the failures, of course. Two of the staff have a history of severe claustrophobia. Both required the help of others to recover, even after power was restored. Only a handful of people—most of whom are in this room—would have felt any measure of control as the situation deteriorated."

"What does that mean, in a nutshell?" Deb asked.

"A nutshell." Keene snorted. "In a *nutshell*, Deb, everyone on base is freaked out. If we have another significant power failure, people are going to be stealing snowcats out of the VMF so they can take the road back to McMurdo."

"Is there anything we can do to help restore confidence, get morale back up?" Hanratty asked. As Keene's face twisted in anticipation of delivering a sarcastic comeback, he added, "*Constructive* suggestions."

The psychologist got his face and his retort under control. "The most obvious step is that the station manager should make a general announcement about what happened and why, to calm nerves by reasserting control of the situation."

"All right."

"While you do that, I could work behind the scenes. The Beck Anxiety Inventory is a quick way to take a group's temperature. And I can pull in a few of the real problem cases, like those claustrophobes, and work with them more intensively—"

"Negative," Hanratty said. It was his turn to look down at his shoes.

"What?" Keene looked surprised. "Why?"

"You're the authority, of course. But—no offense, Gerald—it seems to me that, if the base psychologist distributes an *anxiety* questionnaire, we'll end up with exactly the effect we don't want. It would be like asking someone who's afraid of drowning if they packed a life preserver before getting on a boat. Prudent, but not necessarily the best move."

"What do you suggest?" Taylor asked.

"I'll prepare an announcement about the failure, as per Gerald's suggestion, tell everyone we're checking those systems and we'll get to the bottom of it, et cetera, et cetera. In fact, Deb, let's make a big show of it. Get Jennings to check pipes and lines. Taylor, find Leroy—I don't care if he's part of the ice wall down below, let's get him working and visible so people see him fixing the electrical. Gerald, spread yourself around, ask your questions, but don't press too hard. Take temperatures, as you called it, but don't be obvious."

"You're asking the base psychologist to casually join conversations without raising anyone's suspicions?"

"Yes. Just sit and listen if nothing else." Hanratty turned his attention to Taylor. "Same for you, Taylor. Keep your ear to the ground, report back to me."

"Do you want me to short-circuit any doomsday talk or anyone bad-mouthing admin?"

"No. I think it would have the same effect as the base shrink telling people not to worry. But if they want to talk themselves into a tizzy, let 'em talk. I'd rather know who's vulnerable than have them hide their thoughts."

Taylor looked doubtful, but nodded. Hanratty looked around the room. "Okay, any questions?"

Deb started to speak, then hesitated. Hanratty raised an eyebrow and she plunged into her question. "Jack, we still don't know why the electrical went down or why it came back online."

"Correct," he said, nodding.

"So . . . what are we actually *doing*? Reassuring personnel is nice, but we may have a hell of a problem here, with no idea how to fix it or if it'll happen again."

"Deb, I know that this episode has shaken all of us, but I trust that the system is stable. We'll diagnose the problem soon enough. I think the important thing is to keep a strong outward face on things. We don't want the crew to get spooked any more than they are."

"It won't matter how spooked they are if the heat goes out again," she pressed.

"It'll be fine, Deb," Hanratty said, his tone final. "Trust me."

She stared at him for a moment, as if debating whether to argue, then let it go.

"No more questions? Okay, let's get to work, then."

Deb and Taylor shuffled out of the room. Keene appeared to join them, then held back. He made sure the other two had left the outer office, then looked at Hanratty. "Is this the best way to go about things?"

"There's only one way to know, and that's to do it. If we coddle them now, how will they act in a true crisis? 'That which doesn't kill us, makes us stronger.'"

Keene's laughter came out as a high-pitched bark. "The man who said that wound up in an insane asylum."

CHAPTER TWENTY-SEVEN

He had never been so cold.

As a young boy, he'd been through winters on the plains so hard that the cows had frozen and died standing up, but they didn't compare to the warmest day at the Pole, and it was colder than that. Even when he'd first stepped off the plane at McMurdo, in full gear, when the wind had screamed in his ear and the icy fist of Antarctica had slammed him full in the chest—unprepared and weak—he hadn't been this cold.

It hurt to make a fist and his joints ached. His cheeks and the flesh of his chin felt sandpapery and strange. A few days ago, he'd wiped his running nose and realized he hadn't felt the touch of his own hand on his face. But worst of all was the simple, hurtful cold. He couldn't escape it and he couldn't remedy it. Short stints with a fabric tent held over the propane stove chased it away, but then the waves of shivering came on twice as bad and his muscles would rattle and flinch until his body acclimated once more.

A voice in his mind—weak and distant—reminded him that he could be warm again. All he had to do was leave the nest he'd made for himself, trek back through the tunnels, and climb the steps to the station above. There were blankets and beds, hot drinks and warm forced air blowing through the halls. All he would have to do was listen to the wind once more.

He cried as he thought about the voice of the wind, talking to him, shrieking at him constantly. The people around him had begun to look at him strangely and fall away, but they didn't understand the restraint he'd shown, the strength of will it had taken to fight and refuse what he was being commanded to do. When he'd felt himself begin to buckle and weaken, when the wind began to make sense once again, he'd headed for the tunnels, where the wind was a timid thing and—sometimes—blissfully, wonderfully nonexistent.

With the wind silenced, however, the cold had moved in and the only thing that seemed to take his mind off it were the blue and pink pills he'd found back in his room. At first, after washing them down, they made him feel edgy and irritable, but the sensation went away if he kept his mind cleared and tried to stay calm. Before long, he was lying on the frozen floor of his nest, bundled in full parka, boots, and gear, almost warm under six layers of ancient carpeting he'd torn up from the floor.

Dimly, he wondered what would happen when the pills ran out. But for now it was enough that he was holed up deep in the ice, away from the people, away from temptation, and—most important—away from the wind.

CHAPTER TWENTY-EIGHT

Elise Simon saw blinking lights everywhere and all the time. They forced their way into her thoughts, even when she wasn't working, showing up in conversations and idle moments. They went along for the ride into the frustrating slide into sleep that so often didn't come, and slipped into her dreams when it did. She wanted to scream sometimes, when her sleep-self—gently tipping into the soft, velvet bank of slumber—chose that moment to invent the lights of an imaginary emergency call on the inside of her lids, yanking her awake with her mouth dry and her heart pounding.

Sometimes after waking in the absolute darkness of her berth, she would lie with her eyes oyster-wide and stare at the ceiling, sure she could see the square, gem-like greens and reds from her switchboard arrayed above her bed. Fascinated at what her mind conjured out of thin air, she would watch the imaginary calls come and go, and fill in the backstories of the people on the other end. What they needed and why. Who and where they lived. She pushed hard against reality, inventing benign calls for help, like cats up trees and requests for fire engines to make a big show at the Fourth of July parade.

When her mind ran out of happy stories and her memory started replaying what she knew actually went on behind an emergency call, the horrific reality of experience, she knew it was time to get out of bed and get to work, no matter what time it was or how little she'd slept.

This was one of those times. Elise rolled over and tapped her clock. She'd slept three hours and sixteen minutes. She groaned. A new record. Glancing to her left, she checked the small field radio she was required to keep next to her bed to cover emergencies during her off-hours. All clear; it hadn't squawked, beeped, or buzzed. *Congrats, you woke up all on your own.* She kicked the blanket to the floor, slipped out of bed, and got dressed in the dark, trying not to think about the exhaustion that would set in later . . . or the mental fog that came along with it.

Unfortunately, it didn't matter how tired she was or would be. Communications was one of the few jobs at Shackleton that didn't work toward a goal: she didn't paint sheds, she didn't record computer results, she didn't fix busted pipes. Her job was to answer calls and patch through radio broadcasts for the same ten hours every day, day after day. She'd commiserated with Pete, who had a job like hers; it didn't matter how hungover or tired you were, breakfast got served in the morning, lunch at noon, and dinner at night. Every day. Period.

She nodded wordlessly at the few people she passed on her way to her work cube. The base was a twenty-four-hour operation, so there was always *someone* around, haunting the halls, but no one who was awake now was interested in chatting. A few, suffering from long-eye, stared right past her. She didn't take it personally, since they weren't really there. For all intents and purposes, they didn't see her and wouldn't unless she said something. That was fine with her, so she floated past them like a ghost on her way to the admin offices.

Her prework ritual had boiled down to the same few motions: stop to grab a cup of coffee and fill her water bottle, tie her hair back to keep it from getting caught in the receiver's earpiece, and slap the seat cushion where she'd be planted for the next four hours. Once the necessary items were out of the way, the coffee went on her right, the water bottle on the left, and her butt went in the chair. Ready, she faced front with a sigh.

The dashboard was dark.

Not a single light was on. For a split second, her memory and imagination imprinted a false set of blinking lights, but she squeezed her eyes shut and opened them. No lights.

She punched several of the call buttons to no effect, then lifted the receiver. The familiar tone was there, but when she tapped the space bar on her computer's keyboard and checked her screen for the network signal, a red "X" covered the familiar connection icon.

Frowning, she pushed her chair back and crawled under her desk. A short stint at a corporate IT help desk had taught her to never be too proud to check the obvious: Was it plugged in? It was. And so was everything else. Dusting herself off, she rebooted the computer, turned the dashboard on and off, checked all her connections. Nothing changed.

Elise sat for a moment, thinking things through, then picked up the receiver and called her own room. The line rang a half-dozen times before she disconnected. So, internal comms was up, external was down.

She cleared her throat, picked up the receiver again, then dialed another internal number. It was answered on the second ring, the voice on the other end creaky but clear and awake.

"Jack?" she said. "It's Elise. We've got a problem."

CHAPTER TWENTY-NINE

"So the test continues?"

"Tests," Cass corrected, trying to get comfortable and not really succeeding. It was a challenge to talk on a radio on one's side while simultaneously hovering over the hatch to watch for eavesdroppers, all in subzero temperatures and wearing the equivalent of a spacesuit. Comfort wasn't really in the cards. "Yesterday, the furnaces for the station shut down, so we lost heat for almost an hour. Just as people calmed down, the electricity went out."

"Both were restored?" Vox asked.

"Yes, but not before there was a panic. Some people were hurt."

"You have no backup systems? Redundant generators and so on?"

"Hanratty claims the backup was down as well. But just before the crew became hysterical, both were magically restored. Everyone started to relax and we all went back to our routines." Cass shuddered. "Then, this morning, all communications went offline. Everything. Shortwave, satcom, you name it. Complete radio silence."

"How is the crew taking it?"

"They're on the verge of a collective nervous breakdown. Hanratty called for an all-hands meeting later today to explain what's going on."

"This is, how do you say, bullshit."

"Yes," Cass said as she rolled onto her belly and peered down the hatch. Nothing. Just the dim, white slice of ground below. "It's all just the latest in one of Hanratty's idiotic tests."

"No one is questioning your manager about this?"

"They think he's incompetent, not manipulative. I've privately asked a few people if they think he's been doing these things to us intentionally, but no one wants to hear it."

"It is more comforting to think your superior is stupid than evil," Vox said. "It is a popular Russian attitude."

"It scares me, though. If no one is willing to see what's in front of their faces, then he can get away with anything he wants. It won't be long before people disappearing is considered normal."

"It seems so." He paused. "If something bad should . . . happen to you, do you want me to reach out to your colleagues at McMurdo?"

Cass considered. She knew it was a risky proposition, and she was touched he'd offered. Although he could probably make contact anonymously, of a sort—McMurdo would know it was someone from Orlova who had reached out—he couldn't be sure of the reception he'd get. He would, after all, be attempting to convince an American authority that one of its base administrators was insane and guilty of running mind-control experiments on his own crew, with no other proof than the word of a Shackleton mechanic with a spotty emotional and psychological history.

And that was just on the American side. If word eventually got back to his superiors that he'd been maintaining clandestine radio contact with an American crew member and had radioed the main American base, he'd probably be reprimanded, at best. The Cold War was long over, but the relations between America and Russia weren't exactly chummy. Vox might be punished for just trying to help.

And what if she was simply, catastrophically, wrong? Maybe everything she'd surmised and assumed had a more reasonable explanation. Talk about proof. Where was hers that Hanratty and his cronies had cut the communications on purpose? *You've had a history with making assumptions before. Or had you forgotten?* The thought was bitter.

"No. Thanks, Sasha," she said reluctantly. "I'm going to give Hanratty enough rope to hang himself on this. And, who knows, maybe this time it really *is* an accident. We'd both be risking too much to be wrong."

"Please, call me Vox," he said. "You are afraid of being mistaken. Why?"

"Vox, I . . ." she began and choked. *How do I explain?* "I've been wrong, very wrong, about some things in my past. Important things."

"Who hasn't?" he said lightly.

"It's not something I'm willing to take a chance on."

"Tell me. I will listen to you."

She was quiet a long, long time. Memories rose to the surface of her mind and she groaned out loud. *I don't want to remember.*

The voice from the tunnel came back into her head. *Face it. Remember.*

"Cass." Across the airwaves, the sound of his voice was metallic and toneless, but the concern it carried was unmistakable. "What happened?"

"I was part of an inspection team in . . . no, I won't tell you where. I don't want you to look it up. We were contracted to do inspections of a subway tunnel renovation. Mundane, boring, everyday stuff." Starting was easier than she thought it would be, which wasn't the same thing as easy. With each word, a band around her chest tightened until she felt she couldn't breathe. "But we were brought in with only weeks left on the project, not nearly enough time to do the job right. We should've rejected the work, but the department was proud of our track record of saying yes and making good on that promise, so we took it."

She was quiet for a moment. They'd known they were being rushed, that they had almost no margin for error. But that's how good they were. How good they thought they were. How good she thought she was.

"I won't bore you with the details. The outcome was clear enough. We cut corners and raced through checklists. One of the structures failed while in use. People died. Others were injured. I watched it on the news, knowing the entire time why it had happened. And who was responsible."

Vox was silent.

"I . . . the tunnel suffered from a series of cascading failures, that much any engineer could've told you. But I knew, and I suspect my team knew, that it was my work that started it all. Nobody on the team was blameless, but I was the first link in the chain that broke. The rest came after. And it was the whole that killed those people."

"Were you . . . arrested?"

"No, nothing so dramatic," she said. A sour taste filled her mouth. If there had actually been consequences, some defining moment of punishment, would she have been able to leave it behind? "The company's insurance coverage paid the survivors and their families and the mayor threatened criminal action, but it was all bluster, forgotten a few weeks later. None of us even lost our jobs. But I quit anyway. I knew what I'd done and I couldn't work with people who knew it, too."

"What did you do then?"

"I bounced around, taking odd jobs in stranger and stranger places. Oil rigs, mining ops, lumber camps. Trying not to put myself in a position to hurt people with my mistakes. But, eventually, each job petered out and it was clear just how trivial the work was, leaving me feeling worse than before. I needed another big job with bigger stakes, to show myself I could pull through. With my track record, no one would hire me for a large contract, but then I thought maybe they had trouble finding people crazy enough to go to Antarctica. So here I am. Hoping I can find myself without hurting anyone."

The last was said in a whisper. A long moment passed before Vox's voice cut through the silvery hiss.

"You are very brave to tell me this, *vozlyublennaya*. That you feel so bad so many years later confirms for me something I already knew—that you are a *good* person. That you are intelligent, thoughtful, and care about the people around you. You do not have to fear being wrong when you know this is the truth."

The simple words pierced Cass, but rather than her emotions translating into tears, she felt suddenly lighter and more lucid than before. The muscles in her throat relaxed. "Thank you, Vox. Those words mean more than you'll ever know."

"Good, I am glad. I was afraid you would cry. I never know what to do when women cry. I try to tell jokes, but I only know two and they are both about physics. And are in Russian. And not very funny."

She laughed, her voice shaky. "You'll have to tell me them sometime."

"You promise to laugh?"

"I promise." She peeked down the hatchway and froze, thinking she'd seen a shadow slide through her field of vision. But there was nothing. "Thank you for offering to call McMurdo. But don't do anything yet. If they don't hear from us soon, they'll send their own people out eventually."

"You are sure?"

"Yes. But let's keep our next date. If anything strange happens—stranger than what's already occurred—I want to be able to get in touch with you."

"Is not good enough, Blaze. We should stay in touch more often. If something happens to you, that is too much time to have passed. I will check every third day, yes? I will run up and down channels, to make sure you can reach me."

"That takes time, Vox. Won't you get in trouble?"

"My time is now my own," Vox said. "Comrade Konstantinov is confined to his quarters after slipping in the dining hall and breaking his leg."

"What happened?"

"He made the cook file a report that said the floor had not been cleaned properly, but we all know he tried to drink all the vodka on base in a night. Some stereotypes are true, you know. Besides, I would do it anyway just to feel a glow twice in my heart. Once for defying that pig of a man and again because I know I am keeping you safe."

Her breath caught in her throat. "Thank you, Vox."

"Believe me, it is my pleasure," he said, then sobered. "Cass, be careful. Maybe you think you are wrong about this experiment. Perhaps you do not trust your own judgment. But, remember, there is always the chance that you are right. If so, you are only halfway through the winter. There are more dangers to come."

CHAPTER THIRTY

"Bad luck is one thing," Deb said, both palms pressed to the side of her head, as if holding in the contents. "But this is ridiculous. Jack, what is going on?"

"Deb, we've got problems, there's no doubt. And they've all decided to roost at once, or nearly at once. But that doesn't mean—"

"Bullshit. I've seen winters that were worked on a long leash and other crews that had their problems, but this is insane. No one has this kind of bad luck. This is intentional. This is sabotage."

"Is that all you're saying, Deb?"

She glanced to her left at Keene, but the psychologist kept his gaze trained on the manager. Her face paled, but remained resolute. "You know something. I don't think you're part of it, but you know something you're not telling us. So, here's your chance. Tell us."

"Or what?"

"Or, as deputy manager, I'll take the steps necessary to set this straight."

A moment of thick tension held the room still. Hanratty sat motionless. Ayres stood near the door, ramrod straight and frowning. Taylor's eyes flitted back and forth between him and Deb. Keene had dropped his gaze and was staring at his hands.

Just when it seemed to break the room, the strain went out of Hanratty's face as if a valve had been released. "That won't be necessary. You all deserve an explanation. Hell, *I* deserve an explanation."

He looked at each of them enigmatically, as though waiting for one of them to speak. When no one did, he came around his desk and sat on the front of it, propping himself up with his hands gripping the edge.

"Historically, the purpose of the South Pole station has been to further scientific study in such a way as to benefit mankind, and the fields most often expected to deliver those benefits have been a blend of applied and hard disciplines. Astrophysics. Biology. Geology. Science with numbers and tests, theories and results."

He cleared his throat. The room was very quiet. "Life in Antarctica, however, has always had ancillary benefits in medicine, psychology, and sociology. How are bodies and minds changed by three or four or nine months on the ice? They were never distinct or primary fields of study, but it's impossible to ignore how the isolation and extreme conditions of Antarctica affect the most interesting subject of all: us."

Hanratty glanced around the room. Taylor watched Deb and Ayres, unsure how they were going to react and ready for anything. Keene, of course, had already figured it out for himself. The faces of the deputy manager and the base's doctor were the blank, noncommittal expressions of those experienced in receiving bad news and saving their assessment and recriminations until later.

"When TransAnt took over operations here," Hanratty continued, "they saw an opportunity to remedy that lack of study. Why waste what was already happening, they argued. The science could continue as it always had—no loss there. But science, with just a few tweaks, could double its money by taking advantage of a ready-made lab, specially built to test theories in psychology and sociology."

"We're part of someone's goddamned clinical trial?" Ayres asked in disbelief, his jaw muscles bunched and released.

"You specifically? No." Hanratty's voice was even. Keene stirred, but said nothing. "Others on the base? Yes."

"You're . . . TransAnt's really experimenting on personnel?" Deb asked. When Hanratty nodded, she sat back, unbelieving. "I can't believe this. I can't believe that you'd take part in it."

"Their reasons make sense once you hear the entire premise. I believe the end result is worth the methods they use."

Ayres, shaking his head, asked, "What's the point? What are they looking for? What do they hope to learn?"

Hanratty shifted his eyes. "Keene?"

"Salutogenesis." When his statement was returned with blank stares, the psychologist smiled and repeated, "Salutogenesis. The theory that some of us have it in our DNA to bring out a dormant . . . superman, for lack of a better term, when we are pushed to our physical or emotional limits. The theory was forwarded after studies of certain Holocaust survivors showed that a surprising number of them had not only made it through the worst mental and spiritual trial imaginable, they'd achieved a level of emotional and psychological growth that, frankly, shouldn't have occurred."

Deb frowned. "We're part of a study on 'the tough get tougher'?"

"No. It's not a platitude. It's the belief that salutogenesis is a core human trait that actually manifests and grows only under extreme physical and emotional duress. It's not just *survival* in the midst of a crisis, it's the ability to *transform* under it, to bloom and become something better than you were before the crisis took place."

"What a load of horseshit," Ayres said. "I could name a hundred marines at Camp Lejeune who fit that description. TransAnt doesn't need to set up a base in Antarctica for that."

"TransAnt doesn't have access to the marines at Camp Lejeune. And, frankly, marines expect to be put under duress. It's not much of a study when all of your subjects can predict what's coming or might be faking their reactions in order to conform to a preconceived notion of what it means to be a marine. Having said that, however, I'd be amazed if the government hasn't run their own salutogenic tests that would make a Marine Corps boot camp look like a walk in the park."

"But what's the point?" Deb pressed. "Why bother?"

Keene shrugged. "What's it worth to a government to groom soldiers who excel under the harshest combat conditions? What's it worth to an intelligence agency or a space program to know—and really know, not guess—they have operatives or astronauts who never falter? What value would society put on a clutch athlete or a politician or a hostage negotiator who became better on the job, not in *spite* of the worst possible events unfolding around them, but *because* of them?"

The room was quiet as they digested what Keene had said.

"It all sounds wonderful," Ayres said, breaking the silence. "What are the chances the theory is real?"

Keene considered before answering. "It's an attractive, though not fully credited, concept, I'm afraid. Antonovsky, who pioneered the idea, certainly scratched a popular itch when he proposed it. Who wouldn't like to think she's the heroine of her own story and has it in her to win the day, if only the circumstances were right? But in my experience, we're all better off if we disabuse ourselves of the idea and just work with what we've got. On the other hand, I might believe that because I know I don't have what it takes."

"How does TransAnt hope to make use of this?" Deb asked. "Are they going to interview those of us who don't lose our minds?"

Keene looked at her with bleary eyes. "I didn't say 'something in our DNA' by accident. Antonovsky believed that only thirty percent of the human population possesses salutogenic capacity. It's only a theory, of course, because it's like making educated guesses about suicides—you can't prescreen a segment of the population inclined to kill themselves, then study the results afterward. Not to mention, most cases of extreme duress can't be replicated without, ah, breaking the law. But since most children aren't trained from birth under extreme conditions of duress—if we take nurture out of the equation, in other words—the assumption is that salutogenesis is, in fact, genetic. That we can actually distill the mythic Hero Gene. So, yes, TransAnt will probably want to take DNA samples at the end of the season."

"They won't need to," Ayres said grimly. "We all underwent blood tests and basic disease screenings stateside when we signed up. I'm sure the waiver for additional testing is in the fine print of our contracts. They simply need to wait and see who hasn't lost their squash by November."

"But you said we weren't the . . . test subjects," Deb said, glancing between Hanratty and Keene.

"There are twelve Shackleton staff members who were identified to me as test vectors. Four of those were considered prime candidates," Hanratty said. "All had overcome considerable emotional or physical trauma before arriving at the Pole. The assumption—correct me if I'm wrong, Keene—was that those prior experiences were the first cracks in the shell, so to speak."

Keene nodded. "It would make sense that people who had survived and even flourished after some kind of crisis had already exhibited a salutogenic start and that those qualities would appear fully upon the application of additional stressors. If this experiment is following normal protocols, the so-called mentally healthy personnel would form the anxiety baseline, then data would be collected from the four prime subjects as well as the other eight at-risk candidates."

"'Additional stressors'?" Deb asked.

"Orchestrated events meant to . . . push the subjects' buttons, so to speak."

She looked confused for a moment, then her eyes widened. She looked at Hanratty. "The power failure was *planned*?"

The station manager's silence told them all they needed to know.

"What else was there? Is there something around the corner?"

"The psych staff at TransAnt planned only two major events," Hanratty said calmly. "The power outage was the second. The first I'm not at liberty to reveal, but I can tell you that it has already occurred."

"'Not at liberty'? Jack, these are our lives you're talking about."

"I know this is all a shock and you have a right to be angry." Hanratty spoke slowly. "But that's why I'm filling you in now. It wouldn't do you any good to know what the other event was; it happened almost four months ago. The effects were recorded, assessed, and the ramifications long gone."

"Jesus Christ. I can't believe this." Ayres pinched the bridge of his nose. "And you and Keene are in charge of this shit show?"

"No. Originally, only Taylor and myself knew about the experiment. Keene figured it out after studying the psych profiles of the crew. He came to me with his suspicions, so I filled him in."

"But he's not in charge of the experiment?" Ayres asked. Hanratty shook his head. "Then who is? Just you?"

"Not exactly. I'm responsible for the stressor events and making sure they don't get out of hand. The script and action parameters for those events were handed to me by TransAnt."

"I hear a 'but' in there."

"*But* I was told that there would be a member of the crew who would be monitoring the tests and gathering data. To help keep the study clean, I assume, that person's identity was kept hidden from me and I still don't know who it is. I've taken to calling him the Observer."

The room was quiet as they chewed on the information. Finally, Ayres spoke. "I've got a question."

"Go."

"Things turned ugly after the power failure, and I can't say I'm happy with any of this garbage about some kind of experiment, but from your perspective, we have the situation relatively under control. No one's been killed. Injuries have been moderate, but treatable. Comms going down is not good and has raised anxiety considerably, but we're handling it and are otherwise stable. This . . . Observer is collecting a bevy of test results, so he should be happy."

"Correct."

"So, why are you telling us all of this now? What's changed?"

"It's the third event," Deb said.

Hanratty nodded grimly. "There is nothing in the action protocol calling for external communications to be disabled. We didn't do this."

"And you don't know who it is?"

"No."

Ayres put his hands in his pockets. "What if the comms failure was an actual systems breakdown? Every season has its share of hiccups."

"We've been over the system with a fine-tooth comb. It wasn't an accident. It wasn't an equipment failure. It was sabotaged thoroughly and effectively and we've found out that even satcom and the data streams from the labs like COBRA were affected. We can't call out or receive communications, nor send an emergency signal to McMurdo for extraction. Hell, we can't send Morse code over the wire."

"The Observer?" Deb asked.

Hanratty nodded. "Taylor, Keene, and I think so."

"But why?" she asked, baffled. "We aren't part of the experiment."

Keene picked at the dirt under a fingernail. "We are now."

CHAPTER THIRTY-ONE

"What the hell do you mean our communications are out?"

Hanratty swallowed and passed a hand over his throat self-consciously. He'd called for an all-hands meeting in Shackleton's gym, hoping that the appearance of transparency would keep everyone calm and united behind him. The gym had seemed a strategic choice not only because of its size, but also to stop cliques from forming, as might have happened in a more familiar locale like the galley. By keeping everyone on their feet and mixed as a general population, he'd planned to increase the feeling of isolation among individual crew members.

Unfortunately, herding all the people on base into a single large room seemed to have had the opposite effect, breeding a single, larger organism filled with anger and fear. Perhaps he'd misjudged his audience. His old leadership instructors at Fort Benning would not have been pleased.

"I understand what you must be feeling right now." *State the problem.* "Many of you are upset and scared. Communications is the lifeline that connects us to the outside world, and that lifeline has, admittedly, been compromised."

A murmur of discontent, amplified by the tile floor and hard concrete walls, rippled through the room.

Biddi Newell raised her voice. "Jack, what happened, exactly? How is it possible that all of our comms went down at once?"

"We're looking into that. It has been suggested that an electrical surge from the recent heat and power outage might've caused some damage that began to accumulate and only now resulted in a circuit failure."

Hanratty swept his eyes over the crowd, trying to gauge the effect of his words. The mutters picked up volume. *Control the message.*

"In any case," he hurried on, "we're working on solutions, not theories or recriminations. What other questions do you have?"

"What about work? I'm worried about data loss," Anne said, her expression pinched. "Those transmissions are critical to what we're doing down here."

"We have on-base backups as a fail-safe," he said. "None of your work will be lost."

"What about a satellite phone?" someone asked from the back. "Can't we just pick up the line and call McMurdo?"

"We can't find it."

A swelling growl of disbelief met his statement. "You've got to be joking," Dave Boychuck said from the middle of the pack, his beard bristling. "And what do you mean 'it'? We only have one?"

"That's correct," he said, getting ready for the storm. "I don't know how the need was overlooked, but we were left with one sat phone on base. And that one is missing."

Calls of "Bullshit" and "I can't believe this" rose in the crowd. Hanratty raised his hands over his head. *Show common cause.*

"Again, I understand you're upset, you're scared, and—since much of the science can't happen without reliable communications—pretty pissed off. Believe me, I am, too. I didn't sign up for this any more than you did."

He looked at the two-score people in front of him, their pale faces watching him for comfort and reassurance. He wished he could give it to them. *Get them to unite behind you.*

"But the most important thing we can do right now is, you guessed it, stay calm. Going ballistic when we have no way of reaching the outside world isn't going to help matters. Blaming me or the admin staff might feel good in the short term, but it's not going to restore our satellite uplink. I called all of you in here today so you could see we're doing our best to solve the problem. We are still in a safe, stable environment"—a snort met his statement, but he bulled on—"and we're just a short time away from returning everything back to normal."

He felt the gazes of Taylor, Keene, Ayres, and Deb boring into him, but he refused to look in their direction. They'd all agreed—with dissension on Ayres's part, but eventual capitulation—that it would be in everyone's best interests to maintain the fabrication that the communications failure was an accident and that normal comms would be restored soon. They could continue spooling out excuses for weeks if they had to, but the truth, he knew, would start a riot. *End with a positive message.*

"In the meantime," he began, but *Jesus Christ* just as he was set to launch into his message the lights in the gym went out, plunging the room into darkness.

For one startled moment, he thought he could still see thanks to the impression burned on his retina. Then someone screamed and he was jostled as people began moving, shouting, gasping.

"Taylor!" he shouted, though he had no idea what his security chief could do in the absolute blackness.

Just as the pitch of the voices began climbing the ramp to hysteria, the lights came back on as suddenly as they'd gone out. The forty-some crew members froze in place, looking around wild-eyed and frightened.

Hanratty dove into the pause as though nothing had happened. "*In the meantime*, please return to your duties as posted or required. I know it's a difficult thing to do, but bear in mind that the early South Pole crews went *all nine months* without contact. Even just a few decades ago, the base passed the winter without a single radio broadcast. We are no less capable than any of those brave explorers. We've got technology, the accumulated experience of decades, and our ability to work together, all on our side. As Ernest Shackleton himself said, 'Difficulties are just things to overcome, after all.'"

But the crowd was unmoved and he soon found himself pressed by a half-dozen scared and angry Polies. At his signal, Taylor, Keene, Deb, and even a reluctant Ayres moved forward to mingle with the crowd and start damage control while he fielded questions from the angriest crew members, willing to be the lightning rod if it meant keeping the crew at large calm.

The worst part, he thought as he nodded sympathetically to a red-faced Dave Boychuck, was that someone in the room—someone he'd be talking to, reassuring, and making empty promises to—knew exactly what had happened, why, and what was coming next.

CHAPTER THIRTY-TWO

"Do I have to remind you that midwinter comes but once a year? Please don't make me come dig you out of that filthy garage."

Cass smiled. "Oh, you won't have to."

Biddi looked at her in the mirror above the sink. "You sound so sure of yourself. Are you a social butterfly now?"

"Pete said they've been hoarding goodies for months to celebrate. And I, for one, am tired of eating white lettuce and Wonder bread for every meal."

"I hear you. What was last night's dinner supposed to be, again? It was disgusting."

"Beef stroganoff."

"The hamburger was the color of used bubble gum."

"Stop right there," she said, pointing the toilet bowl brush at her friend. After four months of living in a confined space, the crew at Shackleton had become a little lax in their personal hygiene and bathroom habits. It was her turn to clean commodes and she didn't need any more grotesque thoughts in her head.

"And the noodles were like the insides of a fish's belly, all wiggly and white."

She started to laugh. "Oh my God."

"And the gravy? It was like they had dumped a tub of man juice over the top—"

"Biddi! For Christ's sake." Cass leaned against the side of the stall, shoulders shaking with laughter. Clad in rubber gloves, she had to use her forearm to wipe the tears away.

Biddi turned around. "It's good to see you laugh again, lady. You've been as sober as a judge for weeks now, and I don't mean in a good way. You should get out more."

The comment was meant as a question, but Cass gently deflected it. "You're making up for both of us."

Biddi harrumphed, taking the hint. "What do you think of Hanratty's little hootenanny in the gym?"

"About the fact that all of our communications are down or the way in which he told us?"

"Both. Either. Whatever suits your fancy."

"Comms going down is terrifying in one way, but, as much as I hate to admit it, Hanratty had a point. None of the explorers who came before us had anything like our safety nets." Cass squirted blue cleaner into the toilet and swirled her magic wand around the bowl. "We'll have a few nervous days, they'll fix whatever's wrong, and in a month we won't even remember that it happened."

Biddi grunted. "It doesn't bother you a tad that half of those explorers died?"

"I think that's where the technology and living in the twenty-first century come in. We have slightly more advanced gear than reindeer-hide sleeping bags and paraffin stoves."

"You sound awfully upbeat. What if they don't get it fixed?"

"They'll figure something out. I mean, it's not as if it was broken intentionally, right? If it's broke, they'll fix it." *Right after Keene takes his notes and adds them to our psych file.* "I'd rather focus on the party, to be honest. At this point, if I got a really good meal, comms could be down for the rest of the winter, for all I care. Speaking of which, is there anything else planned for tomorrow night?"

When there was no answer, Cass leaned out of the stall. Her friend was staring down into the sink. "Biddi?"

"Hmm?"

"I asked, is there anything else planned for tomorrow night after the dinner?"

"Oh. Sorry, love. I got a bit of the T3s there. Activities for tomorrow night, right." She cleared her throat. "Officially or unofficially?"

"Both?"

Biddi turned to the mirror and sprayed it with a frothy cleaning solution, then set about rubbing the daylights out of it. "Officially, there will be some champagne after the dinner and some disco music, followed by a midnight screening of *The Shining*."

"After what we've been through? Who the hell thought *that* was a good idea?"

"Think of it as exposure therapy."

"As long as it doesn't turn into a documentary." Cass flushed the toilet and watched the blue whirlpool for a moment. "What about unofficially?"

"Nurse Beth—she's a wild one, she is—told me some of our more adventurous colleagues are planning an ice party down in the warehouse whilst the movie is showing."

"The warehouse is sixty below zero. Why would anyone have a party down there?"

"Well, apparently, someone with a degree in chemistry has been nicking a bit of sugar from the approximately ten thousand pounds of it in the warehouse and using it to fuel a small distillery in the back of the generator room, which, as you know, is not that far away from the warehouse."

Cass leaned out of the stall to stare at Biddi. "*You* wouldn't happen to have a degree in chemistry?"

"No. But my ancestors were bootleggers."

"So, it's just more drinking? Homemade hooch isn't going to do much for frostbite," Cass said. "It's going to get ugly when body parts start freezing and falling off."

"Ah, well, as to those body parts . . ." Biddi said, her voice trailing off.

Cass leaned out again, curious. A note of embarrassment had crept into Biddi's voice, something Cass had never heard before. "Yes?"

"Evidently, there will be more than just drinking going on. It has been suggested that certain . . . calisthenics are planned."

Cass looked at her blankly. "Calisthenics?"

"Yes, Cassie." Biddi, impatient at having to explain the obvious, did a quick bump and grind. "Calis*then*ics."

Cass's jaw dropped. "No way."

"I shit you not, love." Biddi snapped her washrag and moved to the next mirror.

"How do you find *out* about these things?"

"Sanitation engineers are the great levelers," Biddi said haughtily. "We might be bloody fucking janitors, but we talk to everyone and everyone talks to us."

"*I'm* a janitor, and no one told *me* about the orgy."

"That's because you're down in the VMF all the time, fondling engine parts when you could be fondling . . . other parts. I, on the other hand, prefer to walk among the people."

"So Mr. Boychuck and his hose will be there, I take it?"

"Um, well. Yes." Biddi cleared her throat. "You should join us, Cassie. For the boozing, if nothing else. People think you take things too seriously."

"Thanks but no thanks. I've got a date with a real plate of food, a glass of wine, and that's it."

"That nice man Jun looks lonely."

"He's married, Biddi."

"Not for long, I hear."

"What?"

"He's been in the doldrums for some time now. Anne told me he's having trouble at home. Didn't you know?"

Tears, spilling from his eyes. "He told me a few things and I guessed the rest. Is there something new?"

"An American wife, a domineering family, pressure from his school, gone to the South Pole for nine months," Biddi said. "The math is pretty easy, love."

"It's a sad situation."

"Perhaps you could give him a hand, then. You never know what a little bit of tenderness might do for the poor man," Biddi teased. "An ice wife might be just what he needs to cheer him up."

"Can we go back to talking about food, please?"

"You brought it up, darling."

The conversation turned to more neutral topics, like what Pete would be putting on the menu, whether the champagne would be drinkable or better used to scour toilets, and laying bets on whether Hanratty would smile. Time flew by as their chatting turned the bathroom duty into an afterthought, and they were done before they knew it.

Throughout the rest of the day, Cass felt a sense of excitement infect the station as the crew began to anticipate the midwinter celebration. It was a nice change from the anxiety the communications outage had caused, although there was a reluctance to talk about the celebration openly, as if mentioning it out loud would cause Hanratty to cancel it out of spite. But it was impossible to ignore the look of anticipation on everyone's faces as she passed them in the hall or sat down to eat in the galley. Even the previously tasteless lunch buffet took on a richer flavor as the crew whispered to each other how much better the next night's meal would be than the gruel they were eating now. The day couldn't pass quickly enough.

The next night, long lines formed outside the galley while the smells of cooked food—the kind no one had experienced in months—wafted down the halls. It was virtual torture and the crew shifted from foot to foot, antsy and barely able to contain themselves, trading jokes and telling stories to keep their mind off the dinner that was so close. Cass had heard of one's mouth watering in anticipation before, but she'd never experienced it, at least not like she was now.

Colin and Anne were standing in front of her, with Colin trying unsuccessfully to remember the punch line to a joke, though based on Anne's expression, it wouldn't have helped. At one point, with her back half turned to Colin, she rolled her eyes at Cass, who bit her lip and turned away.

"Cass?"

She turned. Pete, wearing his white cook's apron, had appeared at her elbow looking harried and carrying an insulated cooler with a thick handle. He was a small man, perpetually hunched over as though carrying the combined weight of the one hundred meals he had to prepare every day. A few strands of dark, stringy hair had escaped his hairnet and were plastered against his forehead.

"What's up, Pete?"

"I hate, really hate, to ask you this, but I need a favor."

Her heart sank down to the depths of her stomach. "As long as it doesn't mean missing dinner."

"No, not quite," he said, then hurried on when he saw the look on her face. He gestured with the cooler. "Almost everyone on base is here for the dinner, but there are a few people who can't make it. It doesn't seem right that they have to miss the big blowout."

She groaned. "You want me to deliver it to them?"

He nodded. "I would do it, but it's going to take everything I've got just to get the real meal on the table for everyone."

Cass tried to ignore the flip-flops her stomach was doing. "What are you offering?"

"The eternal goodwill of your fellow crew members?"

"I can't eat goodwill," Cass said. Out of the corner of her eye, she saw Anne grin. "Try again."

"I can promise you an extra dessert."

"Two. Plus a bottle of wine."

"Good Lord," he said. "Not a chance. Two desserts and an extra glass of wine."

"Got any candy bars hidden back there?"

He looked at her slantwise. "Maybe."

"Two desserts, an extra glass of wine, and a couple of candy bars."

"Done." They shook and he handed her the cooler. She frowned, thinking of something. "Wait, why the cooler? Whose meal am I delivering?"

"Jun's."

She glowered at Pete. "You are *not* going to tell me he's out at COBRA."

He grinned and started moving back toward the kitchen. "Afraid so."

"Jesus Christ. It's going to take me an hour."

"No take-backsies, Cass."

"You son of a bitch! I want three desserts," she called, but he'd already disappeared through the swinging door with a wave.

Anne, Colin, and the others around her shot her a sympathetic look, but no one offered to take her place, she noticed. The way the food was smelling, ten desserts wouldn't be a good enough trade.

"If you follow the flag line, it's not too bad," Anne offered with a pained smile.

Grumbling, Cass broke out of line and carried the cooler down the hall to her room, where she went through the laborious process of suiting up in full gear, including three under-layers, a parka, bunny boots, and the two-tiered glove system—a neoprene layer under bear claws—needed for the cold. She kept the hood down and the balaclava off until she reached the airlock for Destination Zulu, the ground-level exit, but before long it was time to put both on and cinch them down tight.

Gritting her teeth, Cass turned on her headlamp and opened the outer door. The initial paralyzing cold was held at bay by her layers of clothing, but the brute physical force of the wind pushed against her as though she were a sail, and she had to lean into the first step just to get through the door. She exited the base, stepping into the night, and slammed the door shut behind her.

Fat flakes of snow pelted her face and Cass blinked in reaction even though her ski mask protected her face. Pausing for a moment to adjust, she tromped down the steps to the ground level, then turned her headlamp back toward the base of the stairs, illuminating a metal pole that had been planted to the right of the door. Welded to the pole was a group of lanyards. Lashed to each lanyard was a colored polystyrene rope, different than its neighbor, and tied to each line was a small nylon tag with a handwritten word on it. Fighting the wind, Cass fumbled with the rope until she found a red one marked "COBRA." She glanced down its length. Every fifteen feet, held up by a small pole, a scrap of red nylon was tied to the line, though only the first two flags were visible in the dark. Cass shook the line and the rope bounced, sending the flags dancing frantically in the wind.

She stared for a long, long moment into the looping continuation of white snow and black night. The vision made almost no sense, as though she were staring into the sea, trying and failing to find a measurable length of space. There was no way to bind it, no way to put a limit on the endless. Though seemingly only an arm's length away, the end of the rope was tied to the infinite.

Cass cursed and shook herself. Thinking like that would get her killed. Life wasn't measured in the limitless. You paced it off, one step at a time.

She adjusted her grip on the cooler with her right hand, tightened her left on the flag line, and plunged into the darkness.

CHAPTER THIRTY-THREE

Despite reading the diaries of expired explorers, and listening to all the warnings, and enduring TransAnt training sessions with titles like "How to Survive the First Hour," Cass had never actually believed she might die in Antarctica. Too many people had come before her, too many safeguards were in place, life was too *modern* for her to die from something as mundane as the weather. Pulling Sheryl's body—or what she'd thought was Sheryl's body—onto the sled had shaken that confidence badly, but as time had passed, she'd gradually returned to the belief that life in Antarctica was, at its core, safe, that it was almost impossible that she could die from simply *being* at the South Pole.

Until now.

With her left hand clutching the flag line, she staggered forward against a wind that, had she tried to fall, would've held her perfectly upright. The flurries were so savage that they turned the spray of ice crystals into a physical attack that largely ignored her three layers of clothing, dotting her neck and face with searing pinpricks and hitting her hood with a sound like radio static at full volume.

Visibility was zero. She knew that several red signal lights topped the COBRA lab building and, at just over a hundred meters away from the main station, she should be able to spot the lights from here, but the whiteout was total—she could see nothing but billions of snowflakes whipping past her face, barely illuminated by the frail red light of her headlamp.

The single piece of good news was that, with the wind rushing at the speeds it was, there was little buildup on the ground, and so no drifts to push through. If she could simply put one foot in front of the other one hundred and ten times, and not let go of the flag line in the meanwhile, she would find herself at the door to COBRA. She could drop off the cooler, put both hands on the line, and walk back to claim her reward from Pete. Struggling against the gale, feeling the ice begin to make its way down her neck and between her shoulder blades, it crossed her mind that she'd come across as seriously cheap at nothing more than two desserts and an extra glass of wine. She must've been food-drunk.

To occupy her mind, she began counting steps, kicking herself for not starting the moment she'd left the base. She might as well begin counting now . . . but how far had she come? Granted, it might seem like she'd been walking forever but, in truth, she'd been moving slowly, forging one step at a time. She'd only come thirty steps at best, so thirty it was. *Thirty-one, thirty-two.*

Her mind wandered, lighting on subjects then taking off again, landing nowhere for very long, blown off course like the flurries around her. She thought back to the conversation she'd had with Vox, about the potential that she was the subject of a psychological test meant to push her to her emotional limits, and what she should do about it.

From a number of perspectives, it seemed unlikely that she was the only one being tested. What kind of findings would they get by testing one person, under a single set of circumstances? It wouldn't be worth it. Assuming that the theory of a station-wide test was real and not just a function of her suspicions, that meant that others were being tested in the way she was. But how many? And how often? And to what extent?

Forty-five, forty-six.

The answer was important, because three people staging a protest wouldn't be effective, but ten times that number would. But how was she supposed to compare notes with the crew without tipping off Hanratty and whoever else was involved? What if half the base were subjects of the experiment . . . but the other half knew about it?

She shivered, and not just with the cold. Imagination was the cork in the bottle of paranoia. Open it up and there was no end. What if this season's winter-over had never been meant to have any scientific research benefit? What if the crew members had been recruited with some kind of experiment in mind? Was she delivering a meal to Jun the astrophysicist or to Jun the psychology post-doc brought in to test and record her emotional and mental reactions?

Fifty-eight, fifty-nine.

She shook her head, a futile physical gesture. Giving in to her suspicions wouldn't work; she needed allies. And, anyway, she'd spent too much time with them to believe she could be fooled by Jun or Ayres or Biddi. No one could keep up an Oscar-worthy performance for that long.

She cursed out loud, the words muffled by her mask and scarf. She didn't have to give into paranoia, but that didn't mean she was going to be someone's guinea pig. Armed with the knowledge—or belief, at least—that she was being manipulated, she would stay alert, record the things that were done to her or around her, and face them all down once she was safely back stateside.

Seventy-three, seventy-four.

Seventy-four divided by one hundred and ten was . . . sixty-seven percent. She was two-thirds of the way through risking her life to deliver a single meal to a man because she felt bad for him and had been bribed with sugar. Actually, she corrected herself, she was just one-third of the way through. She still had to return to Shackleton to claim her reward.

She pulled back hard on those thoughts like she was sawing on the reins of a horse. Think too hard about how far you had to go on the ice, and you were laying the groundwork for surrender. Focus on the task at hand.

Eighty-two, eighty-three.

Her body swayed in the wind like a mast as she paused for a minute to orient herself. The lights of the lab were still hidden. Moving with exquisite care, she turned in place and looked back at the way she'd come. A hollow feeling raced through her chest. Shackleton, normally lit bright by red spotlights at each corner of the building, was gone.

Fear clutched at her and she squeezed the rope in her hands. *Easy. Take it easy*. Shackleton wasn't so much gone as she was blind to it—her headlamp illuminated a curtain of snow that effectively blinded her beyond three feet. Even if the station wall had been an arm's length away, she probably wouldn't have seen it.

Well, there's an easy way to test that, isn't there? Swallowing her anxiety, she put the cooler down and slowly reached up to turn her headlamp off. Absolute darkness engulfed her and she had the disorienting sensation that she'd stepped outside her body. Only the relentless wind gave her any sense of place. She looked back the way she'd come.

Shackleton was nowhere to be seen.

A slight groan escaped her mouth; she clamped down on it. *Relax. Nothing's changed. You're no more than a football field away from the station*. Visibility, even for a one-thousand-lumen lamp, was reduced to just a few feet. If she'd used her brain and thought about it before turning around, she would've laughed to think that the lights of the station would be blazing like a lighthouse.

The vista abruptly vanished as she turned her headlamp back on and forced herself to face front, away from the endless black. Carefully and intentionally clearing her mind, she returned to the march toward the lab, focusing on each physical step forward—literally looking at her feet and letting the flag line guide her—instead of listening to the wanderings of her mind.

Ninety-seven, ninety-eight, ninety-nine. One hundred!

Cass raised her head. The deep, dark vista she'd been staring at for twenty minutes stared back at her.

COBRA should be ten, *maybe* fifteen, steps away. But there were no lights, no building.

She stumbled forward—*to hell with counting*—the cooler banging against her leg. With the beam of the headlamp jogging up and down, she followed the line as she ran, five steps, six steps, her breath coming in rasps, until she saw that the flags simply . . .

. . . stopped. One last post kept the cord in place for the final eight feet, but the excess whipped back and forth in the wind like a dying snake. The flag line led precisely nowhere.

Cass stared at the end of the rope, unable to reconcile what she was seeing with what she'd been expecting. She took a few hesitant steps forward, then stopped. Where did she think she was going to go?

The other end of the line leads back home. The thought was the only thing that kept her from panicking. Once again, she turned in place, swapping hands on the line as she did a slow-motion pirouette. Kneeling, she put the cooler down on the ice and pocketed the one or two portable food items, then left the cooler behind. It was a shame Jun wasn't going to get his entire midwinter meal, but she had bigger problems than one man's disappointment right now. She wouldn't be heading to COBRA tonight—or ever, if she had her way. She was going straight back to Shackleton.

She took obsessive care to count her steps on the way back. At twenty, she raised her head to check her progress. There was still no beacon coming from the direction of Shackleton, but to her left, she suddenly saw a bright red flare, like a bloodshot eye staring back at her in the darkness.

Is that the lab? It didn't seem possible she could've missed it—and that still didn't explain why the flag line had veered away from the lab instead of heading right to it—but this was about the same place where she'd put her head down and stared at her boots for what she'd thought would be her final push to COBRA. She'd been concentrating on her steps and the flag line, trusting it to take her to the lab, not looking around. So . . . she'd missed it. But that wasn't the real question.

What was she going to do now?

If she wanted to head for the light, she'd have to abandon the flag line. Untethered, she'd be like an astronaut on a spacewalk, with about the same amount of risk. Or she could do the sane thing and return to base. After what she'd been through, she'd still be claiming those extra desserts or Pete would risk losing a mouthful of teeth.

She looked at the light again, trying to calculate the distance. How big did a light have to be to figure out how far away it was? She glanced along the flag line, then back at the red light. When she'd looked back to find Shackleton, she'd been no more than seventy-five meters away—maybe closer—which would seem to suggest, naturally, that the COBRA lab was less than that. As long as the light didn't go away, she could march right to it.

The idea was ridiculous. Nobody in their right mind would let go of a flag line so they could deliver a mauled midwinter's dinner.

Then she thought about the day in the galley, and the look on Jun's face as the tears had rolled down his cheeks as he told her about his wife.

How much was a small kindness worth?

Squaring herself to the light, she let go of the line.

CHAPTER THIRTY-FOUR

Cass stared at the red light without blinking. Thirty paces after letting go of the umbilical cord that was the flag line, she calculated that she was a little less than halfway to the lab, but what scared her was that the wind had started to pick up and what had been a bright, if baleful, beacon was now flickering and disappearing as the increased snow started to blind her. She realized belatedly that when she'd first caught sight of the light from the flag line, a momentary lull in the wind had increased her visibility. She hadn't counted on the gale force returning and cutting off her vision.

The main culprit was the light from her headlamp, which, as before, was bouncing off the sheet of white blowing a foot from her face. Reluctantly, wondering if she truly had gone insane, she reached up and turned the light off. The plunge into darkness was enough to make her heart stop, but as her eyes adjusted, the red star of the COBRA lab shone more brightly than before. She reoriented herself and trudged forward.

At fifty paces, her stomach muscles began to relax as two more red and one very small green light appeared. The whine and roar of the wind were deafening.

At eighty paces, the red light was almost directly overhead, the only guide she had to keep from running into the wall. She put a hand out until she finally felt something solid. Looking up, the two-story outline of the COBRA building was barely visible above her. Keeping constant contact with the wall, she walked the building's perimeter until she found the door dimly illuminated by a red spotlight so encrusted with ice and snow that it gave off nothing more than a weak pink glow. Struggling against the gale, she opened the door and tumbled inside.

The muted silence inside the building's airlock was almost unnerving after the endless, shrieking wind. Cass pushed back her parka's hood, stripped off her mask and balaclava, and savored the feeling of safety. By normal standards, the tiny room wasn't really warm and the squall had pushed snow through the millimeters-wide gap between the door and the wall to lie in drifts on the floor, but it was a refuge after what she'd waded through.

She kicked the snow away from the inner door, then pushed it open. A blast of warmth hit her and goose bumps raced over her body at the sudden temperature shift. Beyond was a mudroom of sorts. She slammed the door shut with a boom and stripped off her parka and bear claws, the bulkiest parts of the ECW gear.

Once past the mudroom, the COBRA lab building expanded into a colossal space the size of two or three barns. Dominating the center and reaching up to a height of about sixty feet was a single massive dish antenna that she'd been told could both project and collect through the domed roof that sheltered the lab proper. The dish was on a ten-foot-tall concrete pedestal that served as a de facto wall for about ten office cubes surrounding its base; scaffolding and metal stairs led up to the pedestal from the concrete main floor. The atmosphere was hushed; COBRA provided enough shelter that the sounds of the frigid hell outside had been reduced to a soft white noise, interrupted only by electronic noises and the whirring of computer cooling fans.

She cleared her throat, but her voice came out as a croak. She wasn't used to yelling. "Jun?"

There was no answer. She frowned. You might not hear the outer door, but no one could've missed the noise of the inner door slamming shut. She set off through the forest of desks and computer racks.

"Jun?" she called again, but the sound seemed swallowed by the dense equipment and mountains of scientific gear surrounding her. A large monitor caught her eye, distracting her as it frantically updated a chart. A solid blue line peaked and valleyed constantly as it recorded some kind of astrophysical data every half second.

Wandering around the antenna, she came across a workstation that seemed more lived-in than the others. A quilted winter coat hung over the back of a chair. A cup half filled with green tea sat on the desk. Deep dents on the seat of the chair indicated this was probably command-central for the lab. The rest of the workstations were only lightly used; perhaps manned only in the summer.

From her pockets, she pulled out the food she'd rescued from the cooler: a foil package of steak, a plastic container of mashed potatoes with the gravy already mixed in, and a single squashed dinner roll. Hunger tied her stomach in knots at the smells of the food, but she placed the packages on the desk noticing, as she did so, a single sheet of paper resting on top of the keyboard. Cass tilted her head. In an environment as hostile and scientific as the South Pole, seeing paper that wasn't already in a book was almost weird. Glancing guiltily over a shoulder, she leaned forward. She only meant to skim the contents, but when she saw the opening line, she picked up the paper and started to read. It was a printed e-mail.

Jun, it began, *this is a terrible thing to send you in the middle of your time down at Shackleton, but this isn't something that can wait.*

With a growing feeling of dread, she read the rest of the page, although she knew what it was going to say. Jun's wife was leaving him. Unable to wait the five more months until he returned, she had filed for divorce. The words of the e-mail expressed regret and even some reluctance, but the intent was clear and unmistakable.

Sick for Jun's sake, Cass carefully put the paper back. What kind of heartless bitch would drop that kind of bombshell while someone was trapped at the South Pole for nine months? She looked back at the sheet. And an *e-mail*? She hadn't had the guts to make a satellite call for something this important?

Cass raised her head, flushed with guilt. If Jun wasn't responding, there might be a good reason for it; he didn't want to talk to anyone after getting news like this. On the other hand, he could probably use someone to talk to. She wasn't exactly in Keene's league, but she knew something about getting through tough times.

She continued around the pedestal, feeling like a prowler. The stillness in the air made her jumpy, a kind of anxiety increased by the occasional surge in the distant wind as it suddenly shifted direction and went from the soft hiss she'd noticed to an audible assault on the building.

Halfway around the circuit of the antenna pedestal, she distinctly felt as though she were alone in the building. There had been a set of ECW gear in the changing room by the door that she'd assumed was Jun's, but it wasn't unusual to have extra nearby as a precaution. He could've been so dismayed by his wife's e-mail that he had grabbed his set of gear, suited up, and returned to Shackleton to nurse his pain before Cass had even set out for COBRA.

The idea made rational sense, but rang hollow to her. Jun was too much of a professional—everyone at Shackleton was too much of a professional—to let even the worst news interfere with his work. Had he cut out of a twelve-hour shift early to get some alone time in a different setting, he would've asked Anne or one of the other astrophysicists to take over. Maybe he'd lie about being sick or find another excuse, but he wouldn't simply abandon his post.

She was standing still, considering the idea, when she raised her head to look at the concave inner face of the enormous antenna. Most of the interior lighting was on the workstation side of the building, so the greater part of the structure was in shadow, giving the dish the appearance of a waning moon. Its surface was smooth, with a dull gray finish. Beneath the dish was a steel framework superstructure that acted as a support, but Cass guessed from the sight of hydraulics that it was also used to position the antenna.

Her eyes followed the edge of the dish, running around the outside of it like a finger would trace the rim of a bowl, until her gaze stopped on the object that had drawn her gaze inexorably upward.

The simple, final horror of what she was seeing was too much for her to process in the first few seconds. The collection of scientific debris and paraphernalia made Jun appear, at first sight, like simply another piece of equipment. It wasn't until her eyes, following his body downward, stopped at his shoes—the small, battered sneakers with a hole in the toe—that the full impact of what she was seeing hit her and she began to cry.

CHAPTER THIRTY-FIVE

She kept her cool until Taylor reached for her arm.

When, frantic and almost hysterical, she'd been unable to raise anyone on the building-to-building comm system, Cass had thrown on her parka and gear, then raced out of the COBRA building. Luck was with her—the wind had mercifully died down to a stiff breeze, allowing her to use the weak light from her headlamp, her own occasional footprints, and some dead reckoning to make her way back to the flag line.

Some sense of self-preservation was screaming at her to slow down, but the vision of Jun's body slumped against the curved frame of the antenna overruled everything. Gasping and crying, her tears freezing to her face, she tripped and jogged as fast as she could back to Shackleton, barely maintaining a hand on the flag line and, at some points, just keeping the nylon rope in sight so she could keep up her speed.

She made it back to the base in fifteen minutes, banging open the door to Destination Zulu and shucking her parka and gear, dumping everything inside the foyer. She raced along the hall to the galley, following the noise of a party in full swing, wiping her face and pressing her hands to her face as she went.

Cass burst into the room unnoticed thanks to the carousing. The lighting was a hellish patchwork of overhead bulbs that had been removed to make a kind of mood lighting and a single tiny disco ball turning forlornly in the center of the ceiling. Hip-hop music blared tinnily from speakers in one corner. Most of the crew was on its feet, dancing or shouting conversations at one another, happy to forget the fear and anxiety of the last few days. The heat was on, the electricity worked, and life at the South Pole was back on track.

Cass scanned the room, frustrated, trying to find someone to talk to, someone to scream at. The smell of the food was nauseating now. Ruddy faces, drunk on good times or just drunk, mugged at her like fun-house distortions, the fumes of the booze on their breath making her want to vomit. Someone, Tim, maybe, made as if to steal a kiss. While bobbing away from him, she caught a glimpse of Hanratty, sober as a judge, watching the party from a corner of the galley as though observing a social science experiment.

"Hey, take it easy," someone said as she shoved her way through the crowd. A hand plucked at her shirt as if to slow her down. She chopped down and the fingers disappeared with a curse.

There. From across the room, she could see Hanratty watching her. Something in her face must've alarmed him; he turned to Taylor, who had appeared almost magically at his side, then the two of them intercepted her before she'd made it halfway through the galley.

"What is it?"

"You son of a bitch," she yelled, but the music was too loud for anyone but Hanratty and Taylor to hear her. "You and your fucking test just killed a man."

His dark eyes shone dangerously bright, shrinking and growing as the lights flickered. "What are you talking about?"

"Jun. You know, Jun? The scientist?"

"What about him?"

Hands balled into fists at her sides, Cass barely kept herself from punching the man in the teeth. Faces began turning their way. "Harmless, polite, nobody Jun killed himself because of your little social science experiment and you're not going to get me to follow him."

"Jun's *dead*?" For the first time since she'd known him, Hanratty looked shocked.

"Yes, you cocksucker. He hanged himself from the middle of that great-goddamned antenna in the COBRA building. And you had Pete send me out there to find him."

Shaken, Hanratty turned to Taylor, who bent his head close to catch every word. The security chief's eyes widened, then he jerked his head toward the door to the galley. Hanratty turned back to her. "Jennings, this isn't the place to handle this. Let's go to my office and you can debrief me fully."

"Debrief? Debrief? Jun is *dead*. He just committed *suicide*." She clawed at Hanratty's shirt, balling the fabric in her fists and screaming into his face. "You want a debrief? Here's your fucking debrief. You're through experimenting on me. You're through experimenting on us. You're going to call McMurdo now and we're going to shut down this station *tonight*."

The last words came out as a shriek that she couldn't contain. The accumulated suspicions and fear she'd been harboring, the residual guilt and paranoia, bubbled up and out in a scream. Some of the crew, seeing Cass grab Hanratty, stopped what they were doing and stood or turned their way or stepped closer. Someone turned the music off abruptly.

"Nothing to worry about, everyone," Hanratty said, his voice jerky. "Cass here has had a little too much to drink."

"I am not drunk," she yelled, furious. She pivoted to address the room. "I just came back from COBRA. Jun Takahashi killed himself tonight."

"Jesus Christ," Hanratty said. The galley was deadly silent, as though the air had been sucked out of the room . . . then the crowd erupted in groans and whispered "nos." Anne buried her face in her hands. Carla and Colin, stunned, stood with mouths literally hanging open. Biddi and Dave, along with others who hadn't quite understood the message, were asking what had happened; those who had understood began shouting simultaneously, demanding details from Cass, an explanation from Hanratty.

"They're using us like rats in experiments," she yelled at the top of her voice, trying to convince the crowd on the strength of her voice alone. "This whole winter-over is all just a goddamned psych test. They're using you, using all of us. Sheryl's death was faked! The power outage was planned!"

The words came out in a garbled rush, but enough of the message got through that people started yelling questions.

"What?"

"What did she say?"

"What does she mean, Sheryl isn't dead?"

Hanratty, glancing at the outraged crowd, gestured. "Taylor, get her out of here. I'm going to have to handle this."

The security chief nodded and reached for Cass's arm.

The patronizing, take-charge gesture broke her last remaining thread of self-control. As the man's fingers curled around her bicep, she screamed incoherently and drove the butt of her palm into his face. Taylor's nose buckled with a crunch and blood exploded across his face. Shocked by the assault, the security chief looked at her in disbelief, then shook his head like a bull and swung.

His fist caught her on the side of the head, a clumsy punch that stunned her but galvanized the onlookers. The room broke into full chaos, with crew members surging forward to try and separate the two. Taylor, not a popular man, had as many hands restraining him as Cass, although someone grabbed her from behind and shouted in her ear, "What the hell were you thinking?"

Hanratty was shouting for Ayres and Keene to help him. Taylor, his face a nightmarish mask of blood and anger, struggled against the hands restraining him. The crew split into camps, with some trying to tug Cass out of the galley under Hanratty's shouted orders, others trying to subdue Taylor, while still others tried to quell the panic and rage that had destroyed the night's festive atmosphere with an explosion of violence and recrimination. Jun's suicide seemed forgotten.

While Ayres and Beth Muñez tried to pacify the crowd, Hanratty, Deb, and Keene bundled Cass out of the galley and down the hall toward the administration offices. Taylor followed them, cursing and holding a napkin to his nose. The procession was an awkward tangle of bodies and emotions, with Cass struggling against the three of them. The shouts and bellows of the uproar behind them faded.

They dragged Cass through to Hanratty's office, where she was shoved into a guest chair. Cass, caught between crying and snarling, bruised, simultaneously cold and white hot, seethed.

Hanratty tossed a box of tissues from his desk to Taylor. "Clean yourself up and get out to the lab."

"Make sure you get rid of the evidence," Cass called as Taylor walked out holding a wad of tissues to his nose. He shot her a dark look as he left.

Hanratty signaled for Keene to close the door, then he came around his desk to sit on the edge. He stared at Cass with a searing, predatory look. "Talk."

"Talk? About what? About how you've been setting us up? Pushing buttons and watching the results while people *kill* themselves?"

"Start from the beginning. Why were you at COBRA in the first place?"

She struggled to stay calm. "Pete asked me to take Jun's midwinter dinner out to him since he couldn't join the party. I tried to follow the flag line out to COBRA, but someone had pulled up and relocated the last dozen stakes and the end was simply . . . fluttering in the wind."

Hanratty's eyebrows shot upward and he glanced at Deb. "Catch Taylor and warn him about the flag line."

She nodded and hurried out of the office, calling after the security chief. Hanratty turned back to Cass. "You're saying someone sabotaged the flag line? Misplaced it on purpose?"

"No, I'm saying *you* or someone you ordered to move the flag line did it on purpose."

"I didn't. But let's leave that for a moment. What happened then?"

"I made it to the lab and went inside," Cass said. "When I called for Jun, there was no answer. I searched the cubes, found an e-mail lying open on his desk supposedly from his wife—asking for a divorce—and a minute later, I found Jun hanging from the top of the dish antenna."

"And you think Jun killed himself because of the contents of his wife's e-mail?"

"You mean *your* e-mail?"

Hanratty sighed. "Jennings, do you realize how delusional you sound? I'm not a wizard, manipulating people so they kill themselves upon my command. If I had that much control, why didn't I calm down that fracas that you started in the galley? Or smooth things over after the power outage?"

"You don't have to control a fire in order to start one," she said levelly. "You're not interested in containing what you do, you're interested in studying it."

He leaned back and crossed his arms over his chest. "And how do you know that?"

"All of these accidents, all of these crises, they've all been just too easily turned on, then turned off when things got out of control. No one saw Sheryl's body after she died, not even the only doctor on station. The power went out, but was magically restored precisely after the crew had reached an emotional tipping point."

"And I suppose Jun's suicide was just another facet of the experiment?"

"Everyone on base has known for weeks he's been having personal issues at home," Cass said bitterly.

"So someone wrote that e-mail to push him over the edge. Just to see if he'd kill himself?"

"*Yes.*"

He blanched. "That's insane."

"Any more than faking someone's death?" Hanratty opened his mouth, but she cut him off. "Look me in the eye and tell me that Sheryl Larkin actually died out on the ice back in February. Look me in the eye and tell me you didn't turn the power off just to see how they'd react. Look me in the eye and tell me this isn't all some kind of experiment."

Hanratty raised his head and quirked an eyebrow at Keene.

"No." The psychologist shook his head slowly. "It's not her. She's saying the right things, but I can't see any reason for her to storm into the party like she did and hope to get any useful data."

"Does it make any more sense to arrange for her to find Jun? It amounts to the same result."

Keene shook his head again. "Not even close, Jack. It's the difference between *being* the messenger and *observing* the messenger. The first would make no sense—being frog-marched to your office for an interrogation is an easily predictable outcome. If she's the Observer, where does that get her? She's neutralized and sitting in your office."

"But the second scenario is logical if he manipulated Cass into starting the panic," Hanratty said reluctantly. "Then he gets to sit back and record the crew's reaction."

Keene nodded. "Exactly. Cass is not our man. Put simply, if she were, she wouldn't have allowed herself to be brought here to your office."

"God damn," Hanratty said softly, looking back at Cass almost fondly. "I really thought it might be her."

"What are you talking about?" Cass demanded, turning in her chair to try and take in both of them. It was unnerving that Keene continued to stand behind her.

Hanratty ignored her. "Either way, we've got a hell of a mess on our hands and we need to contain it. Suggestions?"

Before Keene could answer, there was a knock on the door and Deb stuck her head into the room. Hanratty frowned. "What?"

"Taylor radioed." Deb tried speaking, couldn't, cleared her throat. "Jun is dead."

"Damn it." Hanratty's eyes flicked from Cass to Keene and back to Deb. "What's happening with the crew?"

"People are losing their shit, is what's happening." Her voice started high and climbed the scale. "Jack, you need to make an appearance or we're going to have some major issues."

"Get Taylor on the horn and tell him to get back ASAP, then head for the galley and help Ayres stabilize things. I'll join you in two minutes." The door closed with a soft bump. Hanratty looked at Keene again, his eyes slightly wild. "I need some ideas, Gerald."

"We need to calm people down and start looking for the Observer. No more tiptoeing. No more pretending we don't know what's going on. No more playing within his sphere of influence. I'm not sure we're dealing with a rational or even sane person. At the rate the situation is escalating, the next test may not only be lethal, it will be widespread."

"What are the two of you talking about?" Cass demanded.

"What about her?" Hanratty gestured as if she were a piece of furniture.

"She's volatile and a liability. The Observer obviously used her to spark full-scale unrest among the crew. She's smart and generally well liked. If you let her run amok among the personnel, she'll have them burn this place to the ground. We'll never flush out the Observer then, because we'll be too busy keeping our heads above water."

"So . . . ?"

"I think we need to reduce our liabilities."

Cass turned in her chair in time to see Keene reach into a breast pocket and pull out a flat, black case the size of a cell phone. From it, he withdrew a prefilled syringe, removed the cap, and flicked the barrel to force an air bubble out. Eyes wide, she opened her mouth to scream when Hanratty suddenly pinned her in the chair with his shoulder and knee. Ignoring her yell of protest, he grabbed her right forearm in both of his hands and forced her palm upward, exposing the soft, white underside of her forearm and the blue veins beneath. Cass began screaming as she understood what they were trying to do. She clawed at Hanratty's neck with her free arm.

"Hurry," Hanratty said through gritted teeth. "She's strong."

Keene stroked his thumb along the vein that stood out from the skin of Cass's arm, then tried unsuccessfully to push the needle in. "Hold her."

"I'm trying, goddammit."

On the fourth attempt, Keene hit the vein and pushed the plunger to its limit. "Don't let up. This could take a minute."

Cass screamed insults at them as long as she could but, driven by her slamming pulse, the drug slipped like quicksilver up her arm. Even as she started in on a new round of curses, she felt herself falling away, tumbling through layers of gossamer and spider lace until her head slumped forward on her chest and she was out.

CHAPTER THIRTY-SIX

Taylor swore loudly and jerked his head up.

Out of long habit, he'd rested his face against his fist as he read over the report he was crafting. But doing so put pressure right below his broken nose, sending streaks of pain followed by dull, but insistent, throbs up into his cheeks, forehead, and eyes.

Gingerly, he explored a spot behind his jaw where he could put his fist so that he could continue with the report. It was doubly irksome because the document had been Hanratty's idea, not his, a bit of bureaucratic bullshit that the station manager thought might save their asses at trial—if the consequences of what had been done at Shackleton ever made it that far.

It was incredibly frustrating to sit at a desk, writing a report that would never see the light of day, when what they should be doing was getting out into the crowd, cracking skulls and getting in people's faces. But when he'd proposed the idea to Hanratty, he'd been shot down.

The station manager had the same reaction as so many others Taylor had tried to advise over the years; they mistook his hands-on approach as simplistic bullying. But Taylor wasn't a Neanderthal and he wasn't stupid. Sheer physical intimidation wasn't going to silence the kind of people who came to Antarctica. Pressing a crowd already teetering on the edge into doing things, *agreeing* to things, that they might normally find difficult to defend . . . well, that was another story.

Early on in his career—fresh out of training, his sheriff's star still shiny and new, with his security work for TransAnt still years away—he'd learned to use the tactic on prison guards who hadn't liked some of his more distasteful methods of keeping the general population under control. The formula had been simple. Shove them, alone, into the cage with a three-hundred-pound lifer jacked up on hooch and looking at solitary for six months. Give them a baton or a can of pepper spray. Faced with taking a beating or dishing one out, the whistleblowers suddenly seemed more open to the idea of using violence to maintain order. Once the potential whistleblowers had become part of the so-called problem, complaints to oversight boards and humanitarian agencies simply evaporated. Balance was restored.

It was the reason he'd counseled Hanratty to allow Ayres and Deb into their little circle. If the time ever came when they had to answer for the extreme measures they'd taken to keep order at Shackleton, the very people who'd opposed them and could report on their actions the most accurately were suddenly culpable. Extend the idea out to include everyone on base—whether they were willing participants or not—and your ass was covered. As much as it could be with the clusterfuck that had become this year's winter-over.

Unfortunately, that didn't seem likely to happen. Hanratty had convinced himself that all that was needed to salvage the crew's tattered confidence and flagging morale was a stern, honest talk. The man thought he was some kind of great orator, capable of leading the masses by the power of his voice.

The station manager lacked authority—with a single summer and a disastrous winter under his belt, he wasn't veteran enough to impress anyone—but more importantly, he didn't seem to have even a rudimentary feel for people, and more than once Taylor had sensed a bit of false theatricality, as though Hanratty had learned how to lead people from reading it in a book or during a weekend seminar. The possibility that he was a fake scared Taylor more than anything that had happened, because he'd seen what happened when a dangerous population sensed a poser. They turned on you, became a mob, and then there was no getting their trust—or fear—back.

He felt that same danger now that he'd felt walking the halls in lockup. Jennings was the spark that had lit the fuse to the powder keg. A chunk of the crew had stopped working after her performance in the galley, preferring instead to hole up in their berths or hunker down together in labs or workstations to wait. Wait for what, nobody knew, but backing into a corner was an instinctive reaction to danger. The next step was to lash out.

At least he'd convinced most of the operations people to keep going. The cooks and fuelies and other maintenance specialists understood that their collective survival depended on keeping the base running. The scientists, oblivious to the need to keep the infrastructure going, seemed to be the ones who wanted to either pull the blankets up over their heads or come out swinging.

He closed his eyes briefly. It wasn't anything they couldn't handle. As long as they could keep the general population calm or at least subdued, they could start splitting individuals off for questioning until they found the goddamned Observer and stopped the next harebrained stress test.

A shout from the outer admin office jerked Taylor's head up a second time. Several voices, men's voices, swelled, each trying to be heard over the others. You didn't have to hear the words to know the emotion: they were angry. He shot to his feet and headed for the door, the report forgotten. He had a feeling that the spark had reached the keg.

CHAPTER THIRTY-SEVEN

As it probably had for every prisoner in history, the sound of the key turning in the lock woke Cass, pulling her up like a fish from an ocean of sleep.

With her heart thudding like a trip hammer, she rolled to a sitting position, ready to defend herself, attack, or run, not knowing which option was best. The door opened a crack, then widened by cautious inches until Biddi stuck her head into the room like a turtle poking its head out of its shell. "Anyone home?"

"Oh, my Jesus Christ." Cass almost cried at seeing the familiar moon face. "How glad am I to see you?"

"Loads and loads, I hope," her friend said, coming into the room and shutting the door behind her quietly. She gave Cass a hug, holding her at arm's length and looking her over. "You're keeping well."

"Jokes? At a time like this?"

Biddi motioned for them to sit on the edge of the bed. "Is there a better time? The bloody world—by which I mean our little microcosm of said here at the South Pole—has gone barking mad. If you can't laugh now, there's no hope for you. And, look, they even installed you in the VIP suite. The last person to grace this room was a senator."

"It's because it has its own bathroom," Cass said bitterly. "Not because they want to treat me well."

"Oh, well. At least it has a queen-sized bed, love."

Cass sighed. Lovable, unflappable Biddi. But what she needed was information, not a cheerleader. "So, nothing's changed? They're not letting me out?"

A look of sympathy said it all. Cass's heart sank, but it had been a forlorn hope to begin with. Hanratty wouldn't have sent Biddi to spring her if they'd changed their mind—he would've done it himself or sent Taylor or Deb to do it—but she'd had a wild hope that that's why her friend had showed up.

"So, what are you doing here, Biddi? Not that I'm ungrateful. You're just taking a risk, is all."

Her friend jerked a thumb behind her to indicate the rest of the station. "Mr. High and Mighty pulled everyone together for another one of his helpful all-hands meetings in the gym. I listened to the first half then snuck out, recognizing that it was the perfect time to come visit my fellow janitor. The only time, really."

"No one knows you're here? How'd you get in?"

Biddi looked at her with pity. "Love, we're janitors. The first day I came down, I made sure they gave me the keys to every door in the building. Never heard of a master key?"

Cass laughed despite herself. "You're shitting me. Any chance you could, say, lend me that key for a minute?"

Biddi shook her head. "I'm afraid not. Not because I don't want to, Cassie, but because . . . where would you go? This place is as good as Alcatraz. Better, really."

"It would just be nice to have some freedom back." The mania subsided, replaced by a black anger. "Those fuckers drugged me."

Biddi's mouth made an "o" of shock. "I should've guessed they would need to do something that extreme to toss you in the hoosegow, but I never imagined they'd actually go through with something so . . . wrong."

Cass put a hand to her forehead. "I don't even know how long I've been locked up."

"You don't?" Biddi asked, curious.

"How would I?" Cass said, rubbing her forearm. Aside from bruises where Hanratty's hands had held her down and the puncture wounds where Keene had fumbled for a vein, there were small red dots near the crook of her elbow. "But judging from this, they kept me under and maybe even stuck an IV in me for a while."

Biddi looked at her brightly. "Good news, love. You've been out for four months. Winter is over."

"Biddi, goddammit."

She gave a small, apologetic smile. "You found Jun—poor, poor man—at midwinter's. Today is the twenty-sixth, so five days."

"My God." Now that she had an actual number, a wave of anger and nausea rippled through her body. "I've got to get the hell out of here."

"And I repeat, dear heart, to do what? Go where? When Hanratty or his little minion Taylor catches you in the hall, what will happen?"

Cass shivered. *Another needle. And this time, maybe no waking up.*

"For right now," Biddi continued, "they've got you locked up, sure, but they can't imprison you any more than they already have and they can't keep you any longer than the normal winter-over."

"They've gone over the edge, Biddi. They could dump me in the middle of an ice field just to get rid of me."

Biddi hesitated. "I don't disagree with you, Cassie, but—while I think there are some who sided with you when you read the riot act to our esteemed leader—there are others who might feel relieved to hang a scapegoat, if only to have someone to blame. It's bollocks, I know, but if you sit tight and don't bring attention to yourself, you won't give any of them an excuse to do something drastic. You're safe as houses staying here compared to the madness raging out there."

"That's the second time you've mentioned it. What's going on?"

Biddi hunched forward conspiratorially, but she was already whispering. "Things have been falling apart since they tossed you in the dungeon. The things you, ah, mentioned at the midwinter party seemed to hit quite a nerve."

"About the experiment?"

"Yes. It made sense to quite a few people. Two of Dave's fuelie comrades, Jeremy and Sam, went to the manager with their concerns."

"And?"

"And he had them thrown out of his office. Upon which, they made an attempt to take over the administration office and place Mr. Hanratty under arrest."

"Jesus. What happened?"

"Taylor made short work of them, sad to say. Apparently, while the two of them were tinkering with fuel lines and playing video games, Mr. Taylor was earning his black belt in any number of martial arts."

Cass blanched. "Are they . . . ?"

"He hurt them bad enough to put them in the trauma center. Dr. Ayres was very upset and told me privately he's going to bring charges against Taylor as soon as all of this is over. My sweet Dave is beside himself."

"When did this happen?"

"The day after they tossed you in here. Our dear leader has a near mutiny on his hands and knows it. I believe he's hoping by bringing everyone together he can present his side of the story and save his hide by shifting the blame to someone else."

"Someone else? Who?" Biddi had said the words matter-of-factly and without emphasis, but now she tilted her head, giving Cass a pointed look. "*Me?* What do I have to do with it?"

"I left before people started asking questions, but he said that there was, indeed, an experiment of sorts going on. Then he started holding forth about some kind of psychological mumbo jumbo beyond me. I'm just a bloody fucking janitor, after all."

"He actually admitted it?"

"I just said so, didn't I? That wasn't the real revelation, though. He claimed that he was as much a subject of the experiment as anyone else. Someone else, another crew member posing as a staffer, has been pulling the strings the whole time."

"Who?"

Biddi rolled her eyes. "*You*, obviously. Haven't you been paying attention?"

"Jesus, Biddi."

"I'm sorry, bird," she said, and now Cass could see her friend, for all her banter, was worried. Dark blue smudges hung beneath each eye and her normally rosy cheeks were sallow. She raised a hand to tuck a loose lock of hair behind her ear; the hand trembled. "It's not a joke, I know, but the whole thing has been terrifying."

"Who is this mastermind supposed to be?"

"Hanratty calls him—or you, I suppose—the Observer, like some comic book villain."

"Keene said something about that when they had me in Hanratty's office. I didn't know what they were talking about," Cass said, scowling at the memory. "And people believe his bullshit?"

Biddi shrugged, deflated and out of jokes now. "It makes as much sense as anything else, doesn't it?"

"And he's trying to convince everyone that I'm the one? I'm this Observer?"

"I'm afraid so." She paused. "People are scared, Cass. Hanratty knows he doesn't have to be right, he just has to sound good. Whatever will keep the crew from turning on him. And you, as a distraction, will do."

Cass put her face in her hands and spoke through them, her voice muffled. "It doesn't make any sense. Why would I come screaming back to base and accuse him of running the experiment if I'm actually the one behind it all?"

"He'd simply say you were upping the ante on the test, I imagine. Stoking the fire and turning people against him just to see what they'd do. Like the bit about Sheryl still being alive."

"She is," Cass said bitterly. "I'm sure of it. But he'd simply say I was taking advantage of a psychologically traumatic event in order to utilize it for the experiment."

"Now you're thinking like a true bastard," Biddi said. "I do believe you know how his mind works."

"What happens now? Are they going to listen to him? Is the lynch mob coming?"

Biddi clucked her tongue. "Don't get too maudlin, darling. They're not all mad dogs. I imagine that even if Hanratty persuades them to his way of thinking, he'll do no more than tell everyone to leave you right here and let the 'authorities'—whoever that is—decide once they get communications back up or, God forbid, after the winter runs its course and the first plane comes back."

"Christ," she said, trying to imagine the next four months in a literal, instead of figurative, prison. Then a thought occurred to her. "What happens when the 'accidents' keep happening? What's Hanratty going to do then?"

"Good news! You'll be exonerated."

"And someone else might be dead. That's not good enough," Cass said. Then, when her friend hesitated, "Spit it out, Biddi."

"Before Commander Jack's dog-and-pony show, a few people were talking."

"About?"

Biddi paused, then sighed. "I think it's madness, but a few of the younger crew were talking about trying to make the trek overland to Orlova for help."

Cass's mouth fell open. "That's thirty miles away. In the dark. At a hundred below zero."

"You forgot the one-hundred-mile-an-hour winds."

Cass calculated the journey in terms of the obstacles, not the distance. With the darkness, the low temperatures, and the wind, the journey would take several days even by snowmobile or snowcat . . . but would you really want to drive it when, if you wandered even slightly off the SPoT, you could plunge headfirst into a two-hundred-foot crevasse? Walking, with the ability to plumb for ice bridges and faults, would be safer, but then you were talking a top speed of just a few miles a day. It would take a week to make it to the Russian base. No one on earth had the stamina and strength to survive the journey. She shook her head.

Biddi had been watching her and nodded grimly. "It's suicide."

"But they were willing to give it a try before Hanratty's speech?"

"They were willing to *talk* about it." Biddi gave a dishwater-thin smile. "Then they did the same figuring you just did and decided to hear what their station manager had to say for himself instead."

"So, my situation is to hang tight and let some kangaroo court decide my fate," Cass said bitterly. "While one of them is manipulating everyone. In fact, whoever the Observer is must've predicted this, right? When all the social norms start to break down and accusations start to fly, a full-scale revolt is the only logical outcome."

"If you say so. My bet is on Keene."

Cass waved her hand dismissively. "He's not smart enough."

"Maybe playing dumb is part of his master plan. Maybe it's an act."

Cass snorted. "Nobody's *that* good."

Biddi smiled again, then her face fell into sober lines and she stood. "I've got to get going, Cass. If anyone catches me here, they'll lock me up, too. Then where will we be?"

Cass grabbed her friend's hands and squeezed them. "Thanks for sneaking in, Biddi. Be my voice, okay?"

"Of course." Her friend looked at her closely. "Are you holding up all right?"

Cass thought about it. Her initial reaction upon waking up had been fear and shock that Hanratty and Keene had actually stooped to imprisoning her. But those emotions had been burnt away by a cold, seething anger . . . and a desire to get even. She wasn't sure where the newfound confidence was coming from, but if it was fueled by anger, she was prepared to use it.

"I'm good. Ready to punch Hanratty in the mouth if I get a chance. But good."

Biddi nodded, satisfied. "That's exactly how I predicted you'd handle this. Take care, birdie. I'll be back when I can."

Cass watched her slip out the door, closing it quietly behind her and turning the key in the lock, the sound every prisoner in history had dreaded.

CHAPTER THIRTY-EIGHT

"You're sure there's nothing I can do to help?"

Carla's smile was a just-courteous baring of her teeth. "Unless you double majored in astrophysics and advanced biology, no."

Anne's face closed down like a light had been turned off. "Sorry. I'll just sit in the corner, then."

Carla turned back to her desk, her smile turning into a grimace. Her friend had a martyrish streak to her that hadn't been obvious before things at Shackleton had started going to hell in a handbasket. As the chaos around them had gone from the manageable to the unimaginable, Carla had fled to her work in the lab for solace, counting on the structure and stability of science to help her make sense of the madness that had taken ahold of the station.

Withdrawal wasn't a logical reaction, she knew. Sticking her head in the sand made little sense; rationally, the deaths of some colleagues and the imprisonment of others meant that the survival of the base was at stake. And, if the station—as well as her life—was in jeopardy, then it followed that her work was, by most measures, irrelevant.

But Shackleton had changed her. She had attempted to take charge during the power outage, trusting in and valuing her own innate authority and intelligence. The results had been terrifying, even aside from her own injury. Even now, remembering the chaos and the primal fear that had overtaken the crew took her breath away. Forced to sit in her darkened berth for days, nursing her concussion, she'd come to the conclusion that they'd all been at the mercy of the environment since stepping foot onto the continent. Whether it was through the actions of other people as Cass would have them believe or freezing to death on the godforsaken plain outside the station, she'd come to realize that drive, ambition, and intelligence didn't mean shit in Antarctica. Your plans, hopes, and dreams were about as meaningful and permanent as footprints in the snow on the other side of this wall.

The thought jogged her memory, and she remembered some old-timer during training telling them that Antarctica wanted to kill them. He'd been wrong. It didn't just *want* to kill them; it *would* kill them.

In the face of that, she was comfortable with, perhaps even proud of, her own newfound myopia. If extending oneself outwardly didn't work, she might as well turn inward, and for Carla, that meant her work since her time in the lab was simply an extension of her identity. To lose her life would be only slightly more jarring than losing her work—ergo, she'd prefer to die rather than sacrifice her experiments. Had she been a laborer on the *Titanic*, she would've been polishing handrails and setting tables while others jumped for the lifeboats. Let someone else man the oars or shout hoarsely from an upper deck.

Anne, on the other hand, seemed unable to cope with either the change of circumstances at the station or the particular tragedy of Jun's suicide. She had refused to go back to work at the COBRA building or even the in-station astrophysics lab down the hall, putting a huge amount of stress on the remaining two astrophysicists to do the work of four and drawing Hanratty's ire. Many of the other staff members, without the luxury of being able to stop working, weren't happy with her, either.

Carla, unable to comprehend the mind of someone who preferred not to work over any other option, would've resented Anne, too, had her friend not come and begged her to let her stay in the biology lab. Initially reluctant, Carla had given in after one of the scientists had told her something that only a few knew: Anne's father had hanged himself when she was a little girl. On the first shift after Jun's death, Anne had trekked out to the COBRA building to sign on for her twelve hours, only to return screaming, claiming she'd seen her father's body hanging from the top of the antenna.

But now Carla was barely hanging on to her own sanity because Anne—in emotional turmoil, but still possessed of a scientist's mindset—had insisted on helping Carla with biology experiments she was unqualified to perform. The stress of the situation on base plus Anne's insistent presence had brought Carla's concussion-induced headaches back full-time, making her snap at the slightest provocation. Now the two of them were both on edge, no work was getting done, and Carla was close to kicking her friend out into the hall.

Instead, she gritted her teeth for three seconds, relaxed her jaw, and turned around with as genuine a smile as she could muster. "This sequence really is a one-person job. If I could clone myself, I still wouldn't be able to help. But what I *could* use is a good jolt of coffee. If you wouldn't mind playing intern for a minute, could you run down to the galley and grab me a cup?"

"You're serious? You want me to fetch coffee?"

"Don't think of it as fetching," Carla said brightly. "Think of it as providing field support. If I'm going to get the most out of this latest round of tests, I've got to stay awake and alert for the next twelve hours. Only coffee and good conversation is going to make that happen."

Anne looked wounded, but nodded and said, "Black, right?"

"Just like my test results," Carla quipped. She got a slight lift of the lips in return, then Anne headed outside and down the hall to the galley.

Carla stifled a sigh. Anne was going to have to either lighten up or get back to work, or there'd be more than a couple casualties before the winter was over. She winced. She could be an insensitive bitch at times. She didn't know where it came from. Jun had been a nice man, after all, and Sheryl had always been polite and cheerful. Carla frowned. Assuming Sheryl was actually dead, of course; Cass's accusations had gotten everyone talking, but Carla preferred to deal with the facts that she could see in front of her. Until she saw the proof that Sheryl's death had been faked, the woman remained dead to her.

She sighed, getting back to the problem at hand: Anne. She'd racked her brain trying to come up with things for her friend to do around the lab, but the work wasn't just specialized for someone with a PhD in biology; most of the tests and experiments had been specifically devised by Carla for herself to perform. Space for busy work—mentally, physically, and professionally—just didn't exist. In truth, Anne's running out to get coffee was probably the most useful thing she could've done. Carla let her eyes meander around the lab, trying to dream up fake tests and bogus tasks she could give Anne when she got back, a kind of work placebo, but nothing came to mind.

Stop wasting time, she chided herself. The only thing that could make the situation worse would be if Carla squandered the time she'd been given after successfully getting Anne out of the lab. She'd just toss her another bone when the time came. Carla cleared her mind and bent over the slides she'd been working on.

❄

Anne stalked down the hall toward the galley, seething. Rationally, she could understand Carla's need to get rid of her—if the situation had been reversed and Carla had insisted on pestering her in the middle of an analysis of COBRA data, she would've hit her with a laptop—but she had trouble, had *always* had trouble, when her friends had appeared to abandon or dismiss her. It fostered in her a profound sadness that twisted and transformed into a deep-seated anger she had difficulty defusing.

Worse, with an analytical mind like hers, she knew exactly where the anger came from. But no amount of left-brain analysis had ever overcome her right-brain emotion. Simply put, if she could, she would go back in time and kill her father.

She'd come to the conclusion long ago that the burden of guilt she would bear from killing a parent couldn't compare to the cross she'd been forced to bear when, as a seven-year-old in a daisy-patterned dress, she'd discovered her father hanging from the second-floor banister of their Providence brownstone. Anything would be preferable to that.

Two of her friends had come over to play, and when she'd turned to them, hysterical, for help and advice, they'd laughed at her and accused her of making up stories. Since then, any time thoughts of her father and an image of his slack body resting still and motionless in the stairwell invaded her head—when she'd looked up at the dish antenna and was sure she'd seen him hanging from the steel catwalk, but shod in Jun's threadbare sneakers—they were accompanied by the light, scornful laughter of little girls.

Anne pressed her hands to her face, willing the image and the sound away, desperately trying to put the look of pity and impatience on Carla's face into perspective, trying to rationalize to herself why her friend's charity and tolerance might be wearing thin enough to send her on a bullshit mission in search of coffee.

"Get ahold of yourself, Klimt," she said out loud, startling herself, but the sound died in the dead walls of the station. No one was around to hear her, which, not long ago, would have struck her as strange. Even on a winter-over, she should have run into a familiar face or two on the way to the galley, but since Cass's announcement at the midwinter party, people had chosen to hunker down in their berth or bury themselves in their work. Like some people she knew.

If she had any doubts that life at Shackleton wasn't proceeding normally, entering the galley put them to rest. The dining room was as empty as the halls and that was *definitely* not right. People on base ate and drank constantly for comfort and camaraderie. Not long ago, half the station would've congregated in the galley simply to be close to one another. Now, the room stood empty, and she could imagine herself as the only one alive on base. Alone, wandering the halls, looking for someone, anyone to talk to . . .

Stop that. Yes, there'd been two deaths, and a blistering chaos of violence and accusations, but forty-odd crew members still lived at the station. She wasn't the only human being left on earth, for Christ's sake. She moved deeper into the galley, hoping to see someone she'd missed.

"Pete?" she called, figuring the cook, at least, had to be around. When there weren't meals to be made or served, there were dishes to be washed and appliances to be maintained, right? But there was no answer. Despite the fact that she'd just left Carla in the biology lab five minutes before, the sensation that she was utterly alone returned in full force. It was like a ten-pound weight had suddenly appeared in her gut, dragging her to the floor.

Timidly, she walked across the galley to the coffee urns that were a mainstay at the base. Ignoring the decaf, she grabbed two porcelain diner cups from the rack and tilted the REGULAR urn forward, but she knew it was empty as soon as she touched it.

"Goddammit." She slammed the cup against the counter, cracking it, and turned to look around, as if there were a roomful of people to share her exasperation. Under normal circumstances, running out of coffee would have started a riot.

She grimaced. *Riot. Nice word choice.* While the fracas at the mid-winter party hadn't quite fit the definition, it had been close. And for better reasons than running out of coffee. But still, where the hell was everyone?

Anne called the names again, hoping that one of the kitchen grunts simply had their head in a bin and hadn't heard her, then bellied herself across the countertop, trying to see into the prep area without actually crossing the line from the dining room into the kitchen—a big no-no that earned an ass-chewing from Deb for violating sanitation guidelines. But there was no one.

Looking around again, this time guiltily, Anne scooted her butt onto the counter—*how's that for a sanitation violation, Deb?*—spun in place, and landed on the other side. No Pete. Maybe they'd run out for supplies?

In the meantime, there had to be coffee somewhere. Gingerly at first, then with more and more assertiveness, she proceeded to ransack the kitchen, tipping open boxes and peeking into cabinets, first in search of coffee and then, she had to admit to herself, simply because it was so much fun being nosy. A grin, unfamiliar but welcome, spread across her face. If she'd known it would be this much fun to snoop, she would've risked a demerit weeks ago.

Coffee was still her primary goal, however, and she continued the hunt into bins, boxes, and cupboards, but to no avail. She was about to open an upper cabinet when one of the freezers kicked on with a click and hum, scaring her half to death. One hand pressed to her chest, she leaned against a counter, trying to recover. Her heart hammered in her breast like a bird beating its wings against the bars of a cage. When the rhythm returned to normal, she moved on to opening boxes and plastic crates piled by the outer door, marveling at the amount of food needed to keep forty-four people alive.

Well, forty-three, now. Or is that forty-two? The thought came ugly, unbidden, and she recoiled, disgusted with herself, wondering where the hell it had come from. Childish laughter, light and cruel, lit along the edge of her mind and she slapped herself.

She stood there, panting, dissecting her thoughts and wondering if she were going insane. Her cheek burned where she'd struck it. She needed to move, needed to do something, or she was going to lose her mind.

Spastically, she began tearing open the lids of boxes, ripping open bags, knocking canisters, jars, and pots off of shelves. Tears trickled down her cheeks as jars tumbled to the ground and broke, scattering sugar and salt across the floor. The kitchen was filled with the reek of vinegar and cheese, the must of dried spices, the malted smells of rice and flour. Gasping, she hurled a box of dried milk across the room. It burst into a cloud of white powder and she gagged as a sickly sweet smell reminiscent of infant formula floated on the air.

"Jesus H. Christ on a stick."

Anne froze at the voice, slowly turning to face the bulging eyes of Pete Ozment. He stood in the doorway to the hall, one foot holding the outer door open. Trailing behind him was a large cart with boxes stacked three deep.

"Anne? What in blazes are you doing?"

Her mouth opened, unable to articulate a sound at first. Granules of powdered milk floated downward in the space between them. Finally, when his eyebrows hit the top of his hairline, she said simply, "I was looking for coffee."

"Coffee?" He pushed the cart into the kitchen. It made small grinding sounds as it crushed salt and sugar crystals beneath its wheels. "This whole damn thing is full of coffee. I just busted my ass to bring back a hundred pounds of it from the warehouse and you wrecked my kitchen while I was doing it."

She stared, fish-mouthed, at the boxes, then up at Pete's frowning face. She couldn't help herself, and started to laugh. He looked as if he was going to explode, then threw his head back, put his hands on his hips, and started to laugh, too. More tears, from laughter this time, cascaded down her face. She choked out an apology in the middle of her cracking up.

"Coffee." He shook his head as his laughter wound down. "The girl wanted coffee."

They looked around at the mess she'd made and then they both got the giggles again. As Pete put his head back to guffaw once again, a large figure suddenly appeared in the hall behind him. Anne gasped.

Following her gaze over his shoulder, Pete started to turn, making it only partway before the figure raised an arm, then chopped down like a gate swinging shut. Something hit the cook on the top of the head with the sound of a wet hand-clap.

Pete made a burping sound, then took two tripping, tipping steps backward into the kitchen, sprawling across his cart and knocking boxes to the floor. Blood spilled from a rift in the crown of his head. His feet kicked once like a toy thrown to the ground.

Anne looked down in horror at the body, unable to comprehend what she'd just witnessed, then screamed as the bulky figure that had loomed in the doorway moved into the kitchen. A scream joined hers, playing counterpoint to the water-bright laughter in her head as the arm rose and fell.

CHAPTER THIRTY-NINE

Carla looked up from her microscope, annoyed. The noise that had broken her concentration, she realized, had crescendoed from a distant murmur into a collection of shouts and pounding feet that was impossible to ignore.

She frowned, only just remembering that Anne had gone in search of coffee for the two of them. She glanced at the clock . . . Jesus, she'd banished the poor woman almost an hour ago. Her mind, keen and pitilessly logical when it came to matters of biology, moved sluggishly in other circles and it took her a minute to connect the possibility that the fracas outside and the fact Anne hadn't come back yet might be related. She hesitated, then hurried for the door.

A crowd had bunched at the far end of the hall. Voices, punctuated by the occasional gasp or moan, filled the air. A primal sense of shared fear and crisis emanated from the group, causing doors to open and heads to pop out into the corridor. Carla took small, hesitant steps, drawn magnetically to the gathering.

"On your left," someone barked behind her, and she pressed herself against the wall. Dr. Ayres trotted past her with a trauma kit in one hand, his face a professionally blank mask that scared her more than any amount of screaming or yelling. She hurried after him. The knot of people parted to let Ayres through, then re-formed behind him. In that brief second, she got a glimpse of a body sprawled on the ground, legs askew, a scarlet pool welling underneath the boots.

Carla's cool, scientific detachment vanished, like a hat knocked off her head. In an instant she knew that she hadn't really managed the anxiety that had been building inside her, she'd only packed it away and smoothed it over with a veneer of professional detachment. At any moment, all that had been needed was the right set of circumstances to pry open that box and unleash every pent-up emotion she thought she'd jettisoned. This was that moment.

A scream rose inside her as she pelted down the hall toward the boots and the blood.

❄

Hanratty paced his office floor, wiped his hands on his khakis, then frowned at the mannerism. It smacked of weakness, of sweaty palms and regret, and he clasped them together to keep it from happening again. He was in the soup, no doubt about it, but things were far from over.

The meeting in the gym had gone as well as could be expected. He knew from the start that he'd win some of the crew, he'd lose some of them, and some had long since left his sphere of influence. It was a lesson learned in Afghanistan, when his vision had blurred and he'd stopped seeing his men as individuals and instead seen groups of bodies, factions breaking along lines of personality and temperament.

There had been three simple divisions. The men in the center were the bravest. The ones along the sides, clumped together, had courage but questioned everything he said. And the ones haunting the back were the cowards.

He'd hated the last group, despised them. Not because of any innate moral judgment. Not because society had told him to. Not even because, soldier-to-soldier, you feared and loathed the ones who wouldn't be there for you when you needed them most. He hated them because he knew them as he knew himself.

He was a coward. Always had been. Always would be.

In twenty-three years of traveling the world to do America's dirtiest jobs, he'd never had to prove his courage one way or the other. That was the modern army. You could fight for a lifetime and never see combat, even while your country was at war. Acting angry and barking orders didn't take any special courage or talent. You just had to act the part and everything seemed to work out.

Until that day when he'd seen his men broken up into those groups, knew which one he should've slunk over to and joined . . . but couldn't. Because he had to lead them, lead them all. Right up that valley, where the kill rate was fifty percent and every inch of the floor had been marked off and measured by their snipers. Then all of you began to jog and your kit was flapping against your back and hitting your legs and your lid was slipping down over your eyes and you were waiting for the slug to hit you like a truck and oh, Christ, two of your men had had their heads taken off and now the rest were scrambling for cover and shouting to you, screaming, wanting to know what you were going to do to save them. *Help me, Captain! Captain, please!* He'd crouched behind a rock, bleeding tears, watching his men die. Jesus Christ, he would've given anything at that moment, done anything, to know why he was frozen in place, his mind an uncomprehending mass of fear, to know how he could've been built differently to help his men, to help himself . . .

"Jack!"

Hanratty spun in place, staring at Taylor as though he'd been dropped from the sky. His chief of security must've come through the office door, but if he had, Hanratty hadn't heard him. He looked down at his palms. Not sweating now, but bleeding from where his nails had pierced the skin. He put on his best CO scowl. "What is it?"

Taylor's face, normally impassive, was apprehensive. "We've got a problem. Dave Boychuck has some of the techs wound up. Sounds like they might try storming the castle like those two idiots."

"They're coming here?"

"Not yet. They saw what I did to their buddies. I think they'll try something at night, try to catch us napping, literally."

"How in the world do you know that?"

"I've got a source."

"Who is it?" Hanratty asked, annoyed. He'd had his own tattletales in the crew, but he could've used a little edge before things had gone down the shitter.

Taylor opened his mouth to reply when the door to the outer office banged open. Taylor moved aside as Deb appeared in the doorway, breathless and trembling.

Hanratty's stomach dropped. "What's wrong now?"

Her face twisted like a wrung dish rag. "Jack. Oh, God."

"Tell me."

"Beth just found Anne and Pete in the kitchen. They've . . . someone beat them, badly."

"Beat them? Beat them how?"

"I don't know." She looked sick. "With a pipe or a hammer, maybe?"

"Jesus H.," he said, coming around the desk and brushing past her to head for the outer door. "Has Ayres seen them? Did you get them down to trauma?"

"Jack," she said, and he stopped. She hadn't followed him. "They're not hurt. They're dead."

❄

In all the time he'd spent in recovery centers observing patients who'd given up their lives to controlled substances, over the course of the many years spent in psychiatric wards charting the symptoms of PTSD, grief, and mental illness, Keene had never heard a scream like the one that rang down the hall from the galley.

The scream had straightened him up in his seat and he'd snatched open the door before he was even aware that he was standing. Paralyzed, he stood in the doorway, aware of a commotion down the hall to his left, but unable to command his body to move. A moment later, Hanratty, Deb, and Taylor were running down the hall to his left. Their backs were stiff, body language alarming. He called for them to stop or explain, but they ignored him.

As he watched the trio disappear, a feeling of finality came over him, the sensation that something he'd been waiting for had finally shown its face. A flush of blood curled from his scalp to his scrotum. He savored the feeling, analyzing it. *Is this what terror feels like?*

He debated with himself. Follow and identify the danger? Ignore it at his own peril? Follow . . . better to know than not. He turned to close his door—*what a curiously civilized, meaningless gesture*—and found that his hand was shaking. He hurried down the hall.

The group was gathered outside the door to the galley's kitchen. Hanratty and Taylor were both shouting, trying to restore some kind of order, but managing only to increase the tension. A second scream rang out, then, a true banshee's wail, starting low and rising almost out of hearing. The flush he'd felt moments before came back, but it seemed to well out of his heart and rush upwards to the tips of his ears. He realized he'd bared his teeth and his hands were balled into fists. Keene slowed as he approached the group, unable to tear his eyes away from the scene.

A pool of blood had run out into the hall from the kitchen doorway, filling in the gap between a pair of legs resting akimbo. Several people had gotten too close; the pool now had footprints along its edge, the tread marks making the scene somehow more horrific. A handful pointed beyond the body, hands to mouths. Intrigued despite himself, he moved so that he could see what had captured their attention. Taller than most, he could look over the crowd directly into the galley kitchen.

The room was a tableau of hell.

Blood bathed the sinks and counters and appliances; it had clumped with flour or salt to form obscene cakes on the floor. The source was the back of what was left of a man's pulped skull, unidentifiable due to the damage and the small mercy that he was lying facedown. Boxes and bins of food were scattered everywhere, their contents littering the floor and tabletops, thrown into corners and draped over chairs. Farther inside the kitchen sprawled another body, a woman possibly, although it was hard to tell. Ron Ayres and Beth Muñez were working frantically on the inert form.

The scream rang out a third time, jerking his attention back to the group. The source of the scream was a woman bundled in the center of the crowd, with an almost unobstructed view into the kitchen. Keene realized with a start that it was Carla Bjorkholm; her face, twisted with horror, had been unrecognizable at first.

The sound seemed to galvanize the knot of people. Heads turned to confront Hanratty and Taylor. Faces were contorted, pale and red and purple, squinting with anger. Voices, low and ugly, sheared off into the hysterical, screaming for answers. Taylor, with his limited, one-gear mentality, was barking at people, assuming he could clear them out and restore order through sheer force of will. Keene almost felt sorry for the man, who didn't understand that bullying only worked on a population receptive to it. A crowd of people driven by anger or fear to ignore authoritarian hierarchies was not just immune to being shouted at, it was inflamed by it.

Keene watched as Taylor, frustrated by the lack of response, shoved Dave back from the pool of blood. Dave cursed and grabbed the security chief's wrist. Taylor, moving fast, reached out and twisted the fuelie's entire hand upside down. Something in the wrist seemed to give, Dave's face went white, then the big man bellowed in pain.

That was all Keene needed to see. He turned and retraced his steps back to his office. It didn't take a psychic to sense the group was a hair away from exploding. If Hanratty had been possessed of real guts and a defter touch, he might've talked them down. But he didn't and he couldn't and Taylor was precisely the wrong catalyst, a rock-head with too much authority and the problem-solving sensitivity of an ape. The man was so ill-suited to the task of calming a distressed group of people that Keene wondered idly if the Observer's reach was so great that he'd somehow arranged for Taylor to be present at precisely the wrong place at the right time.

He picked up his pace as the shouts took on a different tone. Anger, of course. Outrage. And the most frightening of all, release.

He had tried to warn both Hanratty and Taylor that the crew—ostensibly selected for their self-sufficient, take-charge attitude—couldn't be put off forever, that they wouldn't be satisfied with half-truths and orders to obey some arbitrary chain of command. They were used to thinking and acting independently. It was obvious that, between the scripted accidents and whatever insanity the Observer had planned, everyone on base was being primed to reach a breaking point. How and when they handled it could spell the difference between a group that worked together to get out of a jam or an all-out riot spiraling down into anarchy and violence. Keene knew which way the group was tipping.

He reached his office nauseated and shivering, perhaps a delayed reaction to the scene in the kitchen or maybe anger at the inevitability of it all. He'd told Hanratty to do some major damage control sooner, long before midwinter and the communications debacle. Then Jennings had stormed in, dropped her fucking bombshell, and suddenly it looked like all of them were in a conspiracy. The moment had been lost and now this was the result.

Keene had started making plans of his own as soon as he saw Hanratty and Taylor marching down the garden path. With the fitness level one might expect from a fifty-one-year-old psychologist, there was no way he was going to risk an overland trek to the Russian base, but neither was he going to hole up in his office with the desk blocking the door. At some point, someone was going to decide that the base psychologist had to have been behind the experiment and he wasn't going to wait to see what kind of mob showed up looking for answers.

A few days after the power had gone out, sensing a seismic shift in how Shackleton's psychic environment had changed, he'd started making nightly treks down the Beer Can and into the ice tunnels, moving his most important files, batteries, food, and other supplies into a hidey-hole just off the main artery. He had no illusions about surviving the four months until help arrived in November; he just had to hunker down, stay safe, and wait until the fire had burnt itself out. Then, maybe, he could resurface, perhaps reestablish communications and leave this nightmare.

In his office, he moved quickly, staying long enough to scoop only the most critical pieces of his work into a backpack. He spared a last look, feeling nothing but revulsion for the little space—the books, the paintings, the stupid fucking fish—then flipped the lights off and hurried out, locking the door behind him.

He paused to glance down the hall: the knot of people was seething, wrestling, breaking each other's bones and hearts and trust. Involuntarily, his lip curled. *They got what they deserved.*

He turned in the opposite direction and headed for the Beer Can. When the shots rang out, he stopped in his tracks, shocked. Then he broke into a run, realizing in a wash of insight that even he had underestimated just how bad things had gotten.

❄

Hanratty didn't know when the situation had gotten so out of hand.

Someone had punched him in the side of the head and it ached from the cheek up to the temple, while a dull throbbing emanated from his thigh where someone else had kicked him. One hand held the collar of someone's shirt—the face was so twisted with anger, he couldn't recognize him—then the face was whipped away, replaced by a woman's clawed hand raking at his eyes.

Throughout the melee, he was aware of Taylor shouting hoarsely, threatening people with detention if they didn't clear out. Hanratty fought the urge to laugh—the fool was telling the genie to get back into the bottle *or else*. It had explained a lot, he thought, when he'd found out that Taylor was not nearly the international mercenary soldier he'd initially claimed, but instead had been a sheriff's deputy at a Louisiana jail before working security at a few TransAnt facilities. And now his inexperience was coming home to roost.

Hanratty pushed the woman—he finally recognized her as Beth Muñez—away and shouted to Taylor, "Back up, back up! We've got to get to the office and regroup."

Taylor, his normally flat expression twisted into fury, didn't seem to hear him. He was struggling with Dave Boychuck, who, even with his wrist broken, was still wrestling the security chief one-handed. From nowhere, someone took a swing at Taylor, landing a weak punch that the chief caught on a hunched shoulder. The second attack seemed to trigger something in Taylor; he lashed out a kick that buckled Dave's knee, punched him in the throat for good measure, then backed up.

Hanratty felt he was seeing something in reverse that he'd already viewed; he knew the results even before they played themselves out. Taylor's hand shot to his waistband, reached under his shirt, and came out with a pistol, black and square and ugly.

Hanratty yelled something incoherent and dove toward his security chief. As bad as things were, what he was seeing now was sheer insanity.

Taylor backpedaled, trying to give himself separation, while simultaneously bringing the pistol up in a two-handed grip and taking aim at the crowd. A few of the crew saw the gun and screamed as they began scattering, diving, and running away.

Hanratty found himself alone in front of his chief. He reached for the gun. In his mind's eye, his hand wrapped around the barrel, twisted it away, and saved the day.

In reality, Taylor simply saw another body hurtling toward him, an outstretched hand reaching for his weapon, and so he fired. Two bullets hit Hanratty: one in the chest above his right nipple, the other above his collarbone, tearing away a length of his jugular vein and carotid artery.

Hanratty clapped a hand to the blood leaping from his neck and fell to the floor, looking up at his chief in disbelief. His mouth gulped like that of a fish out of water. Taylor, his eyes impossibly wide, took two steps back, then fled down the hall. Shouts and shrieks of the terrified crew came to Hanratty down a long, narrow tube, growing more muffled and faint as his blood pumped out to join that of the others scattered around him.

In the thirty seconds left of life, Hanratty gifted himself with the thought that he would be remembered, if not as a hero, then at least not as a coward, if he were to be remembered at all.

CHAPTER FORTY

Taylor ran along the hall—gun in hand, head swiveling—ready for anything.

It was all over. Hanratty was dead. Keene was nowhere to be found. Ayres and Deb and half the crew were crazy or gone or dead, he didn't have time to figure out which. He'd had a suspicion it would end this way, had tried to warn Hanratty to stop *talking* to people and start *leading* them. Draw some fucking lines in the sand. Kick people back into their corners. Take charge. But instead Hanratty had decided to reason with people, talk to them. *Well, we saw how that worked out, didn't we, Jack?*

He felt no responsibility for Hanratty's death. If the moron hadn't tried to grab his gun, he wouldn't have pulled the trigger. But he was a trained professional, indoctrinated to handle insurrection brutally and effectively. What had Hanratty expected? What was he *thinking*? When the world went to hell, you fired first and sorted things out later. If someone put themselves in front of the barrel, that was on them.

It hadn't occurred to Taylor just where he was running to; he just knew he needed to get away from the mob and get out of the base before someone did for him like he'd done for Hanratty. He was halfway down the stairs in the Beer Can, taking the steps two and three at a time, when he realized his feet had already decided for him. He'd have to hurry; he wasn't dressed for the sixty below of the service arches, but if he kept up his calorie burn, he might get through without losing too much to frostbite.

At the base of the stairs, he stopped briefly to listen. The lower level, always fairly quiet, was eerily silent now. He was too cold to stop for long, however, and jogged through the hatch and toward the arches. His labored breathing and the squeaking crunch of his steps along the ice became the only sounds.

Had he been moving at any slower than a full run, he might've been intimidated. But with the very real dangers of the crew behind him, imagined dangers were more easily dismissed, although it occurred to him that, despite the bloodbath upstairs, no one knew who had killed Anne and Pete. For all he knew, the killer was down here with him, as well. He covered his mouth with a sleeve to warm the incoming air and picked up his pace.

Humans were not built for sixty degrees below zero. At just over a minute in the tunnels, he could feel his body shutting down, his vision blurring. Gasping and shivering uncontrollably, he reached the VMF seconds before collapse. He had just enough sense left to wrap his sleeve around his hand before reaching for the metal latch to the garage or he would've lost all the skin on his palm and fingers. With his hand covered, he threw open the door and flicked on the lights while his breath poured out in great billows of white vapor.

His eyes darted around the garage. The VMF was warmer than the tunnel, possibly in the low teens, but that only meant his death would be prolonged if he didn't find a source of warmth or protection in the next few minutes.

"Come on, Jennings, you bitch," he snarled into the empty space. "I know you kept spares."

There. Tossed casually on a stool was a set of Carhartt overalls covered in grease. He hurried over and started tugging them on, cursing at the tight fit. He was hopping around on one leg, trying to shove his body into the overalls, when he shouted in victory. Hanging from a hook in the corner: Jennings's spare ECW gear.

He abandoned the overalls and snatched the parka. A light sheen of sweat that had formed on his brow and back had already frozen, and he ran a hand along his face to break up the ice. He began throwing on the gear as fast as he could, fumbling with the zips and buckles. His hands had lost feeling, the fingers thick as sausages and just as clumsy. In thirty seconds, however, he had the entire set on and the tremor in his limbs slowed to an occasional twitch. The gun he stashed in an inside pocket, which was a shame, but he no longer felt quite as exposed as he had back in the halls of Shackleton.

Now he needed wheels. He jogged over to the station's fleet of Skandics, parked neatly in a row. Moving as quickly as the bulky gear would allow, he checked their gauges and general state of wear. He needed something tanked up and in good working order; his life depended on which machine he chose.

He finally settled on one of the older but more reliable-looking sleds, started it to get it warmed up, then ran to a supply shelf, where he rummaged through pre-stocked saddlebags meant for outside workers who needed to grab-and-go. Cannibalizing several, he managed to put together a bug-out bag of two first-aid kits, a GPS system, flares, a radio, and a basic survival kit. He tossed this onto the back of the Skandic, strapped down an extra can of gas, then trotted over to the large garage door to open it. The great bay door whined and ground its gears, unused to fighting the massive snowdrifts that had piled against it since summer. It rose slowly, inevitably, and the warmth of the VMF disappeared as the black cold of the South Pole night flooded in like water bursting over a dam.

Staggering against the push of the wind, he returned to the snowmobile, threw his leg over the saddle, and headed out of Shackleton for the last time. As he crossed the threshold, however, a thought occurred to him. He slowed the Skandic, then stopped. The idea was vicious, and possibly self-destructive if anyone with any authority ever caught up to him, but it suited his sense of completeness and right. TransAnt wanted to see if the crew of the Shackleton base could handle adversity and stress? Well, he'd give it to them.

Jogging back into the main floor of the garage, he pulled a fuel hose twenty feet out of its reel, then nicked the hose with a pair of shears. Back at the fuel dashboard, he punched on the flow button and kicked the lever. Gas pulsed out of the hose and pooled on the floor, filling the garage with evil-smelling fumes. He ran back to the Skandic, kicked it in gear, and tore away from the garage as fast as he could.

A hundred feet away, he parked and looked back. The bright lights of the VMF formed a perfect square in an otherwise velvet black world. He couldn't have asked for a better target—it was literally the size of a barn door. Reaching into the saddlebag, he pulled out the flare gun and aimed directly for the center of the square, like he was shooting the heart of Shackleton itself.

The flare, blown slightly off course by a savage wind, barely sizzled and tumbled its way into the garage. But, as he'd hoped, an errant spark met the spreading gas fumes. The square blossomed into a flower of fire.

The shockwave hit Taylor hard, nearly knocking him off the snowmobile. But he kept his balance, then turned and sped off, the weak beam of his headlight showing the way into the night.

CHAPTER FORTY-ONE

Leroy woke crying. He'd been dreaming of the ocean and pale sand the color of a peach, the warm breezes he'd felt once on a trip to the Gulf, and the feeling of the sun hot on his back. The dream dimmed, and out of the darkness, he saw his sister, her face first scared, then smug and cruel, slipping and molting into another woman's face, someone dark-haired and screaming.

He lay under the mounds of carpeting and nesting material he'd scavenged, trying to calm the tumult in his head. Guilt, anger, pain, hunger, fear. And cold. So incredibly cold. He couldn't seem to stay still and he was always cold, so he'd taken to stalking up and down the ice tunnels, hitting himself and slapping the walls like they were sides of beef to reassure himself he could still feel. But now the cold seemed to be inside of him, freezing him from the inside out, and there seemed to be no answer to it.

His days and his nights had been filled with suffering. His mind seethed with impressions of the wrongs done to him, or those that might be done. For the pain, he took the pink pills—the blue pills had run out long ago—but they seemed to do little except excite his imagination. Scenes of blood and the visceral feel of a wrench breaking bone passed through his vision and he groaned, realizing he was replaying memories—recent memories—not visions.

Starving after nearly a month of living in the tunnels under the station, eating only what he'd managed to bring with him and the little bit of food he'd grabbed from intermittent raids up above, he'd begun wandering closer to the base, eventually coming across someone hauling supplies from the warehouse on a cart. Leroy had followed him, frustrated when he'd taken the freight elevator, and so he'd ascended the steps to the base for the first time in a week. Smells from the galley had pulled him in and he'd begun panting at how warm everything was. He'd followed the cook quietly, only meaning to knock him out and steal the food he needed. But then he'd seen *her* and suddenly the only important thing was to obliterate the person who reminded him of a lifelong source of guilt and fear.

When he was done, he'd grabbed what food he could and fled back to the safety of his nest. Exhausted, he'd fallen asleep immediately, only to be ripped awake by his nightmares. When he was awake, however, the visions of blood were still vivid and alive in his head . . . Then he looked down at his hands and saw the real thing.

They'd come for him eventually, he knew. He could've lived down here indefinitely if he hadn't bothered anyone, but now that he'd killed, they'd want to capture him and drag him back for their judgment. The thought made him twitch under his layers, and his mind careened off into a new clutch of anxious thoughts. He croaked threats and curses into the air.

He froze in mid-curse. A dull, distant *whump* had reached his ears. Considering how far away he was from the occupied parts of the base, it must've been earsplitting at the source. The sudden noise was a shock in a place where, aside from the creak of ice and burble of fluid through the sewage pipes, he was the only source of sound. Had he actually heard it? Or imagined it?

Throwing off the blankets and pieces of carpet, he struggled to a sitting position. He held his breath, listening intently.

He heard nothing. But he *felt* something.

It began with a light, feathery touch, caressing the sliver of exposed skin on his cheek. A few seconds later, it was pressing insistently. His scarf, frozen permanently in the shape of his face, crackled as he peeled it away.

The wind, forced through the halls and corridors under the station, moaned its greeting, then, squeezing and tilting through tiny spaces, it pitched upward until it was a constant, insistent shriek.

Leroy scrambled to his feet, his heart racing. Without thinking, he began shrieking along with the wind, his voice rusty and breaking from disuse. In his mind, he saw nothing but colossal movements of color and emotion. A part of him made a weak attempt to hook reason onto his actions, but in the end, he gave up and gave in. A cracked smile broke across his face as he shuffled out the door of his nest and into the ice tunnel beyond, still singing the song of the wind, looking for its source.

CHAPTER FORTY-TWO

Cass was shivering.

She hadn't gotten a real night's rest since being locked up—no surprise, of course. More than once she woke gasping, crying, or shivering. This time, she lay flat in bed with her eyes shut, willing herself to become calm and serene. Something was tickling her cheek, though. Still half-asleep, she reached up to scratch and felt a crust of ice on her eyelids.

She sat bolt upright in bed, blind.

Frantic, she rubbed the ice away and opened her eyes with difficulty. The room was dimly lit, illuminated not by the normal overhead lamp, but from a weak battery-operated emergency LED above the door, one of the same ones that had kicked on during the station-wide power failure. She stared at it, her vision obscured by her fogging breath.

Her muscles, shocked by the cold, rippled and twitched as she rolled out of bed and began throwing on every scrap of clothing she could find. Taylor hadn't allowed her any outdoor clothing, but Deb had secretly brought Cass her books, clothes, and personal items from her berth. Mouthing a thanks for the woman's kindness, Cass pulled on five layers in all, then crawled back into bed, pulling the blanket up over her nose as she tried to get warm. Tiny ice crystals, formed by her breath as she had slept, clung to the ceiling above her head, glittering and twinkling like tiny stars. Her mind, almost as frozen as the rest of her body, lay dormant and blank, but after long minutes, the shivering slowed, then finally stopped, allowing her to think.

Something had happened to the electrical system that was bad enough for the emergency lights to kick on . . . again. But this time, it wasn't just cold, it was below freezing in an internal room of Shackleton. For that to happen meant the power had been off for some time. And if *that* were the case and no one had come to check on her, then she'd either been forgotten or the situation on base was so bad it amounted to the same thing.

Cass kicked off the blanket and rolled out of bed again. Stiff from her clothes bunching at the elbows and knees, she went to a bag in the closet and pried off one of the zippers. With the small metal tab clutched in one hand, she went back to the bed, upended the nightstand lamp, then used the end of the zipper tab as an impromptu screwdriver to loosen the base. After a minute of fumbling, the screws fell out and the base popped off. Fishing around inside, her fingers closed around a mini multi-tool from her belongings that Taylor had overlooked in his enthusiasm to lock her up. She'd hidden it as soon as she'd found the right place.

Rummaging around in one of her bags, she dug out a flashlight and her trusty headlamp. Aside from the multi-tool and clothes, they were the only other resources she had. She flicked through the tools and chose the flat-head screwdriver, then went to work on the hinges of the door to her room.

Never meant to act as the entrance of a prison, the door was hinged on the inside, which should've made the process of removing the hinges easier, but her hands were numb and she had to jam them under her armpits several times to warm them up. After ten minutes of patient manipulation, she had the screws out and the hinges dangling in place.

She turned around and gave the door the hardest mule kick she could muster, driving all of her anger and outrage through the heel of her boot. The door flew open, twisted momentarily at the lock, then fell into the hall.

Cass poked her head out. The VIP suite was on the bottom floor of the base. The galley and offices were located on the upper floor, so the bottom deck was normally the less busy of the two floors, but even for here it was quiet. Emergency footlights lit the hall every fifteen feet, providing a dim, uncertain light. She sniffed cautiously. The faint smell of gasoline floated in the air and she blanched; if the generators had blown the contents of their fuel tanks, the base was doomed.

If Biddi was right and Hanratty and Taylor had managed to make a scapegoat out of her, the entire base might blame her for everything that had gone wrong since the last plane had left for McMurdo. Her only defense was that the second power outage had happened after she was imprisoned; surely no one could still believe she was the mastermind behind some insane experiment *after* she'd been locked up? She shook her head, trying to put theories out of her head; right now, she needed to get warm and for that she needed proper gear. Her first stop had to be her own berth, though as she padded down the hall, she peeked into several of the labs, hoping to find someone, but all were empty.

After reaching the A4 wing, she headed straight for her room. Her stomach sank when she found no sign of her ECW gear, although the rest of her things were intact. Rummaging through her bags and rucksacks, she threw on every layer of clothing that fit, then pocketed a few personal items that included her headlamp, a flashlight, and the battery to her crude shortwave. Her nascent diary and the copy of *The Worst Journey in the World* she left behind, feeling just a twinge of regret at abandoning both.

She backed out, leaving the little space that had been her home for much of the last year, then continued on, opening doors and poking her head into room after room. Each was deserted. Half cups of coffee sat abandoned on desks, pens and pencils rested on open notebooks. Had the electricity been running, she was sure she would've seen monitors showing unfinished e-mails and incomplete reports. A shiver went through her. The crew had left in a hurry.

Unfortunately, ECW gear—the one thing she could've used—was also missing from every room. Cass circled back to check the dorms; it made sense people might retreat to their own quarters in the event of an emergency. Her footsteps rang hollow and empty on the floor and she closed each door gently, unable to bear the thought of the sound they would make if they slammed shut.

But room after room was empty. Few were locked, and she glanced in to make sure some kind of . . . plague hadn't laid the crew low. In some cases, the rooms resembled the offices she'd looked in: deserted in a hurry, with half-opened drawers and personal items strewn over beds and on floors. In others, the occupants had departed more strategically, with little left behind. What few things remained were the time-killers: books and CDs, impractical clothes, decks of cards, handheld games. But in every case, the critical element was the same—no crew members were left.

Each room was equipped with an on-base phone; she tried every one of them and was greeted by the same flat silence. She'd thought that calling out loud for people was ridiculous, but after the fifth empty bedroom, she started yelling names, shouting *hello*. Her voice was a rusty croak, growing louder and more desperate as the five empty berths became ten, then twenty, then thirty.

She was getting colder by the minute and her breath steamed in the cold. Feeling only mildly guilty, she lifted a few items from some of the sloppier berths—another cap, a second set of gloves, a spare flashlight, extra batteries—but if she didn't find a heat source and some answers soon, filching clothes was going to be the least of her worries. She hadn't checked the entire base yet, of course, but if there was no heat, no power, if all of Shackleton was compromised, options for getting warm and staying alive were few.

A thrill of panic ran through her. *No gear, crew left in a hurry, no power, gasoline leaking.* Had the entire crew decided to evacuate and leave her behind? Surely Biddi or Ayres or someone had thought of her before they simply fled for . . . for wherever they'd decided.

The real possibility that she'd been abandoned started to overwhelm her until she stopped in the middle of the hall and literally smacked herself. *Idiot. Stop looking for people and start looking for places.* Any sanctuary that had the elements she needed to survive was also going to be where others would gather: maybe the gym, possibly the galley, but most certainly the Lifeboat, an entire area devoted to keeping Shackleton's crew alive in the case of a catastrophe. It had food, its own heat and power supply, and enough space to house an entire winter crew.

Cass tucked her hands under her armpits and began to jog down the hall toward the room of last resort. The base, as deserted as it had felt sometimes during the winter-over, had never been dead silent. Background noises—small electronic burps, the distant murmurs of conversation, the almost subsonic hum of air moving through vents overhead—had always been present, a kind of constant proof of life. Now, there was nothing. The base was dead.

Her steps faltered as she caught sight of something odd in the hallway. She was nearing the galley, itself only forty feet from the door to the Lifeboat. Between her and the entrance to her best shot at survival was a jumble of shapes lying on the floor, propped against the wall, draped over each other. In the dim gloom of the footlights, the shapes were indistinct and ugly, but they stood out because normally the halls were required to remain clear. But nothing about Shackleton was normal any longer.

Cass shuffled down the hall in a stupor, unwilling to discover what her instincts told her was waiting up ahead, but unable to resist a strange, morbid pull to confirm it. A low, involuntary moan escaped.

Her mind refused to process what she was seeing, pushing back hard in an attempt to assimilate the scene. Swallowing with difficulty, she pulled out her flashlight and pointed it forward.

Bodies, four or five altogether. Black pools of blood, spooling out from skulls, guts, limbs. Slack faces limned in ice. She forced herself to check faces, if not bodies. Dave Boychuck. Beth Muñez. Her eyes slid away from a colossal head wound on another corpse, only recognizable as Pete Ozment by his apron. There were two or three others she could barely identify.

Hanratty was propped up against a wall, as though he'd grown tired of standing and waiting for her and had decided to sit. His hands were folded over his stomach in a pantomime of napping, but they couldn't hide the furrows in his shoulder or the crusted blood frozen in plaques on his chest. Covering her mouth, she leaned closer. The others had obviously been beaten or been involved in some kind of fight; it took Cass a long moment to realize that the wounds she was looking at were gunshots. *Taylor*. Only he would've had a gun.

She put a hand out to a wall for support, dizzy and sick. It was as if a wave of madness had grabbed everyone by the throat and hadn't let go, even in death. One of Dave's arms had been bent back at an obscene angle; Beth's face was twisted savagely in fear and anger. Glancing through the doorway in which Pete was sprawled, she spotted the shoes of another casualty, the feet crossed in an awkward jumble that no living person would tolerate.

Cass stumbled away, gulping down the bile in her throat, her head screaming at what she'd seen. *Leave it, get it out of your head, start over.* Her mind clawed at something it could hold on to, found purchase on a goal that would keep her stable and safe. *The Lifeboat. The Lifeboat is ahead of you.* Five doors separated her and it on the right, three lockers on the left. She'd idly counted them months before when she was bored, in the same way that, as a bored child on long family trips, she'd tapped forefinger to thumb for each passing truck and car. Now the habit was a tenuous strand that barely kept her mind in one piece.

As she approached the emergency shelter, she slowed, puzzled at the strange look of the entrance. Initially, she thought it was because the fire door was shut, which of course it would be if the Lifeboat were actually being used. It simply looked odd now because the massive emergency door had commonly been kept propped *open*, a safety rule that had never been violated since the first day she'd arrived at Shackleton.

But then she realized it wasn't just that. Two strange pieces of metal as long as her arm, struts or braces lifted from some other part of the base, were jammed at an angle against the door, planted into the ridge in the hall floor that was normally used to lock the door open. Hesitating, she grabbed one piece and tried to move it without success; pressure, bulging outward, was holding the metal as though it had been welded in place. Running her eyes along the jamb, she could see where the door had warped outward as though by some great force from within.

Determined to get inside, Cass kicked the strut, aiming out and away from the door. The first try was ineffective, but on the third, she flinched as the metal strut sprang away and shot down the hall. The second did the same. She closed her eyes for a brief second, then turned the Lifeboat's latch.

The door was even colder than the air around her. She jumped at a faint scratching sound that started as soon as she began pulling it open—something was leaning against the other side, sliding down its face. She swallowed and opened the door the rest of the way.

A blast of frigid air hit her full force. She jumped as an object flopped through the open doorway. It was the frozen hand of Ron Ayres. His body, no longer propped up by the door, rocked in place, preserved by the cold in a stiff, bowed curve. His arm and hand were a claw that had been draped over the inside latch and now hung in the air above his head in a grotesque *croisé devant*. Beyond him, softly lit by the emergency lights, were the stiff, crystalline bodies of twenty or thirty people, huddled together to conserve a warmth that had been leached out of them by degrees and dissipated into the Antarctic night, slowed only marginally by the insulated walls. If the Lifeboat had been heated, there was no evidence of it now.

Cass backed away from the door, her mind simultaneously screaming and numb. Her eyes tried to unsee the twinkling crystal forms arrayed in a row, unsee Ayres's frozen face, unsee the struts that had transformed the Lifeboat into a tomb instead of a sanctuary. She turned her head away, only to face the bodies sprawled across the hall near the galley.

Thoughts of rescue or hunkering down to wait out the crisis were gone. The idea that the atrocities that had occurred were either accidents or arranged by Hanratty evaporated. Someone was responsible, someone had made this happen. There might not be a reason, but there was an answer. She just had to live long enough to find it.

Cass turned and ran down the hall, chased by the cold and the frozen gazes of the dead.

CHAPTER FORTY-THREE

As Shackleton's security chief, Taylor had spent little time looking out over the ice fields that made up the world around the base. If he'd noticed the outside at all, it was in the early days of last summer, when the sunlight bouncing off the bright snow irritated him enough to snap closed the blinds or pull a blackout curtain across the window.

On the rare occasion when he gave himself the time to wrap his head around the immensity of the ice, the intimidating expanse of white, his thoughts ran toward the impossibility of traversing it. The fact that men had attempted to travel over it with dogsleds, ponies, and even on foot was stunning. Sometimes, when he saw the cliffs and crevasses, felt the screaming wind, comprehended the absolute *nothingness* that lay in every direction, he had to sit down on the floor to get back in touch with something solid, man-made, and real.

The vision of that immensity and the fear that those thoughts provoked began enveloping Taylor as he skimmed over drifts and fought the giant, insistent hand of the wind. Even though the great white desert had unnerved him, the constant darkness—with the same uninterrupted, featureless face, just black instead of white—was no better. The beam from the Skandic's headlight died an arm's length in front of him, illuminating nothing more than the next snowbank or the toothed ridges of the damned frozen sastrugi that made his teeth slam together in his head.

Only the GPS kept him on course; there was no chance he could use a compass, and sight, of course, would be useless until he was almost on top of the Russian base, his final destination. His situation was still dicey, of course, but he permitted himself to feel a tiny amount of optimism for the future, because even if those bastards back at Shackleton survived his parting shot into the VMF and the subsequent fire, the fever that had consumed the high-strung and volatile crew was enough to finish the job. They'd been on the verge of tearing each other apart; it would be a miracle if anyone else made it out of that hellhole alive.

All of which meant that, if he made it to Orlova, *and* they didn't turn him over to whatever secret police they were using these days, *and* he managed to make it back stateside, his future was set. As Shackleton's sole survivor, the story he'd tell the press would keep news cycles running for a week. He'd make a few appearances, describing the deplorable living conditions and the psychological stresses, then hit them with the biggest surprise of all: it had all been an experiment to drive people crazy. He'd sue TransAnt, write his memoir, sign a movie deal. These last four or five shitty months would turn out to be the meal ticket he'd been looking for his whole life. Not bad for a piss-poor kid who used to dream about owning a pair of shoes.

A gust hit him sideways, lifting the right side of the sled a foot into the air. He leaned into the rise and slammed the snowmobile back down to the ground. The track's teeth slipped and spun, then bit into the ice. With his heart slamming in his chest, Taylor wrestled the sled back under control and reluctantly slowed the Skandic down to a crawl. At high speeds, the machine was the equivalent of an expensive kite, and getting dumped onto the ice was not an optimal outcome right now.

The gust presaged a shift in the wind. Snow hit him full in the face, cutting visibility down to nothing, and he slowed the sled down even more. Slow enough, in fact, that he risked a glance behind. In his imagination, he'd assumed he'd see a starlike pinpoint of light from one of the outside spotlights or maybe even the Halloween glow of fire from the explosion he'd triggered in the garage.

But Shackleton had long since disappeared from view, and the world behind him was as dark as the bleak, flat night in front of him. *Nothing ahead, nothing behind.* A hollow pit opened up in his stomach, despair and dread and naked fear fusing together . . .

It took longer than it should have to realize that the twisting, careening sense that the bottom of his world was dropping away was real, not imagined. The Skandic's headlight tipped forward and away, a plank of light teetering over the crumbling edge of a crevasse. Taylor tried to roll backward from the sled, but it was too late. Man and machine tumbled into the darkness, the single headlight playing over the blue-black walls.

CHAPTER FORTY-FOUR

Cass unwound the scarf from around her neck and doubled it over her mouth and nose. The smell of gasoline was strong enough to make her gag and she had to squeeze her eyes hard to clear it of tears that formed and froze. Rationally, she knew that the Beer Can, always unheated, couldn't be any colder than it had always been, but it somehow seemed darker and less protective than ever as she started down its metal steps.

The central shaft of the staircase appeared to her flashlight in muddy sections. The familiar sterile lights of each level were gone, as was the sluggish glow at the bottom of the shaft that she associated with the service lights of the ice tunnels that led to the arches and the VMF. Just one emergency footlight glowed at the top of the Beer Can. Her flashlight was the only other illumination.

Her steps made a hollow, staccato rapping as she descended the staircase. She wanted to move quickly, but the muscles of her calves and thighs twitched and shivered, making both her steps and her judgment risky. Her only source of heat was movement, which might be good enough for now, but as she failed to replace the calories she'd lost, her body would start to break down, slow, and die.

The dark maw of the ice tunnels loomed in front of her. She swung the light back and forth, expecting, perhaps, to see more bodies lying in the tunnel, on the ground, propped against the icy walls, but there was nothing. The sound of her breathing was loud in her ears. The layers of cloth swaddled around her head kept her warm, but also kept her isolated and deaf.

The smell of the gas was stronger. Moving slowly but steadily, she made it to the conduit intersection in twice the time it normally took with the power on and the lights guiding her way. Tugging the cloth aside from one ear, she listened down the tunnel.

Nothing.

But the arches weren't her destination, not yet. She moved to the plywood door that led to the rough ice tunnels, her feet crunching and squeaking on the ice floor. She wrapped her hand around the rope handle of the door and yanked it open, thrusting her flashlight into the opening like a sword.

The light showed nothing but the round-roofed shaft leading into darkness. The silence beyond was absolute, sepulchral.

She closed the door behind her and shuffled forward. The walls of the older tunnel were serpentine, and the beam from her flashlight illuminated only a few feet ahead, refracted by the next turn or aberration in the tunnel. The smell of gas was less oppressive here, but there was a new, brassy odor she couldn't place. It sat in the back of her throat like a pill half swallowed.

She moved down the tunnel slower than she ever had, her muscles and eyes twitching, her breath coming in a quick, one-two rhythm just shy of a gasp, trying to inhale and exhale without tasting the air. The first turn was coming up.

Steeling herself, she rounded the corner with the flashlight held steady and straight. Light splashed over Jerry's screaming bust.

Then, Cass's vision shifted violently, as though she'd been blindsided in traffic, and she realized Christ, oh God, it *wasn't* Jerry, it wasn't a bust of snow tinted with axle grease or human shit; it was smaller and more articulate than the crude sculpture had been. Gaskets were still there where the eyes should be and the vacuum hose still made the outline of the mouth an "o" of surprise, but this head had a long nose and a bearded chin, gold-rimmed glasses crushed into a face crusted with ice and covered with a stain that spread over the rim of the ice shelf it rested on, forming rusty brown stalactites that hung from the ledge.

She clawed the scarf away and doubled over, vomiting onto the ice. *The beard, the long nose, the glasses. It's Keene*, she thought as she heaved. Tears collected and instantly froze around her eyes and she had to gulp in deep breaths of the brassy, tainted air to make them stop. She stumbled blindly down the tunnel.

Weaving like a drunk, careening off the ice walls, she pressed forward, not quite caring if she ran into whoever or whatever had killed the psychologist. She had one goal at this point and it was impossible for her brain to move beyond that single point, although her eyes registered that drops of the rusty brown stain decorated the ice floor in front of her every few feet . . . and were appearing with more frequency.

A distant part of her mind edged through the fear and the growing scream that was building inside of her. *Come on, girl. Just fifty more feet.* She concentrated on counting off the remaining distance in strides. *Thirty more feet. That's just ten strides sprinting, fifteen walking, thirty crawling. Do it.*

The path was familiar, at least. Even without the flashlight, she could've found her way to the small corridor that peeled off the main artery toward the sewer bulb. She panned her light over the floor, the rungs, and the dark shaft that led into the darkness above.

Coffee-colored stains speckled the ground at the foot of the icy ladder and decorated several of the rungs. She stared at the dots, paralyzed. She didn't want to think what they meant overall, let alone what it meant for accomplishing her single goal. *You can go up there and find out or you can curl into a ball and die right here.*

Cass held her breath, listening. Nothing.

Swapping the flashlight for the headlamp, she began climbing, chasing the red light up the shaft. With a surgeon's care, she placed her cramped hands and aching feet precisely on each rung before moving to the next. Every few seconds, she paused again to listen, trying to hear past her own heartbeat. Only silence greeted her and, halfway to the top, she allowed herself to feel a small flush of success. She tilted her head back so she could shine the beam directly up the shaft and her heart stopped.

The hatch to her hideaway was open.

The light from her headlamp punched through the open hole, illuminating the ceiling of the Jamesway hut above it. She was unable to move or swing the light away, holding in place so long that her arms and legs started to quiver from the strain.

What's it going to be, Cass? Do you have any other choice?

Shaking, she climbed the last five or six rungs, expecting at any minute to see someone hurtle out of the hole at her, or a face to pop into view.

With agonizing care, she raised her head and shoulders above the floor of the hut, flashing the light in quick half-circles around the tiny room, ready at any second to slide down the icy ladder and take her chances falling to the floor below rather than confront whoever had killed Keene. Debris from previous generations of Polies littered the room, throwing strange shadows against the walls of the hut.

Nothing moved. There was no sound. She slowly crawled the rest of the way out of the hatch and into the Jamesway, whipping the headlamp around to try and see in every direction at once. Only after she was standing to her full height did she see it.

Propped up in a corner was a body dressed in full expedition gear. The head had been torn away and the hood of the parka pulled up to frame the empty space where it should've been. A wave of black blood stained the torso down to the belt line, starkly contrasted against the scarlet material. One arm was held up by the back of a chair in a pantomime of a wave of greeting or warning. Rigor mortis had curled the arm back toward the body as though it were gesturing to itself.

Cass stared at the corpse, then slowly closed the hatch and backed away as if it would stand and start walking toward her. Without taking her eyes off the body, she maneuvered her way toward the small patch of carpet where her shortwave was hidden. She knelt and, working by feel, reached for the piece of ancient shag carpeting that covered the false floor hiding the fragile components of her homemade radio.

But nothing felt the way it was supposed to. Risking a glance down, she trained the light of the headlamp on the space. A low moan slipped from her chest as she saw the gaping hole where the hidden cache should be. In the depression, lying in a jumble, were the smashed fragments of her only remaining link to the outside world.

CHAPTER FORTY-FIVE

Only the pain told Taylor that he was both awake and alive. Coming to in complete darkness and cold had been so much like being unconscious, he couldn't tell the difference.

He thought, at first, that he was sitting. He was bent at the waist, but peculiarly so, and in such a way that he couldn't feel his legs. Raising his head, he hoped to see just how far he'd fallen, but the darkness was total. It was so absolute that, afraid that he might've been blinded somehow in the accident, he ran a hand over his eyes. When he felt no damage, he reached for a small penlight he kept in a pocket of his parka, breathing a sigh of relief when he saw the cone of light bounce off the walls of the crevasse.

Taylor panned the light around him, assessing. The snowmobile, its front end smashed up to the seat, lay wrecked twenty feet away. Had he not scrambled out of the saddle when he had, he'd be part of that wreckage. Then again, he thought as he looked around, maybe it would've been a better thing.

The wind, savage and unrelenting on the surface, was softer down here. Taylor pushed back the hood of his parka and peeled off the balaclava. It was no warmer—his ears immediately began burning from the cold—but he could hear the engine of the Skandic ticking as it cooled, and now that his mask was off, he could smell the stink of gas and motor oil leaking out of the machine.

After composing himself, he pointed the flashlight at his legs. The left wasn't so bad—only turned a little strange at the ankle, like he was stretching funny—but the right was bent up underneath him so that the sole of his foot was touching the side of his hip. The pain was a dull ache right now—maybe shock and cold were keeping it at bay—but he'd be screaming soon. Of the other bumps and bruises, few were worth mentioning except what he thought might be a broken rib or two, courtesy of the 9mm Glock he still carried in an inside pocket.

He swung the beam of his light back toward the Skandic. The saddlebag he'd packed had been torn or thrown free in the fall and lay a tantalizing ten feet away. Ten feet that could be measured in many different ways. Three strides, if he were walking. Less than two body lengths. Or, as it turned out, fifteen minutes of crawling, gritting his teeth and crying and spitting as the pain from his leg began to explode.

He gave a grunt of satisfaction as his fingers wrapped around the strap of the bag and pulled it close. Holding the penlight between his teeth, he clawed through the contents. The first-aid kits were less than useless: bandages and zinc oxide tape and sterilization pads weren't going to help him solve a multiple compound fracture. He looked skeptically at a bivy sack and foil space blanket wondering just how long they could keep him alive, but he tucked them nearby anyway. A repair kit—rivets, extra nylon webbing, and a sewing kit—had him laughing so hard he started to cry.

At the bottom, his hand wrapped around the blocky dimensions of a Saber field radio, the first truly useful thing he'd found so far. With trembling fingers, he turned it on, grinning like a skull when the yellow face of the channel display lit up.

Hugging it against his body to keep the batteries warm and alive as long as possible, Taylor began hailing on every channel, making a call once a minute up and down the dial. Time passed, but he refused to look at his watch. Time was irrelevant. His calls transformed from understandable English into gibbering moans. Shivering set in after the first half hour and he had trouble flicking the channel dial. For the first time since leaving Shackleton, he realized he truly might die.

When he could no longer feel his feet or his fingertips, he decided it was time. He could strip off his coat and let the cold take him, but the pain from his ribs was now on a whole new level—did he want to lie here for hours, waiting for hypothermia to set in while screaming in pain?

Carefully setting the radio down beside him, he scooted his back up against the wall of the crevasse and got comfortable. He reached under his coat and pulled out the pistol. Then, croaking out a "Sorry, Jack," he put the barrel in his mouth and pulled the trigger.

Beside him, the Saber crackled and spat, barely audible in the soft wind of the crevasse.

"*Zdravstvuj? Zdravstvuj? Hello? Is anyone there?*"

CHAPTER FORTY-SIX

Cass staggered down the tunnel, her mind enclosed in a hard shell, as removed from her own existence as though she were watching her body propel itself along a preconfigured track laid out on the ground. Behind, the track led from her berth, through the base, down the tunnels, and out into the cold. Nothing she could do would change the direction of the track. Vaguely, she hoped that meant nothing that got in her way would do so, either.

Looking at the shattered pieces of her shortwave lying on the floor of the hut, her emotions had circled the drain. She might escape Shackleton and whoever had engineered the murder of most of its crew, but without external aid, she would still die. *Never forget. Antarctica wants to kill you.*

She had stared at the pieces of the sabotaged radio until her teeth started to chatter. Then, as though planning to return later, she'd carefully stowed the shortwave away and left. She averted her gaze from the corpse in the corner as she moved to the hatchway and slipped down the ladder to the ice tunnel below.

Vox or no Vox, Orlova was her only hope now. She needed to leave the base, and quickly. For that, she needed transportation and supplies. The VMF and warehouse could provide both.

If they were still there. Rolling black smoke stained the ceiling and the petroleum stink had grown so bad that she had to double up her scarf and press it hard to her mouth and nose to breathe. She had forcefully kept her mind away from thinking about the source of the gas smell, but her engineering mind provided the answer anyway: unless a Hercules had landed on the strip outside Shackleton and spontaneously combusted, either the fuel depot for the base or the petrol tanks in the VMF had been sabotaged. Nothing else within a thousand miles of the South Pole had enough fuel to send fumes all the way to the Beer Can and beyond.

If the fuel depot had been tampered with, that would explain the power failure and would also confirm that Shackleton was doomed. If it was the VMF, her plans for escape were gone. Living or dying depended on the answer.

She hadn't gone a hundred feet down the tunnel when she got it. Smoke spilled down the side artery to her garage in great clouds, blackening the walls and ceiling. The acrid stench of petroleum joined with the fresh-tar odor of burning tires and the chemical stink of evaporated solvents. Cass pushed down the hall anyway, even dropping to her hands and knees to try and slip beneath the smog of smoke and fumes, but she was turned back, choking and gagging, before she'd gotten halfway down the corridor. Residual heat had begun to melt the ice forty or fifty feet away from the entrance, and the walls and floor were slick with water.

Back in the main corridor, she crawled up to a wall and sat with her back against it, staring blankly at the ice opposite her. Almost immediately, the chill started seeping through her coat. She didn't care.

Trekking overland on a snowmobile or a snowcat in the middle of an Antarctic winter would normally be considered suicidal, but—in light of the living hell that Shackleton had become—the term had lost any meaning. With enough fuel and maybe an emergency kit or an MRE or three under the seat, a snowcat would give you even odds of surviving long enough to get to Orlova. A snowmobile, open to the elements, would be a shot in the dark, though still better than freezing to death or waiting to be killed and having your body parts propped up in a shrine.

But with a fire hot enough to melt the walls fifty feet away, there was nothing with a track or a wheel or a tire left whole in the VMF. And that meant there was just one way to escape: a thirty-mile trek alone, on foot, during winter, in the darkest night. Something no one had attempted in the hundred-year history of Antarctica. Because it wasn't possible.

"I can't do it," she whispered to herself. "I've got nothing left."

Is it time to give up?

She groaned. "Leave me the fuck alone."

That's not what this trip was about, the voice persisted. *You were supposed to dig down deep and find out something about yourself you didn't know before.*

"I didn't sign up for this."

No one signs up for the hardest thing in their life.

"Jesus Christ."

Get up.

"Fuck off."

Get up. Or die.

Crying, spitting, cursing, she rolled to her hands and knees and crawled. First, a few yards, then thirty. At fifty, she staggered to her feet, away from the reek of the burning garage, and stumbled down the corridor. Ahead was the warehouse—with enough food to keep her alive for twenty years, but nothing to keep her warm unless she set fire to the place—and the power plant, which might be intact, but likely sabotaged or damaged beyond her ability to fix.

She banged through the door to the warehouse and on into the cavernous warehouse. Her light illuminated once-familiar racks of dried goods and supplies; in the complete darkness, though, it seemed like she'd wandered into some post-apocalyptic storehouse. Her footsteps rang hollow on the metal floor as she hurried down the center aisle. She flicked her flashlight from side to side, washing the sacks and boxes in a brief, stark light, before pointing the beam in front of her to guide her steps. Her goal was at the back of the warehouse and it was her last shot.

She sniffed. The air had become fresher and cleaner as she'd moved away from the VMF. *The Beer Can is functioning as a chimney, drawing the fumes and smoke away*. A small consolation, but she was at least able to stop pressing her hands to her face just to breathe. Great. She could die with a cold, frigid lungful of air instead of asphyxiating.

"Shut up," she said savagely. The time for giving up and dying was over. If she hadn't thrown her hands up and cashed it in after discovering the fire, then now wasn't the time to take cheap shots at herself.

"Cass?"

She stumbled back at the sound of her name, gasping as though a cold hand had slipped inside her chest and seized her heart. It clenched painfully in her chest before starting again with a reluctant thud. Whipping the flashlight to her left, she got a brief view of a short, round figure bundled in the thick layers of an expedition parka, fat gloves, and enormous bunny boots before light flooded her eyes, blinding her.

Cass winced and threw up a hand. "Biddi?"

The light left her face and the figure peeled off a glove to pull down the mouth covering of the balaclava. The apple-cheeked face of her friend peered out of the fur-lined hood, giving her a weak grin. "In the frozen flesh, dearie."

Cass exclaimed an inarticulate noise and hugged Biddi, barely able to feel her friend's body through the thick layers of the parka. Biddi hugged back, then pushed her away to look at her. "Speaking of frozen flesh, what the hell are you wearing?"

Cass wiped her tears away before they could freeze. "Seven shitty layers of clothes stolen from half the rooms on base."

Biddi made an "oh" sound and tugged her arm. "Get over here, you dummy. There's a whole cage full of emergency supplies lying here in piles just waiting to be used."

Her friend turned and waddled away, playing the beam from her flashlight over the stiff, steel wire of the emergency rack. She carried a mountaineer's ice axe in her other hand.

"Biddi, what the hell happened while I was locked up? There are . . ." Cass choked as images flooded into her head. Instinct and self-survival had compartmentalized all the horrors she'd seen, tucking them away so she could focus on basic survival. But asking Biddi the simple question brought all the scenes back in a rush. "I saw bodies. Hanratty and Dave. And the Lifeboat."

Biddi opened the gate to the ECW cage and threw it back with a clang that made Cass wince. Her friend searched her face. "They didn't make it?"

"You didn't know?"

Biddi shook her head. "The day after I visited you, there was a terrible riot. It was a . . . a mutiny, of sorts. A bunch of others were hurt in the aftermath."

"Oh my God."

"It was pure anarchy. Doc Ayres rallied whoever was left after the fracas and made for the Lifeboat. I think he hoped our radio silence had triggered some kind of alarm at McMurdo and that all they had to do was wait out the crisis. They should send help sometime, right?"

"You'd think so." Cass moved quickly down the line of clothing, folded and organized by size. She found a set that fit and began slipping the parka and expedition pants on over her clothes, shivering at the change in temperature. Bunny boots followed. Armed with the kind of gear meant for eighty below zero, her body finally began to warm itself.

"What happened to them?" Biddi's voice rang hollow in the empty space.

Cass cinched the parka's hood down tight, then turned to the non-clothing gear. Rucksacks and web belts were mounded in piles, while axes and testing poles leaned in a corner of the cage. Cass helped herself to one of the axes. The heft of it in her hand felt good. "Someone had braced the doors shut. They . . . froze to death."

Biddi stared at her, silent.

Cass felt her throat tighten. "Biddi, they were . . . huddled together. Trying to stay warm. They died that way." She took a deep breath, fighting to get her emotions under control. "I am just so glad you weren't with them. How did you not get trapped there, too?"

Biddi shook her head. "I know the good doctor meant well, but . . . huddle together with everyone else in a single room so we could all die a slow death on some lunatic's timetable? No thank you."

Cass shuddered. "You made the right decision. It was . . . terrible."

"I can't imagine what seeing that was like. How are you holding up, dear?"

"I don't know if I am." Cass put her hands to her face. "It's hitting me, but the pain is coming from a thousand miles away. I think I've suffered as much shock as I can at this point. Something inside me is saying, get out of here first, *then* deal with the madness."

"I think that's a wonderful idea," Biddi said, then paused. "How do we do that?"

"You don't have a plan?"

Biddi flapped her arms like a giant stuffed bird. "You're looking at it. I thought maybe I could set fire to the powdered milk and live off dried jerky until the cavalry came."

"We'd probably kill ourselves if we tried to set a fire. Assuming whoever did this doesn't come for us first."

Biddi hefted the ice axe. "Let him try, dearie. But I get your point. Can you think of anything better?"

Cass paused. "Orlova."

Biddi looked at her blankly. "What about it?"

"We head for it."

"On foot?"

"Yes." Cass explained herself in a rush. "It's far, but with good gear, the right supplies, and two of us checking for crevasses, we have a chance."

"A chance is right. You didn't happen to grab a GPS before you stumbled in here, did you?"

Cass shook her head. "But the SPoT highway passes within a few hundred meters of the Russian base. If we keep an eye on our watches and keep track of the stars, we should come close using dead reckoning. Then we'll just have to look for Orlova when we think we're near."

Biddi stared at her. "Dead reckoning? You want us to re-create Ernie Shackleton's bloody fucking journey, is that what you're after?"

"No, he did it in a boat," Cass said calmly, and with more confidence than she felt. "We'll be walking."

"So, you're saying at least we won't drown? Fantastic."

"It's either that or stay here and freeze to death. Or be killed."

"My God," Biddi said in a whisper, looking at the supply racks. After a moment, she said, "I suppose there's nothing for it. Is there anything of use here?"

"Grab a few MREs to eat, but not too many. More than a couple will weigh us down and if it takes any longer than a few days to reach Orlova, well, more food won't really make a difference."

"Well, you're a cheerful one, aren't you? Where does it come from?"

"Some deeper inner reservoir of strength," Cass said. "Also, I'm scared shitless."

They grabbed rucksacks, threw a few dried meals in each, then shouldered them and headed out of the ECW cage. Biddi turned to face her in the aisle. "How do you want to get outside?"

"I remember the engineering schematic showed an old station tunnel leading east for a hundred meters or so before it exits out a stub-up on the surface. It's going generally toward Orlova. If we use it, we'll be out of the wind the whole time."

"With just over forty-nine and a half kilometers to go."

"Do you have a better idea?"

"No," she sighed. "Let's go."

She and Biddi headed down the central causeway of the warehouse to the door. Just before they passed through, Cass glanced back. The hangar-sized cavern seemed isolated and safe in comparison to the rest of the base. But at sixty below, they would both slowly die of hypothermia and frostbite, no matter how many layers of ECW they put on. Assuming they weren't murdered in their sleep. As crazy as it sounded, walking overland to a base fifty kilometers away made more sense.

They trudged back down the corridor that connected the arches in silence. The smell of gas began to increase and Cass pressed her scarf closer to her mouth and nose. As they pulled even with the side tunnel to the VMF, Cass asked over her shoulder, "Who set fire to my garage?"

"I wish I knew, dearie," Biddi said, her voice muffled by her scarf. "It was already like that when I separated myself from the Lifeboat group. No doubt it was the same whacko who dreamt up this nightmare we're going through, this Observer Hanratty spoke of."

"Do you have any guesses as to who that is?"

"Personally, I'd nominate Mr. Gerald Keene."

"It's not him."

"Oh? And how can you be so sure?"

"Someone cut his head off and put it in one of the shrines."

"I see," Biddi said, pausing briefly to absorb the news. "Only his head?"

"The rest of him was in one of the Jamesway huts."

"Jesus, Mary, and Joseph. How do you know *that*? I thought Hanratty had you locked up this whole time."

Cass hesitated, faced with a strange reluctance to reveal her last secret. But there was little reason to hide anything now. As they walked, Cass explained how she'd discovered the shaft up to the abandoned Jamesway over the summer and made it her sanctuary. Guilt assailed her as she described the little shortwave she'd managed to cobble together.

"You had outside radio contact *this whole time*?"

Cass frowned at Biddi's tone. "I was locked up and sedated, remember? By the time it could've helped anyone, I was being kept in a trance."

"And you didn't reach your Russian friend just before you got here?" Biddi asked, her voice anxious.

Cass shook her head. "Someone found the radio. It was destroyed."

"Positive?"

"Yes, Biddi, I'm positive," Cass snapped. "What's the matter with you?"

Biddi's voice was tart. "Pardon me. I thought for a minute there might be a way out of this madhouse aside from walking fifty bloody kilometers in the dark."

Cass clamped down on her anger. They desperately needed each other if they were going to have even a remote chance to survive the trek to the Russian base. "So, if Keene wasn't the Observer, who else is there?"

"Well, seeing as how Taylor shot his own boss in cold blood, then ran off, he seems like a good runner-up. Unless you found *his* head in a niche?"

"I didn't. But Taylor wasn't smart enough to do something this sophisticated."

"You might be right about that. Chief Taylor had a fine body, but never struck me as the sharpest knife in the drawer."

They continued in silence, the *rusk, rusk* of their boots and Cass's own harsh breathing the only sounds for long minutes. At the conduit intersection, Cass moved right, opened the plywood door to the entrance to the old base, then stopped cold.

Biddi tried to look around her, her voice high-pitched. "What? What is it?"

Scattered just inside the door, as though they'd tumbled off a grocery cart, were a random collection of food items—two or three candy bars, a can, some pieces of fruit that were now frozen into icy glass sculptures. One of the pieces of fruit, however, had been smashed underfoot and frozen in place, preserving the front crescent of a large boot print.

Cass moved aside so her friend could see what she'd discovered, then put her own foot beside the print. It was large, even compared to her oversized winter boot. The tread pattern was different, as well, more of the alligator-skin markings of a work boot than the light ridges of a bunny boot.

"Taylor?" Biddi whispered.

"I don't know," Cass said in the same low voice, but inside she was thinking something else. *Taylor isn't that big.* She squeezed the handle of the ice axe. "Let's keep going."

"Are you kidding? That fucking gowk has a gun."

Cass turned to face her friend. "What choice do we have?"

That ended the conversation, and they continued down the rough-hewn passage, their combined flashlights bobbing and swaying back and forth.

Minutes later, Biddi whispered, "How do you do it?"

"Do what?"

"Stay so calm."

"I'm not calm. I'm terrified."

"You'd never know it by looking at you," Biddi persisted. "I wish I could bottle you up and sell you."

"Why, are crippling neuroses and self-recrimination in this season?"

Biddi snorted. "You're too hard on yourself, Cassie. You've come through this with flying colors."

"We're not through it yet."

"True, but anyone who knew you before could've seen it."

"Knew me before?"

"Before the accident. The tunnel. It was never your fault."

Cass said nothing and continued down the frozen tunnel. Divots of ice that had been carved out by hand decades before gleamed like the facets of fist-sized diamonds embedded in the walls. The *scritching* noises of the hyper-frozen snow underfoot—the sound of walking in a world of Styrofoam—were loud in the small tunnel, creating the illusion that the walls were drawing inward and the ceiling shrinking until she was sure her head was brushing the roof above.

Her back felt wooden, as though a plank had been slid under the skin along her spine. Her hands and feet began to tremble, and she stumbled slightly, sending the light of her headlamp wobbling uncertainly. Tears began to well up and she shuddered with a barely contained sob.

"Cassie."

She turned. Biddi had stopped in the middle of the tunnel. Covered in cold weather gear from head to toe, no part of her face was visible.

"You never told me about the accident, did you?"

Not trusting herself to speak, Cass shook her head.

"Ah, that was foolish of me, wasn't it?" A pregnant pause followed, broken only by their breathing. "You know, my money was always on you."

Cass rocked back on her boots, but didn't move. "Why?"

"I handpicked every one of the subjects. Ferns, we called you. Do you know why? Because you were 'plants.' Some idiot at TransAnt came up with the name. But it fit better than they knew. Some of you stagnated, most died. But only one flourished."

"Biddi, start making sense," Cass said, her voice a whisper.

"You were part of a grand experiment, love. You guessed as much, as did the feckless Mr. Hanratty, who believed in his own delusion of control. But his scope, much like his heart, wasn't big enough. Only the bombastic Mr. Keene guessed the truth. You were *all* part of the experiment. Even me. I might have been in charge of conducting the test, observing the results, but of course I'd been shipped along with all the other rats, hadn't I? Dumped into the same maze, despite having never agreed with the psych team's petty goals. Such small minds, such limited ambition. And yet, here I was, right in the mix. I was angry at first, of course. Then, I thought, what better opportunity to put my own theories to the test while simultaneously thumbing my nose at those little shites back in the lab? So I simply . . . accelerated the study."

"It was you?" Cass swallowed. "You really killed everyone?"

"Of course not. Not directly. I inserted a catalyst here, removed a social barrier there. Not so very different than what happens in any true crisis, isn't that so?"

"Why would you do that? What could be worth all those lives?"

"Oh, Cassie." Biddi sighed in disappointment. "Think of every drought, every natural disaster, every man-made catastrophe you've ever heard about. What happens? Social constructs we've built up over thousands of years disappear in a flash. People kill one another for a crust of bread or a gallon of gas."

"What's that got to do with any of this?"

She lifted an arm, gesturing upward to include all of Shackleton. "The crises I fabricated here are nothing compared to what we're going to face in the future. If we want to continue as a species, it's not enough to know who can face up to a crisis and *survive*, we need to know who's going to *transform*. And, more importantly, how."

"You're telling me this year's winter-over was a dry run for the apocalypse?"

Her face was obscured, but Biddi's smile came through her voice. "A wee bit melodramatic, perhaps, but yes. And you needn't be so negative, dearie. We're on the cusp of colonizing other planets, creating habitations in the Sahara and at the bottom of the sea, aren't we? Extraordinary achievements that might be accomplished by exceptional individuals . . . but what happens when ordinary people are asked to do the same?"

"Did you learn what you needed to? Was it worth it?"

"On the whole, no. Our tests are already sophisticated enough to weed out the weak and the infirm. My models predicted nearly everything that happened—from Jun's suicide to the final riot—on the basis of the psych surveys all of you took a year ago. But TransAnt's little team of pinheads decided there was nothing like a field test to confirm the theory."

"And did it?"

"Yes. The prognosis is not good. We started with forty adventurous, intelligent, resourceful subjects. Two of you seemed to show signs of crisis growth. You and Ayres had faced enormous personal, professional, and emotional setbacks only to come out stronger and better than when you went in. Both of you thought of yourselves as failures. Psychological messes. Dangerously fragile. But the truth is, you're just the kind of people the world needs if we're going to survive."

"But you killed Ayres. And all the people he was trying to save."

"He allowed too many people into the Lifeboat—ten might've survived over the long term, but not thirty. He knew that and brought them in anyway. Our future can't be left in the hands of someone so sentimental."

"So you locked them in and shut off the heat."

"Yes. And to the station as a whole, of course. That was a nice feature installed on the power plant last summer." She shrugged. "The TransAnt folks will be mortified, but they'll come around when they see that I took the experiment to its logical conclusion. Haven't we always benefited from pushing science through its moral hedgerow and finding out what lies on the other side? It takes someone with true courage to keep the greater good in mind."

"But why kill everyone? You had your . . . results."

"Forty-odd legal inquiries would taint the value of my conclusions, I'm afraid. Better to purge the subject pool and deal with the fallout later, don't you think? Dead men tell no tales, as those rascals the buccaneers used to say."

"Biddi," Cass said, grasping for words. "You're insane."

"It's just big-picture thinking, my girl. You're disappointing me, by the way. I was ready to rank you as the highest performer. But now I'm not so sure."

"Does that mean I'm to be purged, too?"

"Cass, the ugly reality is that, in any experiment, even the rat who finds the cheese is killed at the end."

Biddi's ice axe was an overhand blur, the spiked head aiming for the top of Cass's skull. But at the first sound of the change in Biddi's voice, Cass had begun leaning away, and as Biddi moved toward her, swinging the axe like a lumberjack, Cass threw herself backwards, backpedaling and scrambling to get away.

Hampered by the awkward cold weather gear, Biddi's swings were clumsy and poorly placed, throwing her off balance. Cass turned and ran down the darkened tunnel. She'd thought briefly about standing to fight, but couldn't imagine trading blows with the person she'd called her friend, no matter what madness she'd just confessed to.

Her breath came in gasps and spasms as she shrugged off the rucksack as she ran, trying to shed weight. The ice axe, she kept.

Behind her, Biddi crooned her name, calling for her to stop. Cass pelted down the tunnel, the light from her headlamp bobbing in time with her panicky strides. She struggled to pull in clean, steady breaths; she *felt* the bite of that axe in her spine, and the fear caused her breathing to stagger and choke in her mouth.

Calm down. Breathe. In through your nose, out through your mouth.

She raced for the oldest ice tunnels of the original station, the area where she'd first discovered the sewage leak. The only sound was the scrabbling sound of her boots and her heaving gasps, broken only by Biddi's occasional yell for her to stop.

Put your foot down, bring that boot up. She is slow. You are fast.

Then why do I feel like I'm dragging the world behind me? I don't think I can feel my legs. I'm swimming in mud.

You were kept sedated and imprisoned for a week, the voice reminded her. *You're fatigued and rusty. That's all. Keep moving.*

Cass ripped the scarf away, feeling like she was being asphyxiated. The icy air hit her lungs like a dagger stabbing her through the mouth and chest, but the shock of the coldest temperatures on the planet jolted her into greater effort—for a moment, her stride lengthened to its normal spread, her arms swinging like she had hit her runner's high in her best marathon.

But then she hit an uneven patch of ice and her ankle, the bad one, wobbled and buckled. A twinge ran up the side of her leg and she gasped at the old, yet familiar, pain. *Please, no*. Her runner's pace evaporated, the ache sending her limping and stumbling forward into an intersection of the tunnel. She would never be able to outrun Biddi like this. She would have to fight.

As she came even with the cross-section, however, a figure lurched at her out of the side tunnel. Cass had a brief flash of a gaunt, terrifying face—black nose, cauliflowered ears, frostbitten gray cheeks—before he clubbed her in the head with a soft, heavy arm, sending her sprawling. She lay on the ground, stunned, as the figure shambled around to face Biddi.

A hoarse shout of rage and recognition emerged from the man. Biddi yelped and swung the axe, but it was a clumsy attempt, and it only raked harmlessly down Leroy's arm. His clawed hands reached for Biddi, but the woman windmilled the axe desperately, keeping him at bay. A sustained, high-pitched shriek emanated from him as he batted Biddi's swings aside.

From the ground, Cass backpedaled in a panic, skidding along the ice as she watched the melee. Gasping, she rolled to her feet and stumbled down the tunnel, slamming into walls as the grunts and yells from the desperate fight behind her faded. She navigated her way past the ancient rooms and the fragile wooden struts, the sight of which caused a prickle in her scalp as she remembered the accident she'd had months ago.

Retracing her steps in the near dark, she tried to conjure the base schematic from memory. *The common room, where the pipe was. Ahead?* Yes. There it was, the tiny, cramped opening. She dropped to the ground and crawled through the opening.

The sharp stink of human feces—not sewage—and the overall stench of close living hit her, permeating even the layers of the mask and scarf. She played the light over the room, steeling herself.

Cans and tins of food littered the floor, while the furniture and debris that she remembered from her first visit lay stacked in bizarre towers and shapes. The old shag carpeting had been ripped up and formed into a kind of cocoon in the middle of the room.

Cass crossed the room quickly, keeping an eye out for anything at this point: traps, rotten floorboards, things to slow or injure her. If she remembered the schematic, the old station only had one main stubby corridor that ran from its entrance to the common room she was in right now. Dorms and labs split off from that main artery like flowers on a vine, but it should be a straight shot to the exit.

Careful not to touch anything, she moved across the room and shoved her weight against an old foam-core door. It wouldn't budge. She tried again, with minimal result: she managed to create a half-inch gap between the door and the jamb.

"Shit, shit, shit." Desperate, Cass flicked the beam of her flashlight around the room, looking for anything that could help her. Freeze-dried couch cushions, battered old tables, splintered chair legs—none of it was of any help. She fought down panic. No matter who won the fight behind her, the winner would come after her.

She scoured the room. In the far corner, to the right of the entrance, she found something promising: the wall's paneling had been torn away, exposing a supporting structure of rebar and two-by-fours. With a dozen desperate yanks, she managed to pry away one of the lengths of rebar.

Cass ran back to the stubborn door and squeezed the tip of the rebar into the opening she'd created. Using the metal pole as a lever, she pried open the door first an inch, then a half foot, and eventually a space wide enough for her to slip through.

The hallway beyond had the dark, still atmosphere of a tomb. Crystal mounds of ice and snow had invaded the old base through microscopic cracks, forming alien, curved sculptures along the ceiling and walls. Her heart leapt into her throat at a roar from far behind her in the tunnels. She jogged down the corridor, sparing only a flash of her light and a glance for each room as she passed. At the end of the short hall, a simple set of stairs climbed two stories, ending in a small antechamber and what she'd hoped would be the door to the outside, but turned out to be nothing but a rounded snowbank.

Gasping and crying, she hacked at the pillows of ice with her axe. After a sweaty minute, breathing heavily, she had managed to expose the door. But all her efforts to move it weren't even as successful as moving the common room door an inch.

She slumped against the wall, then slid to the ground and put her head down on her arms, beaten. A half mile of snow and ice could be pressed against the other side of the door. It was true, after all: Antarctica would kill her. Her death might actually come at the point of Biddi's axe or Leroy's curled fingers . . . but it would be the continent itself that defeated her.

Had the early explorers, living so much closer to the edge than the modern expeditions, ever felt this way? Death, always just on the other side of a door or the walls of your ship. Even the scientists of the early twentieth century had to have lived with fear most days, especially during a winter-over when the chances of rescue in the case of a disaster were truly nil. How they even went about their daily work was hard to imagine . . .

The thought stopped Cass. *Their daily work.*

Slipping and skidding, she hauled herself to her feet and jogged clumsily back down the hall. The early base crew knew that they'd never get the front hatch open during the winter. They must've done their work by using observation tubes at the top of the stub-ups she'd been told about. Popping her head into room after room, she found what she was looking for on the fourth try: the telltale horizontal bars of a hatchway ladder leading upward.

She hurried past the relics of a former workstation and flashed her light up the shaft. The ladder ended at what looked in the darkness like a bubble or tiny observatory.

Breathing heavily, she began pawing her way up the ladder. Her axe, hanging from its lanyard, banged against the side of her leg. After twenty slippery steps upward, she found herself at the top of the observation tube, a tiny circular room with a Plexiglas dome for a ceiling. Scratched and scoured after decades of ice storms, it was almost opaque now, but originally was meant to allow someone standing on the last rung a one-hundred-and-eighty-degree view of the night sky in the winter. Primitive by any modern standard, it would've been the only way to do basic astronomy in the original days of the South Pole station.

Cass ran her light along the edge of the dome, looking for a weakness or a seam, finally finding it behind her. Wedging herself against the wall of the tube, she pocketed the light, grabbed her axe with both hands, and began bashing at the tiny line that ran up the dome.

She stopped after thirty swings of the axe, out of breath and aching. The brittle dome had begun to give way, however, and the wind moaned through the aperture. It reminded her of the inhuman bellow

Leroy had made as he attacked Biddi. The memory made her grab the axe and continue swinging.

At the fortieth whack, the dome cracked a foot up the seam. The wind's groan turned into a scream, and with the next blow, the Plexiglas split with the sound of tearing cloth. The dome rattled in place for a brief second, then was torn away by the gale. Cass, almost knocked back down the shaft by the force of the wind, pulled out her flashlight and grabbed for the rim of the tube.

Before she could haul herself over the lip of the tube and out, a noise from below made her focus the beam between her feet and down the shaft.

There was nothing but the black hole leading down into the hell that was the old base. Errant flakes of snow, long held at bay by the dome she'd just shattered, floated down into the shaft. Cass's imagination took hold and she almost saw Biddi, her mask and balaclava covered with blood, or Leroy, with his nightmarish, frostbitten face, looking up at her from the bottom of the ladder.

Cass turned and clawed her way hand over hand around the opening of the rim. Finding a clear spot, she shoved herself belly-first onto the rim, then dumped herself over the edge of the tube. She slid down the slope of ice and snow that had built up around the tube like a toboggan, coming to a stop ten feet below.

Stumbling to her feet on the uneven ice, she spun in place several times, trying to get her bearings in the dark, resisting the fear that was screaming at her to start walking no matter what the direction. Picking the wrong direction now would be fatal.

The wind shrieked in her face and the pitch-black darkness surrounding her was almost overwhelming. At a guess, she was about two hundred meters from base, maybe more, but Shackleton's red lights and the normal illumination visible through the windows were gone. Panic welled inside her when she couldn't find even a simple reference point, but then a windblown cloud was pushed out of the way, giving her a momentary view of the base carving out a blocky, black silhouette against the stars. Taking several quick, deep breaths, she oriented herself against the angle of the silhouette and forged ahead, aiming for the southeast corner of the base and the start of what would be her pathway to survival—the SPoT road—if she could find it.

Each small patch of progress forward was contested by the wind, the ice, and the darkness, at times pushing her off her feet or suspending her body in mid-step. The wind shifted unpredictably, causing her to stumble as it went from nearly standing her up to buffeting her from the flank. Every few meters, Cass was forced to stop and pan the flashlight back and forth, looking for the telltale road flags, without which she was truly dead.

Numb from the cold and the constant battering wind, with the endless roar in her ears, her perception of the trek took on a surreal, alien feel, a detached journey dialed in from a light-year away. Time was measured only in how many steps it took to close the gap from one highway flag to the next . . . whether it took a minute or an hour to cross that distance was irrelevant.

The moon was full, casting a wavering ghostly image on the ice in front of her that grew in definition and detail as the scud moved off, pushed by a wind crested into a high-pitched shriek even as a shadow behind her became perfectly, crisply outlined in the snow.

Too tired to turn, the best Cass could do was throw herself to the side, letting gravity take her out of the way of the swing of Biddi's axe. Moving with glacial speed, she rolled over and over in the snow, trying to build up the momentum she needed to get to her feet. Biddi chased after her, swinging the axe in wild, drunken passes. Cass, mesmerized by the motion and her own exhaustion, watched as Biddi raised her axe and brought it down in a two-handed chop.

Cass slipped out of the way, scrambled to her feet, and threw her shoulder into Biddi's torso, pushing more than striking her. The woman stumbled back, flailing her arms to keep her balance. Clutching her axe in two hands, Cass followed her with desperate swings, missing by wide margins. Staggering, tripping, running, she followed after Biddi. In the face of Cass's onslaught, Biddi slipped and went down on one knee.

Putting all her accumulated rage and fear into a final swing, Cass brought the axe down in an overhand arc, catching Biddi high in the chest. The point of the axe, sharp as a beak, traveled through the thick layers and lodged deep in her flesh.

Her friend gave a single, strangled cry and collapsed, dropping her axe as she fell. Exhausted, Cass dropped to her knees, then sank to all fours with her head hanging down. The capricious wind died for a moment, leaving the icy plain strangely quiet. Biddi moaned; whistling, burbling noises rose from her chest.

Blood, black and shiny in the stark moonlight, spilled from the gap between Biddi's parka and scarf. Cass's axe was still stuck obscenely in her chest and Biddi pawed weakly at it for a moment, then her hands slowed, then stopped, then fell away.

Cass crawled the few feet separating them. Reaching out, she gently pushed back the scarf and the blank inhuman mask of the balaclava, exposing Biddi's face. Her friend's eyes, open to slits, widened slightly, then sunk back again. Her lips were moving. Cass bent forward.

In the suddenly silent icy world, Biddi sighed. "Cassie, love. Save us, won't you?"

Her breathing thickened, then stopped.

Cass sunk onto the ice next to her, lying there for a long moment as the wind picked up again. Flecks of snow began to collect on Biddi's face, sticking to her nose and eyelashes and cheeks. In only a minute, ice had covered Biddi's eyes and snow had filled her mouth, transforming her from something human into a feature of the landscape, another part of the ice.

When she could no longer recognize her friend's face, Cass rolled onto her back and looked up at the stars. The light of her headlamp shone skyward like a bloody beacon. Sleep, beckoning, pulled her into a black abyss and her arms spread wide, as though asking for a hug or making a snow angel.

An aurora, like a ghostly green ribbon, tore across the sky. *It's beautiful*, she thought, glad to have seen it. A feeling of peace enveloped her. The voice in her head nagged at her to get up, to fight, but she gently shut it away. Her struggle was over, and it was enough to have tried.

She wished for the people she had failed—in her past, in the present—to forgive her.

So she forgave herself.

And then she closed her eyes.

CHAPTER FORTY-SEVEN

In the distance, pinpoints of light wavered and winked like stars. Minutes passed and the tiny, flickering lights, spaced as orderly as diamonds on a necklace, became round moons, then pale planets bobbing and moving in a line until they materialized as the headlights of a convoy of giant Vityaz snowcats wending their way along the SPoT road.

Ice crystals, thrown into the air by the deep-toothed tires, glittered as they fell back to earth. Shackleton was the obvious goal, but just as the snowcats poked their nose toward the base, the herd slowed, then veered toward the red beam of a headlamp shooting toward the sky. Pulling close, one of the giant machines stopped with a lurch. Frozen, nearly unconscious, Cass turned her head to watch as the door opened, only mildly interested. Four men, big as bears, hopped out of the cab and waddled over to her.

One of them knelt by her side and, pulling his scarf down, he flashed her a bearded smile she hadn't seen in nearly a year. "*Vozlyublennaya*, what's a nice girl like you doing out on a night like this?"

"Oh my God." Cass clutched at him. "Vox."

He put a mittened hand along her face. "It is just Sasha now, Blaze."

With his arms around her, he helped her to her feet. Step by step they walked to the snowcat. The three other men, with the painstaking care reserved for a child or a saint, raised her into the cab. White clouds billowed into the night as the door opened, then was shut quickly.

The Russians held a quick conference, then three of the Vityaz continued on toward the American base. The last turned and headed for the safety of Orlova, leaving the wreckage of Shackleton, and the lives of the crew who'd manned it, behind.

AUTHOR'S NOTE

The fictitious Shackleton South Pole Research Facility, as stated in the text, is based on the very real Amundsen-Scott South Pole Station, but I've taken poetic license in describing its construction and usage, as well as the lives of the people who live and work there. Ice-heads who have spent time at Amundsen-Scott will, I hope, forgive the many liberties I've taken and appreciate the facts when I've used them.

I've played fast and loose with the salutogenic theories of Aaron Antonovsky, but his work is fascinating and worthy of study, as are the investigations into the phenomenon of T3 syndrome. Any misunderstandings of his work or the broader field of Antarctic psychology are my own.

The Lyubov Orlova station is fictitious and was invented solely for storytelling purposes; to my knowledge, there is no base, Russian or otherwise, near the Amundsen-Scott facility. The name of the station is my homage to the MV *Lyubov Orlova*, the ship I took on my sole visit to Antarctica (though not the South Pole), which has since been decommissioned and lost at sea. The ship, in turn, was named after the lovely and talented Lyubov Orlova, "the first recognized star of Soviet cinema."

ACKNOWLEDGMENTS

I would not have been able to write this novel without the help, direct and indirect, of the following people, places, and things.

The love and support of my family and friends form the foundation for any novel I write. I include in those two groups my extended family at Thomas & Mercer, who have helped and mentored me along the way. Thank you all.

Special thanks goes out to my editor Jacque Ben-Zekry for believing in the project from the start and providing great advice and humor along the way; Caitlin Alexander, who improved this book by several orders of magnitude over one incredibly intense month of editing; and Jon Ford, whose eagle eye caught the many mistakes that (somehow!) slipped through the first dozen drafts. Thank you all for your patience, sensitivity, and expert advice.

The blogs of the legendary Bill Spindler (www.southpolestation.com) and world-traveler Jeffrey Donenfeld (www.jeffreydonenfeld.com) were so instrumental to my research that this book wouldn't exist in its present form without them. Additional invaluable information—including some breathtaking photography—came from the personal blogs of Marc Ankenbauer (www.glacierexplorer.com), Jeremy Bloyd-Peshkin (www.ulterior-motors.com), and Marco Tortonese (www.marcopolie.blogspot.com).

Other helpful online resources included the National Science Foundation's United States Antarctic Program website (www.usap.gov) and the *Antarctic Sun* (antarcticsun.usap.gov), the continent's largest (only?) newspaper.

For an inside view of the lives of some of the quirkiest, bravest, and most singular people on the planet as well as achingly beautiful cinematography, nothing beats Anthony Powell's documentary film *Antarctica: A Year on Ice* (www.frozensouth.weebly.com). If you have a chance to view it, you'll find that, far from exaggerating what it's like at the bottom of the world, I barely did it justice.

Written resources include Kim Heacox's *Antarctica: The Last Continent*, a poetic and sensitive treatment of the continent's history and significance; Kim Stanley Robinson's *Antarctica*, a novel that delivers profound ruminations about the future and past of Antarctica, as well as humanity's role on it, while spinning an entertaining tale at the same time; Apsley Cherry-Garrard's *The Worst Journey in the World*, the stunning and eloquent account from a man who nearly gave his life in those heroic early days of Antarctic exploration; and Caroline Alexander's *The Endurance: Shackleton's Legendary Antarctic Expedition*, with its awe-inspiring photography by Frank Hurley and, of course, the even more jaw-dropping account of Ernest Shackleton's unprecedented voyage.

Background on the psychological effects of wintering over, confinement psychology, and general information on Aaron Antonovsky's fascinating theory of salutogenesis was gleaned from "The Psychology of Isolated and Confined Environments: Understanding Human Behavior in Antarctica" by Lawrence A. Palinkas.

Technical details about snowmobiles and their maintenance were cribbed from the excellent *American Snowmobiler* magazine (www.amsnow.com).

I received encouragement and sage advice from Jil Simon, David Jacobstein, and Maria Schneider. David Mugg and his wife, Sarah

(McMurdo, 2013), gave generously of their time, sharing their pictures, stories, and knowledge of life at the bottom, including the disappointment that comes from discovering you only have mint Irish cream liqueur to drink until the next flight arrives from Christchurch.

This project would've stalled out at two chapters without the coffee and shelter provided by the baristas of Swing's, Killer E.S.P., Stomping Grounds, St. Elmo's, and Grounded.

For musical inspiration, I turned most often to Radical Face and Kishi Bashi, but especially the dark, atmospheric works of composers Petri Alanko, Roque Baños, Jason Graves, and Garry Schyman.

Lastly, to the readers who've made this career possible, thank you. You've made this writer's dreams come true.

ABOUT THE AUTHOR

Photo © 2014 by Sally Iden

Matthew Iden is the prolific author of the Marty Singer detective series—*A Reason to Live*, *Blueblood*, *One Right Thing*, *The Spike*, *The Wicked Flee*, and *Once Was Lost*—as well as several acclaimed standalone novels. Iden's eclectic résumé includes jobs with the US Postal Service, international nonprofit groups, a short stint with the Forest Service in Sitka, Alaska, and time with the globe-spanning Semester at Sea program. Trips to Iceland, Patagonia, and Antarctica have given him a world of inspiration. Iden currently lives in Northern Virginia—close enough to the woods to keep his sanity, close enough to the Washington, DC, Capital Beltway to lose it. Visit him on the web at www.matthew-iden.com, or find him on Twitter @CrimeRighter and Facebook at www.facebook.com/matthew.iden.